Chance Meeting

A naked woman stood knee-deep in the water, facing away from him.

After a few stunned moments, Chance saw that she was Bold Nose, her wet body gleaming like new bronze in the moonlight. As he watched, the girl scooped up a double handful of water and let it flow over her breasts, shivering as the cool stream trickled down her body and legs.

Bold Nose started to turn toward him, and he moved swiftly, wading out to her and clapping his right hand over her mouth.

"Don't be afraid, girl," Chance whispered.

Chance slowly removed his hand from her mouth and, when she made no protest, replaced it with his mouth. Breaking off the kiss, he lifted her out of the water and carried her over to where she had conveniently spread her blanket on the sand and carefully laid her down.

When he knelt down and pulled her legs apart, her breasts rose and fell rapidly as she panted like a small animal run to ground.

Chance tried to be gentle, but when he pressed his body full upon her, he was no longer in control. The hot raging fury within him demanded release. Chance found her breasts with one hand while the other gripped her hair and pulled back her head.

From her concealed position in the willows, Winnedumah watched the activities on the blanket approvingly. It was about time things started to work out right for her. There was still much work to be done, but Bold Nose had made an excellent beginning. . . .

Chance Fortune

Bill Starr

PINNACLE BOOKS   NEW YORK

CHANCE FORTUNE

Copyright © 1981 by Bill Starr

An original Pinnacle Books edition, published for the first time anywhere.

First printing, September 1981

ISBN: 0-523-41141-3

Cover illustration by Bruce Minney

Printed in the United States of America

PINNACLE BOOKS, INC.
1430 Broadway
New York, New York 10018

California, like Hell, can always use more water and good people.

—Mark Twain

Los Angeles is the largest city ever built in a desert.

—A newspaper filler item

*First to dwell in the valley were the legends—
ageless when the wind began to hone its razor
edge on the Sierra whetstone, subtly carving the
land's spirit before the immortal raindrops and
sandgrains etched its face, hosting the mysterious
sojourn of ancient makers of rock pictures.*

*Thus even the Paiutes, who arrived with the
beginning of time, found a rich storyhouse await-
ing their occupation. And after new gods stole
away the valley's weeping heart to nourish distant
dreams and dances, the legends breathed on in
the unloved land. They had grown too old to
remember how to die.*

CHANCE FORTUNE

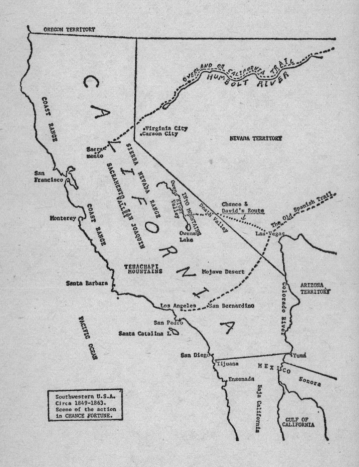

OREGON TERRITORY

CALIFORNIA

OVERLAND OR CALIFORNIA TRAIL

HUMBOLT RIVER

COAST RANGE

Virginia City
Carson City

NEVADA TERRITORY

Sacra-
mento

San
Francisco

SIERRA NEVADA RANGE

SACRAMENTO/SAN JOAQUIN RIVERS

Monterey

COAST RANGE

INYO MOUNTAINS

Owens River
Valley

Death Valley

Chance &
David's Route

The Old Spanish Trail

Las Vegas

Owens
Lake

TEHACHAPI
MOUNTAINS

Mojave Desert

ARIZONA
TERRITORY

Santa Barbara

Los Angeles

San Bernardino

Colorado River

San Pedro

Santa Catalina I.

San Diego

Yuma

PACIFIC OCEAN

Tijuana

MEXICO

Ensenada

Sonora

Baja California

GULF OF
CALIFORNIA

Southwestern U.S.A.
Circa 1849-1863.
Scene of the action
in CHANCE FORTUNE.

Chapter 1

October 17, 1849

They were almost beyond caring when they came at last to the valley.

First to glimpse the narrow green trough between the hills was Kenneth Malcolm, peering over old Winnedumah's bowed head as they emerged from the rocky ravine that was as dry and dusty as they were. For a moment the teasing vision was too much for Kenneth's thirst-crippled mind. He felt a hysterical urge to retreat back into the desert barrier they had paid so painful a toll to cross. At least the flame-breathing sands, melancholy sun, and sucking winds were familiar demons, while this promise of relief might be only a cruel mirage sent to soak up the last of their hope.

But the impulse passed quickly. An instant later his panic became joyful anticipation and his bloodied feet, more decorated than protected by trailworn boots, took him beyond the Indian guide at a limping run.

David Wheeler followed him, as he always had, leaving Bold Nose, the other Paiute female, to bring up the rear of their small column. As far back as David could remember, it had always been "Kenny and Davy" when folks spoke of their boyhood activities. Not that ranking second had been without compensation. Since the more daring Kenneth was

1

known to be the instigator and leader of any mischief they were caught doing, he always got the hardest lickings.

David had been reliving some of those long-gone pranks as he stumbled along in an exhausted stupor that made cherished memories seem more real than their present dull surroundings. For a minute he could almost feel the crisp bite of autumn in the Catskills, with maple leaves glowing like frozen fire against the rolling hillsides. It was then that Kenny would insist—not that David needed much urging—that they ditch school and chores to go apple stealing or just rambling through the woods. Winter thoughts were better distractions from their sweltering ordeal, but David's imagination couldn't quite make snow and ice convincing. Always his mind went home to October days where seasonal changes meant something, unlike this contrary land where the sun never stopped burning the sweat off a man's neck even before it had time to get wet.

With the heavy farm work of spring and summer finished, the brief after-harvest pause was a vacation for two frisky lads out for some fun. And fun was to be had, especially when they could lure Judy Trent into a hayloft to play doctor with them. Good old Judy—so pretty and so wild with the boys that it was a wonder she'd managed to stay out of trouble until her wedding night, as Kenny later assured him was the case.

David had been as smitten by Judy's developing charms as the other young fellows thereabouts. But he had learned by then the futility of trying to compete with Kenny for so desirable a prize. When Kenny set his heart on something, he usually found a way to get it, even if that meant running audacious risks that discouraged other men. His daredevil willingness to take chances had earned him his favorite nickname, Chance, and had made the more stolid David his most devoted companion. So it had been with brotherly love and no little envy that David had served as best man when Chance inevitably took Judy to wife. And it was with growing sorrow that he had watched their marriage turn sour, while his own happiness with Margaret had blossomed.

Abruptly David was jolted out of his reverie as he rounded the final bend in the ravine and nearly blundered

2

into Winnedumah. The gaunt old squaw stood beside Chance, watching his tongue move restlessly over his cracked lips at the sight of the valley below them. David halted with them, blinking hard to make his sun-blurred eyes and numbed brain accept the obvious but incredible existence of a river the color of bullet lead angling southward with an almost jubilant air of purpose. Most of the valley floor was still green with summer ripeness; only here and there over the grassy meadows poplars and oaks flickered yellow-orange to tease David's homesick memories. To the north a few strings of smoke rose in the windless sky, and on a reed-choked backwater a flight of wild ducks settled down to feed. David saw Bold Nose move silently past him to her grandmother and for a moment they all stood motionless—two expressionless Indian women and two west-hearted white men with long rifles upon their shoulders.

Winnedumah was the first to break the pose. "There river, like I say."

"Right you are, old woman," Chance said. "Lucky break for you, too. I was about ready to shoot you for a liar."

"Now, Chance, you've no call to talk that way to her," David said patiently. "Didn't Captain Ward tell us you could always count on a Paiute to lead you to water? After all, that's what their name means. 'Pai' is the Ute word for water, so they're water-Utes."

Chance's bearded mouth curled mockingly at his friend. "Davy, you ought to have been a schoolmaster, the way you like to tell folks things they already know."

David smiled back. As always, a taunt from Chance was more pleasing to him than a compliment from anyone else.

"Sure is a pretty sight, ain't it?" David mused. "I imagine the Nile Valley must've looked that nice to Joseph's brethren when they came starving from the famine in their own land."

"Well, let's hope we get as friendly a welcome as they did." Chance directed Winnedumah's attention to the smoke columns. "Your people?"

"Si, señor. Paiutes. Many." The old woman opened and closed the fingers of both hands several times to give her impression of great numbers.

3

"Are they friendly or hostile to whites?"

Winnedumah stared blankly at him.

"She don't understand our big words," David said.

"I think she savvys more than she lets on," Chance grumbled. "Your Christian spirit does you credit. But you have to learn not to trust people so much. Especially women and Indians."

David was tempted to argue that point with Chance. Everything they had heard about the Paiutes—dating back to the earliest exploration of the area by Jedediah Smith over a quarter-century ago—described them as a peaceable tribe. And Winnedumah had served her white employers faithfully as she guided them across the Great Basin, where they had encountered a few scattered bands of Paiutes who displayed no sign of hostility.

But David hated to dispute Chance on a matter involving defense. After all, Chance had served in the Mexican War with such distinction that he had been personally commended by General Zachary Taylor, the recently elected President. So instead David questioned Winnedumah about the valley Paiutes, with awkward sign language and simple baby talk, until she fully understood him.

The old woman shook her head vigorously. "*No*, Señor! Paiute no kill white mans—never. Paiute sometime kill Ute. Sometime kill Shoshone. But no kill Mescan. No kill 'Mercan. Never."

David looked at Chance, who gave a slight shrug. "All right. If they're peaceful, we won't give 'em any reason to change their ways. We'll just be here long enough to let our oxen get their strength back and lay in enough dried meat to carry us over the mountains, and I grudge losing that much time. I don't aim to let somebody else pick up my share of the gold, even if they do say the nuggets are scattered as common as pebbles along the streams."

David's rifle swung heavily over his head as he brought the butt to ground and leaned his weight on the barrel. Removing his hat, he scratched his naturally fine brown hair that dirt and sweat had coarsened to the texture of buffalo wool. Reflecting on his dilapidated condition, he marveled at how Chance had remained almost debonair in comparison. Both men were ragged, foul-smelling, and

4

rawboned by weeks of hard travel on short rations. But whereas David slouched wearily like the typical picture of a lanky, lantern-jawed, jug-eared Yankee farmer, Chance's more compact body stood erect, his handsome squarish face full of purpose, with the old hopeful gleam still bright in his deep-set gray eyes. Even the crescent scar on his left cheek seemed to grin impishly through his matted whiskers.

"Well, even if there is that much gold in them mountains, it makes a man wonder if it's worthwhile climbing over 'em," David pondered as his tired gaze moved up the sheer granite masses that towered like the shoulders of a headless giant along the valley's west flank. Along the jagged crest thin fingers of old snow seemed to grasp at much whiter clouds billowing against a sky so blue and deep that his eyes ached to fathom it. Already the broken peaks blocked enough of the afternoon sun's rays to carpet the western valley floor with purple shadows that crept toward the opposite slope where they stood. Winnedumah had told them the Indians called these east-bordering mountains Inyo, "place of a great spirit." That seemed a more apt description of the mighty range facing them, but homesick Spaniards had christened it Sierra Nevada and common usage had made the name as permanent as the rocky cliffs themselves.

"Man alive, I never would've believed there are such mountains," David said. "They look taller than the Rockies."

"That's only because they have no foothills on this side," Chance said. "That makes 'em look impassable, but don't you fret about that. There are enough passes marked on my map for us to find our way through to the gold fields well before snow flies."

"The same map that led us into the Valley of Death?" David asked dryly, thinking of the dismally perverse desert they had just traversed. He did not know if the area had been officially named, since they were evidently the first white party ever to have the misfortune of seeing it. But his choice of a title seemed fitting and a tribute to the oft-quoted Twenty-third Psalm in their prayers of deliverance. Only God's personal guidance could have saved them from that hellish nightmare, David believed, overlooking the fact that it was Winnedumah who had found stingy waterholes along the way and pointed out the most direct route to the river.

Chance accepted his friend's jibe with a sheepish smile. "You're right to fault me on that score, Davy. I should never have insisted on leaving the wagon train at Las Vegas. But, all things considered, I think we've come through the ordeal in pretty fair shape."

David nodded. "Aye, we still have our lives, thank God. And with a little luck, pluck, and hard work we should soon recoup our losses. I find no fault with you, Chance, only with the lunatic or scoundrel who drew the map showing a well-watered trail through the desert. We all were to blame for wanting to take the quickest way to the gold."

Chance nodded absently, too accustomed to David's good-natured tolerance to think it worth acknowledging. He licked dry lips again as his eyes darted up and down the long verdant gash in the mountains' flesh. "A veritable Garden of Eden. Or, as you said, a Nile to the starving Hebrews. I don't know why we're standing here jawboning over it, when we could be down there wetting our whistles with that wonderful elixir of life."

He started forward impatiently but David caught his arm. "We ought to wait for the others to catch up."

"They won't have any trouble following us." Chance pulled free of the restraining hand. "We can have a campsite picked out for 'em when they get there, and maybe even bag some fresh meat for supper."

"All right, you go ahead and do that, then. I'll go back and tell 'em the good news."

David watched Chance stride eagerly forward, thinking it was just like him to rush headlong into a new experience and leave his companions with the task of maneuvering their wagons down the rugged slope. Winnedumah, seeing the men separate, instantly told her granddaughter with a flick of her eyes which of them they would accompany. Bold Nose obediently followed the older woman downhill after Chance.

Walking back up the dry streambed, David was amazed at how the mere sight of the river had restored his physical

6

and emotional strength. An hour ago he had been plodding along on his last legs, cursing himself for taking Margaret into this godforsaken land where they must surely die. Now he stepped lightly and laughed at those foolish fears. Why, they hadn't been anywhere near as bad off as he had imagined. They still had about twenty pounds of beans, ten pounds of flour, some salt pork and even a little coffee and sugar left, not to mention the bag of seed corn he had hidden among the farming supplies. And in a pinch they could have butchered their few remaining oxen.

True enough, things had looked bleak back there in the Valley of Death, when they had lost most of their animals and were forced to abandon the wagon carrying the trade goods they had hoped to sell to the California miners for a good profit. But any time healthy young Americans like them couldn't endure a little hardship and still walk across the country smiling, they ought to give it back to the Indians.

Once more David was glad Chance had talked him into joining the hordes of California-bound goldseekers. It had taken some persuading at first, what with them doing so well with their general store in Oneonta and the skeptical disbelief that greeted the early reports of gold discoveries in the Sierra Nevada foothills. Such tall tales as the one about Captain John Sutter complaining about gold dust and nuggets clogging his sawmill on the American River were too much to swallow. What did those frontiersmen take their eastern brethren for—ignorant greenhorns fresh off the boat and looking for streets paved with precious metal?

But the derisive smirks had disappeared when the first sizable gold shipments started arriving at the Philadelphia Mint late in 1848. After that it seemed that the whole world was eager to believe what Chance had told David— that just about anything was possible in the vast new territories the U.S.A. had annexed after the victorious war with Mexico. Even David had felt the burning bite of the gold bug, much to Chance's delight.

Only David's concern for Margaret's condition had held him back. After her two miscarriages, he was determined that her latest pregnancy should have the best possible care. Yet he could not bear the thought of leaving her be-

7

hind for even the brief year or less in which he assumed he would make his fortune and return. Margaret herself resolved the dilemma by stating that she was just as anxious as David to "see the elephant," as some unknown wag had dubbed the California craze. Besides, Margaret insisted, there was no good reason why a big, strong young woman like her could not carry a child across the continent and deliver it in a climate that everyone said was far superior to anything the States had to offer.

Many times since then David had regretted the ease with which he had allowed himself to be convinced that Margaret was not making a great sacrifice just to please him. But at the time they all were too frantic with gold fever to think of anything else. It was an experience quite unlike anything the world had ever seen before, when hopes were boundless and speed counted for more than common sense.

It seemed that everybody and his brother was dead set on grabbing a piece of the golden dream, whether they traveled overland to California or took the equally dangerout sea routes around South America or across the disease- and bandit-infested isthmus of Panama. During their torturous ordeal on the western trail, David had wondered if anyone would ever tally up all of the human lives and property that were lost in the Gold Rush. It would be interesting to see how that score balanced against the amount of gold that was actually found. But it was doubtful that that would have discouraged anyone caught up in the mad stampede for El Dorado.

David heard the squeal of ungreased wagon wheels ahead of him. Hurrying around the next bend, he saw the two Conestoga wagons drawn by emaciated oxen lurching slowly toward him. Seventeen-year-old Michael O'Neal, marching ahead of the wagons, still managed to find some pleasure in playing soldier with his absurdly long-barreled squirrel rifle. But the youth had manfully assumed his dead father's duties in looking after his formidable mother and three younger brothers.

He wouldn't mind having a son like that, David thought, looking beyond Michael at Margaret pacing heavily beside the first wagon. Hunger and exhaustion had exaggerated her swollen abdomen and made her natural unloveliness seem almost hatchet-faced. Even so, she still had the strength to carry Chance's five-year-old daughter Vicky Beth on her shoulders for brief stretches.

A fresh wave of pity for the poor little tyke swept through David. Chance had been cruel to subject the child to their arduous trek. Almost as cruel as a man who would drag along an expectant wife, David reminded himself with an appropriate twinge of guilt. But Chance, as he had often demonstrated, was not the kind of man who lightly gave up something that belonged to him.

As David thought of the good news he was bringing to his travel-weary companions, Margaret caught sight of him and smiled happily. She always could read his face like an open book.

Getting the wagons down into the valley was a slow process, but not as difficult as David had anticipated. Gravity relieved the weakened oxen of much of their labor and the tedious job was accomplished with a great deal of careful steering, braking, and curse-laden instructions from the Widow O'Neal. That such a small woman could contain so much energy, volume, and profanity so amazed David that he counted it a blessing when her thick brogue rendered her incomprehensible. He feared that her echoing shouts would alert every Indian in the valley of their arrival. But then, as Margaret had once observed, any Indian who knew what was good for him would stay clear of Susan O'Neal.

Chance, after selecting a level stretch of riverbank bordered by willows and poplars, had sent Bold Nose back to guide them to it. By nightfall they had the wagons drawn up beside a cheery campfire where Winnedumah was roasting a fat buck antelope that Chance's rifle had brought down. After drowning their thirst in the gurgling river, they watered the livestock and turned them loose to graze on the rich grass. The O'Neal boys were eager to strip off and plunge into the water for a frolicsome swim, but a curt command from their mother made them sullenly content just to wash their hands and faces for supper. Under a sky of blazing stars they gathered around the fire to savor the long-denied luxury of a carefree meal preceded,

9

at David's insistence, by a prayer of thanksgiving for their safe passage through the desert.

The red meat, fresh water, and the knowledge that they could at last relax in some degree of security was a tonic to their bone-weary limbs, reviving their old hopes of finding wealth and happiness at the end of their journey. Little Vicky Beth best summed up their newfound euphoria when, pausing from the demanding task of gnawing on a greasy joint of meat, she rolled her great blue eyes up at Chance and asked seriously: "Papa, we really eatin' now, ain't we?"

The question was a pinprick to her elders' nervous energy, released in roaring gusts of laughter. Chance lovingly cradled the child in his arms and kissed her repeatedly. "Yes, Princess, and a year from now—no, blast me, six months from now—we'll be eating even better off of solid gold plates."

"Sure, and drinking the finest champagne from crystal goblets!" Mrs. O'Neal seconded.

Margaret, seated on an overturned bucket at the edge of the fireglow, listened half-interestedly to the banter about acquiring and spending easy fortunes. Her light infection of gold fever had burned out long ago. Now her only concern with this tomfool business was to be with David and see him occupied at any work that would satisfy him and give them a good living. If gold mining did that, then all well and good, although she would have preferred farming. So would David, she was sure. But Chance had pretty well put an end to that dream when he persuaded David to leave his father's farm and become a storekeeper with him. Not that they'd ever had reason to complain about the money they made, but still. . . .

Margaret flinched at the jerky movement of the baby and tried to shift her weight to a more comfortable position on the bucket. The increasing activity in her womb seemed to confirm her growing suspicion that Doc Hutchings back home had been wrong. By his reckoning she should have another month—time enough for them to get over the mountains to the mining camps where there ought to be some sort of doctor to attend the delivery. But, judging from the signs, she could go into labor at any time now.

The prospect of giving birth so far from all civilized conveniences almost made Margaret regret her decision to come along with David. Well, there was nothing she could do about it but grit her teeth and hope she was as tough as her pioneering forebears who had helped tame the New England wilderness. Family tradition had it that an ancestor of hers had borne a son while being held captive by the Iroquois, and later returned safely with him to her people—a feat that Margaret would rather admire than emulate.

On the other hand, Margaret was grateful that she and David would be together for the birth, and she would have the experienced help of Mrs. O'Neal. It was an inspiration, though a harrowing one, to hear the Irishwoman describe how she had brought her children into the world in the wretched squalor of the poorest and most British-oppressed part of County Galway.

With conditions so bad in the Old Country, it was understandable that the O'Neals had migrated to America. Of all the followers of the Gold Rush that Margaret had met—except for Chance—Susan O'Neal impressed her as the one most likely to acquire the great riches of which they all dreamed.

Peering across the fire at the small woman's stringy black hair and ruddy pumpkin of a face illuminated by intense brown eyes, Margaret saw that her iron determination remained undiminished. It was too early to tell if Susan's four sons had inherited her spirit along with her looks. But as long as Susan was around, they didn't need it. She would drive them on until they became successful or fell broken by the wayside, as their father had done.

Poor old easygoing, hagridden Frank O'Neal. Margaret hadn't needed to know them very long to see who wore the pants in that family. She hated to say it about anyone, but it had probably been a relief for Frank when he finally gave up the ghost to pneumonia back on the Kansas prairie. Certainly his widow wasted little time grieving over his grave before ordering her boys to get their wagon back into the train.

Something moved at the edge of Margaret's vision and she turned her head to see Bold Nose approaching from

11

downstream where old Winnedumah was building a wick-iup frame of willow branches. An angry flush surged through Margaret as she observed that the girl was wearing only a tattered blanket over her brief rabbitskin skirt—the standard costume of a Paiute maiden.

When Winnedumah had attached herself and her grand-daughter to their party at Lake Utah, Margaret had given them some of her dresses and insisted that they keep themselves decently covered when they were around white men. But these savages had no shame and would go near-naked as often as they thought they could get away with it. The Mormons back there should have done something about that, the way their leader Brigham Young was always talking about bringing the Indians the Word and helping them become civilized. Not that you could expect much in the way of respectable behavior from people who went in for polygamy and God knows what other strange practices.

Bold Nose shuffled up to the fire, her eyes demurely downcast, and held out an iron cooking pot. Margaret sniffed the odor of boiled *taboose*, the nut-flavored root tubers of a plant that somewhat resembled small potatoes. The Indians had learned to make use of all edible vegetation within their range, and Winnedumah's knowledge of what could be safely consumed was a valuable aid to their survival. The girl indicated with sign language that she wished to trade them the *taboose* for more antelope meat.

David bustled to make the swap, blushing as he tried not to stare at Bold Nose's considerable amount of exposed skin. Chance and the older O'Neal boys, however, were not at all reluctant to let their eyes linger on the girl's dusky bare arms and legs and the curve of her small firm breasts that the blanket only half concealed. In spite of the ravages of their desert crossing, Bold Nose's well-rounded young womanhood was disturbingly evident.

Margaret thought of reprimanding Winnedumah for the girl's appearance, but she was too tired to walk over to the old woman's wickiup. Scolding Bold Nose herself would do no good, because she understood very little English. So Margaret only sighed and joined the men in studying the naively unaware object of their lust. She had taken an in-

12

stant liking to the shy maiden and tried to help her learn the ways of white society.

But the cultural barriers between them were so great that they had achieved little communication. Aside from reading Bold Nose Bible verses that she did not understand and teaching her to dress modestly most of the time, Margaret had to admit that her efforts to improve the poor heathen's lot had not amounted to very much, although she also had managed to protect Bold Nose from the lecherous menfolk—so far. Now, with her time of confinement coming on, Margaret shuddered to think what might happen to the child. She was sorry that she couldn't do more for Bold Nose, who was such a sweet little thing and rather pretty, except for the oversized, owllike beak that had inspired her name.

Bold Nose completed her trade with David and returned to her grandmother, much to Margaret's relief. As the conversation returned to fabulous gold finds, she gazed fondly at the way Chance held Vicky Beth tenderly on his knee. At times he could be such an angel that she secretly envied Judy their brief hectic time together. Not that she was ever seriously interested in anyone but David, of course, but every woman had a right to her daydreams.

And Chance had been such an awful flirt when they were growing up. He still was a terrible tease with the ladies, for that matter. Like the fantastic stories he told about the scar on his cheek. Usually he claimed it as a mark of valor received from a Mexican bayonet at Buena Vista. But when fancy or drink moved him, he would as likely as not spin a tale of a saber duel with one of his messmates over a coquettish señorita.

Not that Chance was ever really *bad*, just high-spirited and adventurous. That was why they all loved him. It seemed to Margaret, as she let her thoughts drift back, that nearly all the high points of her and David's lives were marked by Chance's adventures. When they were sixteen they had promised themselves to each other, and about that time Chance had run off to Boston to sail as a cabin boy on a whaling ship. Three years later he had returned with wonderful stories of the South Seas and swept Judy off her feet—making Margaret and David's wedding a few weeks later pale in comparison.

After David and Chance went into business together, it had seemed natural—if not entirely fair—for Judy to have the first baby. The little girl inherited most of her mother's beauty, except for a square chin and dark curls that made her the spitting image of Chance when she set her mouth stubbornly. Chance named her Victoria Elizabeth for the two queens, and promised her everything due royalty.

Fatherhood had made a new man of Chance and for a while it appeared the two couples would be content to stay put and raise their children together. But then President Polk's war had come along and Chance had to be in on it. In a way, Chance had been to blame for giving Judy two lonely years at a time when she was least able to handle them. But that was no excuse, and Margaret could still cringe at the way Judy had openly carried on with Seth Gifford, finally even moving into his house.

Small towns being what they are, word of the scandal reached Chance long before he came home to what should have been a hero's welcome. Everyone expected him to try to kill Seth, or leastways raise a terrible ruckus.

But Chance, unpredictable as always, had accepted the situation calmly. He only shrugged, saying it was useless for him to try to win back a wife who no longer wanted him, and offered no resistance to Judy's divorce suit. He did make a half-hearted effort to get custody of Vicky Beth, until he saw that the law was firmly against him on that score, despite Judy's undeniable guilt. After that Chance seemed to put all thought of his ruined marriage out of his mind, as he became absorbed in the news of the Gold Rush.

Margaret and David encouraged Chance's hankering to go west, thinking it best that he seek a new life in a new country, and they were happy to see his zest for living revive as he threw himself into preparing for the venture. When David agreed to continue their partnership "clean across the continent," Chance insisted that he and Margaret should go ahead as far as Pittsburgh, while Chance stayed behind to sell off the last of their property. That would enable David to treat Margaret to a belated honey-

14

moon, Chance said, while transporting their two wagon-loads of trade goods and personal belongings to the river landing where they would take a steamboat as far west as St. Louis or Kansas City. Margaret was so excited to be taking her first big trip away from home that it never occurred to her that Chance might have another reason for arranging their moves in that manner. So it had been a shocking surprise to her when Chance had joined them in Pittsburgh the day before their steamer shoved off, leading a frightened and tearful Vicky Beth by the hand.

Watching the child nod sleepily against her father's chest, Margaret finally forgave Chance for having stolen her away from Judy and Seth. The first few weeks of the journey, when Vicky Beth had cried constantly for her mother, had been heartbreaking for Margaret, but eventually the child had turned into a brave little trooper. Now Vicky Beth seemed—like the rest of them—to be forgetting the old life in her eagerness to reach the new.

Margaret hoped that would include a new, more reliable mate for Chance, even if it cost her the pleasure of acting as Vicky Beth's substitute mother. But with real parenthood nearly upon her—as she was reminded by another kick in her lower ribs—Margaret figured she would be too busy to miss the little girl very much. Her eyes lovingly met David's over the fire and she thought of how he was going to be every bit as good a father as Chance. Even better, because he would never have to worry about losing her.

Chapter 2

Winnedumah sat crosslegged outside the doorway of her wickiup and sucked on a pipeful of crushed yerba santa leaves. She was dying for a real smoke, but she had decided to save her remaining pinch of tobacco for a more suitable occasion. Inside the uncompleted structure behind her, Bold Nose lay curled up exhaustedly in her blanket. Winnedumah listened to the girl's deep, even breathing and thought disgustedly of how soft the younger generations were becoming. Well, let her sleep. She had more serious matters to occupy her attention.

She stared unblinking at the main campfire, where the white people had finished their meal but not their talk. Her gaze focused on the *patrón* called Chance, as her mind worked ceaselessly at the challenge he presented to her. In some ways these gold-seeking *yanquis* were the most puzzling members of their race that she had yet encountered. They were even harder to understand than the Mormons. Fortunately she had enough experience with men to comprehend the vital key of their nature, regardless of their varying skin colors or tribal distinctions. White men were as eager as Indian braves to kill one another and take their women—they just didn't like to talk about it so much. Keeping that in mind, gaining control of white men became simply a matter of giving them what they really wanted in ways that didn't appear too obvious.

Winnedumah's education in the art of pleasing and manipulating men had begun early. As a maiden she had been captured by Apache raiders who knew the value of a strong, comely female slave. After making good use of her themselves, they eventually brought her to Santa Fe and sold her for two horses and an old musket to Don Francisco Gomez, a local rancher. Her new owner and his wife did not treat her too harshly, by the standards of the times. Winnedumah was content with her existence on the ranch, even when Don Francisco exercised his full proprietary rights to her body. Doña Maria Gomez was willing to overlook her husband's peccadillos—but not when they produced unsavory results that interfered with the servants' work.

The infant was stillborn, but by then Winnedumah had been traded to a less humane neighbor. After several runaways, whippings and changes of ownership she landed in Pepe Varga's cantina and crib house, where she was to spend much of her adult life. She was not unhappy there. The *aguardiente* fired her blood, she enjoyed gossiping with the other women, and servicing the customers was the least demanding work she could imagine doing.

She met a considerable variety of men over the years. From American traders and fur trappers she acquired some English and heard fantastic tales of great cities to the east. But Winnedumah, having learned quickly not to put much stock in anything men said, was never disappointed when they sobered up and moved on.

Eight more children were born to her, with three of them surviving to adulthood. One of the boys, Diego, showed enough promise in the mission school for the padres to send him to Mexico City to study for the priesthood. But all of them, when they grew old enough to become aware of her profession, turned away in shame and sought more respectable lives in other areas. Winnedumah accepted her losses stoically, finding solace in work and drink, unmindful that their impact on her highly perishable youth was steadily reducing her value to her master. When the inevitable day came that even the most intoxicated can-

17

tina patrons no longer found her desirable, she was unceremoniously given the freedom that she had long since ceased to want or know how to handle.

For a few years she wandered aimlessly, living hand-to-mouth on what little work and charity the frontier offered its outcasts, until good fortune brought her to the plaza at Abiquiu one day when several newly captured Paiute women and children arrived. The Ute slavers and their customers were having trouble understanding the terrified captives, whose dialect was similar to Winnedumah's, so she volunteered to interpret for them. While engaged in that, she was impressed by a tall, grim-featured Ute warrior who stood out strikingly from the other heavily armed, fierce-looking flesh traders.

Winnedumah soon learned that he was Walkara, Hawk-of-the-Mountains, a chieftain whose courage and ruthless daring had made him the leader of the most dreaded band of raiders north of Apache country. Young braves fought for the honor of riding with Walkara and no woman could resist his animal attraction, not even one who was too old to hope to arouse his interest.

It was a simple matter for Winnedumah to insinuate herself into Walkara's band until they accepted her as an unofficial camp follower. From that moment, she was caught up in the whirlwind of the chief's driving ambition as he galloped restlessly over the Great Basin as far as the Sierra in search of booty and slaves. All the tribes in the area were his prey, especially the nearly defenseless Paiutes, who made up much of the involuntary labor force on the great ranchos of Mexico's northern provinces.

Winnedumah, serving as the raiders' interpreter and cook, found it an exhilarating life—until one morning on the Little Humbolt River when Walkara grew bored with her company. As casually as the great chief had accepted her into his band, he discarded her beside the trail, along with a sickly ten-year-old female captive with a grotesquely large nose.

Winnedumah was tempted to give up and die then, but somehow her tough survival instinct enabled her to find sustenance in the wretched wilderness. Realizing that the child was her only remaining asset, she carefully nursed her back to health.

In the following five years Winnedumah taught Bold Nose to call her Grandmother and worked on her natural docility to make her a good servant. When the girl's body started to ripen, the old woman decided it was time to realize something from her investment.

Winnedumah first thought of an outright sale, then shrewdly judged she could do better than that. As she well knew, some white men were unbelievably sentimental. With the right handling, one of them might be induced to marry Bold Nose and take on the support of her only living kin. It was about time Winnedumah thought of doing something about her old age. At a rough guess, she was forty-five, looked sixty, and felt even older when her rheumatism acted up.

The closest white settlement was the Mormon community near Utah Lake, so Winnedumah traveled there to test the bride market. But she quickly learned there was no shortage of wives in that area. In casting about for more likely prospects, her attention was naturally drawn to the throngs of California-bound emigrants. There were plenty of single men among them, and several appealed to Winnedumah as good grandson-in-law material. But when she saw Chance Malcolm's resolute figure standing out of the crowd like a stallion among geldings, all other suitors were wiped from her mind. Not since her first sight of Walkara had she been so moved by a man's dominating presence. Surely this gray-eyed Anglo was destined to become a great chief among his people, with ample wealth and power to keep his women in idle comfort.

A little unobtrusive research confirmed the old woman's intuitive guess that Don Chance had no woman of his own—a serious handicap for a man with a small child, despite the considerable help given by the homely wife of his friend Señor Wheeler. Assured that her chosen victim was fair game, Winnedumah moved in with all her subtle skill at currying the favor of white people.

At first Margaret, suspicious of all Indians, was reluctant to accept the withered crone and half-naked adolescent girl into their party. But she relented when Winnedumah offered their services as all-round camp helpers in exchange for their food and whatever cast-off items the whites wished to give them. Chance, having gazed admiringly at Bold Nose's bare bosom before Margaret sternly ordered it covered, strongly supported hiring the two Paiutes—precisely the reaction Winnedumah had hoped for when she displayed the girl to him.

As the wagon train moved southwestward along the Old Spanish Trail, Winnedumah carefully studied Chance and worked out the strategy of her campaign. She was under no illusion that a white man would be inclined to honor Bold Nose with an innocent courtship and wedding, as the romantic fools often treated their own women. No, he would have to be given a sample of the wares to make him a serious buyer, when ample titillation had inflamed his desire. After that, Winnedumah knew she would need all of her wiles to keep that desire burning in a virile man who would be likely to lose interest in a woman once he'd had his pleasure with her. But by carefully instructing Bold Nose in the art of giving and withholding her favors, Winnedumah felt confident she could gradually get Chance into the habit of thinking of the girl as a permanent and necessary part of his life.

It was a daringly ambitious plan that might have succeeded, except for Margaret's interference. At first Winnedumah had welcomed the sharp-featured *patrona*'s help in safeguarding Bold Nose's virginity from the young swains who came prancing and sniffing around her like rutting bucks. But when Margaret proved equally determined to keep Chance away from the nubile maiden, the old woman sadly watched her hope of a comfortable retirement trickle away.

All across the western plains, Winnedumah could only seethe with silent frustration as the white woman conscientiously chaperoned her young ward. At times the disgruntled squaw was tempted to even the score by pairing up Bold Nose with David while Margaret was busy watching Chance. But fortunately she recognized David as a one-woman man, and she wanted no trouble with him.

Even after Don Chance led their small party away from

the wagon train, Winnedumah found scant opportunity to get Bold Nose away from Margaret's protective vigilance, although their mounting hardships soon gave them more serious causes for worry. Winnedumah could have warned them of the dangerous course they were taking, but as usual no one bothered to consult her and she knew better than to offer unasked advice to men.

Even so, the desert crossing had not been too strenuous, despite the whites' reluctance to take full advantage of the mesquite beans, lizards, and insects that provided an abundant food supply for Indians. Sometimes Winnedumah despaired of ever being able to teach these obstinate people the simplest facts of wilderness life that any Paiute child knew. Just this afternoon, while digging *taboose*, she had uncovered some tasty-looking wild parsnips that a hungry, ignorant white person would have greedily devoured—with fatal results.

Now, sitting before her wickiup with a dead pipe and the night chill stiffening her rheumatic joints, Winnedumah angrily brooded on the injustice of not being allowed to sell her property freely to Don Chance. She knew she must do something about that, and soon. For the longer they stayed in this Paiute-frequented valley, the more the odds mounted against Bold Nose retaining her high marriage value. Already Winnedumah's keen hearing had discerned in the surrounding darkness the faint stirrings and simulated birdcalls of wary scouting parties. For a while the valley Indians would be too fearful of the white men's guns to show themselves. But eventually some amorous brave, far more stealthy than the clumsy white men of the wagon train, would succeed in luring Bold Nose away from Margaret and into the bushes. Once that happened, Winnedumah knew she would have little chance of holding on to the girl.

Suddenly Winnedumah's eyes narrowed intently on the whites' campfire. Most of the exhausted travelers over there had already crawled into their bedrolls under the wagons. Only Chance and David remained talking by the fire. As the old woman watched, David straightened from his heel-hunkering position and moved wearily toward his wagon. Chance banked the fire, then took up his rifle and strolled down the riverbank where their oxen were grazing. Winnedumah forced herself to wait several minutes, then rose and went into the wickiup. Bold Nose protested sleepily when she was kicked awake, but she obediently moved to carry out Winnedumah's orders.

Chapter 3

Chance paused at the edge of a small meadow, watching the famished oxen fill their bellies with fine long grass, while a lopsided waning moon struggled to lift its brilliance over the Inyo Mountains. David was right—this was a hospitable valley, with plenty of good soil and water. It was almost a shame that they were on their way to become rich in the gold fields. A man could make a good life for himself and his family here, if he was inclined to turn his hand to farming. Chance was sure, despite his map's inaccuracies, that this must be the Owens River Valley. Somewhere to the south the river flowed into Owens Lake, a salt-thickened body of dead water with no outlet. But here the water was only slightly less clear and sweet than where it originated in the Sierra snowbanks.

Life abounded with ironies, Chance reflected somberly, thinking of the way fate had made sport of him. It seemed that some people were singled out to be fools and the harder they fought it the more foolish they became. But by heaven, Chance swore he would fight it, as long as he had a leg to stand on and a hope of regaining the old luck that had seen him through so many hazards.

Maybe his ill fortune had already taken a turn for the better. That they had gotten this far safely was a good sign, although it would be dangerously late in the year by the time they were ready to attempt the high mountain passes. His gaze traveled up the naked Sierra escarpment, silvered by moonglow, and he thought of the cannibalistic tragedy of the Donner Party somewhere up there, just three years ago. It was in hope of avoiding such a disaster that they had decided to take the southern route along the Old Spanish Trail to Los Angeles, then travel north through the San Joaquin Valley to the Mother Lode country. That was the most sensible course, but too slow to satisfy Chance's impatient craving for action. So he was ripe for a change when they met an eastbound traveler named Alvah Ward, who claimed he had already made his fortune in the gold fields and showed them a map of the area that he swore was true as gospel in every detail.

"So much for trusting the word of strangers," Chance muttered, starting to limp back to the camp on his rock-torn feet. He was thankful now that no other members of the wagon train, except Widow O'Neal and her brood, had been gullible enough to join his mad rush into the desert. It had been a costly blunder, and Chance pondered the risk of committing another one in a freezing mountain pass. Perhaps they should turn south and try to catch up with the wagon train at Los Angeles. That would be playing it safe, but it would also cost them much valuable time while other gold hunters poured over the mountains and staked out the best claims. Again his eyes probed the towering saw-toothed range, with the fabled gold fields lying so tantalizingly near on its opposite slopes. If only he could sprout wings and fly over that frustrating barrier . . . .

As he passed a copse of willows that grew right down to the water's edge, Chance suddenly halted at a splashing sound louder than the river's steady murmur. Instantly he brought up his rifle and slipped his finger inside the trigger guard, straining to see through the thick growth. He doubted that an Indian prowler would be so noisy; probably it was just some animal visiting its accustomed watering place. But he had better investigate, just in case. A wolf or bear could wreak havoc on the debilitated oxen.

Chance pushed his way into the shadowy thicket, hoping that whatever was on the other side would hear him com-

24

ing and run like the dickens. He really didn't feel as vigorous as he had let on to David when he insisted on taking the night's first tour of guard duty and if it was up to him, he would just as soon avoid trouble until he had his full strength back.

For all its density, the tangle of young trees and underbrush was only about a dozen feet wide. Almost before he realized it, Chance had passed through the leafy screen and stepped onto a small tongue of sand that licked out into the water from the bank. His first glimpse of the scene before him brought him to a dead stop, his breath caught in his throat.

A naked woman stood knee-deep in the water, facing away from him.

After a few stunned moments, Chance saw that she was Bold Nose, her wet body gleaming like new bronze in the moonlight. He tried to think clearly, wondering whatever had possessed her to come out for a bath at this time of night. But his mind was too busy contemplating her straight bare back and the curve of her lean hips and thighs to give thought to anything else.

As he watched, the girl scooped up a double handful of water and let it flow over her breasts, shivering as the cool stream trickled down her body and legs. Chance shivered, too, but not from the cold. His weariness was swept away in a hot, surging revival of his long-dormant manhood and he looked around uneasily, half expecting to hear Margaret's prim mouth scolding him for being so naughty.

Chance quietly leaned his rifle against a willow sapling and continued to stare at the picture of naked innocence, comparing it with other female bodies he had observed. He was reminded of the Pacific island beauties of his sailing days. What an experience that had been, with the laughing girls happily feeding his insatiable appetites for food and love.

Then there was Judy coming shyly to their wedding bed. How proud he had been that they had restrained their young urges and waited until then to consummate their love. And how stupidly he had believed her promise of eternal faithfulness!

The memory brought back some of his bitter resentment

at Judy's later betrayal. But Chance forced that out of his mind. No sense in blaming it all on Judy. He was at fault too, for leaving her alone so much.

Besides, as Margaret repeatedly told him, there were plenty of other women in the world—good, loyal women who would help him forget his unlucky first choice. Chance supposed she was right about that. But while he was waiting for such a woman to come along, there was no reason why he shouldn't enjoy the company of other kinds. Especially when opportunities like this one presented themselves.

Bold Nose started to turn toward him and he moved swiftly, wading out to her and clapping his right hand over her mouth. She only had time to struggle briefly before his left arm encircled her body and locked it to his.

"Don't be afraid, girl," Chance whispered. "I won't hurt you."

He smiled reassuringly, not knowing if she understood his words. Her flat brown eyes stared blankly at him and her tense body relaxed.

Chance slowly removed his hand from her mouth and, when she made no protest, replaced it with his mouth. Her lips lay flaccid against his, her body unresponding as his hands roved freely over her shoulders, back and buttocks. Chance would have liked her to be more lively, but the feel of her cool, smooth skin set his heart pounding with enough excitement for both of them. Breaking off the kiss, he lifted her out of the water and carried her over to where she had conveniently spread her blanket on the sand and gently laid her down on her back.

Bold Nose stared at the dark figure hastily stripping off his clothes over her. She was uncertain and fearful of what was going to happen to her, but also quite curious. All white men were awesome creatures to her and this one seemed a veritable god. She did not think she could have denied him anything, even without her grandmother's commands. When he touched her in the water she felt strangely moved and at the sight of his emerging hard, male nakedness she tried to close her eyes modestly but could not. When he knelt down and pulled her legs apart,

26

her breasts rose and fell rapidly as she panted like a small animal run to ground.

Chance tried to be gentle. He had always prided himself on being a considerate lover with even the crudest women. But when he pressed his body full upon her, he was no longer in control of it. The hot, raging fury within him demanded release, driving him into her welcoming softness with no regard for the tender barricade that was so roughly penetrated. Chance found her breasts with one hand while the other gripped her hair and pulled back her head. He tried to kiss her again, but her big nose kept getting in the way until their absurd contortions made him laugh even as she groaned and bit the air.

From her concealed position in the willows, Winnedumah watched the activities on the blanket approvingly. It was about time things started working out right for her. There was still much work to be done, but Bold Nose had made an excellent beginning. Leaving the girl to proceed on her own, the old woman crept silently away to celebrate the occasion with a pipe of real tobacco.

Chance opened his eyes to full daylight and stretched contentedly, enjoying the warmth of his blankets against the autumnal nip in the air. He felt ravenously hungry, but vibrantly refreshed by the soundest sleep he'd had in months. Recalling the reason for his total relaxation, he smiled and stole a glance at the Indian women's camp. Winnedumah was seated before her wickiup, while Bold Nose busied herself with the breakfast fire. Both of them were expressionless and seemed totally uninterested in the whites.

" 'Bout time you were up," Margaret's voice called cheerfully. "Move those lazy bones, if you want some breakfast while it's still hot."

Chance looked at her stirring a fire-blackened kettle, as a vagrant breeze brought him the tempting aroma of bean and meat stew seasoned with wild onions and *taboose*. Even more inspiring was the steaming coffee pot on the coals beside the kettle. "Yes, ma'am. You don't have to call me twice for that," Chance replied, throwing off his blankets and reaching for his boots.

Michael O'Neal, squatting at the fire with Margaret, quickly poured a mug of coffee and brought it to Chance, making no effort to conceal his eagerness to please the older man. Despite his demonstrated ability to cope with adult responsibilities, Michael was still boy enough to be overwhelmed by hero-worship. Chance was flattered by the youth's adoration and responded to it with big-brotherly affection. In his secret opinion, Michael was the only one of the O'Neal brothers who showed any real promise, combining as he did his mother's hard-driving courage with his father's patient intelligence. James and Francis—aged fifteen and fourteen—were too full of high-spirited mischief, and a noticeable streak of cruelty, to take life seriously. And twelve-year-old Peter was a sniveling mama's boy who would probably never develop a mind of his own even if his domineering mother ever gave him an opportunity to do so, which seemed highly unlikely.

Chance willingly conceded that he could be wrong—and hoped that he was—about Susan O'Neal and her sons. But as things stood now, he made no bones about his preference for Michael. Even physically the lad was the pick of the litter, standing nearly six straight feet tall with a gaunt face and frame that promised to fill out handsomely. His reddish brown hair and freckle-splashed complexion had a healthy outdoors glow and his pale blue eyes could face a man squarely with only a hint of shyness.

"Thanks, Mick." Chance accepted the mug and sipped the scalding black eye-opener. "How did things go on your watch last night?"

"Just fine, sir, except for the shot I had to fire to frighten off a bear. But I reckon you heard that?"

"Uh, yes," Chance lied. "I was going to get up to see if you needed any help, but I figured you were able to handle any emergency."

Michael blushed with pleasure at the compliment, suddenly tongue-tied.

Chance laughed and clapped a comradely hand on the boy's shoulder, then bent to roll up his blankets. Nearby, Susan O'Neal snapped orders at her other sons as they fetched water and firewood to a huge corrugated washtub she had set up beside a heaping pile of dirty clothing. As

28

usual, the energetic little woman allowed no grass to grow under her feet when there was work to be done.

After dashing away the last of his sleep in a bucket of chilled water, Chance joined Margaret at the cooking fire, gratefully accepting the plate of stew and scorched pan biscuits she handed him. "Where's Vicky Beth?" he asked, looking around.

"Gone with David to see to the animals," Margaret said. "She doesn't take after her slugabed father, thank goodness."

Chance blew a spoonful of stew cool and wolfed it down. "Yes, I'll have to do something about my slothful ways. Especially now that you're going to have to start taking it easy, for young Davy's sake."

Margaret smiled and laid her right hand on her bulging middle. "I wish I were as sure as you that it's a boy."

"Of course it's a boy," Chance assured her. "I can tell by the way you've been so happy about it. If there was another female coming into the family, you'd be jealous as all getout."

"That's mighty comforting. But it seems to me you said about the same thing when Judy was carrying Vicky Beth."

Chance shrugged away the reminder. "Oh, well, everybody's got a right to make a mistake now and then, as Andy Jackson said when he found out he'd fought the Battle of New Orleans after the war was over."

Margaret hesitated, then decided she had to share her secret with someone. "Yes, everybody makes mistakes, even Doc Hutchings."

For a few moments Chance continued eating and glanced eastward at the sun struggling over the Inyo ridgeline. Then his eyes jerked sharply back to Margaret and widened in astonishment. "You mean——?"

Margaret nodded and modestly lowered her gaze, although there had never been any awkwardness between them about this sort of thing, farm-bred as they were and familiar with the matings of animals. "I think you'd better start building some sort of shelter for me. But don't tell David just yet. I hate to spoil his dream of reaching the gold fields before snow flies."

"Yes, that's right," Chance muttered, thinking that David wasn't likely to be the most disappointed one. It did seem that the women in his life were determined to mess him up with their unpredictableness, even when they were doing the most womanly things. But before he had much time to fret over the matter, the voice of the happy father-to-be called out to them. They turned to see David trudging up the riverbank, with Vicky Beth running excitedly ahead of him, irrepressible joy burning the roses in her cheeks to bright flames as she clutched something in her small muddy hands.

"Papa! Papa! Look what I found!"

And Chance, as he had done with all the countless rare treasures his daughter had discovered on their west-going journey, solemnly accepted and exclaimed over the young pond turtle that stared tolerantly out at him from the safety of its shell.

Chapter 4

In the following days Vicky Beth and the younger O'Neal boys found much in the valley to delight their eager curiosity, while their elders attended to the mundane details of survival. Chance and David spent much of their time hunting, leaving Winnedumah and Bold Nose to construct a snug wickiup for Margaret. Antelope, deer, bear and smaller game were fairly plentiful and, being unaccustomed to firearms, easily bagged. The travelers quickly regained their strength on the fresh meat and jerked the surplus for future use.

Sometimes Chance and David came across Indian encampments that showed signs of hasty evacuation. Chance suspected the inhabitants were watching them from concealment and he cautioned David against disturbing any of their belongings. They even left a few trinkets as goodwill gifts. But the valley Paiutes cautiously evaded contact with the newcomers until the third day, when Winnedumah appeared with a solemn, gray-haired man whom she introduced as Lightning Tracker, chief of the band upon whose territory the whites were camped.

Chance was impressed by the way the old chief stood straight and patient with the calm dignity of his office. While the others looked on curiously, Chance cordially greeted Lightning Tracker and presented him with a new hatchet he had salvaged from their lost store goods. Lightning Tracker impassively accepted the gift and listened as Winnedumah interpreted Chance's statements that the white people came in peace and greatly desired to be friends with the Indians, but were prepared to defend themselves with devastating firepower if they were attacked.

Lightning Tracker replied that his people also wanted peace and the visitors were welcome to remain as long as they wished. His expression displayed none of the impatience he felt at Chance's lengthy speech on how the two races should treat one another. The Indians must not try to harm the whites or steal from them, Chance warned. And the whites in turn would respect the Paiutes' rights. Lightning Tracker had already heard that from Winnedumah, who had claimed that Don Chance was a great chief and warrior with powerful medicine at his command.

Lightning Tracker was not without diplomatic experience in dealing with white men. He had met Ogden, Walker, and Fremont when they had led exploring parties through the valley, and his tribe had had no trouble with them. Besides, at this time of the year Numa—the People, who for some unknown reason foreigners insisted on calling Paiutes—were too busy gathering and storing their winter food supply to bother with another group of drifters. Now, after having tried conscientiously to make that clear to Winnedumah and her companions, Lightning Tracker was getting tired of being told what he could and could not do around white people. Finally, when Chance gave no indication of ever ending his discourse, the old man said abruptly to Winnedumah:

"Tell the white chief what I have said, I have said. My heart is on the ground. Let him look at it, if he cares to."

With that, Lightning Tracker turned his back on the whites and walked away. Chance stared after him in puzzlement, wondering if he had been insulted. David chuckled as Winnedumah relayed the chief's message.

"I guess he told you, Chance."

Chance agreed, laughing at his comeuppance. "He seems

a good sort—straight and trustworthy. But we'll keep our guard up anyhow, just in case."

That was typical of Chance, David thought. But this time his precautions proved unnecessary. In the next few days other valley Indians emerged from hiding to look the white party over. That seemed to be the extent of their interest in the newcomers. After assuring themselves that these intruders were not hostile, the Paiutes went about their business pretty much as usual. It was the time of harvesting the ripe nuts of pinon pines on the high Inyo slopes and foraging parties returning with heavy loads of that vital food were far more important than any number of white visitors. That, along with their other preparations for winter, kept the natives fully occupied most of the time.

However, there was some contact between the two races, as Chance attempted to converse and trade with the Indians. With Winnedumah's help, he swapped a few bits of ribbon and bright cloth for a bushel of pinon nuts, which made a tasty addition to their meals. But Chance's most urgent need was for accurate information about the paths over the mountains, and the Paiutes were able to supply that from their trading expeditions with the trans-Sierran tribes. The Paiutes' most valuable trade item was salt collected from the crusted shores of Owens Lake. The salt-poor Indians on the other side of the mountains were so desperate for it that they would exchange anything—even their daughters—for a few rock-hard cakes of the precious crystals. That was how Lightning Tracker had obtained one of the four wives who had helped him while away his fifty-odd years in the valley.

Occasionally Lightning Tracker and a few of his followers would visit the white camp, ostensibly to observe the habits and implements of a more sophisticated civilization. But actually the old chief had already learned all he cared to know about the ways of the white men. Some of their weapons and tools were quite handy, of course. But in his conservative old age he was content to continue doing things as his people had always done them. The truth of the matter, although Lightning Tracker would not have confessed it under torture, was that he was drawn to the

33

white travelers' camp because Winnedumah fascinated him.

He had never known a woman like her—so much one of the People in appearance, yet so worldly and knowledgeable of white society. He could listen spellbound for hours to her stories about her adventures with the Mexicans and Chief Walkara's raiders, which seemed to him as fabulous as the legends of the gods. Just why he was so powerfully attracted to a mere woman, especially one who had so little to offer a man, was a frustrating mystery to Lightning Tracker. He still had one living wife—Slow Of Speech— who was young and active enough to fulfill his needs, so there was no good reason for him to gaze longingly at the quarrelsome old squaw. His strange emotional disturbance made him long for the more peaceful days of his youth, when his keen eyes and nose had earned him the reputation of a hunter who could follow the track of lightning over the earth. It was ridiculously humiliating for a man of his age to fall in love, but there didn't seem to be much he could do about it except remain silent and keep the shame to himself.

For her part, Winnedumah tolerated the old chief and courted his friendship for whatever use he could be to her while she was in the valley. As she had anticipated, several of the young Paiute braves expressed interest in Bold Nose, and Lightning Tracker was helpful in discouraging them when Winnedumah explained that the girl was already spoken for. Only Lightning Tracker's youngest son Hu-pwi (Desert Thorn) was too smitten by Bold Nose's charms to stay away from her, but he was too shy to do anything but stare hungrily at her from a safe distance.

Winnedumah ignored the lovesick youth and continued to instruct Bold Nose in the womanly wiles of holding her white master's attention. Now that Don Chance had so eagerly taken the bait she had dangled before him, the old woman knew she must play him skillfully to keep him on the hook. Therefore she ordered Bold Nose to go to Chance only every other night and to heighten his desire with a tantalizing display of modest reluctance before surrendering. Winnedumah also taught the girl certain lovemaking techniques that white men were known to esteem, and then waited with fearful apprehension that Don Chance might be put off by such forwardness in one who was so recently an innocent maiden. But, as Bold Nose happily reported later, she need not have worried about that.

Bold Nose had good reason to be happy. She was doing what she had been trained to do—serve her grandmother and please men. And with such a man, it was difficult to say who was being pleased the most. In Chance's powerful but gentle embrace she experienced a soaring fulfillment unknown to most women of her time. Even more exhilarating was the spiritual lift she derived from knowing that she belonged to a man who was judged superior even among his own people. Even Winnedumah's warning that Don Chance might eventually decide to take a white wife and keep her only as a concubine and servant did not diminish Bold Nose's contentment. The security of being his woman in any capacity was far more than she had ever dreamed of achieving and her simple heart could conceive of no greater joy than to spend the rest of her life in devoted bondage to him. She could hardly wait to give him his first son.

Chance, however, had other things on his mind. The girl's warm, eager body was a pleasant distraction, but only a minor one to his all-consuming goal of getting over the mountains while they still enjoyed good weather. From what the Indians had told him, he surmised it would be well-nigh impossible to maneuver heavy wagons through the rugged passes between the towering peaks. That meant they were faced with the possibility of abandoning their remaining possessions and going ahead on foot. Chance was reluctant to ask his friends to make that sacrifice, and he didn't much relish the prospect himself.

Yet he had to go on. He was driven by an irresistible inner force that was more than just a greedy eagerness to get rich quick. It was hard for Chance to explain how he felt, but he thought it was pretty well summed up in the patriotic statement of John L. O'Sullivan, editor of the *New York Morning News*: "Our manifest destiny is to overspread and to possess the whole of this continent which Providence has given us."

Manifest Destiny.

The phrase had a thrilling, idealistic ring, like "life, liberty and the pursuit of happiness." To Chance it meant more than just the physical ownership and occupation of North America by U.S. citizens. It meant the spreading of the free and progressively improving American way of life, with its solid traditions of individual responsibility, honest hard work, and equal justice for all. Chance had had only five grades of formal schooling and his mind was not well suited for deep philosophical thinking. But he sincerely believed in the moral superiority of his country, which he thought could become a shining example to the rest of the world.

Perhaps California's gold was just a lure to bring vast numbers of Americans to the newly acquired western territories. That wasn't important. What mattered was that they *did* come out here, to create new states and populate them with prosperous, happy, growing communities that were the backbone of the nation's greatness. Chance felt that he was living through an important chapter in human history, and he was impatient to get out of this desolate wilderness and play a more active role in writing that chapter.

It was near the end of their second week in the valley when Chance came upon an unexpected solution to his problem.

Chapter 5

David was returning from a successful morning of fowling. With his shotgun over his shoulder and his game bag heavy with wild ducks and geese, he thought happily of the good time they would have around the campfire tonight. Abruptly the three Paiute men with him turned off the path before he saw their small village on the riverbank.

It hurt David's feelings a little to see them stalk away from him without even a thank-you gesture; after all, his shooting had accounted for most of the dead birds they were carrying. But he had learned not to be surprised by the uncivilized behavior of Indians. You just had to make allowances for the poor heathens. He paused for a moment to rest and watch the women of the village grinding acorn meal in stone mortars. It certainly was amazing the way these people could be so ignorant and lazy about most things, and yet were downright ingenious when it came to making the most of what nature provided them. Those fellows who had been duck-hunting with him were a good example of that.

David had found them at a quiet lagoon off the river's main channel and had watched curiously as they floated hollowed-out gourds among a flock of feeding fowl. When the birds were no longer disturbed by the bobbing objects around them, an Indian would slip through the tule reeds with his head inside a gourdshell, peeping through an air hole above waterline. Slowly the gourd would drift over to an unsuspecting duck, which would suddenly disappear as the Indian gripped its webbed foot, jerked it underwater and snapped its neck. The work required much time, skill and patience, and the Indians were glad to have David's shotgun make it easier for them.

David started off on his final quarter-mile to camp. Yes, these Paiutes were nobody's fools. They hardly had any tribal organization to speak of, but the scattered family groups could work together for the common good. A few days ago old Lightning Tracker had shown him how they used digging sticks to make shallow ditches to clumps of *taboose*, rye grass, and other plants they used for food. It was the first irrigation system David had ever seen and it greatly interested him. He spent several hours studying the rich, level ground along the river, imagining what it would look like with a network of ditches carrying water to fields of corn, wheat, oats, and other crops. With such a contrivance freeing the farmer from his dependence on rain, farming could almost be a pleasure. That is, as long as the river always carried an ample water supply, and Lightning Tracker assured him it had never been known to run dry.

It did give a man something to think about.

Coming to their encampment, the first thing David saw was Chance seated on a water keg, polishing his sword. An Indian sat crosslegged before him. David didn't pay much attention to him; he was just another Indian. But the sight of Chance with his shiny cavalry saber was always worth a second look. The weapon, along with his cap and ball Navy Colt, were his most prized mementos of his military service. He often wore the revolver for target shooting or possible defense, but only on special occasions did he take the saber out of his trunk to show off his fencing skill.

After giving his bag of game birds to Margaret, who called Vicky Beth to help her pluck and clean them, David strolled inquiringly over to Chance. "You getting ready for another war, Chance?"

"Not likely. I'm just trying to do some business with my friend here."

"The Paiute?"

"Look again. He's not a Paiute."

David inspected the seated Indian, who stared disinterestedly at the ground. He did seem slimmer and more sharp-featured than the stockily built Paiutes, and he wore the ragged remains of a cotton shirt and trousers instead of the usual animal skin clothing. "Well, what is he then?"

"As near as I can make out, he comes from a tribe called the Salinan, 'way over near the Pacific coast."

"You don't say!" David was surprised. He had heard that California Indians seldom strayed far from their homegrounds, unlike the tribes whose hunting and warring activities took them far afield. "What's he doing here?"

"Trying to be a Paiute. They're not too keen on it and neither is he, I gather. But he figures it's better than starving and they're willing to put up with him as long as he makes himself useful."

"I mean, how come he's so far away from his own stomping grounds?"

"That was what I wanted to know. By the way, his name's Paul the Apostle, and he's a real honest-to-goodness Christianized Indian. The mission padres over at San Miguel baptized him with that name and taught him a few things. Unfortunately he doesn't seem to have learned any more Spanish than I did, but we're slowly getting to understand each other."

"A baptized Indian." David regarded Paul the Apostle with growing interest. "Well, that's something, even if he is a papist. What you fixing to do with him?"

"Business, like I said. He's got something we can use."

"What on earth could that be?"

"That takes some explaining. After the padres got through with him, he worked on some big rancho for a while and learned a bit about tending animals, but not enough. The *patron* didn't treat him right, so Paul decided to even the score by stealing some of his horses. He figured if he took two good ones for breeding stock, he could start his own herd. He pulled that off all right, but he was so afraid his boss's *vaqueros* might track him down that he didn't stop running till he got here."

Chance put aside his polishing cloth and lightly ran a

whetstone along the fine edge of his saber. For the first time, Paul the Apostle betrayed a trace of expression as his eyes narrowed on the bright blade.

"So now you want to get his horses?" David guessed.

Chance smiled. "Not exactly. You see, the animals he took weren't actually horses. They were mules—a fine male and female. Now Paul can't for the life of him understand why he's not getting any colts and fillies out of 'em."

David joined Chance in grinning at the poor Indian's backwardness. Any ten-year-old farm boy worth his salt knew you could only produce a mule by crossbreeding a horse with a jackass. Being hybrids, mules themselves were always barren. "That's about the most pitiful thing I've ever heard of."

"Yes, I think he's about got his bellyful of mules by now. But they're just what we need to get over the mountains. Mules are more sure-footed than oxen and they can survive on what little grass grows up there. I ought to be able to pack enough supplies on them to make it to the Mother Lode country, even in bad weather."

"You mean leave our wagons and most everything we own behind?" David demanded. "Oh, Chance, that'd be making it awful hard on the women and young ones."

Chance looked away from David's worried eyes. "I've given that a lot of thought, and it strikes me that we might stand a better chance if we split up temporarily. I could make a swift crossing alone, or perhaps with Mickey O'Neal, while you take the others down around the southern end of the range. That way, I can stake out a rich claim for us before the country fills up, and I'll spread the word around the settlements where you can find me. With luck, we'll all be together again in a month or so."

David turned the proposition over in his mind and had to agree that it did seem quite sensible. "I just hope we'll be able to get along without you," he said plaintively.

"Of course you will," Chance laughed. "I'm not really as all-fired important as I've led you to believe. Now let me see if I can do some sharp mule-trading with this gentleman." He stood up and made a few fancy thrusts and parries with his saber, watching the Indian's eyes intently follow his movements. *"Quiere esta? You like it?"*

Paul the Apostle stared noncommittally.

"You surely don't mean to trade your sword for his mules?" The possibility shocked David.

"I don't like it either, but this seems to be the only thing we have that interests him. Except for my rifle, and that's out of the question." Chance flourished the saber again and waved the Indian to his feet. "*Vamonos, amigo*. I want to have another look at your animals."

David watched the two men amble off to the northwest. He had no doubt that Chance would get the mules, one way or another, once he had set his heart on them. And Chance was certainly right in declaring that they must soon move on; the beautifully clear, warm weather they were enjoying couldn't last too much longer. Still, David was troubled by the thought of dividing their small force, after having come so far together. His first impulse was to discuss the matter with Margaret, but she seemed strangely distracted as she went mechanically about her chores. For the first time in their marriage they were unable to share their thoughts, and David was at a loss to explain it. There was a subtle but decided air of change in the camp. Even little Vicky Beth appeared to sense it when her father returned a few hours later leading two sorry-looking gray mules over whom he and the O'Neal boys showered lavish care. David tried to cheer up Vicky Beth by taking her for a walk along the riverbank, but he was unable to shake off the feeling that the two of them had become outsiders among their own people.

The feeling persisted throughout the evening, and grew stronger when he crawled between the covers beside Margaret on the feather mattress that had been his mother's wedding gift to them. Hesitantly he asked Margaret if anything was wrong. When she gave no answer, he lay for a long time staring up at the dark dome of the wickiup with dreaded suspicion like a heavy weight on his chest. It was almost a relief when, hours later, he was awakened by a warm, moist sensation along his left flank and Margaret ordering him to go bring Mrs. O'Neal to her—immediately.

Giving birth was all that Margaret had dreamed and feared it would be. There was the expected pain, and moments of barely controllable terror when she thought of dangerous complications. But even as the waves of tension and release swept through her, she was filled with the wonder and glory of her labor. *What God hath joined together . . .*

The minister's words echoed in Margaret's mind with new meaning. It had always been her strongest desire to make a perfect marriage with David, in which their two separate beings would merge into a harmonious whole. In a way they had achieved that from the beginning, feeling and acting together almost as a single person. Now even physically the best of each of them would be combined in a new body and given life by their love. Despite her discomfort, Margaret felt very close to God.

"There, darlin'. Squeeze me hand and bear down hard with the contractions," Susan O'Neal said gently at her side. "Don't try to fight it. Just let nature have her way."

Margaret looked up at the Irishwoman's comforting smile in the smoky glow of the whale oil lamp. Susan leaned over to check Margaret's progress, then settled back on her heels and stroked Margaret's cheek.

"I think I can manage, thank you," Margaret grunted between her teeth. "But I wish I hadn't made such a mess of the bed."

"That's nothing to the mess there'll be when you've finished. But don't worry. It'll all come out in the wash."

Margaret started to speak but was interrupted by another mighty spasm. When she was able to rest again, she said: "Is David all right?"

"No, but husbands never are at times like this. I asked Mr. Malcolm to get him drunk, if there's enough whiskey left. 'Twill be the best way to keep him from getting under foot."

"David doesn't drink."

"Then this'll give him a good excuse to start." Susan looked down at Margaret's exposed loins again. "Dear me! Is it coming so soon?"

"Is it?" Margaret could hardly speak as the grinding pressure nearly crushed the breath out of her.

Susan finally shook her head, as Margaret's pain subsided. "I'm afraid we'll just have to wait and let the little darlin' take its own sweet time. Children never have any consideration for their mothers, I can tell you."

Susan proved to be an accurate authority. Throughout the night and the following morning Margaret's labor dragged on, filling her alternately with hope and despair. Her mind grew dull with the agonizing monotony of straining and releasing her abdominal muscles without producing any noticeable results. It was not until nearly noon of October 31, 1849 that the first white baby was born in Owens Valley. Margaret, completely exhausted by then, forced herself to stay awake long enough to see that he was a fine, big, healthy boy.

"What a Halloween prank to play on your mother, pumpkin," she sighed, holding the squirming red body to her breast.

"And what will we name this precious bundle from heaven?" Chance asked, awkwardly cradling the baby in his arms.

Before David could say that he hadn't given the matter much thought, beyond wanting to have his father's memory honored, Margaret replied: "David Chance Wheeler, of course."

Chance cocked an eye at David. "Can't you do better than that?"

David considered Margaret's determined expression and smiled sheepishly. "I guess not."

"Then I guess it'll have to do, but God help anyone who has to go through life with a handle like that."

"I think David Chance has a nice ring," Margaret insisted. "And I like the initials, too. D.C. They ought to give him a boost in the right direction."

"If that's what you have in mind, maybe you should call him White House," Chance teased.

Francis O'Neal explained the wordplay to his illiterate mother, who repaid his kindness with a cool stare. It was the second day of David Chance Wheeler's life, and his mother had insisted she was recovered enough to be taken outside for some fresh air. Margaret sat with her back against the trunk of the campsite's largest live oak and looked beyond Chance and David at the river's rock-ruffled surface. All the other members of their party were gathered around her, except for Vicky Beth, who was over at the Indian women's camp watching Winnedumah deftly weaving willow withes into a basket. Vicky Beth had been permitted to hold the new baby for a few moments, but she wasn't very impressed by him. She thought it was much more fun to play with her dolls.

Chance carefully leaned down to place the infant in Margaret's arms. "Well, young Master D.C., I don't want to make you feel unwelcome, but you've certainly arrived at an awkward time."

"How so, Mr. Malcolm?" asked Francis O'Neal.

"Because a newborn babe and its mother are hardly up to the strain of a mountain crossing, especially this late in the year. For safety's sake, we had best winter here, or take the roundabout southern route when Mrs. Wheeler has regained her strength."

"Nonsense," Margaret said. A leaf fluttered down to settle on the baby's blanket. She picked it up and waved it enticingly before his unfocused blue eyes. "David has told me about your plan to go ahead with the mules, and I think it's an excellent idea. The rest of us will do very nicely here until we are able to go on."

"I wish I could be sure of that," Chance said uneasily. "But I'd never forgive myself if anything happened to you just because I couldn't wait to get to the gold."

"I'll be all right," Margaret insisted. "Just ask Mrs. O'Neal."

The widow nodded. "Aye, she seems a strong, healthy young woman, and the child is quite normal. The birthing took a lot out of her, but that's usually the case with a first baby. With three or four weeks of rest and good food, she ought to be her old self again, I should say."

Margaret smiled reassuringly at Chance. "You see? There's no reason in the world for you to let me slow you up."

"That's right," David seconded. "We ought to do just dandy here. The Indians are friendly, I've ample powder and shot to keep us in meat, and Mrs. O'Neal will be on hand to give Margaret whatever womanly comforting she needs."

44

Susan O'Neal peered levelly at David. "I fear there has been a misunderstanding, Mr. Wheeler. For it is my intention to journey on with Mr. Malcolm. 'Tis sorry I am if you judged otherwise."

David, taken aback by the unexpected announcement, flushed and spluttered, while Chance said patiently: "I don't think that's a wise decision, Mrs. O'Neal, for the way ahead entails much hardship and sacrifice. And although you've proved yourself an intrepid traveler up to this point, I would advise you to let Michael go on with me as your agent. I'll help him stake out a good mining claim and work it until you catch up with us."

Michael eagerly concurred with Chance, but his mother swiftly silenced him. "Thanks for your advice, sir, but I must do what I deem best for me family. Michael is a fine lad and manly in many ways, but scarcely fit for a mission o' such importance. I could not be true to my dear husband's memory if I entrusted his sons' futures to a mere stripling."

"Oh, Ma!" Michael protested, deeply embarrassed, but to no avail.

Equally futile were Chance's and David's heated arguments on Michael's behalf. Susan was unusually softspoken and careful not to disturb the baby with harsh profanity, but within the next hour it became obvious that Chance had at last met his match in stubborn determination.

"Well, if that's your decision, then there's no more to be said about it," Margaret finally broke into the deadlocked conversation. "I shall miss your company, of course, Mrs. O'Neal. But I suppose I would do the same in your place."

"I'm glad you're so understanding," Susan said gratefully. "I feel that guilty to be leaving you in this heathen wilderness, but charity does begin at home, the Book tells us."

Chance scowled at her. "I'm not sure I agree with that. What if Mrs. Wheeler should need some help that only another woman can give her?"

"Oh, tush, tush," Margaret scoffed. "We're American citizens on American soil. If we're not safe here, then there's no place in this world where we will be safe. Isn't that right, David?"

"I guess so," David helplessly agreed.

"Besides, I'll have the squaws to help me. You don't intend to take them along, do you, Chance?"

Chance gazed over at the Paiutes' wickiup, where Vicky Beth was struggling to imitate Winnedumah's deft basketry with a handful of twigs. He wondered where Bold Nose was at that moment. The warmth of her body and her shy smile glowed within him, but he had already started putting that part of his life away. "No, they wouldn't be of any use to me as guides through the mountains, since the old woman has never been up there. Besides, they'll be better off here with their own people."

"And Vicky Beth? You'll leave her with me, of course."

"Yes, but I don't know how I'll break the news to her."

"Leave that to me." Margaret cuddled her fidgety son. "When do you think you'll be ready to leave?"

"Oh, I should have the mules fully broken to the packs I made for 'em in another couple of days. Paul the Apostle let 'em run wild until they nearly forgot the work they were trained for."

"Then I had better be about sorting out the things we'll carry with us," Susan O'Neal declared, ordering her boys to their feet. "You are welcome to anything we leave behind, Margaret, though I fear 'twill be slim pickings."

"Thank you," Margaret said. "For everything." She watched the Irish family move away to their wagon, then smiled at David as the baby piped out an angry cry. "Now if you'll help me back into the hut, I think this little feller needs some tending to."

After carrying her inside, the two men strolled down to the river's edge. They were strangely silent as Chance scooped up a handful of pebbles and began hurling them as far as he could across the water. After a moment's pause, David did likewise. "You sure you'll be all right here?" Chance finally asked.

David laughed carelessly. "'Course we will. I've already picked out a good spot to put up a cabin for the cold weather."

"Where?"

"Around the second bend downstream. That long level stretch above the highwater line. We'll be right snug there,

46

and the land is good. If you don't strike it rich over there, come on back here in the spring and we'll see what kind of a crop we can raise." David smiled at himself. "But that's just fool talk, because you're going to make us so rich that we'll none of us ever have to do a tap of work again."

"That's right. The only things we'll harvest will be gold nuggets—like this!" Chance snatched a handful of gravel and splattered the river with it. But even as they laughed together, he wondered about the lurking seriousness behind David's jokes about farming. Both David's and Margaret's roots were planted deep in the soil; Chance had managed to pull them up once, but he wasn't sure he could do it again. And, gazing from the friendly valley up at the Sierra's grimly challenging face, he wasn't sure he would want to.

Chapter 6

The morning of their departure was bitingly clear. Light
frost webbed the grass and air as intoxicating as chilled
wine flushed the sadness of parting from their hearts.
David felt almost cheerful as he helped Chance load the
packs and cinch them onto the reluctant mules. By the
time the naked sky had turned into a gray sponge and blotted up the stars, Chance and the O'Neals were ready to
leave. Chance, gulping a final cup of coffee as the sun's
first rays made the toothy Sierra appear to grin invitingly,
gave David's hand a hard squeeze and briefly took Margaret in his arms.

"So long, Sis. You see that you get your rest, now. And
take good care of the future president."

"I will," Margaret promised, smiling at her son as he
slept peacefully strapped to the Paiute cradleboard that
Winnedumah had made for him.

Vicky Beth stood by silently staring at the ground. She
had taken the news of her father's decision to leave her
behind pretty well at first. But watching his travel preparations had filled her with a mounting dread that she could
not understand but dimly recalled as part of the terrifying
experience of being taken away from her mother. Now as
the possibility of losing her only remaining parent became a

48

certainty, the discomforting fear turned into gut-wrenching panic.

"Be a good girl while I'm gone, Princess," Chance said, picking Vicky Beth up and giving her a warm hug and kiss. "Mind Aunt Maggie and Uncle David the same as you would me."

His stubbled cheek rubbed hers as he started to hand her to David. Watching his face go away from her, Vicky Beth saw the scar on his cheek stand out clearly, then blur in a gush of tears. "Take me with you, Papa!" she suddenly cried out, clinging desperately to him.

"Hush, honey! That's no way for my big girl to act." Chance pried her grasping fingers from his arm and stepped back in surprise. "I've told you why I can't take you with me, but I'll be back before you know it."

"No, I want to go with you!" Vicky Beth wailed, squirming against David's restraining arms.

"There, there, Vicky," Margaret tried to soothe the child. But Vicky Beth only sobbed louder as her father moved away quickly to take the mules' lead rope. The balky animals firmly stood their ground at first, but were soon put in motion by switches wielded by the O'Neal boys. As the small caravan got under way, Susan O'Neal quickly embraced Margaret and patted Vicky Beth's cheek. David thought he detected an expression of pity and remorse in the Irishwoman's eyes, before she swung a heavy pack onto her back and strode off after her sons.

"Papa! Papa! Come back!" Vicky Beth screamed, her terrible anguish tearing at David's heart as her tiny hands wildly clawed at his face. Both he and Margaret were nearly in tears as they petted the hysterical child. Young D.C. Wheeler, aroused by the tragic drama, opened his eyes and contributed a soft squall of his own, then dozed off again.

But Chance gave his daughter only a backward glance and a parting wave as he moved steadfastly over the valley's gently rising western floor, his eyes fixed on the towering granite wall before him.

From their own camp, Winnedumah and Bold Nose silently watched the departing travelers. Blank-faced with the long-accustomed habit of accepting whatever fate befell her, Winnedumah swallowed her bitter disappointment. Her plan to make Don Chance her permanent benefactor had been a slim gamble at best, she realized, and now that she had lost there was no point in grieving about it. Sadly but resolutely her gaze shifted from the white man who was leaving the valley to the one who was staying.

But Bold Nose's attention was riveted to Chance. Behind flat dry eyes, her mind burned with pain and puzzlement, unable to comprehend why he was abandoning her so dispassionately. Up till two nights ago, he had seemed so totally satisfied with her fawning eagerness to please him that she had assumed that he would always want to keep her.

For years the girl had been thoroughly trained by her grandmother to think of herself as a creature of little worth, a lowly dog who could only hope to be fed and fondled occasionally by whomever owned her. Unable to imagine a higher station in life, Bold Nose had learned to be content with the role and play it lovingly. And had she not been a good dog to her white master, submissively obedient to his commands while courting his favor with servile devotion?

Then why was she not allowed to follow at his heels and curl up beside his fire, gratefully accepting whatever scraps of food and affection he threw to her? Something about Chance's behavior seemed very wrong to her. She could understand a man dealing harshly with his equals— killing his enemies and beating his wives. But it was unworthy of any man, particularly a great chief, to desert a faithful animal who desired only the pleasure and security of being owned. Having become property, she was nothing if she did not belong to someone. Therefore she could only wait and hope that someday her master would come back to reclaim her.

A half-hour later and a half-mile upstream, old Lightning Tracker stood outside his wickiup and watched the small column of humans and mules move slowly away to the northwest. He had known for some time that most of the white people were planning to leave today. Very little that happened in the valley passed his notice, since his people relied heavily on gossip to hold their loose social structure together. The strangers had made an intriguing topic of conversation among the Paiutes and Lightning Tracker wondered how the remaining white family would fare in the valley.

Perhaps he should visit their camp to see how they were getting along. And if Winnedumah should invite him to sit a while and talk with her, well, he could hardly refuse her hospitality. It still embarrassed him to admit that he couldn't stay away from the old woman, and the situation was made even more ominous by his wife's growing suspicion. Not that Slow Of Speech was the kind to make a jealous scene, but she knew other ways of expressing her feelings that were more subtle but no less disturbing to a man who enjoyed domestic tranquility as much as he did.

Suddenly it occurred to Lightning Tracker that he had a perfect excuse for visiting Winnedumah. Now that the white chief had deserted Bold Nose, her grandmother would have to find another husband for her. His son, Hupwi, was still interested in the girl, so Lightning Tracker could act as go-between and haggle over the bride price. With proper handling, that could be stretched out for quite a while. Silently approving his plan, Lightning Tracker turned to look at Slow Of Speech as she knelt to kindle the morning cookfire from smoldering coals. A man couldn't be too careful in his dealings with women.

About that time, in his solitary camp beside a nameless creek far to the north, Paul the Apostle sat staring at his reflection in the bright saber blade. For the first time in several months, his mind was alive with hopeful dreams that overcame his humiliating failure as a mule-breeder. When he had first arrived in the valley the hungry Paiutes had wanted to make an immediate feast of the mules and it had been a great effort for him to convince them to wait. When the animals began to reproduce, there would be a continuing meat supply for everybody, he promised. The Paiutes, respecting his superior knowledge of the white man's ways, had forced themselves to be patient. But as time passed and there was no discernible change in the she-mule's appearance, they had turned on Paul with scathing

51

ridicule. Ostracized from their community, he had burned with shame and hopeless rage, until his luck had been miraculously changed by the arrival of the gullible white travelers.

Lovingly he ran his thumb along the blade's keen edge, thinking of how it would at last give him the prestige he had long sought. Though not as potent as a gun, the saber was nevertheless a far more impressive weapon than the Paiutes' obsidian knives and arrowheads. With such a distinguishing instrument of death belted to his ragged waist, he could swagger among the valley braves as proudly as the ornate grandees he had envied in his other life beyond the mountains. Now the Paiutes would have to accept him, and let him choose a wife from the most desirable maidens. And if they should ever again go to war over territorial boundaries with the neighboring Shoshones or Washoes, he would be in the forefront carving a bloody path to glory. For had he not been assured by Padre Alonso that he who lived by the sword would cause death by it?

Ten days later the fair weather broke. Great bunches of dark clouds prowled over the Sierra crest, sending raw winds hurtling down the valley's natural funnel for storms. The river's surface was whipped to a dull froth and the cutting air smelled drenched with rain that never fell. In such weather men and animals took shelter where they found it, while birds seemed indifferent to the wild pitchings of their roosting limbs.

Shortly after noon, David emerged from his wickiup and caught the chilling gusts in his open mouth. He stared vaguely at the clouded mountains, wondering if Chance and the O'Neals had gotten through safely. Not that it mattered; there was something else of more immediate importance, although it stubbornly eluded his mind's efforts to get hold of it. Margaret . . . Margaret had told him to do something . . . what was it? And when? He kept getting the days mixed up. Vicky Beth . . . . Yes, it had something to do with her. Where had that child gotten off to now? It seemed she was forever disappearing and causing them no end of worry, especially now that the baby took up so much of Margaret's time.

Lowering his head, he pushed his way through the dusty wind curtains toward Chance's wagon, hoping the tattered canvas would hold up a little longer. Something strange happened, for a brief moment. It was as if he had eyes in the back of his head and could see into the wickiup behind him. There was Winnedumah sitting on the floor, with Bold Nose kneeling across from her holding D.C. on his cradleboard. And between them lay the pale, still form that . . . .

David climbed into the wagon, swaying as the rough floorboards rolled under his feet like a ship's deck. Vicky Beth was there, crouched in the cubbyhole she had made for herself among the crowded chairs, boxes, and other gear. She was playing with her dolls, apparently entertaining them with an imaginary tea party, and she seemed hardly to notice when David hunkered down beside her. "You oughtn't to sneak off like this without telling us," he said mildly.

"Aunt Maggie said I could," Vicky Beth responded, serving tea. She had a real toy teapot but no cups, so she had to improvise with a couple of thimbles and some play-acting.

"Aunt Maggie," David repeated. He picked up one of her dolls, the raggedy black pickaninny. "What's this one's name?" he asked, thinking that he should know all of their names by now; she had told him often enough.

"Liza Jane. And this is Edith." Vicky Beth held up her favorite, a golden-haired china doll. "She has asthma, like Grandma."

"Is that so?"

"Yes, but I'm doctoring her real good, like Winnedumah's doctoring Aunt Maggie."

"Aunt Maggie." The second repetition of the words loosened something inside David. "There's something I have to tell you about her. She's . . . gone away."

"You mean she's dead?"

David nodded, his mind finally able to admit the fact. Now he could remember. He had gone as usual this morning to work on the half-raised cabin, thinking everything would be all right. Margaret had been feeling poorly for only a few days and seemed to be coming around nicely on the Indian herb medicines that Winnedumah had fixed for her. It couldn't have been a serious illness because she had remained in high spirits even when he insisted that she stay in bed. Her last words to him had been a cheerful promise that she would be up and about before he knew it; meanwhile he wasn't to worry because the squaws were taking good care of her and the children. Then he had returned to camp for lunch and found Winnedumah weeping outside the wickiup. Margaret was still warm and right up till the instant he touched her he was sure there must be some mistake.

"Then we'll have to bury her," Vicky Beth said matter-of-factly, with her new understanding of life. She had cried bitterly over the losses of her mother and father, but that had not brought them back. Now she had made up her mind that she would never again cry about things that couldn't be helped.

"Yes, bury her." David stared at the black doll's grinning red lips and returned it to Vicky Beth's tea party. "You stay here until I call you," he ordered, rising unsteadily as another wind blast rocked the wagon.

"Yes, Uncle David."

Outside again, David tried to remember where he had left his rifle. Finding it leaning against his own wagon, he carefully made sure it was still charged and primed. He wished he had a revolver like Chance's, but it really didn't make any difference. The important thing was to get so far away from camp that the sound of the shot wouldn't disturb anyone. The noise of the storm would help, if he went downwind. He started walking south, angling away from the river toward a group of low ancient hills that had been worn down to blunt rocks.

Winnedumah, peering around a lifted corner of the blanket covering the wickiup's doorway, watched David leave. Then she turned to Bold Nose and spoke a few words. The girl scrambled to her feet and, still clutching the baby's cradleboard, left the hut. Winnedumah settled back on her heels beside Margaret and composed herself to wait patiently. From a bag hung on the near wall she selected a stick of venison jerky and chewed slowly on it.

* * *

David, approaching the first rocky knobs of the hills, came to a stream-cut gully about eight feet deep and twelve across. He climbed down the side of the trench and found himself pleasantly sheltered from the wind. Figuring this was as good a spot as any, he sat down and pulled off his right boot. The sock was so riddled with holes that his big toe was already exposed, so there was no need to remove it. He had just gotten to his feet and tucked the muzzle of the long barrel under his chin, when a movement above caught his eye. He looked up and saw Bold Nose standing on the edge of the bank.

The wind at her back whipped her hair around her face and billowed out her skirt to give his upward gaze full view of her legs. But David saw only the small bundle in her arms, with his son's pink face peeping out at him.

"Go back!" David screamed. "Get away from me!"

Bold Nose only stared calmly at him, even as he waved his rifle threateningly at her.

"Leave me be, damn you! It's none of your business."

David looked around frantically and snatched up a stone to hurl at her, but stopped when he realized he might hit the baby. He turned and ran several yards down the dry streambed, the stones painfully jabbing his unbooted foot. When he paused and looked up again, the Indian girl was keeping pace with him, the baby held like a shield before her. "Oh, God damn you to hell!" David groaned, running on and on, hugging his rifle and desperately searching for a place where he would be out of his son's sight. But every time he looked up the girl was above him and D.C. Wheeler's questioning blue eyes were upon him.

"Please, God, please," he begged, and stumbled blindly on.

"Why? Why? Why?" he panted, until it became difficult for him to remember the meaning of the question.

Finally, coming to a boulder that blocked the narrowing channel, he stumbled against it and lay too exhausted to climb over. For a long time he pounded the rock with his fists, sobbing and cursing whatever power was preventing him from doing what needed to be done. But at length his thrashings subsided and an expression of incredible amazement flooded his face as he slowly turned toward the woman and child.

"All right," he whispered, smiling softly. "All right, Margaret. I'll do it. Just let me find my boot first."

Chapter 7

Spring in the western Sierra foothills is a joyous time. Long before winter ceases to rage along the ridgelines, the sweeping mounds and dells of lower elevations explode with fresh greenery and roaring waters. Between brief rainshowers the polished sky and sun-dazzled earth present an invitation to celebrate the triumph of living. The Time of Feeding Rocks, the Indians called it, and it does appear that even the scattered boulders grow as their covering mosses and lichens expand. Animals bestir themselves with renewed vigor and flocks of birds rise and fall like sea waves determined to wash the land bare of all they can pack into their beaks and bellies.

That year, and for much of the two previous years, other waves of restless creatures had pounded over the gentle hills—pecking and scratching for a substance that was as vital to their well-being as were seeds and insects to the birds. The creatures—recognizable as men when singled out of their swarming masses—seemed almost in a feeding frenzy as they snatched up the cherished yellow flakes and lumps with pans, shovels, and crude wooden structures that utilized water to wash away lighter soil and debris. It was hardly a becoming activity for sane men, but who cared for dull sanity when the madness of gold-gathering was so rewarding?

Chance ruminated on that as he stood in the doorway of the store and gazed down on the frantic workings of Goldcock Diggings. All along the rocky creekbed, as far as he could see in either direction, men were busily turning the land upside down and shaking the money out of its pockets with incredible energy and jocularity. He had witnessed the almost exact repetition of the scene many times in several different locations over the past four months, but it never ceased to fascinate him, even when he was part of it. Although he had previously considered himself a knowledgeable man of the world, it was only when he and the O'Neals had stumbled out of the freezing mountains at Mariposa, near the southern end of the Mother Lode area, that he had begun to understand gold's magic power of enchantment.

For centuries men had gone to war for gold and this case was different only in that the enemy was the wild land that held the treasure. The first local troops into the affray had been followed by forces recruited from around the world, until an army of tens of thousands was stubbornly fighting it out along a battlefront that extended over 150 miles, from Mariposa to Downieville and beyond. At the northern mines winter had forced a temporary pullback to the staging centers of Sacramento and Stockton, while in the south, where Chance had remained, the miners had continued their gouging attack in spite of icy winds and frigid water that made their hands as numb as the lifeless pay dirt they worked. But the return of favorable weather had brought forth a new offensive, with every gravel-grubbing warrior determined not to leave a single yellow speck on the field. The easy victories had been won the first year, when lucky members of the vanguard had scooped up fortunes from surface deposits and retreated with honor from the strife. Now those who had come to replace them dug in grimly for their share of the glory and booty.

As in every war there were camp followers. That was where the enchantment shone brightest. Not just a few tawdry sluts and hucksters trailed after the California gold army. An entire civilization had been lifted bodily and transported to an exotic empty country that until a short while before had been the end of the earth. On the Bay of

Saint Francis, a squalid village of little account was depopulated overnight by news of the first rich strikes, then underwent another rapid transformation to a thriving metropolis named San Francisco. Hundreds of ships sailed and steamed through Golden Gate to land seasick cargoes of bonanza-seekers, who as likely as not were followed by the officers and crewmen in their stampede to the hills, where they were joined by their overland comrades. No matter that a sizable navy of vessels was left derelict in the bay; there were plenty of other ships to keep the gold army supplied, for a price. And when the initial excitement subsided, cooler heads realized that the real fortunes in this grand adventure would be made by mining the miners.

With such rich prospects, hordes of merchants and would-be merchants frantically wrote to eastern suppliers ordering every product their customers might conceivably be persuaded they couldn't live without. That resulted in the most fantastic commodities lottery and lopsided inflation the world had ever seen, as shiploads of random goods arrived in unpredictable order. At one time iron cookstoves were so scarce in northern California that they sold for ten or twenty times their purchase price, with the buyers required to unload them from the ships. A few weeks later so many stoves had been received that an unsold consignment of them was used to pave one of San Francisco's muddy streets.

Conditions were even more chaotic in the mining camps, where competitionless storekeepers charged all the traffic would bear, sometimes for the oddest assortments of wares imaginable. A simple prospector accustomed to living on beans and salt pork might pan out enough dust to treat himself to a meal of fresh eggs, tinned turtle soup, lobster salad, apple pie, Swiss cheese and vintage champagne—all enjoyed in the comfort of a silk smoking jacket and slippers. But naturally the biggest sprees were reserved for the more robust pleasures of saloons, gambling houses, and infrequent ladies of easy virtue. It was to provide such pleasures to the hard-working miners of Goldcock Diggings that Chance and Susan O'Neal operated the store.

Chance turned to look around the interior of the store, as much amused as bemused at finding himself in an unpremeditated business partnership with Susan. Being Gold-cock's only sizable commercial establishment gave the place an imposing air of permanence among the motley cluster of tents and log cabins. The store itself had begun life as a large tent enclosed by walls of timber and stone chinked with clayey mud from the creekbed. Additional construction had increased the building's size and profit potential, as indicated by the variety of merchandise displayed along two of the walls.

But a casual glance revealed that the emporium's major trade flowed around close-set tables and a plank bar extending along the north wall. On the bar stood a pair of gold dust scales and on a stool behind them perched Susan, her knitting in her lap. She was surrounded by other tools of her new trade—liquor bottles and kegs, drinking mugs, an oil painting of a voluptuous lady wearing only ribbons, and a metal strongbox and sawed-off shotgun easily at hand under the bar. At the moment she was taking advantage of a lull in business to finish a pair of socks for Peter while she proudly surveyed her domain.

Since it was late afternoon of a working day, only a few tables were occupied by men talking, drinking, gambling and trying to decide if their lust was more important to them than their money. One bearded gentleman evidently answered that question affirmatively and leaned down to whisper his decision into Clara Escobar's receptive ear. Clara responded with a winsome snaggle-toothed simper and rose languidly.

The happy couple ambled over to the bar, where Susan relieved the miner's poke of a half-ounce of dust and wished him much enjoyment with his purchase in one of the tiny log cribs out back. Even during slack hours Clara and her sister Pia, occasionally aided by Gloria Holt, maintained a fairly brisk trade. Until a week ago the store had employed five pleasure girls, but in the woman-starved environment marriage had taken its inevitable toll.

In a few years California would have enough decent women to return the oldest profession to its traditional unsavory position. But for the time being prospectors and tarts coexisted on such equal social footing as to render credible the future poetic claim that "The miners came in forty-nine; the whores in fifty-one. Together they made the Native Son."

Gloria, the third filly in Susan's stable, made fewer visits to the cribs than the Escobar sisters, but not because she was less attractive than they. On the contrary, her outstanding beauty and affability commanded a high price that was beyond the average customer's means. For that reason, her main duties consisted of giving the patrons something nice to look at and operating the establishment's proud centerpiece—a glittering hand-carved roulette wheel.

At the moment the wheel was idle and Gloria stood beside it sipping champagne and returning the men's hungry stares with tantalizing smiles that opened her full red lips and violet eyes like flower petals. Even in the store's dim light her cascading mass of titian hair, heart-shaped face and flawless ivory complexion glowed magnetically. Not surprisingly she had become something of a legend around the mining camps, especially after one of her suitors had made a bawdy pun on her name, calling her the Glory Hole, where a man with the right drilling tool could always strike it rich.

Chance pondered the enigma of a girl like Gloria in a place like this. From the few remarks about her past that she had dropped, he gathered that joining the Gold Rush had been her way of rebelling against her straitlaced New England family.

After being sent to a genteel finishing school whose restraints on her high-spirited zest for life were intolerable, Gloria had escaped with a California-bound lover. What had become of the man was not known. But Gloria had quickly learned that she could do quite well on her own. She loved the rough exciting freedom of the gold camps and the easy money she earned there. Several lucrative marriage proposals had come her way, but her exalted position with the miners was so pleasing that she chose to stay single.

Chance liked Gloria and he thought he understood her feelings, which seemed to reflect his own lust for adventure. But his puritanical upbringing made it impossible for him to approve of her profession. Nor was he proud of himself for being, in effect, her pimp, although Susan took care of that part of the business.

Michael O'Neal, entering through the back door with an armload of firewood, made his way to the potbelly stove beside the roulette table. After stacking the wood, Michael paused to chat with Gloria, much to Susan's scowling disapproval. Susan had made it clear to her sons that they were to have nothing to do with the—in her words—"poxie-doxies." But Chance doubted that Susan, knowing how valuable Gloria was to the store, would offend her by openly reprimanding Michael. Only Susan's tightly pursed lips and increased knitting rhythm expressed her irritation as Michael fawningly bathed in the warmth of Gloria's attention.

To some degree Chance shared Susan's worry about the boy's attachment to Gloria. Michael was growing up fast and ordinarily a little harmless fun with the wrong kind of women would help make a man of him. But this was clearly an intense attack of first love on his part and, with Gloria definitely not ready to settle down yet, any serious involvement with her was bound to end painfully. Her occupation didn't help matters either.

Despite Chance's efforts to help the youth face life realistically, Michael burned with murderous jealousy every time he saw Gloria head for her crib with a high-spending customer. Chance was tempted to give Michael enough money to bed Gloria, and distract Susan long enough for him to do it, in hope that the physical satisfaction would enable him to overcome his obsession for her. But Michael was too bashfully tongue-tied to do anything but worship his love goddess from a safe distance, daydreaming of heroic ways to rescue her from this sordid life and carry her off to a never-never land where she would be all his forevermore.

On her part, Gloria could not be accused of unduly tempting or encouraging Michael. She treated him with the same kindly affection she showed all men, without letting his calf-eyed lovesickness interfere with her activities. It wasn't her fault that she didn't share Chance's concern for the lad's well-being.

In fact, the only man for whom Gloria seemed to display any special feeling was Chance himself. Chance could not tell if she was truly attracted to him or merely willing, like the other girls, to honor his privileged position as her employer and protector. So far he had not cared to investigate the question very deeply. To his amazement, he found himself, for the first time in his life, without much interest in women. The phenomenon was partly due, he thought, to his being constantly exposed to sensuous females whose business was pleasing men. As the old saying went, the best way to cure a sweet tooth is to work in a candy kitchen.

Also, he had many other things on his mind, particularly his worries about Vicky Beth and the others he had left in Owens Valley. Since communication over the weather-locked mountains was impossible, he could only hope and pray that they were safely waiting for him to be able to send for them. It was for that purpose only that Chance had reluctantly agreed to help Susan purchase and operate the store.

At the sight of a miner hurrying up the path from the creek, Chance stepped out of the open doorway. "Knocking off a mite early, aren't you, Bob?" he greeted the newcomer.

The man's beard rolled back in a wide grin as he held up a small leather pouch. "Already made my wages for the day—more'n two ounces. No sense working myself to death till that's spent."

"Then come on in and we'll help you enjoy it."

Bob entered the store and Chance reckoned that his claim must be richer than was originally thought. Most miners considered themselves lucky to average an ounce—$16—a day, now that most of the richer and more easily-worked deposits had been exhausted. That was ten times the daily wage for a laborer back in the States, although it didn't go very far with the high cost of living in the mining communities. But the hearty gold-seekers didn't let that or anything else dampen their optimism. The dream of finding El Dorado kept their spirits high, and when that flagged they could always fall back on their extraordinary youth. Chance, at twenty-eight, was a good five years older than the average Argonaut.

Above the general hubbub of the diggings, Chance suddenly became aware of someone talking nearby. He glanced down and saw Ben Butler, Susan's new husband, seated on a log against the wall and slowly whittling a stick to death as his steady monotone droned on. It was not surprising that Chance had at first failed to take notice of him, for Ben talked incessantly on any subject to anyone who would listen to him. When no one would listen to him, he talked to himself. Right now he was discoursing on the weather with Klaus Dietrich, the German cobbler. Klaus was hard of hearing, knew little English, and was only interested in repairing miners' boots on the last he held between his knees. But none of that fazed Ben; it just meant he had fewer interruptions to put up with.

"Snow?" Ben demanded. "You ain't seen real snow till you've wintered in the Sangre de Cristos. I mind a time me and old Gabe Bridger was makin' a crossin'—must've been in 'thirty-nine or 'forty, thereabouts. Wal, we come to this here snowdrift so high you couldn't've shot a cannonball over it, and stickin' out of it was a human hand."

"A hand?" Chance said with a grimace. "Did you give it a decent burial?"

"Tried to, but the feller it was attached to didn't cotton to the notion. We roasted him slow over the fire till enough color come back to his face for us to see 'twas old Ike Jones, that used to trap with Sublette. Asked him what he was doin' out thar so all froze-up. Said some Injuns had got uncommon fond o' his hair and he figgered hidin' in the snowbank was the only way he could get shut of 'em. Wal, we took him down to Bent's Old Fort and they saved most o' him. Had to take off a leg—don't recollect if 'twas the right 'un or left. But it warn't no matter. Ike got fitted out for a wood pegleg an' said he was glad to cut down the rumatiz by half."

Ben rambled on, as Chance wondered how many of his outrageous yarns had any truth in them. It was hard to say, for in addition to being a wonderful liar, Ben was a true frontiersman who had left his native Kentucky at a tender age and roamed the West as a fur trapper, scout, wagon train guide and jack-of-all-trades. That the nondescript little man with a walrus mustache and sparse fringe of graying black hair had pulled his own weight with such semi-legendary stalwarts as Kit Carson, Jim Bridger, and John Fremont was so impossible to imagine that it had to be fact. As an early arrival on the Mother Lode, Ben had revealed an uncanny knack for finding gold effortlessly and letting it slip through his fingers with equal ease. He had squandered three modest fortunes and was halfway through his fourth, when Susan met him and decided she had better use for it. That was obviously her major reason for returning to matrimony, but why a man so plainly designed for bachelorhood as Ben had let himself be ensnared was a mystery to Chance. Maybe he was so astonished to find a woman who talked less than he did that he hadn't been able to resist her.

At any rate, it seemed to be a compatible match. Ben was glad to have a woman to "do" for him, and Susan didn't object to his shiftless reluctance to move anything but his mouth, as long as he kept out from underfoot while she ran the business. The O'Neal boys also took Ben for granted and Chance wished them well, although he doubted that he would ever get used to calling Susan "Mrs. Butler."

" 'Tain't like the old days," Ben was saying sorrowfully. "What with all the killin' an' robbin' an' claim-jumpin.' Back in '48 it was one big happy family in the mines. No need to steal. Thar was gold a-plenty for everybody. 'Most any pan you washed showed color, an' a man had only to leave his pick or shovel on his claim to prove it war his'n. Onct in a poker game, Joe Bayliss an' Tim Rogers kept a-raisin' each other pinches o' dust till thar musta been thuty-five, forty ounces in the pot. Finally old Joe shakes out his poke an' says: 'Watch the pile, boys, while I go out an' dig enough to call 'em.' Wal, in about half-a-hour he was back with enough dust to win the pot, an' nobody had touched a smidgen o' it."

Ben's story reminded Chance that he should be inside helping Susan keep an eye on things. The later waves of the Gold Rush had brought many undesirables—thieves, swindlers, tinhorns, cutthroats—as well as basically honest men made overly rambunctious by the lawless freedom of the new land. Violent crime had become commonplace in the gold fields, especially at places like the store, where large sums of bullion mingled with alcohol and excitement. For that reason Susan kept her shotgun handy and Chance constantly wore his revolver in a cutaway holster low on his right hip. He hitched up his gunbelt and entered the building, moving slowly as his vision adjusted to the smoky gloom.

At the bar the prospector Bob was happily spending some of his daily two ounces on the popular rotgut whisky called Oh Be Joyful. Susan bantered with him, while Peter stood at her side sucking a stick of horehound candy. Ordinarily Susan tried to keep her younger sons away from the store's unwholesome influences, but as the baby of the family Peter could wheedle special favors. Chance paused beside a table where Willis Trent was dealing faro to three rough-looking miners who seemed more interested in joshing one another than playing the game. Of all of those who worked in the store, only Willis really looked the part of a professional gambler. His swarthy, handsome face smiled easily as his small, well-manicured hands manipulated cards, coins, and gold dust with icy control. He always managed to appear dapper and fresh in his stovepipe hat, frock coat, and lace-ruffled white shirt, with a diamond stickpin winking in his broad silk cravat. Chance was similarly dressed, but he could never seem to remain free of mud stains or the odor of sweaty underwear for long. Nor could he affect the bland air of innocence that masked Willis's deadly skill with the derringer and stiletto tucked up his sleeves.

After admiring Willis's smooth dealing for a few minutes, Chance moved on to a nearby table where two lanky Missourians were debating the question of whether California should enter the Union as a free or a slave state. Although a confirmed abolitionist, Chance decided to play the neutral peacemaker as the argument heated toward the point of drawing bowie knives. By offering a round of drinks on the house and calling Pia Escobar over to keep the men company, he was able to leave them with their friendship intact.

Michael was still mooning over Gloria and as Chance passed the roulette table he overheard the boy telling her of their mountain encounter with an ill-tempered grizzly bear whose winter hibernation had been disturbed. Chance recalled the incident vividly because of its location—a deep valley enclosed by stupendous granite cliffs rising more than 3,000 feet and slashed by mighty waterfalls. Even when covered with wet snow it was a place of enchanting beauty, and at a friendly Indian village in the midst of the valley floor they were treated hospitably. Communication with the Indians was difficult, but Chance managed to learn that the tribe was called either Awani or Yosemite, names that were also applied to the valley. The spectacular valley scenery, as well as nearby groves of gigantic red-barked trees, were marvels that had to be witnessed to be believed. Chance hoped he would someday have time to return and enjoy the mountains at leisure, after he had answered the urgent call of the gold fields.

Upon reaching Mariposa, Chance had remained with the O'Neals long enough for Susan to obtain a well-paying position as cook and laundress for a group of miners and hire out her sons as apprentices to learn the gold-washing trade. Then Chance had sold his mules to a freighter and let himself be swept up in the giddy whirlwind of bonanza-chasing. Twice he had staked out claims of substantial value, only to desert them and join wild-eyed stampedes to new camps where it was rumored that gold covered the stream bottoms like butter on toast. His wanderings had taken him to some highly flamboyant settlements with equally colorful names—Mormon Bar, Mount Bullion, Second Garrote, Jackass Hill, Angel's Camp. Farther north there was even a Rough and Ready, christened in honor of Chance's former commanding general, Zachary Taylor, whose rough and ready attitude in Mexico had contrasted with his more fastidious rival, old Fuss and Feathers Winfield Scott.

There were some fascinating stories as to how the camps had gotten their names, and probably a few of them were true. A typical example was Goldcock Diggings, where the first big strikes were made by Mexican prospectors who had brought along their favorite sport of cockfighting. To enliven an otherwise dull afternoon, the popular account went, the Mexicans pitted two spirited birds in a sandy de-

67

pression alongside a creek that had yielded only faint color in their pans. As the roosters tore furiously at one another, their thrashing talons had thrown up clouds of sand that turned to golden showers in the sunlight. *"Oro! Oro!"* cried the excited spectators, tossing the bewildered gamecocks out of the pit and going at it with their shovels.

By the time Chance drifted into Goldcock, he had soberly taken stock of his situation and realized three irrefutable truths: 1) gold mining was a hard, unreliable way to make a living; 2) without extraordinary good luck, it was unlikely to provide him with the quick fortune he sought; 3) if he wanted that fortune badly enough he would have to find some other, probably less respectable way of getting it. At precisely that stage of his thinking, Susan had appeared with a new husband and a business proposition for Chance.

With Ben Butler's gold at her disposal, Susan had no need of financial assistance in purchasing the store. But she did need a capable male partner to help her run the business and Chance was the only man she felt she could trust. Chance was touched by her faith in him and intrigued by the lucrative opportunity she offered him. The store had been established the previous summer by two Mississippi sporting gentlemen, one of whom had recently finished up an unfortunate poker game with an extra ace in his hand and an extra hole in his head. His bereaved partner, upon learning that his own gambling methods had fallen under suspicion, became eager to quit the area even though it meant liquidating his property at rock-bottom prices.

Chance, after overcoming his aversion to operating a house of ill-fame by telling himself it would only be temporary, had accepted Susan's offer. So far he had not had reason to regret the decision. Much of the gold mined along the creek found its way across the store's bar and tables, and in spite of their high overhead Susan's strongbox rapidly gained precious weight that would soon be shipped down to one of the newly established banks in Sacramento.

Chance's tide of bad luck was turning at last, thanks in no small part to Susan's unexpected genius for commerce.

To the day of her death Susan remained unable to read or write, but she never forgot a name, face, or important event and her mental arithmetic was so swift and accurate that those who did business with her soon learned not to try anything shifty.

Pausing at another table, Chance watched their second dealer, Leif Dahlgren, help two tipsy sports lighten their pokes with lively sets of three-card monte. One of the players was Culbert Hightower, the traveling daguerreotype artist who earned a pretty penny making the miners' portraits with his newfangled black box. His companion was Jack Chevington, a British engineer who had worked for several years in the iron and coal mines of Wales before being bitten by the California bug. He was explaining the local mining methods to Hightower, who said he already understood that placer mining referred to the recovery of loose gold that had been deposited by water erosion at lower elevations.

"And at the current frantic rate of exploitation, all of the economically feasible placer deposits will soon be exhausted," Chevington predicted. "Then we shall have to find the Mother Lode, which is to say the quartz and prophylitic veins from which the gold was eroded."

"You mean like the rich rocks they found over on Fremont's Rancho Las Mariposas?" Hightower asked.

"Exactly. To extract the gold from such deeply embedded veins will require hard rock mining techniques and that, I fear, will be the end of the independent miner working his own claim."

"How so?" inquired Leif.

"Because only large organized companies will be able to afford to sink shafts to bring up the ore and build the smelting and refining facilities required to process it. Those of us who wish to continue working as miners will have to become employees of the companies at set wages. Pity, but I can see no way of avoiding it."

"What will happen when even the vein deposits have been mined of all their gold?" Chance wondered.

Chevington regarded him with a cocked eyebrow. "Why, long before then, my dear fellow, I hope we all shall have returned to our homes with full pokes. For without its gold,

I am sure this wretched wilderness will quickly revert to its naturally worthless state."

"Sure. Why else would anybody want to live in California?" Hightower demanded.

Before Chance could answer Hightower, Leif asked: "Spell me for a minute, will you, boss? I gotta go to the necessary house."

Chance nodded and took the cards from Leif. "All right, gents. Place your bets and see if you can pick out the lady."

Chance showed them the queen of spades, then turned it face down and swiftly rearranged its position with the other two cards on the table. Before joining the ranks of professional gamblers, Chance had thought that monte dealers somehow managed to palm the winning card, as was often done with the pea in the similar shell game. But Willis and Leif had taught him that a quick-handed dealer could keep the suckers guessing without cheating.

Chevington and Hightower, pleading a temporary depletion of funds, declined Chance's invitation to play and left the store. But before Chance had time to miss them, the doorway filled with what appeared to be a small army that poured into the room with wild whoops and clouds of mosquitoes and flies. The group dissolved into four men who ranged along the bar talking loudly.

Susan smilingly moved to gratify their demands for double shots of Oh Be Joyful, but she kept her shotgun within reach. Chance automatically loosened his pistol in his holster, then regretted the action when he saw that Michael had observed it and placed a hand on the gun in his pocket. No sense getting the boy trigger-happy before there were any real signs of danger.

The four men at the bar were fiercely bearded and bristling with weapons. That was a common sight at the mines, but at least three of them had established reputations for being as tough as they looked. Jonas and Ward Gookin had behaved themselves pretty well all the way from Boston to California, via Panama, because their sister was with them. But after she married an up-and-coming San Francisco businessman, they had wholeheartedly taken to the wild ways of the new frontier. They had reached Goldcock with fresh scalps on their belts and a story about being attacked by an Indian tribe that had never been known to harm whites. Since then their swaggering belligerence had gotten them into several brawls and intimidated the other miners sufficiently to enable them to jump one of the best claims on the creek. The Gookin brothers had been aided in their claim-jumping by Henri Buchard, known as the Keskydee. The nickname had been generally applied to all of the numerous French prospectors because of their constantly asking *"Qu'est-ce qu'il dit?"*—"What is it that he says?"—although Buchard himself spoke tolerable English. The fourth member of the gang had only been in Goldcock a few days and was so tight-lipped about his past that he had not even given a name by which he might be called. Because his face had been deeply pitted by smallpox, some of the miners had taken to calling him Pockmarks, but not within his hearing. No one seemed to know how he had joined forces with the Gookins, except that he looked mean enough to belong with them.

While the other three men remained at the bar drinking and talking loudly, Pockmarks looked around, spotted Chance, and silently made his way over to the monte table. Without a word, he opened his poke and placed a pinch of dust in the saucer on the table. Chance moved the cards swiftly, then waited. Pockmarks turned over a four of hearts. Chance poured the dust into the store's poke and showed Pockmarks that the card at his right was the lady. As he started another game, Jonas Gookin left the bar and ambled over to the roulette table, smiling at Gloria. Ignoring Michael's sullen glare, Jonas flicked his head commandingly toward the back door. Gloria arched her brows inquiringly. Jonas took something from his pocket and tossed it on the table. Chance caught a glint of yellow in the lamplight as the nugget thumped dully.

"Found that just for you, sweet thing," Jonas said. "Seven ounces."

Gloria nodded and reached for the nugget, but Jonas put his hand on her wrist. "Double or nothing?"

Gloria hesitated, then shrugged. "Why not?" She reached out to the roulette wheel. "Name your color."

"Black."

The wheel spun smoothly, with the little white ball making its happily clattering dance over the numbered grooves. Gloria watched the wheel, but Jonas's gaze never left her face. Across the table from him, Michael's eyes smoldered. Chance, dealing another hand of monte, heard the skipping ball fall silent and a few moments later Gloria said calmly: "Black."

Jonas threw back his head and let go a howl of savage joy as he pocketed the nugget. He grabbed Gloria's hand and started toward the back door. "Come on, boys. We got ourselves a party!"

"No!" Michael was suddenly in front of Jonas, pale and trembling. "Not all of you," he said, almost pleading.

Jonas stared at him in astonishment.

"It's all right, Mike," Gloria said. "Please don't interfere."

"Yeah, step aside, boy," Jonas added in a good-natured tone.

When Michael hesitantly stood his ground, Ward Gookin called from the bar: "Maybe he wants to help us with her."

Jonas laughed at the suggestion. "Sorry, son. No Irish need apply."

At the hated insult, Michael's nervous uncertainty turned to cold fury. "Take that back, sir!"

The room was suddenly so quiet that Chance could clearly hear Jonas's low, mocking reply: "Make me, sir."

Jonas drew aside his coattails to expose the revolver in his belt. His brother made a similar movement and the Keskydee's right hand went to the hilt of a bowie knife on his hip. Susan watched in confused horror, then reached under the bar while Peter looked on in wide-eyed wonder, still clutching his candy stick. Chance, his heart pounding in his throat, stole a glance at Pockmarks and saw his hand inching toward his knife. He discouraged him by putting his hand on his gunbutt as he shouted:

"Mickey, no! Get out of the way!"

Michael looked at Chance and seemed about to heed him. But then Jonas, looking Michael up and down, remarked off-handedly:

"I never knew they piled shit so high in Ireland."

For a split-second that seemed an eternity, all motion

72

was frozen. Chance felt he had all the time in the world to examine the details of the scene. For the first time he noticed how Pockmarks's long lashes almost beautifully framed his soft brown eyes; the tarnished braid on the Keskydee's army shako; the frayed straw of the Panama hats that the Gookin brothers still wore in spite of the windy weather. Above all, there was Michael's fine young face made even more boyish by freckles and red hair.

And then everything happened.

Michael's hand dived into his pocket and came out clutching his father's pepperbox revolver—a ludicrous weapon with five barrels that rotated on a single trigger and hammer mechanism. The gun shot as miserably as it looked and Chance knew it was no match for the two Colts that were coming out of the Gookins' belts. But Chance had little time to think about that, for Pockmarks had his knife in his hand and was lunging over the table at him as he drew his own gun. Chance snapped off a shot at point-blank range. But that was all he heard—a snap, as the hammer fell on a defective cap.

Before he could recock the gun, Pockmarks was upon him and he was barely able to grip the man's right wrist with his left hand, halting the knifepoint an inch from his throat. Pockmarks's free hand got hold of the gun barrel and they stumbled back against the wall wrestling over their weapons.

Fighting for his life, Chance glimpsed Susan bringing her shotgun to her shoulder as Willis Trent, unnoticed by anyone, raised his two-shot derringer and coolly drilled Ward Gookin through the head as he was about to shoot Michael in the back. At nearly that same instant, Michael and Jonas Gookin exchanged fire. Amazingly, Jonas missed, but Michael's pepperbox bullet struck Jonas in the upper right arm, breaking the bone. The Colt fell from his useless hand and he stared unhappily at Michael trying to get off another good shot.

The Keskydee charged across the room at Michael, sending men scrambling out of his way. Willis's second shot passed harmlessly behind him. Only Susan's shotgun was on the Keskydee; only a twitch of her finger could save Michael's life. Why didn't she fire?

That question screamed in Chance's mind as he made a mighty effort to force the muzzle of his gun against Pockmarks's side, thumbed back the hammer and dropped it. At the muffled roar, Pockmarks jerked bolt upright. Chance flung the twitching body away from him just as the Keskydee sank eight inches of tempered steel into Michael's back. And still Susan held her fire.

Chance gasped for breath as he raised his gun with both hands and shot the Keskydee through the lungs. Chance swung his weapon to Jonas, who threw up his uninjured arm in a gesture of surrender. But in the heat of battle there was no quarter. Through the choking, eye-stinging cloud of powder smoke, Chance took careful aim and squeezed the trigger. The gun bucked and he took brutal satisfaction in seeing Jonas's arrogant sneer wiped away in a crimson blur.

The last body fell in the room that seemed to smolder in hellish brimstone fire. At Chance's feet, Pockmarks's bootheel drummed on the floor as he twitched away his life, while beside Michael the Keskydee gurgled and spluttered through the agony of drowning in his own blood. Men who had dived under tables for cover began to creep out cautiously, while in the open doorway stood Ben Butler—utterly speechless for once in his life.

Gloria pulled away from the wall she had cowered against and took a few faltering steps toward Michael, as Chance picked his way across the room to join her. As she peered down at the youth, her face was a contortion of shock, fear, sick revulsion and—unavoidably—interested curiosity. He was the first man ever to die for her.

Chance stood beside her and saw that there was nothing he could do for Michael. His slim body lay motionless. His wide blue eyes stared emptily up at the beautiful face he would love forever. Chance looked over at Susan as she lowered her shotgun and put a comforting arm around Peter, who was sobbing into her dress. Their eyes met unflinchingly and at last Chance understood why she had not shot the Keskydee. The shotgun was to protect the gold in the strongbox, not Michael's life. She had other sons.

Chance turned his back on Susan and knelt down to press Michael's eyes closed.

Chapter 8

July 29, 1850

"More dig," Winnedumah commanded around the pipe-stem gripped by her almost toothless gums.

"Ain't that deep enough?"

David leaned on his shovel in the thigh-deep, grave-shaped pit and wiped the flowing sweat from his face. No shadow marred the clean raw earth at his feet. Straight overhead the sun was an almost audible sizzling torch that ate through the limpid sky and David's skull.

"More dig."

David sighed patiently and resumed scraping the soil under the old woman's stern supervision. From the nearby wickiup, Bold Nose's loud birth-groans gave fresh strength to his tired limbs. Danged if he would ever understand these contrary Indians, David thought. And except for Margaret's sake, he doubted if he would have the patience to tolerate their heathen foolishness in this matter. After all, Bold Nose was almost a white woman now. Hadn't the westbound preacher who had married them baptized her with the respectable Christian name of Rebekah? Then why couldn't she have her children in bed, like ordinary civilized folks?

Winnedumah would have agreed with David, if they had been surrounded by the white society she craved. But with nothing but Paiutes in every direction, convenience must yield to tradition. The local Indians viewed Bold Nose as one of theirs, so she must bring forth her child in a *cutiavita*—a fire-warmed pit of legendary origin.

In the far, distant, misty reaches of time, when earth, water, and life began (as the elders were fond of telling around the harvest fires), appeared Korawini, Mother of the People. All men fell in love with her, but she killed them one by one until only E-sha, Coyote, was left. E-sha brought her a big feast of ducks, so she decided he was a good enough provider to be her mate.

When the time came for Korawini to give birth to the People, she instructed her husband to make her a *cutiavita*. Then she told him to fetch her some water. When E-sha reached the stream, he found a large sloping rock and began to slide playfully down it. E-sha was a very clever fellow, but being a man, he often acted quite childishly.

When E-sha finished playing and started back to his wife's *cutiavita*, he saw that she had finished giving birth to the People and they were marching off to all parts of the world. There were Shoshoni, Miwok, Modoc and all the other tribes. E-sha called out: "Wait! I am your father. I want to pick my own tribe." But they did not hear him and when he reached Korawini, only the last of her children remained. They were the ugliest and least promising of them all. But E-sha had to love them anyway, so he made them Paiutes.

As creation myths go, it wasn't bad, and Winnedumah thought it had more appeal than the whites' yarn about two naked people in a garden with a talking snake. At any rate, the legend was the basis of the *cutiavita* custom, and Winnedumah saw no great harm in it. When David had added another six inches to the pit's depth, Winnedumah and the other Paiute women present dumped in armloads of firewood and ignited it. The flames and the day's already unbearable heat forced David to retreat to the shade of a cottonwood where he hunkered on his heels, panting and apprehensive. The agonized screams from the wickiup had become so loud that David's teeth were set on edge. He wondered if perhaps her small frame was too weak to deliver a white man's baby and for the thousandth time he felt a guilty twinge for not having turned her away the first night she had crept under his blankets.

But the heartbreaking loneliness of those first weeks after Margaret's death had rendered David incapable of refusing comfort from any source. So he had gathered the slender willing body to him and welcomed the blessed forgetting sleep that his release of energy within her brought him. During the days he and Bold Nose had toiled silently building a thatched-roof hut of sod and stone against the mountains' wintry blasts. When spring revitalized the earth, the shy Indian girl had become such a taken-for-granted companion that at times David almost fancied that Margaret was once more with him. Side by side they tilled a rich plot of bottom land, planting the corn and other seeds that Winnedumah strictly warned the valley Indians to stay clear of.

By then Bold Nose's condition was unmistakable and David was honor-bound to do the right thing by her. About that time the valley was visited by another westering band of gold-seekers, which fortuitously included the Reverend Walton G. Byers, and the necessary rituals were hastily performed, much to Winnedumah's satisfaction. The old woman still often thought wistfully about Don Chance, but she was realistic enough to settle for second-best. David was a good, steady breadwinner who would always provide her with sustenance, if not opulence, and Bold Nose remained fearfully submissive to her. All in all, things had not worked out too badly for her, if only the stupid girl's screams weren't so irritating. For a moment, Winnedumah was tempted to consider mixing another potion of wild parsnip roots.

When the fire in the pit died down, Winnedumah ordered the other women to cover the smoldering embers with earth and blankets. As she turned toward the wickiup, she caught sight of a small figure darting for cover behind the shelter. Winnedumah muttered angrily as she recognized Vicky Beth, with D.C.'s cradleboard on her back. The child had been told to stay at home but, curious and headstrong as always, she had sneaked out to spy on the birthing. David's indulgent habit of allowing Vicky Beth to have her own way was a constant aggravation to Winnedumah, mainly because the little girl's independent spirit reminded her so much of herself. She always felt more comfortable with people she could control, like Bold Nose and Lightning Tracker.

Winnedumah snapped orders to two of the women, who moved swiftly to flank the wickiup and trap Vicky Beth between them. One of the women smilingly took the child's hand and led her away in the direction of David's hut. Vicky Beth cast an appealing look at Uncle David, but saw that she could expect no help from him. His eyes wore the dreamy glow that always meant his mind was off someplace with Aunt Maggie. With a small shrug of her shoulders, Vicky Beth accepted the fact that she was not going to get her way—this time.

Winnedumah nodded with satisfaction as the white child disappeared from view. It was enough trouble midwifing a delivery with just a nervous father underfoot.

David forced himself back to the present when the woman carried his wife's swollen, writhing body out of the wickiup and lowered it into the pit. For an instant he was terrified by the memory of Margaret entering her grave. Then the illusion vanished with the reassuring touch of a friendly hand on his shoulder. He gazed up into the weathered, compassionate face of Lightning Tracker and recognized the man beside him as Pah-ya Che-e—Safe Water—the tribal medicine man. The old chief motioned David to follow him and he went willingly. Clearly there was no room for men here, when the ultimate act of womanhood was about to be performed.

Winnedumah was relieved by the men's departure, and concentrated on the business at hand. Squatting on the brink of the *cutiavita*, she calmly told Bold Nose what to expect and what she must do, as the girl's sweat-drenched body squirmed in the steamy pit. It was a hard delivery, but it came off pretty well. Bold Nose had already undergone her most difficult period of labor in the wickiup. Another two hours of intensive contractions in the hot hole completed the job. Only once did her eyes flash with the blind terror of death, and then the kind understanding smiles and words of her companions enabled her to get on with her work.

Finally the infant and its placenta were expelled with not too great a loss of blood, although the mother was nearly dehydrated from the heat. One of the younger but experienced women tied off the umbilical cord and showed Bold Nose how to bite it through cleanly. Then she was encouraged to make a full confession of her sins, evil thoughts, idle daydreams and laziness. That way mother and child could leave the bed with new life, cleansed and purified of the old, which was buried behind them as the women filled in the pit. No one present attached any special importance to the fact that the first half-breed child had just been born in Owens Valley.

David also was undergoing a purification ceremony. Lightning Tracker and Pah-ya Che-e had led him to the River and helped him strip. Using baskets made water-tight with pitch coatings, they scooped up water and poured it over him, while the medicine man chanted a blessing. Lightning Tracker tried to explain to David that he should confess his sins and shortcomings and petition the gods to reward his good deeds and grant his offspring long life and good luck. The language barrier prevented David from understanding what they were trying to tell him, but he got the impression that they meant well, and he appreciated it. He didn't even object when they wouldn't let him put his clothes back on, although that puzzled him somewhat. Instead, he was given a new suit of Paiute clothing, while his old shirt, pants, and boots were taken by the medicine man as his fee for professional services rendered.

Later, when he returned to the cabin and found Bold Nose and the infant sleeping peacefully, David was so relieved that he didn't even think to ask about the baby's sex. It took Vicky Beth to inform him that he had another son. He chose the name Robert, to honor Margaret's father, without knowing that the Paiutes had already christened the newborn Little Buck. But it made little difference, for the boy was to grow up as Bobby Buck Wheeler to all who knew him. Only Winnedumah took special note of the baby's curly black hair and squarish chin under his mother's unmistakable nose. It gave the old woman sardonic pleasure to know that she had not entirely lost Don Chance.

Chapter 9

October 22, 1850

San Francisco was drunk. Not just on alcohol, although it flowed freely. What had intoxicated the new city's 25,000 residents far beyond the power of any chemical stimulant was news of the most momentous event to befall California since the first gold discovery.

Four days ago all activity in the sandlot cosmopolis had come to a halt and all eyes peered anxiously toward Telegraph Hill. As the people waited with baited breath, the semaphore arms upslanted to announce that a side-wheel steamer had been sighted.

The Pacific Mail Steamship Company's *Oregon* was scheduled to arrive at any time now. Hopefully the vessel would be carrying the answer to the burning question in every San Franciscan's mind. Another movement of the signal arms revealed that the ship was "flying colors," which might mean anything. Finally, with a belch of coal smoke, the steamer paddled around Clark's Point and made for the Long Wharf in Yerba Buena Cove. Flags and banners of all nations fluttered from her rigging, topped by the Stars and Stripes and a long streamer proudly proclaiming: STATEHOOD, BY GOD!

The crowd went wild. Thousands of men, women, and children cheered, laughed, danced, wept and embraced one another mightily. Ships' bells clanged and those carrying guns fired off salutes that were answered by the Presidio's cannons and smaller arms from all over town. For the time being, at least, the polyglot population forgot its racial animosities and praised the U.S. Congress's generous wisdom in English, Spanish, French, Chinese and other tongues.

A year before the Californians had held a Constitutional Convention in Monterey and petitioned Washington to admit their territory as a state of the Union. Finally the federal lawmakers had compromised their way through the sticky pro- and anti-slavery argument and accepted California as a free state on September 9, 1850, although word of the decision had taken longest to reach those it most concerned.

"Welcome to the United States of America!" a tearful giant from Vermont shouted, giving a grinning Turkish peddler a crushing handshake. Someone tried to remind him that California and the New Mexico Territory had been made American possessions by the Treaty of Guadalupe Hidalgo, which ended the Mexican-American War, but he brushed aside such inconsequential details. Statehood was all that mattered in the glorious delirium gripping the settlement.

"Now we can't talk about going home to the States any more," someone else pointed out, almost regretfully.

"Nope, this here is home now, and ain't she beautiful?" said one of his neighbors, fondly gazing down a muddy hillside street that had been deemed to be Not Passable, Not Even Jackassable.

The mayor and city council announced that the occasion would be officially celebrated on October 29 with an Admission Day Parade and Ball. That would give the local military units, volunteer firemen, Masons, Odd Fellows and other civic-minded groups ample time to make the necessary arrangements, including sewing a thirty-first star to their flags. To give the affair an added touch of cultural refinement, the beautiful, talented, and irreproachably respectable Mrs. Elizabeth Maria Bonney Wills was commissioned to write an "Ode of Admission" and train a choir to sing it.

But the general populace couldn't contain their excitement that long. Throughout the days and nights following the *Oregon*'s arrival normal business was suspended and the city plunged into an orgy of patriotic fervor that found expression in every boisterous activity from drinking bouts and horse races to impromptu singing of "The Star-Spangled Banner" and "Oh Susannah," the Gold Rush's unofficial anthem.

Toward sundown, Chance pushed his way through the milling crowds in Portsmouth Square, exchanging cheerful greetings with familiar acquaintances and total strangers alike. From all sides bottles were thrust at him with the happy command: "Drink up to statehood, partner!"

Nursing a lingering hangover, Chance politely declined the generosity as often as he could get away with it and hoped he would survive long enough to attend the Admission Day gala.

Fortunately he was able to slip away occasionally for rest and recuperation in his room over Ah Ling's Chinese Hand Laundry a few blocks up Clay Street. Most of the revelers kept up their frenetic merrymaking until exhaustion overtook them, snatched an hour's sleep under a convenient bar or table, then roused themselves for another go at typing a knot in the Devil's tail.

For although most businessmen had closed up shop to celebrate the occasion, it would have been unthinkable to ask San Francisco to forgo the vital services provided by the Square's hotel-casino-saloon-brothels. Indeed, without those services there could hardly have been a celebration worthy of the name. Nearly every establishment on the Square ran full-blast twenty-four hours a day to feed the lusty male appetite for excitement. From imposing structures bearing such names as the Bella Union, El Dorado, and Sacramento House blared off-key music, the rattle of dice and roulette balls, raucous laughter, agonized wails of gamblers courting fickle Lady Luck, and infrequent gunshots that were seldom allowed to disrupt the general debauchery.

Chance paused before El Dorado and watched the motley human tide sweep in and out of the open door like the Pacific waters squeezing through Golden Gate. On a flag-draped stage played a band of sorts composed mainly of

82

banjos, fiddles, brass instruments and a sad-eyed fifer. Women wearing low-cut gowns and euphemistically called "pretty waiter girls" bustled about urging customers to buy drinks and other wares that were dispensed in small private rooms. At the ornate bar, beautifully set off with crystal chandeliers, mirrors and cut-glass decanters, stood two of the town's best-known citizens. Behind the bar presided Professor Harry Thomas, inventor of the Blue Blazer and the Tom and Jerry, whose artistry at concocting alcoholic delights fascinated even teetotalers.

Standing in front of the bar and sampling the Professor's latest masterpiece was Colonel John White Geary, San Francisco's first mayor. The taciturn Geary was an imposing figure who commanded respect in spite of the rumors that he and other members of the city government were amassing fortunes that couldn't be attributed to their modest salaries. But most of the voters were pretty lenient about that, since it was generally agreed that nobody came to California for purely altruistic reasons.

Chance had heard of Geary in Mexico and he admired his splendid war record. At a time when almost any white man who didn't do manual labor could call himself "Colonel," Geary had earned the title by commanding a regiment of Pennsylvania volunteers at the battle of Vera Cruz. Chance, having risen from the ranks to first lieutenant, knew the value of a nonpolitical commission.

The major attractions in El Dorado were the gaming tables, where men crowded three or four deep in their eagerness to buck the tiger at chuckaluck, monte, faro, *rouge et noir, vingt-et-un,* or what-have-you. Each group of players was a scale model of the Gold Rush—men of all kinds united by the desperate hope that the overwhelming odds against them could be beaten.

In the familiar surroundings where they had grown up, most of them would have adhered to the traditional values of honesty, hard work, and thrift. But here, in an explosive new environment where life was hard and dangerous, they accepted that blind luck was the only certainty and the only virtue was the wherewithal to purchase their hearts' desires. Miners, lawyers, physicians, farmers, muleskinners, ex-clergymen, university students, sailors, soldiers, politicians, ex-convicts and their former jailors all jostled one another to get their bets down with frantic gaiety.

Only the dealers and croupiers seemed exempt from the electric hope that vibrated around the tables. With dead eyes and faultless reflexes they silently sheared the bleating flock. Above them in his high chair sat the Lookout—a hired gunman ready to shoot a crooked player, a dealer attempting to cheat the house, or anyone rash enough to pull a gun on the premises. And even the Lookout had his watchdog. From the second-floor office one of the owners of El Dorado peered constantly down through peepholes at the money-making confusion below.

It was a brutally efficient system that Chance wished he had been able to employ in the Goldcock Store. Perhaps it would have saved Michael O'Neal's life. But he just was not made of the same stuff as the big gambling house owners. They were hard-bitten professionals whose careful attention to detail and ruthless determination made them the most successful businessmen in California. Each gambling den was a heavily armed fortress that the criminal element scrupulously avoided. Instead, the gangs of killers and thieves attracted to San Francisco's wealth preyed on the merchants and other honest citizens who were made vulnerable by Mayor Geary's failure to establish an effective, graft-free police force.

The two most powerful and feared criminal organizations at that time were the Hounds—mostly slum-bred hoodlums from the eastern cities—and the Sydney Ducks—former convicts from the British penal colonies in Australia and Tasmania. Brutalized by their lawbreaking pasts and harsh prison experiences, the thugs subjected San Francisco to the most vicious reign of terror that any American city has ever endured. From their shacks and tents in the area that would come to be known as the Barbary Coast, they sallied forth by day and night to rob, rape, murder and otherwise feed their appetites for loot and violence with impunity. Several disastrous fires had swept through the town in the past two-and-a-half years, with at least a few of them suspected to have been deliberately started by the Ducks and Hounds to destroy evidence of their crimes and enable them to plunder the survivors.

That accusation especially provoked Chance, because the great blaze of June 14 had consumed a warehouse full of expensive merchandise he had recently purchased. The uninsured loss had wiped out most of his capital and his hopes of becoming a prosperous wholesale importer. After that Chance had attended some of the meetings called by respectable citizens in response to the criminal depredations. But San Franciscans were too preoccupied with their own profit-oriented affairs to go to the drastic extreme of taking the law—and the responsibility of applying it fairly—away from those they had elected to administer it.

All around him he could see well-known Sydney Ducks and Hounds cheerfully fraternizing with supposedly decent citizens who just a few days ago were calling for their extermination. Many of the gangsters were easily recognized by the English custom of marking convicted felons with ear notches or brands on the forehead. Then, strolling along the board sidewalk, appeared the most bizarre example of the city's euphoric eagerness to escape reality for a while.

Of the two men pushing their way through the crowd, the slim bearded youth wearing the badge of a city constable attracted the least attention. His companion, even with manacled wrists, and the familiar ugly scar on his low brow, had a roguishly fascinating air about him. He was a powerfully built brute with the face of a mastiff that broke into easy smiles at the friendly greetings he received. One passerby offered him a bottle. "Hullo, Tassie. Have a drink."

"Thanky, mite. Don't mind if I do."

" 'e been be'avin' 'imself, Ralph?" someone asked the constable.

"Oh, sure. Gentle as a lamb." Ralph helped himself to a swallow from another bottle and gazed fondly at his charge.

"It's me Christian upbringin'," the handcuffed man sincerely announced.

He was George Llewellyn, nicknamed "Tassie" to honor his survival of ten years of hard labor in the untamed Tasmanian outback. He had never revealed the specific crime for which he had been deported from his native Wales, but it was general knowledge that he had killed at least five men since his arrival in California a year ago. That wasn't a terribly high score for a leading Sydney Duck, but his latest murder had been such a brazen public affair that even the indifferent local gendarmerie had been forced to act.

Promising a speedy trial, the authorities had confined Tassie to the *Euphemia*, an abandoned ship in the harbor which was being used as the city jail. But when the statehood celebration got under way, the soft-hearted San Franciscans had decided that not even a cold-blooded murderer should have to miss out on such a fine party. So Tassie had been released on his promise that he wouldn't try to escape. For the sake of appearances, it was decided to keep him in chains and send a guard with him. It was a regrettable inconvenience, but Tassie was a good sport about it.

"Hey, Tas, come in and give us a song!" a man inside El Dorado called out. "You can even bring your friend with you."

Tassie looked inquiringly at Ralph, who nodded agreeably. The two men disappeared into the gambling house and shortly Chance heard the Welshman's deep bass boom out "The March of the Men of Harlech," as the band tried to pick up the tune.

Chance turned away smiling to himself. Sometimes he wondered if he had lost his mind, or if he was the only sane man in this madhouse that extended from Mexico to Oregon. He moved along the sidewalk, shivering and turning up his collar as the day's mistiness became a chilly evening drizzle. Inside his constantly damp boots his feet were clammy blocks of ice and he had developed a mild but irritating cough. Just then several horsemen cantered up the water-logged street, whooping and spraying mud in all directions. One of them was a Texan who kept shouting "Remember the Alamo!" and was evidently looking for a Mexican to take the memory out on. Catching sight of a richly attired *caballero* tying a magnificent palomino stallion to the hitching rail in front of the Parker House, the Texan reined in his mount and alighted with a jangle of spurs, adjusting his holstered Colt.

"Hey, Mex, I don't like your looks!"

Chance saw the Latin's back stiffen under his colorful

serape. "*Perdón,* Señor. You weel not address me so, *por favor.*"

"*Por qué no?* You're a greaser, ain't you?"

The young grandee's handsome face turned toward the light and his white, even teeth flashed in an obliging smile. Chance recognized him as Don Nicolas Alviso, wealthy scion of one of San Francisco's founding families. Four years ago Nicholas had been a guest in General Mariano Guadalupe Vallejo's sumptuous *casa* at Sonoma, when Vallejo had graciously surrendered all of Upper California to Fremont's ragtag and bobtail army of insurgents in what had laughingly come to be known as the Bear Flag Revolt. That Vallejo possessed no more legal authority to surrender the province than Fremont had to conquer it had little bearing on the matter. Vallejo, like many other Spanish Californians, had become disgusted with the despotic, indifferent central government in far-off Mexico City and welcomed the change to what he believed would be a more democratic system. Nicolas agreed with him, and besides the conquest gave them an excellent excuse to commemorate their new political affiliation with a fiesta, if a California *ranchero* ever needed an excuse for that.

"Greaser, *si, pero no Mexicano,*" Nicolas said proudly. "I am a *Californio.*"

The man from the Lone Star State looked puzzled, unaware that to be a greaser—one who sold cow hides and tallow to Yankee ship captains—was still considered an honorable calling among the local cattlemen. "Well, uh, you wanna fight anyhow?" he asked uncertainly.

Nicolas shrugged and drew back a corner of his *serape* to expose the knife in his boot. "*A su gusto, amigo.* At your pleasure."

The Texan's hand moved toward his gun, then fell away as the wind threw a spit of rain in his face. "Aw, hell, let's have a drink first. We can scrap any time."

Nicolas smiled again and the two men marched arm-in-arm into the Parker House.

Chance continued to the Bella Union. The warmth of the hotel's smoky, stench-filled interior was a welcome relief from the raw weather. Moving along the crowded bar,

Chance spotted other familiar faces. There was gallant General Andres Pico, victor of the Battle of San Pasqual and brother of Don Pio Pico, California's last Mexican governor. Drinking with him was a 30-year-old former U.S. Army officer turned banker named William Tecumseh Sherman. Three tipplers beyond them stood the laughing, likable blacksmith Peter Donahue, who would soon introduce gas lighting to San Francisco and build the mighty Union Iron Works.

Finally Chance reached his usual corner table, where Dr. Jules Holyrod and three other men were playing stud poker, and Chance settled into the game. Since most of the players were regular customers, the pretty waiter girls didn't try to hustle them but only came around frequently to serve drinks and collect the house's rent on the table. Dr. Holyrod was a genial *bon vivant* whose ready wit gave the table a comfortably relaxed air even amidst the surrounding pandemonium.

"Doc, I hear you just made a solid gold upper plate for a Dutchman that didn't have a rotten tooth in his head," Al Penrose remarked over the clink of coins and soft rustle of cards.

"Yes, I tried to talk him out of it, but he said he wanted to put his money where his mouth is. Ante up, boys. The Lord hates a piker and so do I."

"Doc, I got this terrible pain betwixt my legs. What you reckon it is?"

"Must be galloping consumption."

"How can you call it that?"

"Might as well, since there's nothing I can do for what's really ailing you. Anybody got jacks or better?"

But in spite of the chatter, Chance never let himself forget that the game was a serious enterprise. Although he had long since realized that he would never make his fortune as a professional gambler, he did possess a certain skill at poker and on lucky nights he could win enough to cover a week's living expenses. That gave him enough free time and money to pursue other investments, mainly the buying and selling of the new waterfront lots that were created as the cove was filled in. It was a hazardous business that sometimes almost made him regret having left Goldcock. He had heard that Willis Trent had replaced him as Susan's partner, going even further by making himself Gloria Holt's lover, and was well on his way to becoming the richest gambler on the Mother Lode. But Chance knew he could not have remained with Susan, feeling as he did that she had helped cause Michael's death.

So he had taken his share of the store's profits and moved on, first to Sacramento and then San Francisco, dogged by the old bad luck that he had thought he had left on the other side of the Sierra. After losing his warehouse in the June fire, Chance was just starting to get back on his feet when he finally received word from David Wheeler. Another misguided gold seeker had wandered into Owens Valley and David had given him a letter, hoping he might run across Chance or someone who knew his whereabouts.

The letter had passed through several hands before reaching Chance with the news of Margaret's death. His first impulse had been to rush back over the mountains and take David, Vicky Beth, and little D.C. out of the valley before anything else happened to them. But David assured him that they were getting along quite well. With the Paiutes' help they had survived the winter, and from a few passing wagon trains they had obtained enough goods and supplies to make themselves comfortable.

David urged Chance not to worry about them. The farm he was developing in the valley would support them nicely until Chance made his fortune and returned. Almost as an afterthought, he mentioned that he had married the Indian girl, Bold Nose, and she was carrying their first child.

Chance was glad David had someone to help ease his sorrow and loneliness. It was also good to know that Bold Nose was being taken care of, although he had not given her much thought since he had last seen her.

But the loss of Margaret hit Chance hard. All of the good people in his life seemed to be passing on. President Taylor had died a few months ago, and no one could guess how Fillmore would finish out his term.

Vicky Beth and the baby D.C. were fine, Chance was relieved to learn, as he decided against bringing his daughter to San Francisco's unwholesome environment. Better to wait until he could afford to give her a decent home. That

89

was the goal he must concentrate on, even though it constantly slipped frustratingly out of his grasp.

Fate was still having sport with him, Chance thought dismally, telling himself that he couldn't give up. Somehow he had to fight off the grinding despair that had driven many once-hopeful Argonauts to drink or suicide. He knew the symptoms well enough to recognize them in himself—depression, insomnia, excessive worry, uncontrollable fits of homesickness and fear that things never would get any better for him. And now this damned cough made his life seem even more miserable and pointless.

"I said, it's your deal, Chance!" Al Penrose shouted, jarring Chance out of his stupor.

Chance accepted the offered deck of cards. "Sorry. I wasn't keeping my mind on business."

"That's all right," Doc Holyrod said. "Makes it easier for us to win."

Al suggested the Gold Rush cure for everything: "Have a drink."

"No, I'm all right now."

But Chance still could not shake the fog out of his brain. He played mechanically and was only a few dollars ahead two hours later when Al quit the game and another man slouched into his chair.

"Now let's see some real money on the table, gents. And deal square. I ain't had my usual man for supper yet and my stomach's startin' to growl."

At the familiar voice, Chance looked up from stacking his small pile of coins. The broad-brimmed sombrero was flung back to reveal a wild mop of sandy hair over a freckled face, button nose, and drink-brightened blue eyes. Strange that he hadn't noticed in the street how much the Texan resembled Michael O'Neal. "I'm glad to see the greaser didn't cut you up," Chance said.

"Huh? You mean old Nick Alviso? Oh, me and him's really *compadres*." The Texan scrutinized Chance, trying to place him. "You seen me call him out in the street? I was just showin' off to the other boys. Fact is, I like Mescans. I work for one—Don Carlos Esperanza. He's got a fair-sized spread down Los Angeles way. I just helped drive a herd of his'n up to sell at the mines."

Chance's interest perked up. "You're from Los Angeles? Is it true what they say—that it never rains down there?"

"Well, almost never."

"And the land is so rich that anything you plant is sure to grow?"

"Yeah, they raise tolerable crops and livestock. 'Course it ain't Texas, but what is?"

"You two gonna play poker or chew the fat?" Doc Holyrod demanded.

"Éxcuse me, Doc. I need to stretch my legs a bit." Chance stood up and pocketed his money. "And I'd like to talk to this fella some more about Los Angeles, if he'll let me buy him a drink."

"*A su gusto,* Señor." The Texan rose with alacrity and followed Chance as he elbowed his way to the bar. Over a tot of rum he introduced himself as Simon ("Call me Si") Darcy, born of Louisiana Cajun stock on a cattle spread along the Brazos River.

Chance had been interested in the fabled Eden to the south ever since the bay area dampness had locked the lingering chill from the mountains deep in his bones. The boundless fair weather of southern California had attracted several Yankee emigrants and Chance found it pleasant to dream of lazing in the sun and watching fat cattle make him rich, as Si described the idyllic lives of the Los Angeles *rancheros.*

"What the hell kind of Spanish is that?" Si demanded abruptly, staring at the man draped over the bar to his left. "I've heard everything from ordinary Mex-talk to pure Castilian, but damned if I can make head nor tail of his lingo."

"That's Latin, not Spanish," Chance said, turning to the man whose eyes were closed as he mumbled steadily to himself. He was about Chance's age and height, but with a receding hairline, oversized nose, and sunken cheeks, which made him decidedly less attractive. "Sounds like some kind of poetry."

The man opened his eyes and beamed at Chance. "Ah, you are a linguist, then?" His accent was slight, but unmistakably German.

Chance shook his head, smiling. "No, sir, but one of my

messmates in the war was a professor of languages. He tried to teach me some Latin and Greek, but I couldn't get the hang of them."

"What a pity! But you did understand that I was reciting verses?"

"Yes, and it sounded very nice. What is it?"

"Book twenty-two of the *Iliad*, in which Achilles slays Hector after chasing him thrice around Troy's walls. I've found it's just the thing to clear my head when I've had too much to drink."

"You a schoolmaster?" Si asked suspiciously.

"Oh, no, just an export-import merchant. Permit me to introduce myself: Heinrich Schliemann, late of Hamburg, Amsterdam, and Saint Petersburg."

Chance and Si gave their names and shook the German's hand. Chance inquired if Schliemann's business in California had gone well.

"Quite well, thank you. And the journey has paid an unexpected bonus, for I have just learned that everyone residing here at the time of California's admission to the United States was granted American citizenship."

Chance congratulated Schliemann, and Si said that called for a drink. "My messmate was also fond of Homer," Chance said. "He used to read to us in the evenings, translating it into English. They're mighty exciting stories. But I prefer the legends of Robin Hood and King Arthur myself."

"But the *Iliad* is more than just a story!" Schliemann cried. "It is factual history. Troy actually existed, unlike Arthur's mythical Camelot, and it was destroyed in a war with the Greeks. It is my dream that someday I will be able to afford to search for the ruins of Troy. There must still remain, even after thirty centuries, some evidence that she once stood as proud and beautiful as Homer described her."

Chance aborted an impulse to laugh as he caught the powerful sincerity in Schliemann's tone. He supposed it should not surprise him that such an intelligent, practical-minded businessman could believe in childish fairy tales. He had noticed in other Europeans that strange combination of hardheaded realism and romantic sentimentality that was so rare this side of the Atlantic. But was it really so rare among Americans, or just expressed differently, as in the way their western thrust for land and wealth, mingled with idealistic fervor, had been put forth in John O'Sullivan's almost mystical statement about manifest destiny? Perhaps Schliemann's fascination with the ruins of the ancient past came from the same inner force that drove Chance and his fellow Argonauts to participate in the building of America's future. In the years to come, it would never seem strange to Chance that he had met Heinrich Schliemann in the dream-riddled world of the Gold Rush. It was the most logical place for them to be.

The hell-raising revelry around Portsmouth Square was still going strong when Chance reeled happily out of the Bella Union at 2 A.M. The drinks he had consumed with Schliemann and Si Darcy, along with their inspiring stories about Troy and Los Angeles, had cheered him out of his depression. Even the weather seemed to promise better things for him. The rain had ceased and a few stars were visible through ragged holes in the low clouds.

As he started toward his room on Clay Street, Chance noticed a large crowd of men, some of them carrying torches, in front of the adobe Custom House. Joining other curious spectators, Chance trudged over to see what the commotion was about. A horse and carriage were drawn up under the high beam that extended from the front of the Custom House. Tassie Llewellyn stood beside the carriage, with two men holding his manacled arms. With them was a woman, her figure indistinct under a heavy coat and her face shadowed by a wide hat with lace falling over the brim.

"What's the game?" Chance asked a member of the crowd.

"Oh, they're just gonna hang Tassie," he answered cheerfully.

"Without giving him a trial?"

"He don't deserve none," another man said angrily. "The sonofabitch kilt the constable that was guardin' him and tried to escape. They caught him hidin' on the floor of the lady's carriage."

Someone appeared with a rope and started tying a noose in one end of it. "I'm plumb disappointed in you, Tas," one of his captors said sadly. "Here we give you the free run of the town, and you ain't even got enough good manners to stick around till we could hang you legally."

"Not to mention that you might've got off scot-free," his companion added. "There can be extenuating circumstances to cover little things like murder or arson, but a man that'll break his word don't deserve to live."

Tassie hung his head in deep shame. "I truly am sorry about that, mites. I don't know what come over me. The drink, I reckon. But supposin' I gave you me solemn oath I'd never do it again. D'ye think you could let me off?"

The mob muttered protestingly and the man on Tassie's left said: "Come on, Tas. You wouldn't want to let these boys down after they've all got together to see you off, would you? Be a sport."

While the crowd laughed, the rope was tossed over the beam and Tassie was boosted up on the carriage to stand with the noose dangling before his eyes. "Let's hang his strumpet with him!" someone shouted.

"Yeah, string 'em both!"

"Wait! We don't know if she's guilty or not!" one of the executioners argued. But the front ranks of the mob pressed forward, jostling the woman and knocking her hat off. At the sight of her tumbling auburn curls and lovely pale face, the men drew back with sighs that were almost reverent. Chance stared incredulously, then started pushing his way roughly through the crowd.

"Let me through! That's my sister, just arrived from Boston!" Chance reached the woman and grasped her shoulders as her frightened eyes flared with surprise and hopeful recognition. "Sophie, my dear! What happened? Did this cur kidnap you and force you to help him escape?"

The violet eyes filled with tears. "Yes, it was terrible! He put his hands on me and . . . and . . ." She fell sobbing into Chance's arms.

One of the men leaped up in the carriage with Tassie. "Is what she says true? Speak up, you scum!"

Tassie stared thoughtfully at the girl for a long moment, then nodded.

The mob roared for his life.

"Hanging's too good for a dirty scoundrel that would ruin a decent woman, when we got so few of 'em!"

"Yeah, we might have to send all the way to Boston for another one."

"And that'd leave Boston without any."

The man in the carriage waved them to silence. "All right, Tassie, it's time for you to cash in your chips. You got any last words?"

"Yah, but I can't say 'em dry." A bottle was handed up from the crowd. Tassie drained it and faced his audience with a mocking grin. "So long, you bastards. I'll save places for all o' you in the hottest corner o' hell." He raised his chained hands and placed the noose around his neck. "Bury me face down, lads, and tell the world to kiss me arse!"

He leaped off the carriage as the men holding the other end of the rope gave a sharp jerk. Chance led the girl away, the men chivalrously making a path for them. It was not the most romantic beginning for his first night with Gloria Holt, but it would do.

Chapter 10

October 31, 1850

David led the sad-eyed ox over to the main firepit while the small crowd of Indians looked on. Paul the Apostle stood solemnly holding the saber he had received from Chance. Beside him was his Paiute wife Su-he-be. The ex-mission Indian had achieved acceptance and some degree of prosperity among the Owens Valley tribe, thanks in no small part to his eagerness in using the saber to advance his interests.

Bold Nose looked up from where she sat cross-legged with her friends, making cornbread, and gave her white husband a fleeting smile. David nodded to her and glanced at the southern sun edging toward the Sierra crest. There was no use putting it off any longer, he thought soberly. The ox was the last of the animals that had accompanied them across the continent, and it saddened him to cut another tie with the past. But the beast had outlived its usefulness and was unlikely to survive another winter. Better that it be sacrificed for the combined first birthday party for D.C. and Thanksgiving celebration.

"Let it happen," David said to Paul the Apostle in Paiute.

The Indian unsheathed the saber and plunged it into the ox's throat. Blood spurted, to be caught in pots for soup, while several braves held the kicking, bellowing animal in place.

David looked away, down the broad stretch of cultivated land that sloped gently to the river bank. The stubbled corn stalks were as neatly ranked as soldiers, and David felt justifiably proud of his year's labor in the valley. It had been a good harvest. The storage baskets in the cabin that had grown to three rooms bulged with corn and wheat, with an equal supply of dried and salted meat. Out back, the root cellar was filled with potatoes, turnips, carrots and onions. The Paiutes had also been successful at laying in a goodly store of provisions for the cold months. There would be no starvation in the valley this winter, God be praised. So it was fitting they should commemorate their good fortune with a feast.

When he turned around, the ox had finished thrashing out its life and the Indians were busily butchering it. David oversaw the skinning and quartering of the carcass, which was then spitted over the fire. Paul the Apostle claimed a hindquarter as his share and ordered his wife to shoulder it. Paul never had learned to be very sociable, David reflected, as the Indian couple strode off in the direction of their own camp. Another haunch was carried off by Lightning Tracker's squaw, Slow Of Speech, although her son Hu-pwi remained for the festivities. The Indian lad had never ceased to steal yearning glances at Bold Nose and he took every opportunity to be near her, much to Winnedumah's displeasure. She was exasperated by David's lack of interest in keeping other men away from his wife and she protected the girl's virtue even more diligently than before.

David gave Slow Of Speech an extra portion of corn meal and tried to express his concern for Lightning Tracker's welfare. The old chief was laid up with a severe case of scarlet fever, acquired from a passing party bound for the gold fields. The disease was especially dangerous among Indians, who had no culturally acquired resistance to it, and David hoped he had been successful in persuading Lightning Tracker to remain isolated from his tribespeople until he recovered.

The white travelers had brought considerable new ills to the valley, but the Paiutes had also benefited from their visits. Metal knives, axes, cookware and other implements were appearing in the native camps and several Indians had learned the rudiments of agriculture, which David was eager to teach them.

David's hospitality was always happily extended to the bone-weary but still gold-hungry emigrants and in return he had received many valuable additions to his thriving homestead. Among them were a pair of strong plow horses, a milk cow for the young ones, six laying hens with a strutting rooster to increase their numbers and some seedling fruit trees. Yes, life in Owens Valley was turning out to be as fulfilling for a born farmer as David had foreseen. If only Margaret were here to enjoy it with him. . . .

Of course Margaret would always be with him in the most important ways. But even so, there were times when the warm, helpful companionship of Bold Nose—Rebekah, David reminded himself—was not enough to keep the lingering grief from flooding over him. On some nights he would slip restlessly out of bed to make sure that the children were all right, then walk up to the rise behind the cabin where Margaret's grave commanded a soothing view of the river and croplands. Standing there in the soft starlight, David would tell Margaret about their activities and progress, ask her advice on troublesome problems, and listen as she replied with her dearly remembered love and common sense. That, and a little Bible-reading by candlelight, always enabled him to fall into deep, soul-restoring sleep.

David never noticed that his new wife also had occasional sleepless nights, due to thoughts of another mate. Rebekah was grateful to David for what he had done for her, her son, and old Winnedumah. In a sense, she truly loved him with the servile devotion of her simple heart, blooming into radiant womanhood under his gentle though somewhat absentminded care. But she never forgot that she belonged to Don Chance. He was her real master and someday he would return to reclaim his property. When that happened, she would have to take little Bobby Buck and go with Chance, leaving David and the white child she had come to regard as her other son. That thought filled her with great sadness; sometimes she wept silently for hours into her pillow. But nothing could be done about it. Her fate had been sealed that night on the riverbank, when Chance's hard demanding body had blotted out the stars and become her new universe.

David looked around for Vicky Beth and D.C., then remembered that they had been sent off to play with the other small children while their elders prepared the food and festivities. David decided it was time to start rounding up the little rascals and spoke a few words to Rebekah. Rebekah turned her work over to the other women, rose and swung the sleeping Bobby Buck's cradleboard onto her back. David watched her stride up the path past Margaret's grave and along the irrigation ditch. Naturally, that was where Vicky Beth and her gang of mischief-makers would be found.

Vicky Beth stood knee-deep in the pond, digging freshwater clams from the muddy bottom with her toes and shouting orders to the Paiute children with her. She was naked, as were they all, even hulking Wongata. His name meant "striped" in Paiute and it referred to his strangely discolored and puckered complexion. It was the mark of the hard birth that had cost his mother's life and made him forever a child.

But Wongata saw no misfortune in that. Gentle-natured, trusting all and tolerated by most, he embraced life with loving zeal, his thick slobbering lips wearing their broadest grin when the other children admitted him to their games. Suddenly he stooped and brought up an especially large clam, shivering with ecstasy when the find earned him his small leader's approval.

"That's real good, Wongata," Vicky Beth called. "Now ever'body get in line an' walk real slow. We don't wanna miss any good 'uns."

She looked toward the bank, where fat, toddling D.C. waded cautiously in imitation of his larger playmates.

"Stay there, honey. Don't be a naughty *nah-tse-e*," Vicky Beth ordered, using the Paiute word for little boy.

Her quick mind had absorbed much of the Indians' lim-

99

ited vocabulary and her speech had become a colorful Paiute-English mixture that was somehow understood by members of both races.

D.C.'s foot slipped on the mud and he sat down hard, uttering a loud wail at the abrupt discomfort. His unhappiness was not much relieved by the unexpected emptying of his bladder, although that gave his companions some amusement.

"Oh, hush, you little squirt," Vicky Beth scolded, "or I'll smack your bottom for you."

Having been in charge of D.C. for most of his life, she was as much a second mother to him as Auntie Rebekah, and much firmer in some ways. Vicky Beth tolerated no nonsense from her underlings, including all of the Indian children around her. She was their natural leader, called See-ve Su-zu, East Maiden, and all of her followers obeyed her with slavish devotion.

Nearly seven now, Vicky Beth was lean and strong from farm chores and dashing tirelessly about the Indian camps. The summer sun had tanned her nearly as brown as the Paiutes, leaving only her red lips and sparkling blue eyes to set her apart from her native comrades.

D.C.'s tender baby skin had suffered from sunburn at first. But now he was only a shade lighter than Vicky Beth.

Both of the white children were great favorites among the Paiutes. Only Winnedumah treated them with indifference that barely concealed jealous hostility. The old woman was convinced that her security in David's household rested on her purported blood kinship to Bobby Buck. To strengthen her position, she worked subtly to make the half-Paiute infant David's favorite offspring.

Winnedumah could have saved herself considerable effort and worry if she had better understood David's character. His kind heart and bedrock Christianity would always compel him to provide for his dependents, regardless of their relationships. But Winnedumah was equally compelled to use underhanded methods while dealing with men. A lifetime habit of guarding against male perfidy was hard to break.

As the children waded through the shallows, laughing

100

and clasping hands, small fish darted ahead of them to the reservoir's middle depths. Grassy slopes cupped the half-acre of water and a proud old canyon oak towered over D.C. with powerful limbs reaching wide and low over the ground. Vicky Beth and her bolder friends loved to climb the tree.

David had selected the site carefully, finding it a perfect natural holding tank for irrigation water. Centuries before, the river's floodwaters had cut a loop here. Then silt and gravel deposits had gradually sealed off the ends of the loop and turned it into a marshy backwater.

David had only to open the loop's upstream end and let the depression refill, after cutting a narrow channel at the lowest point in the embankment and fitting it with a crude plank watergate. With the pond bottom being a good fifty feet higher than David's farm, gravity carried the water through a system of shallow ditches to the croplands.

The Indians were impressed by David's innovations. Several of them had copied it on a smaller scale. David was delighted to see his Paiute neighbors making progress toward becoming civilized. All they needed were more white settlers to show them the way, and they could make this valley the garden spot of California and an inspiring example of brotherhood between white and red Americans. With the Paiutes being so peaceful, there would never be a repetition of the eastern states' bloody Indian wars. What could people possibly find to fight about here, where there was ample water and rich soil for everyone?

Vicky Beth held hands with Seyavi, her closest friend. At eleven, Seyavi was only a few inches taller than Vicky Beth, but showing the first swift bloom of puberty in her budding acorn breasts. The two girls had been inseparable from the first moment they met, sleeping together as often as possible and sharing giggly secrets in the private corners of cabin and wickiup. Many a night they had lain around camp hearths with their toes in the ashes, listening wonder-eyed to songs and tales of the People.

On such an occasion, Vicky Beth had first learned of Shoshone Land, that magic world that lies far southward beyond the bitter tideless lake. To reach that country, you must travel waterless days over low hills of sage. From there you come to the place of mottled sands, where the Great Wolf God of Creation spewed his seeds, where the brutal genesis can still be seen in worn craters and hot stinking springs, with steam jets ejaculating from ravished soil. Then you travel through spills of black lava like cold mush, full of sharp twisting cracks, where the cliff faces are marked with ancient picture writings that no Paiute or Shoshone today can read. And finally, on the edge of your endurance, if you drink the raw west wind and utter the proper chant, you may open your eyes to gaze across the sweeping hollow to the blue hills and mesas of Shoshone Land.

All this Vicky Beth heard from Pah-ya Che-e, the medicine man, whose name and wife and children were Paiute but whose heart remained Shoshone. He had come to live among the Paiutes as a youthful hostage in an old war cause that few could now remember. No reason existed any longer for him to remain, except honor, so he did remain, ever yearning and talking homesickly of his beloved Shoshone Land. His Paiute family and friends laughed at his sighing reminiscences but Vicky Beth savored delicious shiverings at the vivid images his words drew in her bright imagination. She vowed that someday she would journey to Shoshone Land and there perform the magic ritual that would return Pah-ya Che-e's longing spirit to its birthplace.

Ta-tsu, Seyavi's mother, gently tried to dissuade Vicky Beth from such foolish notions. Travel, medicine, and war were men's work, Ta-tsu explained. The gods had provided more meaningful functions for women. Vicky Beth had her own ideas about womanhood, but she held her tongue out of love and respect for Ta-tsu, who had become another aunt to her. It was Ta-tsu who had woven the basket caps that Vicky Beth and Seyavi wore over their tangled hair.

The line of clam-diggers swung back toward the bank and Vicky Beth, looking up, saw Auntie Rebekah walking toward them. Vicky Beth sighed and hurried out of the water to where she had left her clothes at the base of the spreading oak. Now that Auntie Rebekah had been introduced to Jesus, she was even more strict than Uncle David about maintaining the civilized decencies. Vicky Beth agreed with her Indian companions that clothing was an unnecessary bother in warm weather. But by the time Rebekah reached the oak, Vicky Beth had herself and D.C. dressed and looking almost like two respectable, well-behaved, white American children. Almost.

Rebekah smiled at the dripping children, adjusting the straps of Bobby Buck's cradleboard to relieve the pressure. Sometimes it seemed to her that carrying a child on her back was even more bothersome than when he had been in front. "It is time, little brothers and sisters," she said, ignoring the fact that Wongata towered over her. "Bring thy brother, stepdaughter," she added to Vicky Beth.

"Yes'm." Vicky Beth gave a little grunt as she lifted D.C. to straddle her right hip. It never occurred to her to correct Rebekah; in their patchwork family, titles were more for endearment than identification.

Rebekah led the chattering gaggle of youngsters back along the trail to the feast site before the cabin, with Vicky Beth and Seyavi at her sides. As much as the young matron loved the white children, it was the Paiute girl who occupied most of her attention. For some of Winnedumah's matchmaking ardor had rubbed off on her foster granddaughter, who saw in the nearly nubile Seyavi the ideal bride for Hu-pwi.

Although Rebekah was almost totally ignorant of the world beyond the desert wastes and mountain shadows that limited her sixteen years, still her woman-wise heart ached compassionately for the young brave's love that she could never return. She was the property of Don Chance, and until he reclaimed her she would be a dutiful wife to her Jesus-appointed husband David. But she could help her lovesick suitor find contentment with another marriage partner, and this she was determined to do. She would teach Seyavi the subtle arts of love and wifehood that she had learned from Winnedumah. Then she would gently offer the younger girl as her surrogate for Hu-pwi's affection.

Throughout the feast that lasted from late afternoon till the highest point of the waning moon's flight, while the People greedily stuffed themselves in honor of the Halloween birthday boy and a little-understood white man's har-

103

vest celebration, Rebekah kept Seyavi beside her. Even as the old pagan songs and strange new Jesus hymns were sung and the blood-stirring *totsoho* dance was stamped out by men in eagle feathers and kilts—to David's puzzled tolerance—Rebekah held Seyavi's head on her shoulder and combed her hair with her fingers.

Vicky Beth watched the unexplained new intimacy between her two dearest female companions with resentful hurt and envy. How could they exclude her from their confidence this way? Was it because she was white? She was *trying* to be as Paiute as they were. If there was any other way that she could become like them, they should tell her. It wasn't fair, she sulked, holding the squirming D.C. on her lap and stuffing food into the bottomless pit of his stomach. Lately she had sensed a subtle change coming over Seyavi that she could not comprehend as the first stirrings of womanhood. She only knew the fear that the change provoked in her, the horrible half-buried memories of losing her mother, father, and Aunt Margaret.

Vicky Beth continued to glower miserably throughout the evening, until D.C. finally had his fill and snuggled down to sleep in her arms with a happy burp. She carried the boy into the cabin and curled up on her bed, holding him tightly. "I'll never let 'em take *you* away from me, honey!" she whispered fiercely into his hair.

Outside, the feasting and dancing flowed on like the steady current of the river. Rebekah smiled at Seyavi, noticing that Hu-pwi was already glancing at the girl with more than casual interest. When the time was right Rebekah would dress Seyavi's hair with clematis blossoms, the white flower of twining, and teach her to sing:

> I am the white flower of twining,
> Little white flower by the river.
> Oh, flower that twines close by the river.
> Oh, trembling flower!
> So trembles the maiden heart.

Rebekah could well testify to the powerful allure of an attractive flower at the river, under the right circumstances.

Lightning Tracker lay miserably on his blanket, trying to ignore his burning brain and the tormenting body rash that he had already scratched to raw bleeding scabs. The white chief Wheeler had warned him against that, saying that the dirt would allow more germs to enter his body. Germs were a new class of evil spirits to Lightning Tracker, but he wasn't surprised to hear about them. The gods had no end of ways to make mortals suffer for their sins.

He wondered for what offense he was being punished this time. Perhaps because he had been stupid enough to marry a fool like Slow Of Speech. He heard her muttering wordlessly around the cookfire outside the wickiup and wished he could shout at her to shut up. But his mouth and throat were too swollen for him to get out more than a hoarse croak. Raising himself on one elbow, he tried to drink some of the watery stew his wife had brought him, but it burned the tender, enlarged papillae on his tongue. "Strawberry tongue," David had called it. Lightning Tracker had never eaten strawberries and, if they tasted anything like his tongue just then, he didn't ever want to.

At least it was reassuring to hear from David that this particular spirit sickness was fairly common among white people, and rarely fatal. That meant he wouldn't have to go to the trouble of sending for medicine man Pah-ya Che-e. Not that Pah-ya Che-e would likely have answered the summons anyhow. He had grown very cautious of the cases he accepted of late, owing mainly to the Paiute custom of killing a medicine man who had three patients die on him in a given span of time. No one could remember exactly how long it had been since Pah-ya Che-e had last lost a patient, but he had never been one to take unnecessary chances.

Pah-ya Che-e's prudence was about the only tolerable quality that Lightning Tracker could find in him. Anyone doubly stupid enough to be both a Shoshone and a medicine man received little sympathy from the old Paiute. Lightning Tracker had nearly entered the medical profession himself.

During his passage-into-manhood rite, after two days of fasting and cleansing himself in the sweat house, the semi-delirious Hour of Visions had given him several vivid dreams. But fortunately he had managed to convince the tribal elders that he did not possess the supernatural gifts of a true medicine man. The elders had allowed Lightning Tracker to follow the less demanding course of understudying his father's position of *Po-ko-nah-be*, or headman of the community, what the whites called "Chief." It turned out to be the ideal occupation for Lightning Tracker. He had led his band expertly through many difficult years, acquiring a shrewd skepticism about the laws of God and man and a realistic evaluation of human nature. He had never lost his commanding presence with anyone, until he fell in love with Winnedumah.

Lightning Tracker groaned painfully as he shifted his weight. He wished Winnedumah was here now. No, she mustn't see him this way. She had only scorn for weakness. He would regain his strength, then go to visit her. To that end, he forced himself to drink the stew water and even managed to gag down a little of the meat. Then he fell into a jerky, fever-torn sleep filled with senseless dreams.

In one of the dreams, he saw war parties of strange new gods invading the valley. Their grotesque forms resembled neither Indians nor whites, but were armed with huge spreading horns on their heads, much longer than those on David's oxen. Then their shapes changed—or at least it appeared to his dazed perception that they changed—and they had other weapons like mighty bows or guns. The new weapons fired out seeds, which sprouted into houses like David's. The houses kept springing up until the valley was filled with them. Then other gods—so terrible that they were nearly invisible—moved devastatingly through the valley, sweeping everything away. Houses, Paiutes, white people, crops, trees, water—all were gone, leaving the valley bare for *Te-lu-gu-pu* to start the creation cycle over again.

During the night Lightning Tracker's fever broke. In the morning he awoke clearminded but so weak that Slow Of Speech had to hold his head up to a bowl in order for him to drink water. Throughout the day the memory of his dream stayed annoyingly on his mind. He told himself that it was just nonsense, but he couldn't help wondering if it had some secret meaning. It was just as well that Pah-ya Che-e had not come to treat him, or he probably would have had to pay the medicine man a fee for some far-fetched interpretation of the dream, just to ease his curiosity.

Chapter 11

"Vaya con Dios, hijos."

"Gracias, Padre."

Chance waited in respectful silence as the elderly priest completed his blessing. Si Darcy, Nicolas Alviso, and the five Indian *vaqueros* rose from their knees in the dust before the mission *convento*. Donning their sombreros and mounting their horses, the small band of travelers took their leave of the sober-faced man of God.

The departure pleased Chance, not only because he was glad they were nearing the end of their journey, but also because the dilapidated condition of the once-proud Mission de San Fernando Rey de España depressed him. All the way down El Camino Real—the King's Highway—he had observed the declining influences of Spain, Mexico, and especially the dedicated friars of the order of Saint Francis of Assisi. The Latin pioneers had been the first to attempt to bring civilization and Christian love to heathen California. They deserved better than to have their works swept aside by the Anglo conquest and the Gold Rush.

As they rode away, Chance glanced back at the mission doors. The hand-hewn, ironbound, thick oak planks were ornamented—as were the doors of all the missions Chance had seen—with the Indians' River of Life motif. The vertical wavy lines carved into the wood symbolized the Indians' mystical reverence for water as a sacred medium carrying all things past and present in its endless flow. It was surprising that the Catholic priests permitted such a pagan mark on their houses of worship. But Chance found it strangely appealing.

Gaspar, a silver-haired *vaquero*, rode beside Chance as they headed due south. The old fellow was delighted to be home again. He was a Tujunga tribesman who had been baptized by Father Fermin Lasuen, the founder of San Fernando Mission and successor to Father Junipero Serra, whose burning vision and tireless labor had created the California mission system.

Stretching from San Diego to Sonoma, the twenty-one missions were intended to convert the territory's Indians to good Christians and useful subjects of Spain. The system had worked remarkably well, at little cost aside from the Indians' loss of their freedom and native cultures. At San Fernando alone more than 3,000 converts were made from such tribes as the Tujunga, Pacoima, Cahuenga and Topanga. The mission's extensive lands yielded rich crops and supported large herds of cattle, horses, sheep and pigs, making it possible for neophytes like Gaspar to become skilled farmers and stockmen.

But in 1822 Mexico won her independence from Spain and shortly afterwards California's missionary period ended with the passage of the Secularization Act. Control of the missions was transfered from the Church to civil authority and most of their lands were sold to raise money for public services. The Indian converts drifted away to find work on the large ranchos or to resume their primitive way of life and the neglected mission buildings, composed of sun-dried adobe bricks and tile roofs, were well on their way to being weathered back into the soil.

But the sad state of the mission churches did not prevent Chance's companions from benefiting from the spiritual services they still provided. Even Si occasionally attended Mass with Nicolas and the *vaqueros*. Si had been born into the Catholic faith and although he claimed to have backslid so many times that he had probably lost his claim to heaven, still it didn't hurt to have a skypilot put in a good word for him now and then. Chance wished he could get as much out of religion as most of his friends seemed to, especially David Wheeler. But, as one of his fellow poker players from a southern state once put it, that old dog just wouldn't hunt for him.

It was a fine clear day, with the Santa Monica mountains that fenced the southern side of the valley shimmering in their evergreen coats of chaparral. The *vaqueros* were eager to reach their home on the other side of the mountains, but they patiently allowed their horses to amble along and nibble the sparse grass beside the trail. The parched ground awaited the start of winter rains and from the dry wild mustard stalks—some taller than a man on horseback—birds and ground squirrels watched the riders pass.

Chance savored the warm sunlight and clean dry air that had almost cured his San Francisco cough. He felt he had made the right decision in leaving the fogbound hellhole to the north, although it had not been easy to tear himself away from Gloria Holt after their exhilarating night together following Tassie Llewellyn's hanging. If only things had been different between them. . . .

Gloria had recovered from her grief as soon as they were safely in Chance's room over the Chinese laundry. Even while he was locking the door, her mouth found his and her rich full body strained against him.

"Let me light the lamp," Chance began when he could catch his breath.

"No! I don't want anything to come between us, not even light," Gloria moaned hotly in his ear. "Oh, Chance, I've wanted you for so long! Why didn't you take me at Goldcock?"

"I don't know." Chance tried to think clearly. "That man, Tassie—"

"Forget him. He was nothing to me."

Chance wished he could believe that, as much as he wished he could overcome his prejudice against Gloria's unsavory past. He wanted her with the raging intensity of his aroused manhood, but not just for the brief, easily forgotten pleasure he could buy from any harlot.

110

Chance's sensitivity to finer things had been so dulled by his coarse masculine surroundings for the past several months that Gloria's femininity was a stimulating tonic. Her mere presence awakened his appreciation for the countless tender refinements a woman can add to a man's life.

Then Gloria kissed him again and the last of his moral reluctance disappeared. They fell on the bed tearing at each other's clothes in their eagerness to be flesh-to-flesh, male-to-female, heart-to-heart. . . .

As he dozed off holding her warm sweaty body against him, Chance happily believed that his luck had finally changed for the better. At last he had found a woman he could truly love. Why should he worry about her former life? He would overlook that and they would make a fresh start in this promising new land. As soon as he could reclaim Vicky Beth they would be a real family. And there would be other children—the kind of strong, brave young Americans California needed to take her rightful place in this great country.

It was a beautiful dream. But like most dreams, it was destined to die in the clear light of the following day, when Chance drew the covers away from Gloria's prone figure and saw the ugly scar on her right buttock. It was a brand in the shape of a T—like the mark of a thief that Tassie Llewellyn had worn on his forehead.

For several moments Chance was too stunned to know what to make of the scar. Could Gloria have been a convicted felon? Where? No American court inflicted such barbarous punishment. Then he understood. She *had* been Tassie's woman. With cruel possessiveness, the brute had branded her as his property, as if she were a cow or a horse.

Leaving the sleeping woman, Chance stumbled sickly out of bed. It was hopeless to plan a future with Gloria. The brand would be a constant reminder of her past. Even if he were man enough to forgive her a thousand times, there would always be a thousand-and-first time when he would turn on her with hatred and scorn. What made that realization especially bitter was that he knew now that Gloria

111

could be a good woman, with the right man. He hoped she would find him.

He quietly dressed and packed his few belongings without waking Gloria, then counted out half of his money on the dressing table. Maybe it would be enough to enable her to make a fresh start without going back to her previous occupation. He thought of leaving a note, but there was really nothing to say.

Pausing at the door for a final look at her lovely face, so innocent in sleep, Chance wished he were like David—full of kindness and charity for the shortcomings of others. Or why couldn't he have been as ruthless as Tassie and taken Gloria when they first met in the gold fields? Why must he always balance in the middle of fortune's scales, never content with the ordinary and lacking the ability for the extraordinary? He might as well put on a dunce cap and resign himself to playing life's fool.

At the Parker House, Chance found Si Darcy and his *vaqueros* drinking with Nicholas Alviso. Si said that they were about to head back to Don Carlos Esperanza's Rancho Agua Fria near Los Angeles and old Nick here had decided to ride along with them. It seemed that old Nick had been seeing a lady, whose husband's unreasonable jealousy made this an ideal time for him to visit his cousins in the south.

"Mind a little more company?" Chance asked them.

Nicolas replied with his lazy good-natured grin and Si allowed he'd be plumb tickled to show Chance the delights of the Pueblo of the Angels.

"But don't expect the same kinda excitin' doin's you're used to around here," Si warned.

"That suits me fine," Chance said.

He was able to buy a good saddle horse at a fair price and by nightfall they were far enough along El Camino Real for him to think about Gloria without feeling too much pain.

They made their way leisurely down the San Fernando Valley, encountering herds of half-wild longhorned cattle that could be dangerous to someone on foot. But the *va-*

queros easily controlled them with their masterly horsemanship and swinging *reatas*.

The impatient younger *vaqueros* urged Si to take the direct route over the mountains and down Canada de Agua Fria—Coldwater Canyon—to the rancho that took its name from the canyon. But Gaspar insisted that the climb would be too hard on their heavily laden pack animals. Si agreed with Gaspar, so the argument was settled. Chance never learned exactly what position the sandy-haired Texan occupied in Don Carlos Esperanza's employ—foreman or *mayordomo* or what—but when he made a decision, it was law to the other ranch hands. And that even included Don Carlos' sons.

So it was agreed that they would take the long way around through Cahuenga Pass. As they turned east, Chance wondered how he would fare in this new territory. Most of southern California's wealth was in the form of land and cattle, Si had told him. There had been a minor gold rush in Placerita Canyon, several miles to the north, in 1842. But that had soon played out and it was generally agreed that no mineral deposits worth bothering with lay south of the Sierra range.

Nearly all of the good ranch land in the area was already owned by old *Californio* families—the Picos, Carrillos, Sepulvedas, Dominguezes, Esperanzas and others who ruled their feudal domains in lordly splendor. But there was a growing class of Anglo businessmen—shrewd merchants such as Abel Stearns, John Temple, and Alexander Bell—who handled most of the town's trade. Perhaps Chance could invest his dwindling capital in a promising commercial venture—say a general store like the one he and David had operated back in Oneonta. He was eager to try anything that would help him make a good home for Vicky Beth and get over his long string of bad luck.

Chance was thinking about that when they rounded the final narrow bend of Cahuenga Pass and paused to take in the broad sweeping vista of the coastal plain sloping down to the Pacific's blue haze. Si pointed out the low southeastern hills that partly obscured their view of El Pueblo de Nuestra Señora la Reina de Los Angeles de Porciuncula—

113

The Village of Our Lady the Queen of the Angels of Porciuncula. It was an ambitious mouthful that Governor Felipe de Neve had given his band of forty-four *vecinos pobladores*—village settlers—upon establishing the outpost of Spanish power on September 4, 1781.

"It's still early," Si observed by the sun. "Might as well ride into town for a drink before we report to the *patron*."

Chance welcomed the opportunity for a firsthand inspection of the community upon which he had based his hopes for the future. His first impression of Los Angeles, however, offered little encouragement for those hopes. In fact, if it had not been for the climate, he might have turned around and headed back to San Francisco.

Chapter 12

The pueblo—actually it had been elevated to the status of *ciudad* (city) in 1835, but it would be many more years before people stopped thinking of Los Angeles as a sleepy Mexican village—had been laid out according to the standard pattern of Spanish colonies in the New World. The original buildings were arranged in a hollow square, enclosing the plaza, for community protection and easy sociability. To the east ran the river, where once had stood the Indian village of Yang-Na. *A zanja madre* (mother ditch) had been dug from the river to carry water to the pueblo and on to the farmlands further south.

Having begun as a dirty little frontier settlement, Los Angeles had since become somewhat larger and much dirtier. When Chance and his friends rode into the collection of dusty flat-roofed adobes, it had a population of about 1,600. Most of the residents were of the *gente de razon*—people of reason, as those of Spanish ancestry still referred to themselves. There were also a growing Anglo and European contingent and several Indians whom no one bothered to count. Many of the *Yanqui* merchants and wealthy *rancheros* had built *palacios*, or town houses, on the plaza and adjoining streets. Most notable were the homes of such prominent citizens as the lusty old rebel Don José Antonio

115

Carrillo, on the south side of the plaza, and Don Abel Stearns, at the corner of Main and a new street that Stearns had named after his beautiful young wife, Arcadia.

With a pack of yapping dogs at his horse's heels, Chance looked over the sunbaked treeless plaza and felt his heart sink. In a nearby mud wallow, a fat sow flopped down to suckle a dozen squealing piglets. Half-naked children played in the dirt, idly watched by gossiping women and loafing Indians. The warm air was thick with the stink of excrement, decaying garbage and dead animal flesh that the scavengers had not completely disposed of. A swarm of black flies hovering about Chance's three-day-old beard stubbornly resisted his efforts to brush them away.

Had he traveled the hundreds of miles from the lavish promises of the gold fields and San Francisco only to find *this*, Chance wondered in dismay? How could he possibly bring Vicky Beth here, even if he were lucky enough to find his elusive fortune in this unlikely environment? Once again he cursed his stupid decision to go chasing California rainbows, when he could have had a good life back east.

"On to Nigger Alley," Si ordered, reining his pony to the right and adding with a deadpan glance at Chance: "'Less'n you'd like to stop at the church for a prayer first."

"No, I need a drink more than anything else right now."

Calle de Los Negros was such a blatantly vile den of vice and violence that for a moment Chance felt he was back in San Francisco's most fashionable district. The name meant Street of the Blacks, but it had been casually Anglicized to Nigger Alley. It was the Spanish habit to call all dark-skinned persons Negros, although there were few individuals of unmixed African blood in California then.

Peter Biggs, the town barber, was Los Angeles' only black American resident. An ex-slave who had come west as an Army officer's valet, Biggs was a fat, jolly, popular fellow whose only failing was a fondness for fair-skinned ladies. That weakness sometimes caused him grief, but not as often as might be expected, for Los Angeles had strong roots extending back to Africa as well as Europe. The majority of the founding *pobladores* had been of mixed Spanish and Negro or Indian ancestry, evidence of which still existed in the swarthy complexions of such prominent local Dons as Pio and Andres Pico.

The southland's early melting pot character provided the major excuse for its northern neighbor's snobbery. The founding families around San Francisco boasted of possessing *sangre azul*—blue blood—the gift of their assumed "pure Castilian" descent. They even had their genealogies recorded at the Court of the Purity of Blood in Mexico— which probably did as much to keep their bloodlines unsullied as the claim of "good breeding" did for East Coast aristocrats. But most Angelenos held the tolerant view that *color no es afrente*—color does not affront—and hardly anyone considered the term "nigger" any more derogatory than "gringo" or "greaser." This was a time when men loved or hated one another as individuals, rather than in bunches.

Passing the plaza bullring, Si and his *compadres* dismounted before the Coronel adobe. A half-dozen wiry, chocolate-skinned *muchachos* dashed up, offering to guard the horses. Si flipped a full *escudo* to the urchins and watched them scramble in the dirt for it.

Then the Texan led the way into the narrow, filthy, noise-and-stench-filled Nigger Alley. Both sides of the block-long corridor were crowded with dark, ugly cantinas, gambling dens and houses of *mujeres de la mala vida*— women of the bad life. Although it was still siesta time, the sin sellers appeared to be doing a fair amount of business. Loud laughter and shouts came from open doorways and windows, accompanied by the clink of coins and raucous singing to gentle guitar strumming.

Suddenly, from an especially dilapidated hovel, a gunshot rumbled, followed by a woman's scream. Moments later a wild-looking, pudgy-cheeked man staggered out with a revolver in his hand and blood oozing from a gash on his forehead. Pausing to fire two shots back into the establishment, he then leaped astride a waiting mustang and raced off across the plaza with a triumphant yell.

Si turned to Chance with a proud smile. "Wickedest damned street on earth, outside of Texas," he proclaimed.

With a flourish, Si ushered his friends into La Marseillaise, which he had glowingly described as "the peach of

117

Nigger Alley." Chance thought it an overripe fruit, like its proprietor—a stout, fortyish Frenchwoman called, for obvious reasons, Madame Moustache.

But the lady evidently had a heart as big as her figure, at least where Si was concerned. As soon as she saw the Texan, she lumbered around the bar and fell weeping into his arms, calling him *"Mon cher agneau."* Si hugged her back and when the two of them started chattering in French, Chance recalled that Si came from a Cajun family—French Canadians who had migrated to Louisiana after England had conquered Canada from France. Chance was happy to see his friend receive such a warm welcome, and even happier when Madame Moustache remembered her duties and ordered the bartender to serve the newcomers a round on the house. When the raw *aguardiente* had burned the hide off of his throat and dulled his senses, he was able to think more kindly of Los Angeles.

The interior of La Marseillaise was more dismal than the vice pits Chance had seen in San Francisco and Sacramento, but that was about the only difference. There were the usual unattractive sluts hovering over tables occupied by men intent on cards, liquor and cigars. Impressive piles of octagonal gold slugs valued at fifty dollars each, as well as $20 double eagles and plenty of silver *escudos* showed that the *rancheros* had profited from the rich northern beef market the Gold Rush had created. But some of the Dons still followed the old barter system and gambled markers for herds of cattle or horses or leagues of land. It was hard for them to stop thinking of their cash flow in terms of *pesetas de cueros*—leather dollars—the name given to cow hides when they were the main medium of exchange for Yankee trade goods.

Chance ordered another round of drinks and went to work learning as much as he could about the latest activities around the pueblo of the Angels. He wasn't sure how much of the information he picked up would be useful to his ambitions, but most of it was interesting. He learned, among other things, that the County of Los Angeles had been established early that year and steps had been taken to convert the town to an American plan of government. But the change would have to wait for the unhurried Latin pace to catch up with it. The city council was still called the *Ayuntamiento* and recently elected Mayor A.P. Hodges was addressed as *Alcalde*. A post office, police force, and fire department had been organized, but on a volunteer basis, which meant that sometimes the manpower was there to handle those duties and sometimes it wasn't. Attempts to establish a public school had been less successful, as no suitable teacher could be found. Dr. William B. Osburn, the volunteer postmaster, had opened the town's first drug store, which seemed to be doing well. Nothing tangible had yet come of talk about starting Los Angeles' first newspaper.

At one point Chance found himself drinking with a soft-spoken army captain who was destined to become a Civil War general and give his name to a California military post. West Point graduate Edward Otho Cresap Ord had been hired the previous year to survey Los Angeles' original Spanish land grant so that lots could be auctioned off to replenish the municipal treasury. One of the lanes on Ord's new town map was labled *Primavera*—Springtime—the nickname of his sweetheart, Trinidad Ortega. She lives on today as Spring Street, between Broadway and Main.

The land auction had gone well and Ord's only regret was that he had been paid his surveying fee in cash, instead of the real estate he had wanted. He strongly advised Chance to invest in town property, as he was convinced that Los Angeles' population would soar to as high as 5,000 in the next decade.

That prediction encouraged Chance somewhat. As the afternoon progressed and the *aguardiente* flowed freely, he became more and more enchanted by Los Angeles. *Viva los Californios! Viva los Estados Unidos! Viva Mexico! Viva* any excuse to raise another glass and prolong the rosy glow that made life in southern California bearable.

The merrymaking in La Marseillaise was getting into full swing when Chance felt a soft touch on his arm. Turning, he met the shy gaze of a young Indian who looked out of place in the cantina; he was wearing a clean shirt.

"*Por favor,* Señor," the Indian began, before his breath was knocked out of him by Si's hand slapping his back exuberantly.

119

"Hey, José! *Como esta, chico?*"

The Indian turned to Si with a flash of ivory teeth and they exchanged a few sentences of rapid Spanish. Then Si explained to Chance:

"José here belongs to Don Alexander Bell. The old man heard we're in town and wants us to come to his *palacio* for a bite to eat and some jaw music."

Chance fingered his beard. "Do I have time for a shave?"

"Don't worry 'bout that." Si shot a command at José, who silently vanished from the room. "I sent him to fetch Nigger Pete. He'll slick you up nicer'n any undertaker could." Draining his glass and giving Madame Moustache a farewell embrace, Si rounded up his scattered companions and rode herd on them out the door.

Alexander Bell was unique even among the rugged early American settlers in California. A Pennsylvanian of Scots-Irish stock, Bell had been bitten by the travel bug when both he and the nineteenth century were in their early twenties. His wanderings as a merchant and adventurer took him through much of Latin America before leading him to Los Angeles in 1842. There he established himself as a trader in cattle hides, tallow, and general merchandise and married a lady of the *Californio* upper class, Maria de las Nievas Guirado. But true to his proud stubborn ancestry, Bell remained an unswerving Presbyterian and patriot. Once a friend remarked on Bell's long absence from America and asked if he ever intended to return.

"Never," Bell snapped. "I will wait for the United States to come to me, as God intends it should."

The Bell *palacio*—one of the town's most imposing structures with the rare distinction of a second story—stood on the southeast corner of the intersection of Los Angeles and Aliso Streets. The house followed the general Moorish-Spanish-California plan—a square of adjoining rooms with small barred windows enclosing a patio made cozy by flowering plants and orange trees. A branch of the old *zanja madre* brought water for irrigation and the gently spraying fountain in the center of the patio. The thick adobe walls provided good insulation from the summer heat and sounds of the rowdy nightlife in the plaza.

From the west end of the mansion a long, low adobe complex, called Bell's Row, extended about 300 feet down Los Angeles Street. In it were Bell's general store and several shops and storerooms rented to other businessmen. But Chance was more interested in the *palacio* than the commercial annex. Swaying before the wide arched front door, upon which Si was rapping vigorously, Chance peered up at the second-floor balcony lined with planter boxes containing red geraniums. Captivated by the romantic imagery, Chance vowed that someday he would own a house like this.

The double doors flung open and Chance blinked at a tall, erect man of about fifty, dressed in a dark broadcloth suit and high wing collar. Thick graying hair swept back from his high forehead and bushy brows shadowed deep piercing eyes, a thin highbridged nose and a stingy purse of a mouth. He looked for all the world like a stern New England preacher, but a hint of *Californio* good humor lurked in his sun-etched features, springing out fully when his tight lips stretched into a welcoming smile.

"*Bienvenido,* Señores! *La casa es suya.*"

Si swept off his sombrero. "*Gracias,* Don Aleck. *Con su permiso . . .*"

Alexander Bell ushered the guests into his house. The *vaqueros* were sent to the kitchen to be fed and wined, while Si, Chance, and Nicolas were taken into *la sala*—the parlor. It was an impressive chamber, measuring nearly 100 feet in length, furnished with teak chairs and tables carved in China, a Louis XIV settee, a china cabinet and sideboard from England, and other exotic items. Crystal chandeliers dangled overhead and a medieval tapestry depicting a unicorn held at bay by hounds looked down on a rug made from a grizzly bear that Bell had shot on a hunt with Kit Carson.

Si introduced Chance and Nicolas to Bell and his wife, a plump, energetic lady a few years older than her husband. After seeing that the gentlemen were well provisioned with platters of *tamales, carne seca,* bread and cheese, *pan dulce,* cured olives, fresh fruit and other snacks, Doña Maria discreetly withdrew and left them to their talk.

Bell put out his best liquors and cigars while asking

121

probing questions about the latest activities in San Francisco. Chance had hardly started to answer them when José entered to announce the arrival of Peter Biggs, the barber. Chance offered to retire to another room for his shave, but Don Aleck wouldn't hear of discommoding his guest. So, while the grinning barber stropped his razor and whipped up a thick lather in his mug, Chance relaxed in a chair that had supported the bottoms of four California governors and, it was rumored, two European monarchs.

It was the best shave Chance could remember ever having received, and word of his arrival spread rapidly. Several townspeople eager to hear what news he brought appeared at the Bell home throughout the afternoon.

The most impressive *Californio* Chance met that day was the incomparable Don Pio Pico. His appearance was as comical as his name. Short, thickset, stubby-legged, his African blood evident in his broad nose and thick lips, Pico had made himself look even more clownish by growing a bushy beard to hide smallpox scars. With few exceptions, Don Pio was probably the homeliest man in California.

It was rumored that once the Pico brothers had attempted to settle the question of which of them was the least attractive by seeking the opinion of an old woman noted for her fearless honesty. After accepting a fee from them to judge the contest, she had shaken her head in dismay and said: "Señores, with two such faces as yours before me, it is impossible to say which is the ugliest."

Yet it was these two unlikely heroes who had led California in her war against the United States. Don Andres served as commander of Alta California's armed forces, while his brother the governor tried to find the wherewithal to support the defense effort. They had lost, but, being *Californios*, they lost magnificently, fighting bravely as long as they could, then obtaining excellent terms of surrender and accepting their conquerors with no hard feelings. Except that Don Pio remained a lifelong hater of all things American with the same passion that he loved his American friends.

Emotion poured from Don Pio in an uninhibited stream, overwhelming Chance's senses and making him understand why the funny-looking little man had been governor and his brother the military leader. Don Andres' dignified bearing, cool courage and ability to make swift, intelligent decisions appealed to the minds of discerning men and women. But Don Pio stole their hearts with his unrestrained gusto and lack of assumed airs. Possessing the contradictory elements of fiery temperament and easy forgiveness, vain illusions and hard practicality, fierce pride before men and humble repentance before God, a romantic compulsion to put honor ahead of all else, as long as it didn't interfere with pleasure—Don Pio Pico was the very soul of old Spanish California. His laughable looks only made him more endearing.

Alexander Bell also seemed to have absorbed much of the Latin temperament. When he spoke English, he was the stern, tight-lipped Scots-Pennsylvanian of his former life, his closed features betraying no hint of his true feelings. But in Spanish he was as emotionally effusive as any *Californio,* laughing easily and obviously relishing the language's sweet music on his tongue. That duality of personalities appeared most strongly in the last words Bell spoke to Chance that day.

When the time came for the visitors to take their leave, Bell and the other homeowners begged the pleasure of accommodating them for the night. But Si firmly defended the prerogative of his employer to give hospitality to the travelers. Bell saw them to the door and gave Chance's hand a firm farewell grip, remarking:

"I'm glad you decided to foresake the golden temptations of the north for our more humble horizon, Mr. Malcolm, when so many are doing the opposite. I feel sure you will do well here. But always remember," Bell's cold eyes suddenly flashed with Latin fire, *"Los Angeles este poesia, no prosa!"*

Chance pondered that as they rode out of town. "Los Angeles is poetry, not prose."

Chapter 13

Their ride toward the setting sun along the Santa Monica Mountains' southern slopes was a repeat of what Chance had seen many times since leaving San Francisco. Ornery-tempered cattle were everywhere, tended by occasional leather-clad riders and sharing the vast range with rabbits, deer, coyotes, rattlesnakes and other wild groundlings and nervous swarms of birds. Chance was beginning to understand the *ranchero*'s proud boast of counting his wealth in "cattle on a thousand hills."

Although it was hard for Chance to understand how even this endless grassland could support so many cows—each of them requiring up to ten acres to feed its restless grazing habits—he was more determined than ever to carve out a piece of the California good life for himself and David. The stimulating afternoon in Alexander Bell's house had sharpened both his ambition and his perception of the area's possibilities.

It was a good rich land, presided over by scattered oaks, sycamores, cottonwoods and willows. But most of the ground covering along the foothills consisted of low, twisted, flesh-tearing shrubs collectively called chaparral, from which the *vaqueros* protected their legs with *chaparrales*, or chaps. They crossed several dry streambeds whose waters, after digging canyons in the hillsides, had twisted down to low depressions to form *cienegas*—marshes. Si told Chance that in the spring the flooded *cienegas* made good breeding ponds for millions of *chapules*—grasshoppers. The Indians had enjoyed feasting on the roasted insects. But to the *Californios* they were a dreaded menace. Vineyardists were particularly fearful of the winged pests, to whom tender young grape leaves were choice morsels.

In the spring there would be a rodeo, when all of the new calves would be sorted out and given the same brands as their mothers. That was the most efficient way for the *rancheros* to keep track of their livestock in the free and easy world of unfenced ranges. Besides, a rodeo provided an opportunity for socializing, with neighboring families getting together in a happy picnic atmosphere.

About five miles from the Esperanza ranchhouse, Si's party was attacked by a band of hard riding, wild yelling *caballeros* who turned out to be a welcoming committee sent by Don Carlos. They escorted them the rest of the way.

An excited crowd waited in front of the ranchhouse and Chance was warmly greeted by Don Carlos, who introduced him to his wife, Dona Luisa, their six sons, an elderly lady called *Tia* Ignacia and other relatives. Chance particularly noticed an attractive young señorita standing beside a man who was obviously another Anglo. He was about Chance's age, but he had the kind of pale dry skin that wrinkles early and a paunch already strained his waistcoat buttons. His thinnig yellow hair lay slickly on his domed skull, as if it had been spread with a butter knife. Chance soon learned that the girl was the Esperanzas' only daughter, Teresa, and her companion was named Farley Hewlett.

"But this is too perfect—two fine *Americanos* in my home," Don Carlos beamed, taking Chance's arm and steering him into the sprawling *casa*. "Now tomorrow's fiesta will honor you and Don Nicolas as well as serve to announce Teresa's *compromiso* to Don Farley."

At the mention of her engagement, Teresa, his daughter, blushed and ducked her head, to the delight of her teasing brothers. Chance politely offered congratulations to Farley

Hewlett, who acknowledged them with a Southern gentleman's slight bow, and an odd half-smile. Chance wondered if it was a nervous affliction.

Inside the *sala*, the newcomers were plied with liquid refreshments and questions. Si, carrying his saddlebags, handed the *patron* a leather purse containing the golden receipts for the cattle he had driven north. Don Carlos gave the purse to a servant with an order to put it in his room, then went on with his conversation. No true *Californio* would insult a trusted agent by counting the coins in his presence.

Between narrating his own experiences, Chance was able to learn a bit about Hewlett, who claimed to be from a well-known banking family in Charleston, South Carolina. He had intended to establish a bank of his own in San Francisco. But the steamer on which he was traveling had run aground off San Pedro.

"Then he saw our beautiful Teresa and decided that Los Angeles had more need of his bank," Don Carlos smiled, drawing more blushes from his daughter and laughter from his sons.

Shortly after that, a maid entered to announce that the belongings of Don Chance and Don Nicolas had been placed in their rooms and a *bano* had been prepared for them.

"Go refresh yourselves, Señores," Don Carlos ordered. "We will continue our most enjoyable talk over supper."

Chance followed the maid from the room hoping he wouldn't get spoiled having both a shave and a bath in one day.

The *cuarto de bano*—bathroom—was located at the end of the long patio near the small shrine to the Blessed Virgin and Infant where the family's religious services were held. The tub was a large, brick-lined pit in the floor, filled with hot water carried by servants from the kitchen. While Chance and Nicolas (Si said he didn't cotton to getting his tail wet unless it was a hot day and the crick was too high to wade) relaxed their saddle-weary bodies in the soothing warmth, they were joined by Ramon, the youngest Esperanza boy.

126

He was a bright-eyed youngster of seventeen, full of eager questions about Chance's travels and adventures. Had the Señor been to such fabulous cities as Boston and New York? Perhaps to Europe? That was where Ramon longed to go. If only Papa could afford to send him to school in England! He could read and write proficiently—an unusual achievement in that rural society where no one saw much value in booklearning. He had collected a small library; his favorite books were the plays of Shakespeare and the great poetry of Byron, Keats, and Shelley, who died so young and so splendidly.

"Don't you think poets and warriors should always die young?" Ramon asked earnestly. "How terrible it must be to grow old and lose one's virility!"

Chance and Nicolas exchanged tolerant smiles, remembering their own boyhood delusions. Shyly Ramon confessed that he wrote poetry himself, an almost shamefully unmasculine thing to his brothers. But fortunately poetry was related to music and for a *Californio* to be born without a song on his lips was as unthinkable as for him not to be born to the saddle.

Suddenly Ramon sprang up from where he had squatted beside the *bano*, an expression of firm purpose on his slim face. "But wait! I will show you something after supper, if Papa will permit it. Something I have been working on a long time. I know you will not be disappointed."

Ramon dashed out of the room, as Chance and Nicolas laughed gently. Chance resigned himself to suffering through a dreamy adolescent boy's attempts at versifying. But it was good to be around lively young folks again, now that the picture of Michael O'Neal's dead face was growing less sharp in his mind. When he climbed out of the *bano*, Chance felt that he had washed off more of the past than just trail dirt.

The dinner table groaned under the weight of crockery heaped with food grown on the ranch and transformed by the magic of Doña Luisa and her kitchen staff. The main course was the *ranchero* favorite, *carne asada con frijoles quisados y salsa de chili verde* (or *chili colorado*, depending on one's preference). It was fresh barbecued beef with

127

refried beans and green or red chili sauce. Plenty of *tamales, enchiladas, gallina estofado con arroz*—stewed chicken with rice—and *pinole*—corn meal gruel much like the Deep South's grits—served as tempting appetizers. The vegetable dishes were represented by *colachi*—similar to succotash, consisting of chopped squash simmered with green beans, corn, chilis, tomatoes and onions and sprinkled with cheese; and *verdolagas*—the lowly pig-weed and other wild greens boiled and seasoned like spinach.

Although Don Carlos was prosperous enough to boast a full array of silverware, *tortillas* were still commonly used as spoons to scoop up *pinole*, *frijoles* and anything else that could not be easily managed with the fingers. Other breads were within reach of each diner, with slices of *queso blanco*—the white cheese that was the rancho's main dairy product. Most *Californios* still disdained milk as a drink except for infants.

For *los postres*—the desserts—there was a great variety of preserved fruit, candied quince, pumpkin and cactus apples, *pan dulce*—sweet bread, rather like coffee cake—*enpanadas*—turnovers filled with sweetened *frijoles*, pumpkin or minced meat—and *puchas*—a rich pie crust cut into fancy shapes and baked flaky and light, then sprinkled with sugar.

Servants were on hand with fresh pots of hot coffee and chocolate. And of course there were ample wines and brandies for the innumerable toasts drunk to the health and happiness of all present, long life to *El Presidente* Fillmore, the undying brotherhood between Latin and Anglo Californians, and so on.

Don Carlos apologized for offering such poor fare to his guests, explaining that the better parts of his commissary had been reserved for tomorrow's engagement party. Chance was glad that he hadn't overeaten at Alexander Bell's house, as he took the seat of honor at his host's right. Ramon claimed the chair next to him and excitedly whispered that all was ready for his after-dinner entertainment. Nicolas sat to Don Carlos' left, with Teresa between him and Hewlett. Doña Luisa faced her husband from the other end of the long table, around which crowded the rest of the family, including the three older sons' wives and children.

The meal was such a confusing riot of eating, drinking, talking, laughing, teasing and trying to control unruly children that Chance was amazed that he managed to make any sense out of it. But the snatches of conversation he did catch were enlightening and he had the pleasure of observing Teresa over the table. She was a charming young lady of nineteen—not really beautiful, but sweetly appealing with her gentle smile and modestly respectful manner. Her large eyes were almost the same deep brown hue as her long braided hair and her glowing complexion would have been as dark as her brothers', if she had shared their exposure to the sun.

From overheard remarks, Chance got the impression that the match between Teresa and Hewlett was mainly her parents' doing. That made Chance feel sorry for Teresa. But it was none of his business, and Hewlett might turn out to be a better person than he appeared.

Teresa also managed to steal more than a few speculative glances at the handsome *gringo*. Not that her interest in Don Chance was inspired by more than a curious desire to learn more about the world beyond her limited environment. As a dutiful daughter, she accepted her commitment to Don Farley, who was rich and respectable. He would provide her with a good home and in return she would be a devoted wife and even try to learn to love him. That was the best life a decent girl of her class could hope for, she had always been taught. Yet there was a strange uneasiness in her heart about Don Farley that she could not overcome or understand. Being such a sweet innocent girl who always tried to think the best of others, it never occurred to Teresa that her feelings might have something to do with the fact that Hewlett was an unbearable ass.

Fortunately Don Carlos was too happily distracted to read any serious meaning into the looks exchanged between Teresa and Chance. His plans for Hewlett and his daughter were working out so perfectly that he would have been horrified by the merest suspicion that anything could disturb them. Every night the stocky *ranchero* thanked God and all the saints for having sent Don Farley to him when he most needed him. Or rather what was in the metal chest at the bottom of Don Farley's trunk.

Guilt struck Don Carlos anew every time he recalled how he had ordered old Prospero, his blacksmith, to pick the lock on the trunk while Don Farley was out riding with his sons. It was an unforgivable sin for a host to commit against his guest's privacy, but Don Carlos had to know the extent of Hewlett's fortune. And *Madre de Dios,* what a fortune! Nearly thirty thousand dollars in gold—an unimaginable sum in a community where nearly all wealth was measured in livestock and land, and that usually heavily mortgaged.

Then and there, Don Carlos had made up his mind that Hewlett would become his son-in-law. The marriage would both provide for Teresa's future and insure Don Carlos a convenient new source of money to pay off his crushing debts. Many *rancheros* sought loans from merchants like Abel Stearns and John Temple to maintain their lavish life styles in lean years. But Don Carlos had become so profligate in his spending and gambling habits that he was in danger of losing his beloved Rancho Agua Fria—something that must be avoided at all cost. For Don Carlos the spectre of poverty was almost as hateful as a dark skin, with both aversions stemming from a common root.

Don Carlos, unlike most of his fellow Southern Californians, strongly believed that color *did* affront. Bitter experience had taught him so. As a starving orphan in Mexico, he had worked as a stable boy for a well-to-do *hidalgo* of proud Catalonian heritage. Because of Carlos' swarthy complexion and black eyes, the fair-haired children of the family derisively called him *El Moro*—the Moor. What made the insult especially degrading to anyone of Spanish blood was the possibility that there could be some truth in it, because for over seven centuries the Moors had ruled Spain as part of a mighty Moslem empire spreading halfway around the world. When Carlos could no longer endure the taunting persecution, he stole a horse and ran away. He was soon brought back in chains and given a long prison term. But, because he was only fourteen, his sentence was commuted to exile to Alta California, which was not receiving enough voluntary colonists to safeguard the empire's northern frontier.

Carlos's California experience began happily. He was

hired by Don Jesus Esperanza, a kind, industrious ex-soldier who had been granted a large tract of land near Canada de Agua Fria. As they worked to build up the rancho, Carlos was treated as one of the family, which consisted of Don Jesus and his wife, their daughter Luisa and the Don's widowed sister, Doña Ignacia.

When Carlos was twenty Don Jesus, having no son of his own, offered to adopt him and make him his heir, if Carlos would agree to marry Luisa. The offer was almost more than Carlos had dared to hope for. He already loved Luisa and he was happy to cast off the last of his miserable past with the name he had worn since birth. And to think that someday Rancho Agua Fria would be his!

With each passing year Don Carlos's happiness and success increased, marred only by the untimely deaths of his adoptive parents. His cattle and horses swiftly multiplied, his Indian workers loved him, and all of his children were born with lighter complexions than his. That was as important to Don Carlos as it was for him to be the most lavish host, the most daring gambler, the most generous giver of gifts in all of southern California. What did a few debts matter, as long as people talked about the great wealth and munificence of Don Carlos Esperanza?

Unfortunately they mattered a great deal to the people to whom they were owed, especially when they grew as large as Don Carlos's current obligations. The money Si had brought back from San Francisco would only quiet his more impatient creditors for a while. But before the others became too demanding, he should be able to obtain sufficient financing from his new son-in-law. Don Carlos smiled approvingly at Farley Hewlett. Not only was he rich, but just look at how white he was!

When the meal was finally over, Don Carlos announced that Ramon and Teresa were going to provide them with a bit of entertainment by performing the balcony scene from *Romeo and Juliet*, a famous play by Don Guillermo Shakespeare. A space was cleared around the settee in the middle of the *sala* and the others sat or stood in attentive silence while Ramon instructed his sister to pretend that the settee was a balcony. Because Teresa didn't know the lines, she was allowed to hold the open book in her lap. With much working of facial muscles and broad gestures, Ramon launched into Romeo's passionate declaration of love.

The boy's untrained posturings made Chance feel embarrassed for him. But he figured it probably wasn't as bad as having to listen to Ramon recite some of his own poetry.

The scene went along well enough until Ramon reached the lines:

> See how she leans her cheek upon her hand!
> O, that I were a glove upon that hand,
> That I might touch that cheek!

The Spanish word for cheek is *carrillo*, the name of a well-known local family. The first time Ramon had used the word, four lines earlier, a few members of his audience had tittered at the pun. The second time he spoke it, his brothers had laughed softly. But the third time, Maximo was unable to restrain himself from calling out: "Oh, *hermanoito*, you want to touch Felomena Carrillo!" referring to a señorita whose saucy ways with the boys were notorious.

At that the entire family broke into loud laughter, much to Ramon's chagrin. His face flushing deeply and his fists clinched in frustrated rage, he shouted for silence. But his anger only provoked more mirth. Even Teresa had to hide a giggle behind her hands. Finally Ramon turned and stormed out of the house, vowing that he would never again try to bring refinement to such crass boors. Teresa, her face expressing alarmed concern, started after Ramon. But Chance waved her back and followed the offended poet into the night.

Chance found Ramon at the stables, trying hard to pretend he hadn't been crying. "Don't take it so hard," Chance remarked lightly. "They were just trying to enjoy the show with you."

"Philistines!" Ramon spat. "I'll show them. I'll stow away on a ship and go find a war someplace and get killed. Then they'll be sorry. No! I'll go to the gold fields and find a fortune and I won't give any of it to them. That will make them even sorrier."

"You might find it even easier to get killed in the gold

132

fields. I knew a fella there who did what you mentioned at the *bano*—he died young, like a good poet or warrior."

Ramon turned to stare at Chance. Seeing that he had the boy's attention, Chance told the story of how Michael O'Neal had died fighting gallantly in defense of a lady's honor. He concluded with the moral that while a glorious young death had its appeal, it would be better if Ramon stayed home a little longer for his mother's sake.

A half-hour later, they returned to the house together. Chance's arm was around the boy's shoulders and Ramon was gazing worshipfully at him.

"It appears that Don Chance has made a conquest," Farley Hewlett remarked to Don Carlos, who only nodded absently, unconcerned by the temper tantrums of his children.

Teresa, witnessing their entrance, sent a grateful smile to Chance. Ramon, the baby of the family, was dearest to her of all her six brothers and she was happy that the friendly Yankee had been able to cheer him up.

Chance missed the smile, as did everyone else in the room except Doña Luisa, who frowned pensively. Reading a great deal in her daughter's expression, Doña Luisa wondered if she should mention it to her husband. She had gone along with Don Carlos' scheme to snare Don Farley, rationalizing that Teresa could do worse in mate-hunting than the pale banker. But something about Don Chance made her decide to let the matter ride for a while. After all, she was still a loving mother and, unlike Teresa, she had recognized Don Farley's asinine qualities from the beginning.

Chapter 14

The fiesta guests started arriving at Rancho Agua Fria shortly before noon. First came the younger *caballeros*, riding swiftly without families or baggage. As high-spirited as their prancing steeds, they strutted about showing off their finery and waiting impatiently for the ladies to get there. The Gold Rush prosperity had enabled the Dons to deck themselves out handsomely in colored silks and gold braid, while equipping their horses in equal splendor with carved leather inlaid with silver. Chance promised himself that as soon as he could afford it he would buy himself a *Californio* costume of a short tailless jacket, tight-fitting trousers flared below the knee, beautifully hand-tooled boots and a red sash wound around a white ruffled shirt. He already had a broad-brimmed vicuna sombrero with a sugar-loaf crown and gold cord with heavy tassels, which he had won in a San Francisco poker game.

Next came the childless young marrieds, with the wife riding sidesaddle before her husband, who had to suffer good-naturedly the laughing jibes of his bachelor friends. In some cases, it was an older woman escorted by a protective male relative. And more than a few of the horseback groups were families headed by stern fathers who insisted that their children must take to the saddle before they could walk.

But most of the families traveled by *carreta*, which meant that they didn't reach the fiesta until late afternoon. In those days of no carriages and few wagons in southern California, the *carreta* was the only vehicle available for transporting people and freight. A crude wooden box mounted on two or four solid wheels crosscut from a large tree trunk, the *carreta* was pulled by oxen at a slow jolting pace over rutted roads. The grinding of the wheels against wooden axles produced a nerve-grating screech that could only be relieved by frequent lubrication from pots of tallow.

But, by whatever means, the guests managed to reach the rancho and were graciously welcomed by Don Carlos and Doña Luisa. Altogether, over one hundred people were gathered at the Esperanza *casa*—gaily gossiping, laughing, drinking, devouring Doña Luisa's magnificently prepared feast and cheering on the young Dons in their horse races and other displays of equestrian skill. Chance lost a fifty-dollar gold slug betting on Don Carlos's eldest son in a game called *la Corrida Para Arabatar el Gallo*—the Race to Snatch the Rooster. It was played with a rooster buried in loose sand with only his head showing. The competitors took turns riding past the bird at full speed and leaning down to grab him by the neck. If the rider missed or pulled off the rooster's head, he was disqualified. If he succeeded in getting the whole bird, he then had to ride back past the other players without them taking it away from him. The game was rather hard on roosters, but great fun for the players and spectators.

With nightfall came music, dancing and romantic flirtations—which, really, were what fiestas were all about. After the torches were lit in the patio, Don Carlos proudly called Teresa and Don Farley to his side to announce their betrothal and offer a toast to their eternal happiness and many healthy children. Everyone drank and called out good wishes while Teresa blushed and Hewlett gazed around with the silly half-smile that Chance found even more exasperating, under the circumstances.

Then the serious fun began.

The music was provided by guitars, violins, tambourines and, somewhat to Chance's surprise, a harp. He had overlooked the large instrument standing in a corner of the *sala*. Si informed him that it had been a wedding gift to Doña Luisa from her father and she had taught all of her children to play it more or less melodiously. Naturally, it was the poetic Ramon who strummed it throughout most of the evening.

Most of the dances alternated between lively *fandangos* and *seguidillas* and more intricate *jarabes* and *contradanzas*. But the foreign waltzes and polkas had also gained some popularity. Chance, being naturally light on his feet, had easily picked up the Latin rhythms and he managed to move well with the fun-loving maidens and their older guardians who regarded with suspicion any man who was both a gringo and a non-Catholic.

But even the highly moral *Californios* offered some outlets for youth's mating urges. A favorite one was the semi-serious courtship game of breaking *cascarones* over attractive heads. A *cascaron* was made by piercing an eggshell at both ends, blowing out the insides, filling it with confetti and painting it with fancy decorations. *Cascaron* in hand, an amorous *caballero* or señorita would steal up on the object of his or her desire and try to strike without being observed. Then, as the confetti flew and bystanders smiled, the egg-breaker would draw back innocently to see how the gesture had been received.

Don Carlos thrust a *cascaron* into Chance's hand and laughingly urged him to play the game. Chance looked around at the smiling younger women and their frowning mothers. Feeling that he had been forced into a foolish position, he suddenly saw a solution. *Tia* Ignacia, the very dignified elderly sister of Don Carlos's adopted father, was seated on a bench against the patio wall, her face turned away from the festivities as she talked with a friend. Casually Chance strolled over and smashed the painted eggshell over the old woman's head.

Tia Ignacia looked up in startled confusion, blinking through the confetti. Chance bowed and asked her for the next dance. Fluttering and simpering like a teenager, *Tia* Ignacia rose and took his offered arm. As they moved onto the dance area, several onlookers cried out *"Bravo!"* and

"Muy galante!" in admiration of Chance's gesture. Don Carlos, grinning broadly, hurried over to whisper something to the lead guitarist. The musicians stuck up a tune that was unfamiliar to Chance. Seeking guidance, he looked at Don Carlos, who clapped his hands and cried:

"*El Son, Tia* Ignacia! *Por favor, el Son!*"

Tia Ignacia shook her head, blushing. "Ah, no, *amigos queridos*. I am much too old."

The others loudly took up the demand: "*Si, el Son!* Give us *el Son*," until finally she bowed in acquiescence. She would honor them by performing *el Son del Pais*—the Rhythm of the Land—an old folk dance for which she had been widely celebrated in her youth.

Chance stepped back to watch as a servant brought a full glass of water and balanced it on *Tia* Ignacia's head. Slipping into the flow of the music, Don Carlos swayed before her, leading her into the center of the floor. Then he drew back to give her sufficient room to maneuver. Unlike most Spanish dances, which provide men ample opportunity to prance about like vain peacocks, *el Son* is all feminine grace and suppleness.

Nimbly *Tia* Ignacia moved with decorous mincing steps into the beautiful minuet, her feet tapping in short staccato bursts. Yet so controlled were her movements that the glass remained steady on her sleek gray hair glittering with confetti and eggshell fragments, the water's surface unrippled. Her eyes filled with long-ago dreaminess as every nerve and muscle warmed to a harmonious ecstasy that burned away the years and melted age-stiffened joints. Once more she was a strong young *ranchera* by day and fiery mistress of the dancefloor by night, able to match any man at pioneering a wilderness empire with calloused hands and artful feet. With her proud head erect she turned to Don Carlos, indicating that she was ready for the most difficult part.

Don Carlos swayed forward again, removed his knotted silk neckerchief and, with a grand flourish, spread it in a circle at *Tia* Ignacia's feet. With many cunning steps and delicate curtsies, she danced into the center of the loop and worked her toes under it. Then, standing stationary with

137

her torso undulating voluptuously but not seeming to move at all from the waist down, she moved the loop up over her ankles until it disappeared under her full skirt.

For several long moments the spectators waited in suspense, until finally *Tia* Ignacia proudly lifted her skirt to reveal the neckerchief about her knees. With equally subtle movements she worked the loop back down her legs to the floor and stepped out of it. The music trailed away. A maid removed the glass of water, from which not a drop had been spilled. *Tia* Ignacia stood in smiling triumph as the crowd exploded with cries of *"Viva!"* and *"Bravo!"* and showered coins at her feet. With that the beautiful young dancer became a shy old woman again and ran from the patio hiding her face in her hands, leaving Don Carlos's sons to pick up the tribute to her artistry.

Across the patio, Teresa stood beside her mother. She too had applauded *Tia* Ignacia's performance, but the major part of her attention was on Chance.

"Oh, Mama, isn't he a fine gentleman?" she sighed. "So kind and thoughtful to others."

Doña Luisa looked into her daughter's shining eyes and glanced around to make sure Don Farley hadn't overheard her. It appeared that she would have to have a serious talk with her husband after all, and soon.

Chapter 15

Chance struggled to control a yawn as he raked the coins across the tabletop. At other tables around the *sala*, small groups of men were laughing and cursing over games of poker, whist, and euchre. But it was Chance's dexterity at dealing three-card monte—and the high stakes involved—that fascinated most of the spectators.

The dancing had ended at two A.M., when the women and the more sensible men had gone to bed. But for Don Carlos and his friends, that was the time to indulge in their greatest pleasure—gambling. The following three hours had seen much lively action in the smoke-filled room, evoking some anguished cries but more often happy-go-lucky grins from the sporting Dons. Now the candles were burning low and the first cock crow could be heard, and Chance was so sleepy that he could hardly focus his eyes on the cards.

That surprised Chance, in view of his phenomenal run of luck. He should be wide awake with excitement, his blood rushing joyously at the sight of the huge pile of coins before him. He hadn't paused to count his winnings for a while, but he guessed he had over fifteen thousand dollars in cash, plus markers for a couple of fine horses and their fancy saddles, three hundred head of cattle and some other items he couldn't remember. It was quite a showing for his original two hundred dollar stake. But monte was a fast game and he had won steadily from the beginning, never having to give up the bank as the gold flowed smoothly to him. That was probably why he didn't feel excited—winning had been so easy, after his long dismal spell of failure, that it was hard for him to believe it was actually happening.

But he did feel some pleasure at knowing that most of the money in his pile had previously belonged to Don Farley Hewlett. The pale Southerner sat facing Chance with both hands on the metal chest that contained what was left of his banking capital. Hewlett had never played monte before and, like most beginners, he had thought it would be easy to pick the desired card from the three the dealer swiftly rearranged on the table. Such gullible overconfidence had fattened the pokes of many monte dealers, even mediocre ones like Chance. Each time Hewlett lost, Chance had looked forward to seeing his obnoxious half-smile wiped off, but so far that had not happened. Don Farley had nerve, if no other admirable qualities, Chance grudgingly admitted. In spite of his losses and heavy drinking throughout the evening, he looked well composed and almost cheerful, as Chance prepared to deal another hand.

"Your bet, sir?" Chance asked politely.

Hewlett's slim fingers arranged two stacks of double eagles on the table, not bothering to count them. "I trust, sir, that you will include the queen with the cards you deal this time."

The remark caused a mutter of protest among the spectators, but Chance calmly went about dealing and switching the positions of the three cards. Don Carlos, standing near Hewlett, frowned disapproval at such ungentlemanly conduct and Si murmured:

"A man oughtn't to buck the tiger if he can't stand the bite."

Chance folded his hands and waited. Hewlett reached for the middle card, hesitated, then turned over the one to his right. It was the four of clubs. Chance flipped over the middle card—the queen of spades—and collected Hewlett's wager.

"Now I'll wish you goodnight, señores. The bank must close and get some sleep," Chance said, stacking his coins for easy counting.

"Looks like you pret' near closed his bank, too," Si observed, to the amusement of the men around him.

Hewlett shot a veiled glance at the Texan, then looked back at Chance. "Why be so impatient to quit while you're ahead, Señor? Are you afraid I may catch onto your tricks and recoup my losses?"

Don Carlos frowned again.

Chance stared levelly at Hewlett for a long moment. Hewlett met his gaze unblinkingly, his half-smile never wavering. Chance returned the monte cards to the deck and shuffled it.

"I'll give you a chance to recoup everything, if you're willing to risk what you have left in the box against my pile on the single turn of a card."

"But you don't know how much is in it," Hewlett replied.

"No, but you can see how much I have. Decide for yourself if the wager is favorable to you. But please be quick about it. I'm very tired."

Hewlett stared thoughtfully into the box. Word of the daring offer spread around the room and the other gamblers paused to look at Chance's table.

Dear God, let him refuse! Chance prayed silently, his guts squirming and his tongue sticking to the roof of his dry mouth. How could he have let his stupid pride get him into such a dangerous position? This money meant everything to him—his future and Vicky Beth's as well. He wasn't a real gambler. He could never hope to have a fortune like this in his hands again. If he should lose it. . . . He tried not to think about that, as he exerted all of his will power to maintain a calm exterior.

Hewlett closed the chest and pushed it to the center of the table. "Very well. One cut of the deck. High card takes all."

"Done." Chance slapped the deck down beside the chest. "Don Carlos, *por favor.*"

Don Carlos picked up the cards with trembling fingers and shuffled them several times, as the watching men

141

crowded closer. He was torn between the agonizing fear of seeing his future son-in-law lose the money he so desperately needed, and the thrilling thought that here in his house was taking place an epic gambling venture that all California would talk about for years to come. If only he could stack the deck in Don Farley's favor! What a curse it was to be an honest man.

The deck was placed between the two men. Chance nodded. Hewlett lifted the upper third of the cards smoothly and held them face-down on the table, waiting. Chance took a thin slice from the remaining deck and turned over the nine of hearts. Farley picked up his wine glass and drained it, then casually showed his card—the five of clubs.

Chance felt so weak with relief that he didn't dare try to speak. Si let out a wild whoop and slapped Chance's shoulder. The other men pressed in to congratulate him with laughter and toasts. In the swimming crowd of faces Chance glimpsed Nicolas's lazy grin and Don Carlos's sad but philosophical acceptance of his fate. And there was Ramon, whom Chance had thought had gone to bed, beaming proudly at his victorious hero.

Through it all Hewlett sat motionless, his half-smile unwavering. It wasn't until Chance recovered sufficient strength to stand and start pouring his winnings into the chest that Hewlett spoke again.

"I commend you on your rare luck and skill, sir, if not your honesty."

Chance, feeling too happy to take offense, merely grinned. "Don't be a bad loser, Don Farley. Come on, let's have a drink."

"A gentleman is particular about those with whom he drinks."

"Don Farley, please do not . . ." Don Carlos began.

"A gentleman demands satisfaction from a scoundrel who cheats him."

"Are you proposing that we fight a duel?" Chance laughed at the absurdity of the idea.

"If you have a scrap of honor, you can do nothing else."

Hewlett's eyes were hard and brittle, but even so Chance couldn't believe he was serious.

"Mr. Hewlett, you may think me a cheat if you wish. For my part, I think you are a damned fool. But I don't think either of us is crazy enough to spill blood over a difference of opinion. Goodnight, sir."

Chance picked up the chest and turned his back to the table. Ramon was instantly at his side, begging the privilege of carrying the chest to Chance's room.

"By all means, have your fancy boy tote your booty."

Puzzled, Chance turned back to Hewlett. "Fancy boy?"

Hewlett's half-smile became even more taunting. "Come, come, sir. I am familiar with your kind, even if Don Carlos isn't. But where I come from, they have the decency to go to establishments that stock colored boys for their pleasure, instead of trying to corrupt their host's children."

Suddenly Chance was no longer sleepy. His heart was furiously pounding blood and adrenaline through him, sharpening his nerves and giving his muscles the energy to leap over the table. His eyes saw only Hewlett's thin throat, which he would tear out with his bare hands.

If Hewlett had been a mind reader, he could not have known better how to goad Chance to murderous rage. Until Chance had sailed as cabin boy on a whaler, he had never known there were men who lusted after members of their own sex. In the course of fighting off many attacks on the long cruise, he had learned that he dared not give quarter. Hewlett had to die.

With a mighty effort, Chance controlled himself and turned to Si. "Will you be my second and make the arrangements?"

"Proud to oblige, *amigo*."

"Señores, I beg you!" Don Carlos cried. "This thing must not be permitted to happen. We are all *amigos*. All *Californios*."

"We all will be that," Hewlett said, "when I've rid this state of its least savory occupant."

Chance took the chest back from Ramon and walked out of the room, leaving the Dons to chatter excitedly.

The evening chill had penetrated the thick adobe walls of Chance's small room. That was good; he needed something to cool his burning flesh and help him think calmly.

143

He lay on the crude bed made of a wooden frame crisscrossed with rawhide lashings, trying to understand the awful mess he had gotten himself into.

In a little while he would kill a man or lose his own life, and for what? A small box of gold? That might make some sense, if that was all this tragic farce was about. But both he and Hewlett were driven by a far more complex motive—the almost mystical ideal of manhood. Women could fulfill themselves through motherhood. But a man must constantly test himself. And in the end he still can never be certain if he has lived as a real man.

Hewlett had gambled to show off his manhood, not because he needed more money. Now he felt that Chance had emasculated him and he could only win back his manhood on what "gentlemen" referred to as a field of honor.

And Chance realized that he was no less guilty of male vanity in feeling compelled to defend himself from a ridiculous insult to his manhood. But was it entirely ridiculous? Could his intense loathing of homosexuals possibly be caused by more than normal manly pride? Had he, perhaps, fought off his shipmates' advances so viciously because he secretly feared he might have a deeply buried hankering for what they were offering?

He had never dared to consider such a possibility before. But now he forced himself to search the dark corners of his mind. Carefully he thought over his relationships with men—on shipboard, in the army, in the gold fields, and especially his almost brotherly closeness to David. In all of his years in the rough-and-tumble world of men, had he ever felt an urge to go beyond the limits of masculine camaraderie?

Probe as he would, Chance could find no evidence to affirm that suspicion. He had loved men freely and wholesomely, looking up to his elders and enjoying the admiration of younger men and boys. Their masculinity had reflected and strengthened his virility, just as his associations with women had enhanced it in more meaningful ways. And above all else, he and David *were* brothers, sharing a much greater bond than mere blood.

Having reached that reassuring conclusion, Chance felt drained of much of his desire to put a bullet through Farley Hewlett's heart. But how else could he hope to save his own skin? Memory of a wartime experience came back to him. Two young officers in a neighboring regiment had had a falling out and decided to settle it with pistols. One of them, being unfamiliar with dueling etiquette, sought instruction from an older man, a Mississippi cotton planter reputed to have considerable experience in such matters. The Mississippian conseled a peaceful settlement of the dispute and, when the young hothead insisted on his right to blow his adversary to hell, said:

"No, that is not wise. If you survive what you are about to do, you must be able to live with it. So try not to have your sleep troubled by the weeping of a bereaved mother or widow and children. Risk your own life, if you wish, but not another's. Aim to wound, not to kill. Or better still, discharge your weapon harmlessly into the earth. Having stood your ground in the face of death is enough to satisfy any man's honor."

The young officer ignored the advice and killed his opponent. However, he didn't have to live with the memory for very long. He was swiftly court-martialed and executed for murder.

But Chance had always thought the Mississippian's words made an admirable code of conduct for a gentleman, providing he had the courage to stick to it. Besides, there were practical repercussions to be considered. If he hoped to prosper in this area, a clean moral reputation was important to him. For him to be thought of around Southern California primarily as a killer, however justifiable the cause, could cause him to lose friends and business opportunities.

Yet, even if he was brave enough to stand unarmed before Hewlett's pistol—which he wasn't so sure about—how could he risk depriving Vicky Beth of a father?

There had to be a sensible way out of the dilemma.

After another thirty minutes of hard thinking, Chance arrived at what appeared to be the best possible solution. It wasn't perfect, but what is? Except, of course, the fact that Hewlett was a perfect ass, which Chance was counting on to make his plan work. He rose from the bed, washed his hands and face in the stoneware basin and changed into a clean shirt. He felt fairly composed and confident when Si arrived a little later to announce that the arrangements for the duel had been completed.

They rode through the first gray beginnings of the new day to a rounded hillock overlooking Canada de Agua Fria. Si told Chance the place was called Monte Roble—Oak Mountain—because of the numerous oaks and other trees growing there. The other men, who had already arrived, stood by silently.

Chance and Si dismounted and walked up to the level crest of the hill, where Hewlett, Don Carlos and his eldest son, Martin, waited. Don Carlos was to referee the contest, while Martin acted as Hewlett's second. There were no traditional dueling pistols available, but two navy Colts charged with a single round each were deemed suitable for the occasion. Ramon stood by with brandy and improvised bandages. Don Carlos made a final appeal to Chance and Hewlett to resolve their differences without violence. Hewlett said he would only agree to that if Chance admitted he had cheated and returned his money with a full apology. Chance said he could not confess to a lie. Don Carlos said this was a sad day indeed for his house, then explained the rules.

The duelists would stand back-to-back and take ten paces, which the referee would count off loudly and slowly. After completing the tenth step, they would halt and, upon the command "Turn!" make an about-face and fire at will. If neither party were injured, and if both were willing, the process would be repeated. Chance and Hewlett said they understood and agreed to the rules. Don Carlos said they would wait a few more minutes, to make sure the light was sufficient for each combatant to see his target clearly.

Chance asked Si to step over to the sidelines with him. Some wisps of morning fog had crept in from the nearby coast and Chance shivered at the clammy touch on his neck. He held out his hand and Si grasped it tightly.

"You've been a good friend, Si. If anything happens to me—"

"Don't talk like that, *amigo*."

"I have to ask one last favor. Try to get the money to David Wheeler in Owens Valley. I've told you how to find him. And ask him to tell my daughter, when she grows up, why I had to do this. You can take a thousand dollars for your trouble."

"You can count on me. But you got nothin' to worry about if you just remember what I told you. Let the gun down nice an' easy, then—"

"Time, Señores," Don Carlos called.

The Colt felt heavier in Chance's hand than he remembered.

His shoulder blades brushed Hewlett's once, before Don Carlos called:

"One!"

Chance walked stiffly, his gaze fixed on a tall sycamore straight ahead of him. Birds sang lustily in the tree and in the hills a coyote called. The eastern sky was pale gold and the last stars were fading. It was going to be another fine southern California day.

"Ten!"

Chance spun around quickly, leveling his pistol at Hewlett's back just as Don Carlos ordered:

"Turn!"

A gasp broke from the crowd at Chance's ungentlemanly action. But no one had time to do anything about it before Hewlett turned around. As Chance had hoped, Hewlett was so astonished to find himself staring into the muzzle of a cocked and ready revolver that he brought down his own weapon quickly and jerked off a shot without taking proper aim.

Chance heard the bullet sing past his ear and nearly lost control of his bladder. But the initial panic passed swiftly and, although his knees were trembling, he was able to swallow the dry lump in his throat. He had survived the most dangerous part of his plan, and he even had the satisfaction of seeing Hewlett's irritating half-smile disappear. For a long moment he held his revolver pointed at Hewlett's chest, while the spectators waited tensely.

"Now don't you agree that this is a silly game for grown men to play, Don Farley?" Chance drawled.

147

"If you're going to shoot me, then do it!" Hewlett snapped, getting his nerve back. "But don't talk me to death."

"All in good time, sir. That's one of the rules, isn't it—that I can take my shot whenever I please?" Chance smiled at Hewlett's defiant glare. Then he decided to get on with it before the gun's weight made his hand waver. "But what if I offered you a profitable alternative to dying?"

Hope leaped to Hewlett's pale face, as Chance had anticipated. "What do you have in mind?"

"I am as anxious to make money as anyone, but I know nothing about the banking business," Chance explained. "So why don't you and I become partners? I'll put up the capital, you run the business and we'll split the profits fifty-fifty."

Hewlett's relief was clouded by suspicion. "Why would you make an offer like that to a man who tried to kill you?"

"For profit, as I said. And for the satisfaction of hearing you retract your false charges against me and beg my pardon."

Hewlett's jaw tightened stubbornly and he drew himself up proudly. Chance closed his left eye to squint down the gun barrel. "Which will it be—eat a little humble pie, or a bullet?"

Hewlett managed to hold his pose for another half-minute, but even an ass's obstinacy has limits. His shoulders slumped and, nearly choking on the words, he admitted he had been wrong and offered Chance a full apology.

The spectators cheered loudly and Don Carlos rushed forward to embrace both men. Everyone was in a high emotional state, with only Ramon feeling disappointed because Chance had not killed his man, but still it was another victory for his idol. They all mounted up and galloped hellbent back to the *casa*, where many happy toasts were drunk to the success of the new business venture and friendship between Don Chance and Don Farley.

A contract for the banking partnership was drawn up, signed, witnessed and celebrated with more drinking and laughter. Chance insisted on giving the chest of gold to Hewlett, saying that he was better qualified to handle money, as long as he stayed out of three-card monte games. Finally fatigue overcame excitement and they all went off to their beds or blanket rolls.

When they awakened late in the afternoon to resume celebrating, one of the stablehands informed them that Don Farley had saddled a fast horse and departed early in the day. Later they learned that Hewlett had found a ship in San Pedro Bay ready to weigh anchor and sailed for San Francisco on it. Don Carlos was crestfallen at having lost a wealthy son-in-law and so consumed with shame that a guest had been robbed in his home that he could hardly face Chance.

"Don't worry," Chance smiled. "I only hope Don Farley can use four pounds of bullet lead covered with a few coins."

That got the fiesta off to a fresh start and it continued fullblast for the next three days, saddened only slightly by Teresa's heartbroken retreat to her room. But the maid who took her meals to her reported that, for a jilted bride, she sure smiled a lot.

Finally the last fiesta guest was seen off and everyone at Rancho Agua Fria settled down to get a full night's sleep. Don Carlos, yawning as he crawled into bed with his wife, grumbled:

"Now we'll have to do the whole thing over again, and this one isn't even as white as the other one."

"Just leave everything to me, *querido*," Doña Luisa said with a serene smile. This was one matchmaking enterprise she could put her heart into.

Chapter 16

It was obvious to Chance from the start that the Esperanzas were determined to mate him with Teresa. But far from being offended, he was only amused by the devious methods they employed to observe the proprieties of courtship among respectable Spanish California families. For Chance had already made up his mind to go into the cattle business, now that he had the capital to undertake a major commercial venture.

He could have played it safe and lived well on the fortune fate had handed him. But the hungry beef market created by the Gold Rush was an irresistible temptation. By investing wisely, he could use this once-in-a-lifetime opportunity to increase his thirty thousand dollars to a hundred thousand in a few years, perhaps even to a million before he was forty.

The thought dazzled his imagination, even as caution warned him of the many pitfalls on the way to his goal. The trail north was made hazardous by rustlers and unreliable grazing lands and watering places. But Chance was confident that a good trail boss like Si Darcy and loyal *vaqueros* could overcome those dangers.

His only serious drawback was his lack of knowledge about cattle raising, particularly as it was conducted in southern California. And what better way could he hope to overcome that than through an alliance with a well-established ranching family? For a while Chance considered keeping his relationship with the Esperanzas on a strictly business level, by loaning Don Carlos the money he needed and using Rancho Agua Fria to fatten his own herd, which he was building from the cows he had won during the now-famous monte game. But conversations with Alexander Bell and his other new Anglo California friends convinced him that marriage was the best way to penetrate the close-knit *ranchero* society, in which family and business ties were indistinguishable. Then, too, there was Teresa herself.

The better Chance got to know the girl, the more she impressed him. She was an intelligent, good-natured, hard-working young woman who would make him a good wife and be a fine stepmother for Vicky Beth. He had liked her from the beginning and he felt that she returned the feeling. Given time and the right conditions, they could learn to love each other and build the happy family life that he now realized he had always wanted. After all, he was getting near thirty—time he gave up his youthful dreams of adventure and romance and settled down to a more sensible life. That was brought home to him even more forcefully by the memory of the hard let-down from his wild fantasy about Gloria Holt.

So Chance willingly fell in with Dona Luisa's matchmaking plans, even agreeing to convert to the Catholic faith. His Methodist upbringing had never meant a great deal to him anyway. Because it was not seemly for a suitor to reside in the home of his intended, and because Chance was eager to put his newfound wealth to work for him, he purchased a house in town from Don Abel Stearns—a rambling adobe south of the plaza on Main Street. The building wasn't much to look at, but it had a large front room that Chance converted to a general store and stocked with merchandise. As a clerk he hired Ramon, who was willing to take any job to be near his idol. An Indian family trained in domestic service was employed to cook, clean, and otherwise keep the household running smoothly.

Thus established as a promising merchant and cattle

baron, Chance was left with plenty of free time to court Teresa and look for other profitable investments. Both activities proved to be highly rewarding. Although the courtship strictly followed Spanish tradition, with a *duena* constantly overseeing the young couple's conduct, Chance never felt hampered in his conversations with Teresa. For one thing, the *duena* was almost always *Tia* Ignacia, who was so thoroughly charmed by the handsome *gringo* that she would have allowed him to get away with just about anything. Also, Chance enjoyed playing the *Californio* Don. When he called at Rancho Agua Fria he was always impeccably turned out in his *caballero* costume, followed by a servant carrying gifts for his *novia* and every member of her family. And during his semiintimate moments with Teresa, Chance delighted her with romantic Spanish phrases that Ramon helped him learn by heart. Chance even tried to master the guitar so that he could serenade his lady love in true Latin fashion. But Si's remark that playing and singing like that could get a man arrested for disturbing the peace persuaded him to leave the music to the more talented Esperanzas.

Don Carlos realized that Chance, his major creditor, was in an excellent position to gain full possession of the property if bad luck caused him to fall behind in his payments. But, because there was nothing he could do about that unpleasant possibility, Don Carlos fatalistically accepted it. If his own sons were unable to keep Rancho Agua Fria in the family, then a son-in-law would have to do. After all, even he was only an Esperanza by adoption. And Chance's eagerness to learn about ranching finally won the affection of his future father-in-law, who grudgingly admitted that he was an outstanding *gringo* in spite of his dark coloring.

The long, lazy courtship provided Chance with many pleasurable experiences. One that would always remain vivid concerned a *merienda*—picnic—on the sea cliffs of Rancho Los Palos Verdes. In mid-December Nicolas's Sepulveda cousins, who owned the beautiful coastal property, invited Chance down for the day.

He made the twenty-mile ride with Teresa, *Tia* Ignacia, a few Esperanza servants and Ramon. The young poet had quickly demonstrated a total lack of business aptitude and Chance had relieved him of his clerking duties in the store. Now Chance was content to keep Ramon around just for his charming company and the entertaining tales of his attempts to entrance local belles with his music and poetry.

It was a warm day washed clean by the first overnight rain of the season. Their picnic location on the wind-combed bluff offered a superb view of the Pacific's restless quest to merge with the sky's lighter blue, with Catalina Island starkly outlined between the two. A hundred feet below, long green waves speckled with kelp broke over rocks where sea lions dozed, while gulls hung motionless on air currents and sandpipers danced in the surf.

Out in San Pedro Channel the gray whale herds were making their annual journey from the Bering Sea to their winter breeding grounds in Baja California's quiet lagoons. The sight of the great cetaceans diving and blowing reminded Chance of his whaling ship days and he entertained his companions with reminiscences of rounding the Horn and finding the exotic South Sea ports of call waiting for him like shining jewels. The names of Easter Island, Tahiti, Samoa, Tonga and Fiji shivered nostalgically along his spine as he spoke of them.

But it was New Zealand, Land of the Long White Cloud, that provoked the most exciting memories of his adolescent age of discovery. British colonists had just recently settled the two islands, which were still largely dominated by the handsome, proud, cannibalistic Maoris. The Polynesian natives were said to be so fond of war that they even blazed new trails through the bush to make it easier for the white troops to find them. When they couldn't stir up a fight with the English, they battled among themselves. Chance told of being invited to a victory feast given by a Maori tribe that had just annihilated a neighboring village. The main course consisted of a delicious meat stew that Chance and his shipmates hungrily devoured—before they noticed the large number of human skulls and bones around the camp.

At that point, the other picnic guests put down their food with sickly expressions and *Tia* Ignacia crossed herself, crying out in horror, *"Por Dios!"* Chance smiled and detected a mischievous twinkle in Teresa's eye, indicating that she was sharing his little joke. Then he explained that the stew had really been made with pork. The Maoris enjoyed the taste of their victims' flesh too much to waste it on white visitors.

And so the courtship progressed. Chance easily mastered the catechism, was duly baptized into the True Faith and even came to find some satisfaction in the solemn beauty of the Mass and other Catholic rituals. The date for a June wedding was set and the banns were posted. Don Carlos gave another lavish engagement fiesta, which everyone vastly enjoyed, with hardly a thought of Don Farley Hewlett, except to wonder what he had done with the bullet lead.

At the same time, Chance's other enterprises also flourished. He found that there really wasn't a great deal to learn about the banking business after all, if he concentrated on making loans at attractive interest rates on the solid collateral of real estate. He learned the cattle business the best possible way—by spending long days in the saddle swinging a *reata* with Si Darcy and his *vaqueros*. By the time the spring rodeo arrived, he owned more than six hundred head of prime beeves. Since most of his animals had already been marked by other owners, he didn't bother to register a brand of his own with the county officials but settled for a distinct ear notch. It was a remarkably successful and joyous rodeo, with Don Carlos receiving the great honor of being elected *Juez del Campo*—Judge of the Plains. The Judge was given the power of settling disputes among cattle owners and Don Carlos discharged his duties with such wisdom, tact, and good humor that all who participated in the rodeo were pleased with his decisions.

Because of the gold fields' rich beef market, Chance prepared to drive his herd north. But he didn't let that make him lose sight of the traditional hide and tallow trade that had first brought California to the attention of America's eastern cities. Following the example of Bell and Stearns, he purchased the byproducts of animals unsuited for butcher shop use and warehoused them at San Pedro to await sale to Yankee sea captains. In doing that, Chance learned why San Pedro was called "The Hell of California"

154

by sailors. Richard Henry Dana, in *Two Years Before The Mast*, had described how merchandise had to be rowed ashore in small boats, carried over slippery rocks and up steep cliffs. Then the process was repeated in reverse with cattle hides and tallow.

Chance and his fellow merchants had some stimulating discussions on the desirability of building a pier to expedite the loading and unloading of cargo. But in the end they all agreed that it was too expensive an undertaking. San Pedro was not really a bay, but a barely sheltered roadstead where ships were anchored in the hope that they wouldn't be blown aground by storms. Nor was there anyplace else along the California coast between San Diego and San Francisco where the weary seafarer could find safe harbor. And Los Angeles, the commercial center of southern California, lay twenty miles inland from San Pedro.

Chance began to understand why Los Angeles had to be thought of as poetry. How could anyone possibly envision a great future for a dirty little pueblo located on a semiarid plain, isolated by desert and mountain barriers, with little natural resources except good but unreliably watered soil and lacking a seaport, major river, railroad, telegraph or even regular postal service to connect it to the outside world? To hold such a view, one had to have fanatical faith that poetry or divine intervention or some other mystical force was guiding the destiny of the Village of Our Lady of the Angels.

Another irrational aspect of the Los Angeles experience became evident to Chance as he pursued his goal of becoming a prosperous landowner. In addition to some of his real estate loans that seemed likely to result in default and forfeiture, he looked around for good rancho bargains he could obtain through direct purchase. That was when he learned why there was so much confusion and controversy over the boundaries of many of the old Spanish and Mexican land grants. The main cause of the problem lay in the practice of *vista de ojos*—surveying by eye. That consisted of two horsemen tying the ends of a *reata* to stakes and measuring distances by one of them standing with his stake on the ground while the other rode to the end of the *reata*. Then he would ground his stake and wait for his compan-

155

ion to ride past him to the *reata's* end, and so on. At the completion of the survey all of the *reata* lengths would be added up—without consideration of how much of the measurement was over level ground, up and down steep hillsides, across running streams or *arroyos* or through such unimportant things as an Indian camp. Then the surveyors would make a *diseno*—a maplike drawing—of the surveyed area and record it with a written description. Some of the descriptions made very colorful reading, but they were enough to drive the precise detail-demanding Yankee mind to distraction. Chance foresaw the coming legal battles over land titles that would drag through the courts for years and impoverish many *rancheros*, and he wanted to have more scientifically exact definitions of any property he purchased. But unfortunately, after Captain Ord and his assistants returned to Monterey, there were no qualified surveyors in the southland.

Also, Chance was having difficulty finding a reliable clerk for his store. Most *Californios* were, like Ramon, inept storekeepers or uninterested in any business that couldn't be conducted from horseback. A few hard-up gringos occasionally drifted into town, either disappointed goldhunters from the north or exhausted overlanders from the east. But none of those that Chance hired stayed longer than it took to get the wrinkles out of his belly and a few dollars in his pocket. Then, while strolling through Nigger Alley one day, Chance suddenly found solutions to both of his problems.

There being no hitching posts in Nigger Alley then, many a drinking Don used the ingenious device of tying one end of a *reata* around his horse's neck and the other around his waist before entering a cantina. That way, he could always find his way back to his mount no matter how *borracho* he became. A light bay mare was so tethered in front of La Marseillaise that day and Chance recognized her as a favorite of Don Sérbulo Varela. As Chance watched, a young, shabbily dressed mulatto walking in the shadow of the building blundered into the rope with enough force to jolt both the horse and her owner. Loud Spanish curses erupted from inside the cantina and a few

156

moments later Don Sérbulo came reeling out with blood in his eye.

Without asking any questions, the drunken *caballero* attacked the black man with vicious blows and kicks, driving him against the wall. The mulatto made no effort to defend himself and seemed destined to take a severe beating, when suddenly a tall, thin white man of about twenty-three appeared, spun Varela around and knocked him to his knees. Don Sérbulo came up snarling and several of his friends poured out of La Marseillaise drawing knives and guns.

Hurrying forward, Chance flung his arm around Varela's shoulders and laughingly convinced him that this was merely a foolish misunderstanding that hardly required the killing of an upstart gringo. He finished his speech by tossing a fifty-dollar gold slug to Varela's friends and begging them to have a drink on him. Don Sérbulo laughed forgivingly and led his *companeros* back into the bar with many happy *"Vivas!"* shouted to Don Chance's generosity.

Chance turned to the two ragged strangers, who were trembling uncontrollably. At first Chance thought that was due to fear or drunkenness. But he quickly judged from their thin, pinched features that they were suffering from hunger.

"I apologize for your rude welcome to Los Angeles," Chance said. "If you'll allow me to rectify that, I'd be honored to have you step around to my house for a bite of lunch."

The white man gave Chance a slight bow and replied in a cultured Southern accent: "Your kindness is greatly appreciated, sir. But we can only accept if you'll permit us to repay the favor by chopping wood or performing some other service for you."

Chance smiled at the youth's grave dignity. "There's always more than enough work to go around. Let's eat first and discuss that later."

While he led the way to his house, Chance learned that the white man was Madison Starr, from Virginia. The mulatto was introduced as Jeremy. When they entered the *sala* behind the storefront, Chance waved Starr to a chair at the

157

table and said: "Your servant will be provided for in the kitchen."

The young Virginian's hazel eyes met Chance's gaze sternly. "Jeremy is not my servant, Mr. Malcolm. He is my brother-in-law."

Afterwards, Chance was proud to remember that he hesitated only a split-second before saying smoothly: "Then of course he will sit with us."

Madison Starr's remarkable tale was quickly told between ravenous swallows of food. He had been born into a wealthy, aristocratic plantation family claiming an impeccable pedigree. His forebears had faithfully served the Old Dominion since its earliest settlement and it was taken for granted that Mad would carry on the tradition. At nineteen he had graduated with a degree in engineering from William and Mary College and returned home bursting with ideas for his future.

The following year, while working as a surveyor in Brunswick County, Mad met a beautiful quadroon slave named Dorcas, who served with her brother Jeremy on the household staff of Ramplier Plantation. Seducing the shy girl was easily done, but falling in love with her was a complication Mad had not anticipated. Purchasing her and Jeremy, he took them home with him and gave them their freedom.

Mad's family could have tolerated a colored concubine, as long as he was discreet about it. But when he insisted on marrying Dorcas, he was disowned and driven from his father's house. With the cocksure confidence of youth, Mad welcomed the challenge to prove himself on his own merits. Deciding to get rich quick in the California gold fields, he sailed to Panama with Dorcas and Jeremy.

Reaching Panama City on the Pacific coast, Mad bought passage for his small party on a sloop bound for San Francisco. Their luck ran out north of Vizcaino Bay, where the sloop's captain tried to rape Dorcas. Mad and Jeremy were unsuccessful in their efforts to kill the captain and found themselves marooned on a barren beach with Dorcas.

Throughout most of their three-hundred mile walk over the dry, bony spine of Baja California, Dorcas cheerfully kept up the men's spirits, ignoring her own failing strength. Even when she knew she was dying, she bravely urged them to go on to the safety she was sure awaited them. They stayed with her until the end, then somehow made their way to San Diego. They lost all of their money and possessions, but not the dignity and faith in themselves that Dorcas's love had given them.

Chance stared at the Starr brothers—Jeremy had taken Mad's surname upon his emancipation—and wondered if there really were miracles after all. How else could a qualified surveyor have overcome impossible odds to reach Los Angeles when Chance most needed him? And when he learned that Jeremy was a diligent worker with enough education to be a storekeeper, he was all the more inclined to suspect that God's hand was active in his affairs.

After the spring rodeo Chance added his beeves to the herds of Don Carlos and a few other rancheros and headed north with Si Darcy and a dozen *vaqueros*. The large trail drive naturally made a tempting target for rustlers and Indians. But Chance and Si had prepared their men with good arms and military training. By carefully guarding the herd at night and emptying a few hostile saddles with accurate long-range shooting by day, they convinced the surviving bad men to wait for easier pickings.

Chance was gone seven weeks, returning with a profit-heavy poke and Si's appraisal that he might make a fair *vaquero* after all. That filled Chance with justifiable pride, for even Si conceded that the *Californios* were the world's greatest stockmen—outside of Texas, of course.

During Chance's absence, Madison Starr had completed surveying the land he wanted to buy and Jeremy's honest, dedicated service had built up a thriving trade for the store. Also, his wedding date was nearing and the Esperanzas were working on the final preparations for the gala affair. All of which increased Chance's sense of self-importance and his impatience to start a new family. Without realizing it, he had become a typical California Don, imperiously expecting his womenfolk and employees to work their fingers to the bone for him and be happy with an occasional grunted word of appreciation. Amazingly, the system worked out to the satisfaction of all concerned more often than not.

The wedding took place on schedule, disrupted by only a few last-minute hitches. Chance had asked Si to be his best man. But the rangy Texan, although a top hand with the ladies, was a devout bachelor who shied away from anything related to matrimony. So it was Madison Starr who stood at Chance's side and handed over the ring with fingers that trembled slightly at the memory of his own tragic love life.

Black silk wedding gowns were the fashion at that time. But Chance had included several yards of white satin with his other prenuptial gifts, enabling Doña Luisa and *Tia* Ignacia to garb their dear Teresa as the unblemished virgin she was. Happiness reflected the bride's inner beauty and set her glowing from her upswept hairdo on a carved tortoise-shell comb to the edge of her lace *mantilla* that fell nearly to the floor. As she walked slowly down the aisle of the Church of Our Lady of the Angels, her gaze fastened on her bridegroom waiting at the altar and all of her nervous uncertainties disappeared. This was her day, and she fully intended to make the most of it.

Chance had disdained the suggestion of Yankee broadcloth for the occasion, stubbornly insisting on being married in his finest *Californio* costume, complete with jangling spurs. The latter made it somewhat awkward for him to kneel before the priest and exchange vows with his bride, but he managed to survive the inconvenience with his dignity intact.

The church overflowed with the cream of Los Angeles society, including all of the prominent southland Yankees. Nor would any Esperanza relatives or friends—which included nearly every *Hispano-Californio* family between Santa Barbara and San Diego—have neglected the happy event. And of course there was Señor Gobernador Pio Pico and his *muy dulcicima* Señora on hand to add copious tears to the emotion-charged atmosphere.

When Chance escorted the radiant Doña Teresa Esperanza de Malcolm into the bright sunlight amidst showering rice and fluttering doves, it seemed to him that the dirty little pueblo wasn't such a bad place to live after all. Gallantly he lifted his bride to the saddle of his waiting horse, then swung up behind her and led the joyous procession to Don Alexander Bell's house where the wedding fiesta was to be given. Behind them came the Esperanza brothers and other musicians, their instruments singing with the sweet tones of the church's bell.

The fiesta continued through the afternoon and late into the evening, with Chance drinking toasts and leading off dances. But always Teresa's face was before him and it was a great relief when he was finally able to slip away with her to his house.

When Teresa came timorously to his bed wearing a long white nightgown, Chance cautioned himself that he must be extremely gentle with her. Teresa's virginity was a treasured gift that he must accept with proper reverence. Still, he was a man, and when he took her in his arms he found the nightgown an offensive barrier between them.

Chance quickly worked the garment over Teresa's head and cast it aside. Then, lying naked upon her nakedness, he was at last able to discover the being to whom he had pledged the rest of his life.

He was not disappointed by the throbbing warmth of Teresa, with her firm breasts, yielding mouth, and grasping thighs. Just for a moment, when he penetrated her and she sucked air between clenched teeth, Chance was transported back to the bank of the Owens River and felt Bold Nose writhing beneath him. But the illusion swiftly vanished and Teresa became the only woman he had ever known or would ever want to know.

"I love you, *querida*," Chance whispered into his wife's ear.

"And I love thee, my husband."

Her reply was barely audible, but more convincing than his declaration.

Chance felt no shame for the weakness of his affection, which he was certain would blossom fully in time. For the present, he tried to concentrate on ending Teresa's ordeal as quickly as possible. The poor girl's groans and whimpers made it obvious that she was only performing her wifely duty of submitting to his demands.

161

Yet the harder Chance tried to increase his thrusting rhythm, the more the desired climax eluded him. Cursing himself for having drunk too much at the fiesta, he was about to withdraw unsatisfied when finally the pent-up tension sprang from him.

Chance rolled off of Teresa with a final kiss and cuddled her tenderly. He felt very satisfied with himself. He had made the right decision in marrying for sensible business reasons. Let the young fools chase the romantic illusion of everlasting passion; he and Teresa would build a more rewarding relationship, with him controlling his sexual urges to spare her unnecessary hardship.

Holding her in a protective embrace, he dozed off inhaling the clean sweet scent of her hair.

Chapter 17

July 17, 1853

Ben Butler put down the hammer with which he had been crushing rock samples and filled his pipe. "Wal, looks like we tried to play a hand without even havin' jacks or better to open."

"No harm done," David Wheeler said. "We gave her a good try, least ways."

He looked around the boulder-strewn pass through the sharp Sierra ridge. From where they sat, two miles above sea level, they could see out over Owens Valley, the Inyo Range, Death Valley, and into the distant wastes of the Great Basin. It was a starkly beautiful spot that matched the two men's austere personalities.

David was glad he had offered to join Ben on his prospecting jaunt up the mountain. He enjoyed the garrulous miner's company and he had greedily pumped him for information about Chance ever since he had appeared in Owens Valley three weeks before, carrying a letter from Chance.

After Susan O'Neal Butler had acquired a tidy sum in Goldcock, she had sold the store and moved to Sacramento with Ben and her three surviving sons. With a desire to turn semirespectable, Susan opened up a parlor house not far from a hardware store run by a former Oneonta neighbor of David and Chance—Collis P. Huntington. As always, Ben found city life confining and soon told Susan that he had a mind to do more prospecting. Susan, who by then had almost forgotten that she had a husband, dismissed Ben with the command to let her know if he made a rich strike.

For another year Ben meandered through the Mother Lode country with indifferent results. Rumor of a new strike in the Tehachapis took him south, where a band of starving Indians ate his mule and stole his gear. Finally he ended up broke and hungry—but still talking—in Los Angeles, where Chance found him.

After helping Ben get back on his feet, Chance hired him as a teamster on one of the wagons he used to haul cattle hides to San Pedro and trade goods back to the pueblo. Ben liked the work, but inevitably his old wanderlust returned and he asked Chance to grubstake him to another goldseeking venture. Chance readily agreed and suggested that Ben try his luck in Owens Valley, which was still virtually untouched by fortune hunters. Ben thought that an excellent idea, unconcerned by Chance's plan to use him to contact David.

David and Chance had managed to exchange a few messages during the three and a half years since they had parted, in spite of Owens Valley's remote isolation. But David's knowledge of his friend's activities was extremely sketchy and he avidly devoured the letter, rejoicing at Chance's good fortune in business and marriage. Already Teresa had given birth to their first child, a boy whom they had named Miguel Zachary in memory of Michael O'Neal and the late President Taylor.

He had planned on several occasions to journey to Owens Valley and fetch them all down to Los Angeles, Chance wrote. But something always intervened. It required more time than he had just to look after his varied enterprises and cope with the hampering influences of nature and men. The heavy rains and flooding of the 1851–52 winter had drowned much stock and delayed the spring rodeo and northern trail drive. Then there were Indian raids and the growing lawlessness among the white population. San Francisco's First Vigilance Committee had reduced that city's criminal element and much of it had relocated in Los Angeles. Mounted gangs led by the notorious Joaquin Murrieta and other bandits ravaged the countryside. Earlier that year, Chance had joined one of the volunteer ranger companies that had been organized to run down the desperados.

The letter closed with a plea that David bring his family to Los Angeles, where a good home and job would be waiting for him. Chance even offered to send some of his *vaqueros* with pack animals to help with the moving. In a postscript, Chance asked David to kiss Vicky Beth for him and tell her how much her father looked forward to being with her again.

Reading the letter left David with mixed emotions. As much as he longed to see Chance again, he hated the thought of losing Vicky Beth. And that must surely happen because David knew he could never leave the valley where Margaret was buried. It saddened him to realize how fate had relentlessly separated him and Chance when they both wanted so much to be together. But David could see no solution to the problem. Owens Valley was his home now; the Paiutes were his neighbors who relied on him for leadership and instruction. He was permanently rooted here, just as Chance was caught in the poetry of Los Angeles. Maturity had taken them in different directions and they could never be boyhood comrades again. But David was comforted by the knowledge that only time and distance lay between them—not loss of love.

That somewhat eased David's apprehension over the thought of Chance returning to claim his daughter. He just wished there was a way he could spare Rebekah—and especially D.C. and Bobby Buck, who adored their "big sister"—that heartache. The only thing they could do, David figured, was to enjoy Vicky Beth for as long as they were allowed to keep her and be thankful for that. When you came right down to it, it was mighty decent of God to give people any pleasure at all, considering what ungrateful creatures most of them were.

"What you reckon this stuff is?" David asked, fingering a lump of the heavy, dark blue ore that he and Ben had gouged out of the mountain's tough skin.

165

"Don't rightly know," Ben answered disinterestedly. "Could be low-grade lead ore." He had learned a little about hard rock mining from Jack Chevington, the British mining engineer, and the traces of gold dust they had found in streambeds at lower elevations had led him to suspect the existence of a mother lode high in the range's broken teeth. But since their long climb up to the pass that the Paiutes called Kah-maht Pohaveche—Sick Bear—had rewarded them with nothing but exercise, Ben was ready to talk about other things.

"Shore is a clear sky," Ben mused, staring out over the valley. "Puts me in the mind o' Gabe Bridger's yarn about the Glass Mountain. You ever hear tell o' that? Old Gabe used to get the greenhorns with it every time. Said he was out huntin' one day and seen a fine buck deer standin' about two hunnert yards away. So he ups his rifle and gets off a good shot straight for the heart.

"But nothin' happens. Durn buck just goes on standin' thar nibblin' the grass. So Gabe rams home another ball an' fires again. Still nothin' happens to the buck. Gabe knows he couldn't've missed two times in a row. So he starts walkin' forward to find out what in thunder's so special about this buck. Wal, he hadn't gone more'n twenty paces when—wham! He hits smack into somethin' hard that he can't see. Reaches out an' feels a solid wall o' glass. Goes feelin' his way 'round it an' danged if it don't turn out to be a whole mountain made o' glass! Reason he couldn't hit the buck was it was more'n two hunnert miles away. The glass mountain made it 'pear up-close, like when you look through a telescope."

Ben chuckled and removed the pipe from his mouth long enough to spit. "Yes, sir. Old Gabe sure could tell 'em. An' oncet in a while his yarns even had some truth in 'em. Like the time he said he'd seen seagulls in the desert an' a big lake saltier 'n the ocean. We all thought that was his best lie ever."

The afternoon was far advanced, but David judged they would have ample daylight to get back down to the meadow where they had left their horses in the care of Lightning Tracker's son, Hu-pwi. The young Paiute had

166

come along as their guide and David was sure he would be happy to hear that they were ready to start for home, where his bride Seyavi was waiting for him. David himself had performed the wedding ceremony that spring. Or at least he had read Bible verses over Hu-pwi and Seyavi.

It had made David feel self-conscious and almost sacrilegious. But Rebekah had insisted on having her protégée's marriage blessed by Jesus and David figured that any kind of Christian wedding was better than the Paiutes' heathen habit of allowing a man and women to take up with one another without even a by-your-leave to the Almighty.

Hu-pwi, at seventeen, was a strong handsome lad and David's best agricultural student. He had cultivated a sizable farm along one of the creeks feeding into Owens River—alone, of course. His father disdained manual labor as being beneath his statesman's dignity. Now Hu-pwi had a good wife to give him healthy sons to work the land. David smiled at the memory of Seyavi looking surprisingly grown-up for her thirteen years, as the young couple proudly showed off Rebekah's wedding gift—two matching pairs of moccasins beautifully decorated with colored glass beads.

Yes, indeed, a real nice wedding, David reminisced as he and Ben picked their way back down the rocky game trail past pockets of old snow and bright patches of creeping white heather. David broke off a sprig of the tiny bell-shaped flowers that, according to an old Scottish fable, "grow where angels have trod" and stuck it in his hat.

Tough old junipers—lightning-blasted and wind-twisted to grotesque shapes—clung stubbornly to granite cracks with clawlike roots. In the lee of one of the trees sprouted the Sierras' most rare and exquisite flower, the alpine columbine. David paused to admire the lovely yellowish blooms hanging downward on slender stems like children's sleep-heavy heads. He had planned to gather some of the mountain blossoms for Margaret's grave. But the columbine's beauty was too much for his conscience. He turned away and left its murder to a browsing mountain sheep or foraging cony.

When they reached the meadow and found Hu-pwi preparing supper, the sun had gone to the other side of the range. But the alpenglow lingered on, a rosy net holding the spirit of the departed light to the mountains' breasts like a lover's memory.

Vicky Beth was climbing high and fast, higher than she had ever gone before in the great oak towering over the irrigation pond. Below her she heard Seyavi's rapid breathing grow fainter as the older girl withdrew from their race up the tree. Vicky Beth's hands and knees were sore from gripping the tough bark. Blood oozed from a dozen scratches. But she continued to the highest branch capable of supporting her weight and perched on it. Peering down past Seyavi's upturned face, she could see D.C.'s blond curls through the leaves as he clung to a lower limb. Below him, she glimpsed Bobby Buck whimpering on the ground because he was too small to join their climbing game.

"Go no higher, sister," Seyavi pleaded. "You will surely fall."

The words gave Vicky Beth a thrill of victory. She would so climb higher, as soon as she caught her breath and her heart stopped pounding at the swaying of the wind-tossed branch. She'd show them. She'd go all the way to the top and poke her head through the oak's green crown and look out over the valley.

Looking down again, Vicky Beth saw a large object move toward Bobby Buck. That was Coso, her sorrel pony, the one thing she loved above all else in the whole world. Uncle David had bought the horse from a band of Mexican traders the previous summer and Vicky Beth had quickly learned to ride bareback.

Vicky Beth clenched her teeth and summoned all of her courage for her final dash up to where the oak trunk fanned out in twisted branches no thicker than her wrists. But before she could move, a shout from the childish, almost incoherent voice of Wongata.

"Wheela come! Wheela come!"

"Daddy's back!" D.C. cried.

"Hu-pwi!" Seyavi smiled and started quickly back down the tree trunk.

Deprived of her audience, Vicky Beth saw no point in finishing her climb to the top. With a flood of relief she would never admit, she followed Seyavi's descent. Oh well, tree-climbing was a childish pastime anyway.

When they were all on the ground, they gathered around Wongata to hear the news that had passed through the Indian camps nearly as fast as the white man's telegraph could have carried it. Full of self-importance, the childman told them that David Wheeler, Ben Butler, and Hupwi were riding down from the north and would be home before nightfall.

D.C. was anxious to carry the exciting news to Rebekah and Seyavi said she would have to hurry to her wickiup and prepare a proper welcome for her husband. Bobby Buck, who was not quite three and hardly understood what was happening, was just glad to have his playmates back with him. Vicky Beth led Coso over to the oak's lowest limb, which made a handy mounting step, and boosted the two boys onto his back. Then she straddled the pony's shoulders and Seyavi got on behind the boys.

With Wongata running ahead, Vicky Beth kicked the pony into a trot.

They rode to the farmhouse first and dropped off D.C. and Bobby Buck. Rebekah, her second pregnancy swelling the front of her skirt, was delighted to hear that the men were coming home.

"You start supper, Aunt Rebekah," Vicky Beth ordered. "I'll be back d'rectly."

Rebekah watched the two girls ride off with a feeling of uneasiness that had been increasing over the past year. Vicky Beth was growing up as wild as the land and neither Rebekah nor David could control the headstrong girl. David insisted on teaching her reading, writing and other simple lessons from the books Margaret had brought along. But that was about as far as they could go in civilizing her.

Vicky Beth was nearly ten now, and big for her age. Already a few young Paiute bachelors had started to notice her. Rebekah shuddered to think of what would become of her if she reached marriageable age with no suitable men of her own race around. Her years of Christian living with David had made her a snob to her own people and convinced her that the white world had much more to offer a woman. But Rebekah was unable to bring herself to discuss the problem with David and Winnedumah was indifferent to the fate of the white girl. The old woman hadn't spoken to Rebekah since hearing about Chance's marriage to Teresa. She was still convinced that her foster granddaughter could have married the now-rich Don Chance, if only she had tried harder.

There was an obvious solution to the problem of Vicky Beth's future, but Rebekah was afraid to think about it. The letter Ben Butler had delivered had reminded her that Vicky Beth was Chance's daughter and someday he would take her away to live with him. When that happened, Chance would also reclaim Rebekah and Bobby Buck and perhaps even this child of David's that she was carrying. That prospect became more terrifying with each passing day, for Rebekah had come to feel true love for David.

It never occurred to Rebekah that Chance might not want her, now that he had a wife and family in Los Angeles. She only knew she could not stop thinking of herself as his property. Her only comfort lay in praying that Chance would never return to Owens Valley; that he would send someone else for Vicky Beth and leave his poor slave Bold Nose to live out her days with her Jesus-appointed husband David.

After taking Seyavi to her wickiup, Vicky Beth stayed a while to help her prepare for Hu-pwi's return. Seyavi sang happily as she stirred up the coals in the firepit and started fixing her husband's favorite dishes. In addition to the new grains and vegetables that David had introduced to the valley, the Paiutes still relied on their traditional wild foods. Carefully crushing handfuls of pinon nuts to a fine meal in her stone mortar, Seyavi sprinkled it with the white man's precious sugar to make the delicious mush that Hu-pwi was fond of. But the delicacy he loved most, and which Seyavi herself craved with mouth-watering gluttony, was *koo-sabe*. It required all of her will power to keep from nibbling a little of their dwindling last-year's supply. But she forced herself to make the sacrifice, thinking that in the fall there would be another bountiful harvest of the pupae of brine flies that bred in the dead waters of Owens and Mono lakes. Millions of the immature insects washed up on the lakeshores, where they were gathered by Indian women.

They were then dried in the sun and the shells were rubbed off, leaving a small yellowish kernel of worm that had an oily, nutlike flavor. So highly did the local tribes prize *koosabe* that once Paiutes and Shoshones had fought a war over possession of one of the rich harvesting grounds.

Between cooking chores, Seyavi straightened their few belongings in the wickiup and set out their matching beaded moccasins. The wedding gifts from Rebekah were their most cherished possessions and they had agreed to wear them only on special occasions. Then she bathed in the creek and gathered fresh clematis blossoms for her hair, humming Rebekah's courtship song about the white flower of twining.

Vicky Beth soon grew bored with her friend's work and fuss for the sake of a mere man. Declining Seyavi's invitation to stay for supper, she remounted Coso and started homeward to welcome Uncle David.

Although she had come to accept Seyavi's marriage and the difference it made in their relationship, Vicky Beth failed to understand what possible satisfaction a girl could derive from living with a man. She was often an overnight guest in Seyavi's wickiup, where Hu-pwi treated her with brotherly affection, and many times she had watched the uninhibited couple making love. But aside from discovering a new meaning for the name Hu-pwi—Desert Thorn; and it was quite a thorn when aroused—Vicky Beth couldn't see the value of all the thrashing about and grunting and giggling on the rabbitskin blankets. It just disturbed her sleep and made her question Seyavi's sense of values. Why go to so much trouble for a man, when she could be having fun climbing trees or smoking corn silk or making plans to travel to Shoshone Land?

Vicky Beth firmly resolved that she would never get mixed up with the foolishness of married life. The only male animal she ever wanted between her legs was a good strong horse.

Chapter 18

April 7, 1854

The two filibusters outside the hut were arguing over whether buzzards or ants smell death first. It wasn't a very energetic argument. None of the remaining soldiers of the Army of the Republic of Sonora and Lower California had enough strength left to do anything energetically.

Inside the hut, Chance half-listened to the droning voices and recognized one of them as belonging to Cecil Shelby, who had an understandable interest in death because of the festering bullet wound in his lower rib cage. On the dirt floor beside Chance, Ramon dozed fitfully with a cloud of flies buzzing over his damp face. Listlessly Chance waved them away. There was not much else the small ragged band of survivors could do for their sick and wounded, with no medicine and little food and water.

Chance supposed he should be grateful that they had a little shelter for their midday rest. After trudging through the barren wastes of northern Mexico for several days, even the miserable hovels of the tiny Indian village were a welcome sight. The village residents had prudently fled at the approach of the Americans. Probably they were now conferring with the pursuing *rurales* on how to get rid of the gringo invaders, Chance surmised. Not that it mattered very much. Another week of this grueling retreat would solve the problem by leaving forty-seven more human skeletons for the sun and sand to play over.

Chance roused himself from such pessimistic thoughts and touched Ramon's brow. It was still burning with fever, but it did seem a bit cooler than before. Ramon's eyes fluttered open and for a moment he seemed to recognize Chance. Then the lids drooped shut again and he muttered a few words about Ysabel and Ito. Chance was glad that Ramon's delirium-torn mind was temporarily on something besides this sordid mess.

Chance remembered the amazement and amusement that he and everyone else had felt upon learning that Ramon's poetic wooing of the Los Angeles señoritas had at last paid off. True, Ysabel Delgado was no great beauty and her family was so poor that she and her mother had to work as servants in the homes of wealthy *Californios*. But the mere fact that Ramon had managed to get Ysabel with child impressed his brothers as much as it scandalized his parents.

Ramon stubbornly insisted that he loved Ysabel and wished to marry her. Teresa, to whom her beloved little brother could do no wrong, staunchly supported him. But Don Carlos and Doña Luisa would not hear of their son marrying beneath himself. Finally the debate was resolved by Ysabel's death in childbirth.

Chance and Teresa became godparents to the baby, who was christened Ramonito—Little Ramon—and called Ito for short. The heartbroken Ramon continued to live with Chance and Teresa, who gave Ito the same loving care she showered on her own lively little Miguel Zachary. All was going well, with Ramon recovering his normal good spirits, when Chance's world was shaken by one of the strange disruptive forces that sometimes sweep through human events.

Word had reached Los Angeles late in 1853 that an expedition of armed Americans had sailed from San Francisco to La Paz, the capital of Baja California, and captured the governor of that state. It was hardly a unique occurrence. Foreign adventurers and mercenaries had been active in Latin America's revolution-wracked nations for years. But this invasion did appear different in that it was

173

led by a man of rare intelligence and idealism, as well as daring courage.

William Walker, the self-proclaimed president and commanding general of the armed forces of the Republic of Sonora and Lower California, was a 29-year-old Tennessean with an exceptional background. His well-to-do family had given him every opportunity to develop his brilliant mind in the best universities of America and Europe. Unfortunately that also brought him into contact with some of the radical political and social ideas that were causing much turmoil throughout the Old World at that time. He was in Germany in 1848 when Karl Marx and Friedrich Engels half-baked a loaf of intellectual gingerbread called the *Communist Manifesto*.

After returning to America, Walker joined the Gold Rush to San Francisco and fell in with a group of ambitious hotheads who discussed many theories for shortcutting the slow electoral route to power. It was then that Walker conceived the brainstorm of setting up his own domain in politically unstable, militarily weak Mexico.

Chance was fascinated by newspaper reports of the remarkable "gray-eyed man of destiny," as an overly enthusiastic journalist had labeled Walker. Here at last was a leader who could fulfill America's Manifest Destiny.

As the Monroe Doctrine had barred Europe's despotic regimes from meddling in the lives of North and South Americans, the Walker Doctrine would free them from the oppression and mismanagement of their own autocratic rulers. In the blinding heat of patriotic pride, Chance saw Walker's campaign as a holy crusade to bring the struggling people of Latin America, Canada, and Russian America (Alaska) into the humane, enlightened march of progress that the embattled farmers at Lexington and Concord had started.

Shiploads of idealists sailed south to join Walker when the Mexican government showed little interest in defending its northern border. It appeared that the two former Mexican states would indeed follow the Texas precedent. Finally Chance could no longer restrain himself from joining the effort to extend Anglo democracy to the downtrodden peons. Among his investments was a small trading schooner that he had rechristened *La Teresa*. Loading the vessel with food, ammunition, and other supplies, Chance left his business affairs in the capable hands of Si Darcy and Madison and Jeremy Starr, kissed his wife goodbye and sailed down the coast to find Walker. Several men had volunteered to go with him and he chose eight of the best marksmen among them to form a rifle squad.

La Teresa was well out to sea when the stowaway Ramon was found. The poet was so pathetically eager to be in the crusade—particularly as it meant serving with his adored brother-in-law—that Chance didn't have the heart to send him back.

But when they located William Walker in Ensenada, the future of the young republic did not look too bright. Instead of greeting the Americans as liberators, the Mexicans called them *filibusteros*—freebooters—implying they were no better than bandits or pirates. The people of La Paz had tolerated Walker's occupation as long as his gold lasted. When the merchants there refused to sell him goods in exchange for the paper currency issued by his bankrupt treasury, Walker had moved his capital to Ensenada. He was having the same trouble there, so the provisions Chance delivered were gratefully received. Because of the donation, and Chance's past military experience, Walker commissioned him a major in his Army. But since Chance was not given any additional troops to command, and four of his riflemen were assigned to other duties, the rank had little meaning.

In spite of that, Chance's faith in Walker's press-created reputation was so strong that it took him a while to grow disillusioned. He was even able to hide his disappointment at meeting Walker himself. The President and General was a small, slender man wth a massive forehead, concave cheeks, thin nose and oversized ears. But, as Ramon pointed out, he did have the beautiful deepset gray eyes of a man of destiny. And there was something about his bearing that seemed to inspire his men, who were usually dirty, undisciplined, drunk and indifferent toward the natives they had come to uplift.

But Chance thought they could be whipped into shape with the proper training, equipment, and leadership. Unfortunately those things cost money, of which Walker was running desperately short. His many supporters in California were still enthusiastic about his project, but hardly any of them were willing to help pay for it. As Walker's popularity in Ensenada dwindled with his declining funds and the news of Washington's refusal to recognize the new Republic, he decided to try his luck in Sonora.

That decision greatly boosted Chance's spirits. An army on the march was something he could understand and function well within, unlike politics.

It was a slow, costly crossing of the peninsula's dry mountains and sandy waste lands. The progress of the 120-man army was slowed by large herds of cattle and horses, most of them confiscated from *rancheros* who weren't too happy about the new government's form of taxation. And there were occasional skirmishes with the Mexican forces that trailed after them. They lost a dozen men before they reached the muddy Colorado River that separates Baja California from Sonora. Indian guides warned Walker that the river current was too strong for their weakened livestock, but the general ordered a crossing anyhow. Nearly one-third of their cattle and horses were drowned and washed away to the sharks in the Gulf of California.

They spent two days resting on the river's eastern bank. On the second morning, Walker awakened to find that more than half of his men had deserted, heading north to Fort Yuma, the nearest American settlement. For a while Walker insisted on going on with his plan to conquer Sonora, but Chance and his other advisors managed to convince him that it was hopeless. Reluctantly Walker declared they would return to Ensenada, where he was certain more recruits would have arrived to rebuild his invincible army. They lost more cattle and horses recrossing the river.

At last Chance understood the major flaw in their grand scheme—their leader was mad. Walker's insane lust for power had so loosened his grip on reality that, although his brilliant mind still held his noble vision, he was no longer able to cope with practical details. That realization saddened Chance, not only because he feared Walker's madness might get them all killed, but because it meant the end of his own dream of Manifest Destiny. He thought the idea was still valid and maybe someday it would work out successfully. But not this time. Walker's crusade in Mexico was already lost, even if he wouldn't admit it.

Chance almost wished he had gone north with the deserters, as they had urged him to do. The survivors of his squad had joined the mass escape, and he had let them go with his blessing. But his sense of duty forced him to stay with Walker and see the game played out to the end. And naturally Ramon had to do likewise.

Chance's regret increased when Ramon fell sick. Soon he was suffering with chills, high temperatures, vomiting, diarrhea and other symptoms of something Chance wouldn't let himself think about. On the third day, Ramon was unable to walk. Chance made a crude litter and begged and bullied the other men into helping him carry Ramon on it. Now he wasn't sure he could persuade them to bear the burden any further.

Unaware that he had dozed off, Chance jerked his head up at a muffled sound. Sunlight pouring through the open doorway cut his eyes and he blinked at the dark figure etched against the glare. The slight frame and broad sombrero were unmistakable even before the tattered door covering fell back in place and the shadowed face of the president of Sonora and Lower California took shape. Walker's uniform was as dirty and ragged as any of his men's, but the two golden sun insignia of general-in-chief still reflected the fire in his gray eyes. Once again Chance was impressed by Walker's air of command that seemed immune to heat, thirst, fatigue and even defeat.

Chance rose stiffly and started to come to attention, but Walker put him at ease with a gesture.

"We will resume the march in ten minutes, Major."

"Yes, sir."

Walker glanced down at Ramon. "How is the patient?"

"Feeling much better, sir," Chance answered quickly. "He'll be strong enough to walk in another day."

"This isn't another day." Walker's child-sized hands hung nervelessly beside his huge pistols. "We have forty miles of hard ground to cover before we see water again, if

177

that spring hasn't dried up. Even some of the sound men may not make it, let alone an invalid."

"He'll make it," Chance insisted. "I'll carry him myself, if I have to."

Ramon was fully awake then, but Walker continued to talk as if he and Chance were alone. "Carrying a dead weight will waste energy that we may need for fighting."

"He isn't going to die, General. It's only a bad case of pneumonia."

Walker's blank face almost expressed irritation. "I was a medical student, Major. I know cholera when I see it."

At last the dreaded word was out in the open, sending a sick shiver through Chance's already weakened legs and stomach. He fought against thinking of the panic that would sweep through the debilitated army at the mere rumor of a contagious disease, and replied:

"With all due respect, sir, you are mistaken. This man does not have cholera."

Walker stared thoughtfully at Chance, then leaned down to look into Ramon's drawn face. *Le duele al respirar?*

"He speaks English," Chance said shortly, knowing Walker was aware of that fact.

"Does it pain you to breathe?" Walker repeated.

"Yes, sir. Leetle bit," Ramon whispered hoarsely.

Walker felt Ramon's brow, checked his pulse and lifted an eyelid to study the bloodshot sclera. Finally he straightened up and led Chance over to a corner of the hut. "I appreciate your feelings for the boy, Major. But it's obvious he won't last another day, and I have the other men to think of."

"Then think of what they might do to you," Chance said, keeping his voice as low as Walker's, but full of meaning, "if I tell them that they have only you to blame for the fix they're in."

Walker's gaze locked with Chance's. "I've had men shot for less than that."

"I know. But I've never seen you shoot anyone yourself."

Chance's right hand flexed at his gun butt. Walker's hands were on the lower rim of his vision and he sensed more than saw that they made no move toward the twin

Colts. They stood motionless a foot apart, gray eyes drilling into gray eyes; one pair aflame with mad ambition, the other cold with stubborn resolve. There is no telling how long they might have remained that way, if Walker's eyes had not slipped down to the old Mexican War scar on Chance's cheek.

The white crescent peeping through Chance's dirty beard was a reminder to Walker that the taller man was an older and more experienced soldier. And that brought back his lifelong feelings of inferiority that he had tried to overcome with intellectual achievement, political rhetoric and eventually fanatical belief in his destiny. From European revolutionists he had learned the importance of concentration on a single goal at the sacrifice of everything else, even sanity. Now Walker realized that he had not quite reached the desired state of mystical self-exaltation that would enable him to walk into the jaws of death serenely convinced that he would emerge victorious. But he did not doubt that he had the will power to accomplish that. He would just have to keep working at replacing the last of his common sense with delusions of grandeur.

By the time Walker had shifted his gaze back to Chance's eyes, he had dismissed the Republic of Sonora and Lower California and was making plans for his next quest for power. He turned away from Chance with the absentminded air of a busy man leaving the funeral of someone he hadn't known very well.

"Fall in at the end of the column and maintain an interval of at least fifty yards, until you decide to rejoin us alone."

Ramon's eyes followed Walker out the door. Then he looked at Chance rolling up his blanket. "Leave me, *por favor*. You must save yourself for Teresa and the children."

"Don't talk nonsense, *hermanoito*. It's only a short way further to the coast. In a week we'll be home getting fat on Doña Luisa's fine cooking." Chance made himself laugh to show Ramon how little he thought of the dangers of their situation.

"It really is cholera, isn't it?" Ramon asked. When Chance didn't answer, he said calmly: "It's better this way.

Didn't I tell you that poets and warriors should always die young?"

"Oh, shut up," Chance snapped, as he emptied his haversack of all excess weight. "You're not a poet. You're a ham actor, always looking for a dramatic curtain line. But in real life, the play never ends. You just go plodding from one dull scene to another. So don't bother me with any more of your foolishness."

Chance leaned down and lifted Ramon in his arms. The boy's body was down to skin and bone but even that, with Chance's rifle, pack, canteen and other gear, made quite a load. Chance staggered as he walked out into the harsh afternoon sunshine.

The first thing that caught Chance's eye was Cecil Shelby, one of the men who had been discussing death, buzzards and ants. That question had been settled, but it was unlikely that Shelby had any further interest in it. He lay motionless on his back beside a shallow grave that someone had started to dig for him but evidently found the ground too hard or the time too short. Busy columns of red ants were swarming over Shelby's face and bloody lower body.

The filibusters formed up and General Walker mounted one of their few remaining horses. As they marched out of the village, they passed a tiny chapel that Chance hadn't noticed before. On its door was carved the Indians' ever-flowing River of Life. Chance stared at it for as long as possible, not knowing when he would see another stream.

Even with the hottest part of the day over, Chance was drenched with fresh sweat within the first ten minutes. For the first mile Ramon continued to beg Chance to leave him; then he fell into a semiconscious stupor and only muttered incoherently. The agony of burning tendons, blister-bloodied feet, laboring lungs and other painful results of a forced march had become familiar to Chance by then. But they still hurt. He looked around for some distraction from his aches and pains. He saw a sidewinder looping over the sand like a fanged rope endlessly uncoiling, and speculated about a wagon using a similar method of belted traction to keep its wheels from bogging down. But the idea did not

180

seem practical. Camels were what a man needed for this sort of terrain. He would have to remember to mention that to his fellow Los Angeles merchants the next time they discussed the difficulties of transporting commodities to and from the eastern states.

Chance forced his wandering mind back to the task of keeping pace with the column. Campaigning in Mexico and crossing Death Valley had taught him the futility of trying to plan too far ahead. Survival consisted of concentrating on short-term goals. Pick a nearby object, like that rock about ten yards ahead, and promise yourself that when you reach it you'll sit down to rest. When you get that far, pick the scarlet-blossomed ocotillo five yards beyond the rock and tell yourself the same lie, and so on. But don't waste energy looking back to see if the Mexican horsemen are still following. Of course they will be there, just out of rifle range, waiting for a straggler to fall far enough behind to be easily captured for a little sport at the end of a rawhide *reata*.

By the time Walker signaled the first rest halt, Chance's mind and legs were functioning so mechanically that it was difficult for him to stop. He sank to his knees on the hot gravel, almost dropping Ramon. The boy lay curled on his side, so still that Chance feared he was dead. But he managed to locate a faint heartbeat and was even able to get Ramon to swallow a little water. He had just started breathing normally again when the march was resumed.

As the day wore on, dulling Chance's senses, he realized that he could not possibly keep up with the column. The time was rapidly approaching when he would have to find a place to fort up against the pursuing *rurales*. He reckoned he had enough strength left to get a few of them before using his last two pistol balls on Ramon and himself.

They came to a line of desolate hills—weathered-down tombstones of an ancient volcanic outpouring.

Chance remembered the landmark from their eastward trek and decided it was as good a place as any to make his stand. He waited until the column was winding along a narrow passageway through the lava mass, out of sight of the following Mexicans. Turning aside, he clambered up over the cracked rocks. He nearly lost Ramon several times before he found a sheltered recess with commanding views of both sides of the stony barrier.

The thought of abandoning Ramon and rejoining the security of Walker's army occurred to Chance. But not very seriously.

After making Ramon as comfortable as possible in the cave, Chance found a good vantage point and waited to see what would happen next. By then the filibusters were out on the broad western plain marching slowly into the sunset. Chance would always carry the vivid image of General William Walker sitting erect in the saddle as he rode away to keep his rendezvous with destiny, which would take him to supreme power in one Central American country and to a firing squad in another.

An hour later, as twilight was melting the landscape, the *rurales* ambled out of the hills in the wake of the retreating gringos. They seemed not to know or care that two members of their quarry were missing.

But Chance remained nervously vigilant until long after the deepening darkness flickered to star-filled life. The evening chill set in quickly. Chance wrapped Ramon's trembling body in both of their blankets, trying to ignore his own shivering.

"Chance?"

It was like a whisper from the grave, startling Chance out of his plans for defending their position in case the *rurales* came back.

"Si, hermanoito?"

Ramon mumbled something inaudible. Chance held his ear to the boy's lips. ". . . made me promise not to tell you. But . . . must. She . . . another child."

"What? Who? Teresa is going to have a baby?" Chance's tired brain couldn't quite get hold of the idea.

"Si. Did not . . . wish you to worry. That why . . . you must leave me and . . ."

Chance gripped Ramon's skeletal shoulders. "Hold on, brother. We'll both get out of this all right."

Ramon's breathing became even and labored again. Chance felt his closed eyes in the darkness and decided to let him sleep. He crawled back to the cave's opening and stared out at the ghostly landscape, trying to pull his scattered thoughts together.

So he was going to be a father again? And Teresa had kept the secret from him so as not to spoil his fun. God, what a hopeless idiot he was! Would he never grow up and accept his responsibilities like a man? Here he was, one of the richest men in southern California at thirty-two, with a loving wife and family, good friends, a promising future—and he had risked losing all that for another fool dream of adventure. He was a fine one to accuse Walker of being crazy.

No, his problem was worse than insanity, Chance admitted. He was childishly thoughtless. All of his life he had been spoiled by those who loved him and considered him something special in their lives, starting with his parents and David and Margaret and going all the way up to Teresa and her family. And, like a selfish child, he had taken everything they had given him without appreciating it or trying to repay the great debt he owed them. Now it was too late. He was going to die in this obscure wilderness and no one would even know where the scavengers had made a meal of his and Ramon's bodies.

But no, he must not think like that. Somehow he would carry Ramon out of this. And when they finally made it back to Los Angeles, he would never again jeopardize the happiness he had with Teresa. With God as his witness, Chance swore, he would spend the rest of his life being a good husband and father and an honest, hard-working citizen dedicated to the peaceful development of his country. Let others carry on the banner of Manifest Destiny if they wished, but nothing short of defending his own home or country would ever cause him to take up arms again.

The long, lonely night became an important turning point in Chance's life and, coincidentally, the history of the United States. The Walker foray into Mexico marked the unofficial end of America's period of military expansionism. There would be other filibustering expeditions and the United States would win temporary custody of a few islands from the decaying Spanish Empire. But for the most part, America's future wars would be defensive and conservative. Henceforth the nation's Manifest Destiny would be realized by the irrepressible forces of industry and commerce. Vast armies of factory workers, managers, and salespeople would take the American way of life to the utmost corners of the world. Only southern plantation owners and Indian tribes would suffer the loss of territory to United States military forces, and since they were Americans, too, they could hardly complain of foreign aggression.

Sometime in the middle of the night Chance was pulled out of a light sleep by Ramon's hacking cough. He crept over and put his arms around the boy, trying to coax a little heat from their wasted bodies. Chance dozed off feeling the nervous bird twitter of Ramon's heart through the blankets. When he awoke shortly before dawn, the bird had flown the cage.

He spent the morning burying the body under a thick layer of rocks that he hoped would keep it safe from scavengers. He tried to remember something appropriate from the Bible to say over the grave, but only the Twenty-third Psalm came to mind. Chance repeated that, hoping it would do some good. There was nothing he could do about his own heartbreaking guilt, except promise Ramon's spirit that he would love and care for Ito as his own son.

"Perhaps poets and warriors should die young," Chance mused as he walked away from the grave. "But they should at least have a real war to do it in."

Ten days later, Chance was found by two Basque sheepherders thirty miles southeast of San Diego. He remained conscious long enough to learn that he was on American soil, then collapsed with a smile on his cracked lips.

Chapter 19

Thus began the long-delayed halcyon years of Chance's life.

After returning to Los Angeles and regaining his strength, he threw himself into the task of keeping his promise to be a better man. He had always considered himself moderate in his vices, but now he determined to cut down on his occasional drinking and gambling sprees in order to spend more time with his family. He even started attending church regularly, although the higher spiritual rewards of religion still eluded him. He became so respectable, in fact, that Si Darcy and his other hell-raising friends grumbled that he was getting to be a pain in the neck.

Business matters still occupied most of Chance's waking hours. He had come home in time to help with the spring *rodeo* and send a trail herd off to San Francisco. When that was out of the way, he was able to look after his other investments. It was then that he began to appreciate his cautious foresight in hiring Madison Starr to survey the lands he was interested in buying. Other land-hungry Yankees had purchased huge ranchos, acquiring all the problems of their upkeep and management. But Chance had carefully chosen several small, well-watered parcels scattered over the county. By having his *vaqueros* rotate his herds around the parcels, he was able to keep his cattle fat without overgrazing the pastures.

Another advantage of resisting the urge to become a land baron was brought home to Chance by the activities of the federal Land Commission that Congress had appointed to certify the old Spanish and Mexican land grants. The haphazard *vista de ojos* method by which the *rancheros* had marked off their boundaries, together with the loss of their deed records during the transfer of governmental power after the war, provided the Land Commission and landowners with many interesting discussions. Even the big Yankee ranchers like John Temple and Abel Stearns had trouble proving their titles to their sprawling estates.

Money problems also endangered the Dons' properties. Most of the ranchos were heavily mortgaged to private money-lenders like Chance, since there were as yet no banks in the southland. Interest rates ran as high as eight percent a month, compounded monthly. Chance's terms were more reasonable than that, but he required solid collateral for his loans, which had become quite extensive over the years. Once, when totaling up his accounts, he made the awesome discovery that if a major disaster should bring about the foreclosure of all of his loans, he would own a sizable portion of the best land between Santa Barbara and San Diego. The thought gave him a giddy sensation of power, until he wondered what he would do with such a vast empire.

How could he hope to make the land more productive than its present owners? More importantly, how could he find new markets for the products in the fluctuating world of California commerce? Already the state's northern appetite for southern beef was tapering off as the Gold Rush hysteria cooled and discouraged miners turned to farming and stock raising in the San Joaquin Valley. Eventually the agricultural areas around San Francisco, Sacramento and the gold fields would proivde enough food to make long trail drives from what the snobbish northerners called the "cow counties" impractical. The cattlemen could always fall back on the hide and tallow trade. But it would take some readjustment of living standards to sell cows at two or three dollars a head instead of twenty or thirty.

Some of the meat could be jerked and salted for shipment to San Francisco by sea, as Chance had already started doing on a limited scale. That experience convinced Chance that southern California's agricultural future depended on improved methods of preserving and transporting food. The area's slowly growing population simply could not absorb the fantastic bounty of its soil and climate. And its sea, Chance reminded himself, thinking of the teeming, virtually untouched fish schools and whale herds in the coastal waters. Potentially California was one of the richest food-producing areas on earth. But what good was that if the food couldn't be moved profitably to the population centers in the eastern states and Europe?

Los Angeles must reach out to the world, Chance insisted in discussions with his fellow businessmen and southland boosters. That meant a railroad and a deepwater port. Travel time between California and the rest of the nation must be reduced to days, from the several weeks or months required by the routes across Central America and around the Horn. But far more urgent was the need for coast-to-coast telegraph and rapid mail service, to enable western growers and shippers to be informed of the latest needs of the eastern markets.

Chance had to tell himself not to put the cart before the horse. It was all right to make great plans for the distant future, but the fact remained that Los Angeles was still just a dirty, isolated *pueblo* and the entire county did not contain more than 5,000 people. For the time being, he would have to limit his driving ambition to the available opportunities. That included learning more about the new method of preserving food in tin cannisters.

That was a tedious, time-consuming process in which the metal for the cannisters had to be cut, soldered, filled and sealed by hand. Often the food in the cans would become contaminated and poison the consumers. But Chance was confident that food canning could become an important new industry, especially if the ominous war over the slavery issue that everyone was talking about should actually break out. A dependable, easily transported and stored food supply would ideally suit the needs of a fighting army, as Chance well knew.

With that in mind, Chance ordered all of the available literature on food canning and set up a small experimental cannery next to his warehouse in San Pedro. To run the cannery, Chance selected Madison Starr, one of the few people in Southern California who shared his enthusiasm for the lowly tin can's place in mankind's future. Chance had concluded that only daringly imaginative young minds like Starr's could cope with the new challenges that world events were bringing even to backward Los Angeles. The *Californios* and the older Anglo settlers seemed to think that the good times brought on by the cattle boom would last forever, that they could go on squandering money on their women and horses and dancing from one fiesta to another, with never a thought of tomorrow. Few of them suspected that their carefree way of life was about to pass into history, and even they dismissed the possibility with fatalistic shrugs. Being *Californios*, they would go as they had come—in the proud gay splendor of a wilderness civilization, and with the quiet faith and courage that had made that civilization, and those that would follow it, possible.

Chance, unable to persuade his neighbors to prepare for the uncertain future, concentrated on safeguarding his own interests. His first step in that direction was to move his family out of Los Angeles, which had become one of the most violently dangerous frontier towns in America, thanks to its lack of strong law enforcement and the influx of criminals from the north. The unsavory element in Nigger Alley had so expanded that for a while the pueblo averaged a homicide a day, with shootings and knifings becoming more popular than the bull and bear fights in the plaza. Even the public hangings lost some of their entertainment value when pickpockets infiltrated the crowds.

To escape the town's unwholesome influences, Chance decided to build a new ranchhouse near his in-laws' *casa*. The home site he selected was Monte Roble, the hill where he had dueled Farley Hewlett for his fortune and bride. Older residents in the area warned him that run-off water from the heavy rains might undermine the building's foundation. But Chance's heart was set on the location because of its spectacular southern view, which on clear days even included the ocean and Catalina Island. And eventually his choice was vindicated when the great flood of 1862 swept away what was left of the old Esperanza place but left the newer house standing high and dry.

Architecturally the house differed little from the Mediterranean boxed-in patio design that Spain had exported to America. But Chance insisted that the rooms be more spacious than usual, with large windows to relieve the confining impact of the thick adobe walls. The main entrance was a huge oak door engraved with the Indian River of Life motif, Chance's reminder to himself of the importance of water in the southwest. When it came to naming the house, Chance was realistic enough to see that the *Californio* customs were doomed. So he called it simply Monteroble, and was not surprised when progress changed that to Oakmont.

The significance of the name was not lost on Chance's father-in-law. Chance rode out often to oversee the building of the house, and sometimes he would glimpse Don Carlos on the plain below. The stocky *ranchero* would sit motionless on his horse, staring up at the hilltop structure taking shape on land that he had once ruled with absolute authority. Officially he was still master of Rancho Agua Fria, but only because of Chance's consideration for his pride. Don Carlos and his sons had never learned to manage their business affairs wisely and by now they all were hopelessly in debt to Chance, who allowed them to continue with their extravagant standard of living. The Esperanzas, for their part, were loath to embarrass Chance by letting it be known that he was supporting them. So, by unspoken consent, they all kept up the polite pretense that nothing had changed between them.

Unfortunately, Chance could not deal as easily with the changed conditions between himself and Teresa, who seemed unable to get over Ramon's death.

For weeks she had been inconsolable, her hysterical weeping tearing at Chance's heart. Finally her tears ceased and she resumed her household chores mechanically, a grim shadow of her former cheerful self. In bed she was so unresponsive to his lovemaking that he eventually gave up trying to arouse her.

Chance told himself that her pregnancy was to blame for

the trouble. After the baby was born they would get their marriage back on its well-adjusted course. Meanwhile, he would keep himself occupied with his work and the construction of the new house. He had endured other long periods of celibacy, so he was confident this one wouldn't hurt him.

They managed to maintain an image of a happy, compatible couple that fooled most observers, but not Teresa's female relatives. Doña Luisa's keen understanding of marital problems quickly perceived that something was wrong in her daughter's household and she had a long talk with her. But Teresa remained unmoved by her mother's impassioned argument about the importance of a wife's duty to satisfy her husband's needs. She still loved Chance, Teresa insisted, but every time he touched her she was revolted by the thought of those hands burying her beloved brother.

Finaly it took *Tia* Ignacia's no-nonsense approach to break down Teresa's stubborn resistance. The two of them clashed one uncomfortably warm afternoon in Teresa's kitchen, while the old woman sat at the table trying to feed the squirming, petulant Ramonito. Teresa was preparing supper on the huge castiron range Chance had given her on their first anniversary, with toddling Miguel Zachary doing his best to get under her feet. *Tia* Ignacia had ridden into town on a high-spirited bronc who had little consideration for her hemorrhoids. She was tired, sweaty, saddle-sore and in no mood to take any foolishness from a sulking girl who didn't know what life was all about.

"Ramon is dead," the old woman said bluntly, cutting short Teresa's explanation for her marriage difficulties. "Let him rest in peace. It is unfair and unprofitable to drag his corpse into bed between you and your husband."

"How dare you say such a thing!" Teresa whirled around so swiftly that she knocked her son flat on his behind. She was horrified by her aunt's words and her own angry reaction. It was the first time she had ever talked back to the woman she revered as a second mother.

"I speak only the truth that you lack the courage to face," *Tia* Ignacia calmly replied. "If Ramon were here, he would join me in telling you to stop punishing yourself and get on with your life."

"Punishing myself?" Teresa was so puzzled by the thought that she was hardly aware of picking up her whimpering Miguel and soothing his tears with kisses as she resumed stirring a pot of simmering beans.

"Of course. You don't think a man as handsome and virile as Don Chance needs to search very far for the pleasure he isn't getting here, do you?" The old woman watched her niece's shocked expression with pity and contempt. "Stupid girl! Why, half of the women in the county would love to take him away from you. If I were thirty years younger, or even twenty years . . ." A wistful look came into her eyes as she remembered how the gallant *Americano* had broken the *cascaron* over her head.

Teresa was so astonished by her aunt's words that at first she could only feel jealousy and fear at the mere thought of Chance with another woman. How could he treat her that way, after all she had done for him? She hated him! No, she loved him. She didn't know what she felt.

Suddenly all of her confusing emotions were overpowered by something far older and stronger—the excitement of a woman rising to the challenge of fighting for her man. She clutched the two living symbols of her commitment to Chance—the child in her arms and the one in her womb—and realized that she could not live without him. In that instant she grew up, interring Ramon's memory with the rest of her dead past. She was no longer the callow adolescent who had gone blindly from the security of her father's home to that of her husband. She was a mature wife and mother determined to save her marriage.

"What must I do?" Teresa asked.

Tia Ignacia's smile was tinged with regret as she thought of her own lost youth. But it was the proud smile of one who had helped rear a girl child to womanhood. Quietly and frankly, she answered Teresa's question.

That night Teresa, complaining of the heat, stripped off her nightgown and slid nude into bed beside Chance. "Are you not hot, too, *querido*?" she asked, pushing down the sheet.

"No, I . . ."

To Chance's astonishment, she started pulling his nightshirt over his head. He had often undressed Teresa and caressed her into an erotic mood, but this was the first time she had taken the initiative. Her actions were so unexpected, in view of her recent coldness, that he could only lie motionless while her hands moved seductively over his body.

According to all of Chance's moral training and firsthand experience, decent women simply did not behave like this. He had been pleased to discover, early in their marriage, that Teresa did indeed enjoy sex. But up till now she had always expressed her pleasure in the quiet, demure way that one would expect of a "nice" girl. Such blatant desire as this almost made him wonder if he had married a wanton harlot. Especially when she—oh, God! What was she doing to him now? He really should stop her.

But what she was doing felt so good, and he was so happy to have her treating him with affection again. He put his arms around her and pulled her warm full body against his side. Teresa kissed him with deep, tongue-probing passion as her right hand settled between his legs. Chance was so confused by having a woman act as the aggressor that he was unable to do anything but relax and enjoy the unique experience, as his wife worked to arouse the part of him that was most useful to both of them.

After making him fully erect, Teresa straddled his hips and slid him into her. As she dug her heels into his flanks and started moving rapidly up and down on him, she recalled *Tia* Ignacia's final warning: "Remember, a man is like a wild stallion. If you don't want yours running other mares, you must see that he gets plenty of exercise at home." When she finished this ride, Teresa vowed, her stallion would be in no condition to do any running around.

Chance was afraid her frantic movements might harm the child she was carrying. But her desire seemed so insatiable that he could only allow her to whip herself into a sweaty, panting frenzy of orgasms. When she had exhausted her energy, he rolled her over on her back and finished the session in a more conventional position.

Lying with her cuddled in his arms, Chance knew they had a lot to talk about. His mind was spinning with the startling new discoveries about women that he had just made, and which paradoxically rendered that sex even more mysterious to him. But just then words seemed unimportant. They were doing all the communicating they required just by being together. He held her close and stroked her hair until they fell asleep almost at the same moment.

A week passed before they were able to discuss the amazing change in their marital relations. Teresa was still modestly tongue-tied by her strict moral upbringing, while Chance was afraid he might discourage her thrilling new bedtime boldness if he insisted on talking about it. But gradually they managed to open their hearts and laugh with affectionate self-consciousness over the mistaken ideas both had previously had about the other's sexual attitudes. Chance never fully recovered from the shock of learning that respectable women, not just whores, could be as sexually aggressive as men. But he didn't let that bother him too much. He had something better to think about. He was falling in love.

Teresa was able to take the latest phase of their life together pretty much in stride. It seemed only natural that her girlish infatuation with Chance should blossom into fully adult love as she matured. She continued to adore him as her protective lord and master, but she found it equally easy to overlook his all-too-human weaknesses and comfort him with the same maternal tenderness she gave Miguel and Ito.

Chance, on the other hand, was overwhelmed by the startlingly different world of emotion and sensation that love opened for him. Always before, he had followed the chauvinistic male practice of revering female virtue, while viewing women in general as a distinct and somehow inferior race. Now he found himself so intimately involved with a real honest-to-God woman that he could not tell where he left off and she began. Why had he never felt this way with any of the other women in his life? It required all of his courage to face the obvious answer to that question: he had not been man enough to complete a woman until now.

After having traveled the world over and survived more

adventures than most men dream of, Chance realized that he had finally grown up. At last he was ready to meet his greatest challenge: to be a good husband and father.

His days continued to pass in a rush of energy-draining hard work and responsibilities. But his nights with Teresa and the children always refreshed him. It never ceased to amaze Chance that the more he learned about his wife, the more she fascinated him by revealing unsuspected aspects of her character. One evening he came home early and found her struggling with a pen and paper at the kitchen table. Almost guiltily, Teresa explained that Ramon had been secretly teaching her to read and write. Now she wanted to surprise Chance with a love poem written in her own hand.

Chance was so moved by her eagerness to learn that he promised to finish Ramon's job and teach her other subjects as well. She would need such knowledge to help him manage their business affairs, now that she had truly become his second half.

Teresa zealously threw herself into her studies and learned swiftly, glowing at Chance's encouraging praise. She appreciated the wonderful new stage their marriage had entered but she, like Chance, was so busy that she had little time to think about it. In the fall they moved to the nearly completed Oakmont and shortly afterwards, while Chance was in San Pedro investigating the possibility of canning whale meat, Teresa gave birth to their daughter Beatriz.

Being the father of another girl renewed Chance's desire to regain custody of Vicky Beth. He had written several letters to David, urging him again and again to bring his brood down to Los Angeles. David's evasive replies puzzled and irritated Chance and eventually convinced him that he would have to go to Owens Valley in person if he ever hoped to see Vicky Beth again. But every time he planned to make the trip, other pressing demands forced him to put it off.

In addition to his many business obligations, Chance's happy home life was extremely time-consuming. He and Teresa fell in love with their new ranchhouse and quickly made it the center of southern California social life. The gracious hospitality of Oakmont became internationally famous as its elegantly furnished rooms echoed with the music and laughter of lavish fiestas that impressed even the party-jaded *Californios*. Doña Teresa, blossoming into radiant young matronhood, proved to be an excellent hostess. With charming smiles and subtle control, she kept the guests entertained and left her husband free to discuss business matters with his cronies.

Much of the talk during those discussions consisted of teasing Chance about his newfangled ideas. There was always some one to ask how many Indians had he killed by experimentally feeding them the canned foods that no sensible white person would touch with a ten-foot pole. Only his courtesy as a good host prevented Chance from retorting that the Indians in his employ fared much better than some of his neighbors' workers who were overworked, abused and given poor food and medical care.

The mistreatment and gradual extermination of the state's Indian population was a scandalous disgrace that made Chance feel ashamed of his race. But that was only part of the casual inhumanity of the times. It was a raw lawless era, with the old Indian and Spanish cultures breaking up and vigorous Anglo adventurers crowding in to claim their former possessions. The struggle for individual survival and dominance was so harsh that those who hoped to come out of it victorious could not afford the luxury of worrying about such refinements as justice and compassion. And Chance, feeling that he had done his share of losing, was determined to be a winner in this game.

Chance's winning streak, with only minor setbacks, continued through 1855 and 1856 as light winter rains left thousands of cattle and horses to starve on insufficient grasslands. At the same time, large herds driven overland from Texas and Missouri started to arrive in northern California. The drought and competition marked the beginning of the end of the southland's beef boom. As the *Los Angeles Star* sadly reported: "The flush times have passed—the days of large prices and full pockets are gone."

Unfortunately the *rancheros'* high interest mortgages did not disappear with their full pockets. As they fell hopelessly behind in their payments, moneylenders like Chance

195

had no choice but to foreclose. It pained Chance to take away the lands and homes of some of southern California's most famous founding families, even though the Dons themselves cheerfully reminded him that business is business. Whenever possible, Chance allowed the ex-owners to continue living on the ranchos and operate them for him. That eased his conscience and enabled him to believe Teresa when she told him he really wasn't a greedy, land-grabbing gringo.

Not that Chance entirely neglected his civic duties in his eagerness to increase his own fortune. He had rejoined the Los Angeles Rangers upon returning from Mexico and was given command of a mounted troop. His men proudly called him "Major" in honor of his service with William Walker, although Chance preferred the simple Spanish title Don.

Chance took pride in his work with the volunteer Rangers who, along with the sheriff's office, made up the only effective police force in the crime-ridden county. He just wished that the law courts were equally well organized. More than once, a criminal suspect that Chance's troop had brought in alive was taken from the jail by an angry lynch mob and strung up without the courtesy of a trial. That was another reflection of the times, when justice was tempered with hysteria more often than mercy, and it further convinced Chance that he had been right in moving his family away from the pueblo's rampant violence and vice.

Even so, Chance's efforts to improve Los Angeles were occasionally successful. As a member of the City Council, he played an important part in getting the first schoolhouse built and he helped found the Catholic Orphan Asylum. His proposals for more sanitary water and sewer systems were given serious consideration because of the striking example his own home presented. Oakmont, with its windmill pump and large brick reservoir, was the first building in the southland to have running water. But Chance's plan to have the streets and sidewalks paved was flatly rejected by his fellow Angelenos. What did a little dust or mud matter, they argued, as long as a man had a good horse under him?

* * *

So the days sped past, full of work and happiness, with frequent aggravations and occasional dangers. It seemed to Chance that he scarcely had time to turn around before Miguel and Ramonito were talking a streak and little Beatriz was taking her first steps. Teresa conceived again but miscarried in her third month, somewhat to their relief. Although they both wanted a large family, it was nice to have the bed to themselves for a while, now that they had discovered how much pleasure they could give each other in it. So it was quite a shock to Chance when, one night near the end of the summer of 1856, he was awakened by the sound of Teresa weeping into her pillow.

"What's the matter, darling?" he asked, putting his arm around her.

"It's nothing." Teresa blotted her tears with the sheet. "Go back to sleep. I'm sorry I woke you."

"Don't tell me it's nothing. I want to know what's bothering you."

"Oh, I'm just a silly emotional woman." She gave him a quick hard kiss on his open mouth. "But it's over now. See—I'm smiling again."

Chance cupped her chin with his hand and studied her face in the moonlight. "Something *is* bothering you. Tell me, or I'll beat it out of you." He lightly spanked her bottom through the sheet to support his threat.

Suddenly Teresa burst into fresh sobs and buried her face in his chest. "You don't think I'm a good mother!"

Chance nearly snorted with astonished laughter. "What? That's ridiculous! You're the best mother in the world. The way you look after the boys and Beatriz—"

"No, you think I'm not fit to rear your children. That's why you won't bring Vicky Beth to live with us."

He raised her head from his chest and peered deeply into her eyes. "Oh, sweetheart! It's just the opposite. I was afraid you might not want her here. You know how it is with stepchildren in some families, where they don't feel loved."

"How could I feel that way about her?" Teresa demanded. "She is part of you, which makes her part of me. I have loved her as my very own ever since you first told me about her."

197

Chance crushed her to him, kissing her wet cheeks. "My darling!"

"Then you will bring her to live with us? Soon?"

"Yes. As soon as possible."

"Oh, thank you!" She squirmed on top of him, more excited than he had ever seen her before. "I can't wait for her to arrive! We will all be so happy together!"

"Well, don't get your hopes up too much. She may have forgotten me, after all this time. It'll take a while for us to get used to each other again."

"You worry too much, *querido*. Everything will be perfect."

Chance, feeling his body start to respond to her passion, marveled anew at the endlessly fascinating mystery of a woman's love. How stupid he had been to think that Teresa might not accept Vicky Beth! No, not really stupid—just afraid to lose his last excuse for not going back to reclaim his daughter. Vicky Beth was a living reminder of his old life, and he was not sure he had the nerve to face that again. Even after all these years, the pitiful sound of her thin little voice crying: "Papa, Papa! Come back!" cut deeply into his heart.

But he wouldn't have to worry about that much longer, Chance thought as Teresa began to make vigorous love to him. She had forced him to make up his mind about Vicky Beth and, however things worked out, he would always be grateful to her for that.

Chapter 20

The sharpened bone fragment worked slowly on the obsidian, probing and prying into a tiny crack. As the chip of glassy rock flaked off, the bone's point snapped.

Hu-pwi sighed and picked up another piece of bone. Making arrow heads the old way was tedious work, but the white man's iron was not suitable for the hunting task he had in mind. Only a stone point could slay *tuvee-che*, the badger. And only a badger skin possessed powerful enough medicine to ward off the evil spirits that often killed newborn babies, as they had killed the son that Seyavi had borne the year before. Now she was pregnant again and when this child arrived, Hu-pwi would wrap it in a fresh badger pelt to enable it to cling tenaciously to life with the animal's stubborn spirit.

Perhaps he would kill two badgers, Hu-pwi thought, as he worked patiently beside the bubbling spring in the midst of Black Rocks. Then he could protect Rebekah's next baby, too. Her second child, a sickly girl, had died only a few weeks after he and Seyavi had lost their son. Remembering how the two women had comforted each other at that time, Hu-pwi glanced up at the nearest cave in the tumbled lava mass. But the deep shadows concealed Seyavi, Rebekah, and Bobby Buck from view.

Hu-pwi reflected on the strange ways of women. One would have thought Rebekah would be as curious and excited as everyone else by the news of Don Chance's return to Owens Valley. When David Wheeler had read his friend's latest letter to his Paiute neighbors, they had looked forward to welcoming back the white man who had become an important figure among his people. But Rebekah had taken her son and fled to this remote corner of the valley.

Seyavi had insisted on accompanying Rebekah and, after a bitter argument, Hu-pwi had gone along to look after them. He was sure that Seyavi knew the cause of Rebekah's alarm, but she refused to give him that information even when threatened with a beating. It was an empty threat, of course. Hu-pwi was much too easy-going to raise his hand to Seyavi. But still the incident left him feeling hurt, confused, and—for the first time in his life—jealous. The secretive intimacy between his wife and Rebekah made him feel like an outsider.

While he was brooding over that, Seyavi came out of the cave to fetch water from the spring. Because it wasn't seemly for a Paiute brave to let on that a woman could bother him, Hu-pwi bent his head over his arrow-making and pretended not to notice her.

At the rear of the cave, Rebekah huddled over a flickering candle and told Bobby Buck about David and Goliath. Her back was cold against the rock wall but her eyes glittered feverishly and sweat ran down her bold nose as she tried to keep her fidgety son entertained.

"I wanna go out and play," the little boy whined.

"We will play in here," Rebekah said. "We will pretend that there are enemy warriors outside and we must hide from them until your father comes to fight them."

"Will he cut off their heads, the way David did to Goliath?"

"Yes. And chop them into tiny pieces."

Bobby Buck smiled happily. "Good! Let's play that."

Rebekah held the boy tightly to her, stroking his thick black curls. If only Chance could see how much his son resembled him. . . . No! She must not let herself think about that. Already her mind was twisted to the breaking point with painful guilt over the way she had escaped being reclaimed by her rightful owner.

After so many years of alternately hoping for and dreading Chance's return, Rebekah could hardly believe that she had been able to defy the strongest urge of her servile soul. Perhaps the death of her daughter and the fear that she and David might not have any more children had given her the courage to make a stand here in this natural stronghold of the Paiutes. Or perhaps it was simply that she, like Teresa, had grown into a mature woman capable of thinking and acting for herself. Whatever the reason, Rebekah knew now that she loved David so much that she would do anything to remain in the valley with him, even if that meant stealing herself and Bobby Buck away from Chance.

But her stubborn resolve often melted away in unguarded moments when Chance's overpowering memory left her weak with desire. Rebekah could only endure those moments of agonized yearning by clinging to her son and praying to Jesus.

Rebekah might have lost much of her fear if she had known how far she was from Chance's thoughts when he made his triumphal return to Owens Valley. With Jeremy Starr, three *vaqueros*, and a sizable pack train, Chance had journeyed up the San Joaquin Valley to the Kern River and crossed the Sierra at Walker Pass. That route bypassed the most desolate stretch of the desert trail north of Los Angeles, but the searing wind that greeted them when they left the mountains told them how much the Mojave had suffered in the recent drought.

Indian runners and smoke signals sped the news of the travelers' approach up the valley to David, who was too impatient to wait for Chance to reach him. He bridled one of his plow horses and rode south, with Vicky Beth and D.C. tagging along on her pony. They found Chance's party surrounded by a hundred or more Paiutes eager to see the famous white chief they had heard so much about. But Jeremy was much more interesting to those who had never seen a black man before. They watched him curiously, wondering if his color would rub off.

David reined up alongside Chance's horse and greeted his old friend with a crushing handshake and a hug around the neck. Then they both sat back and looked at each other with durnfool grins all over their faces.

"Well, doggone if you didn't finally come back after all," David said. "Well, doggone!"

"You didn't think I'd let you keep this valley all to yourself, did you, Davy?" Chance joshed. His gaze went beyond David to the wild-haired girl who sat easily astride a sorrel pony and stared at him with the bold impersonality of an Indian.

At twelve, Vicky Beth's body was a long string of rawhide knotted to thin, work-toughened arms and legs. The homemade dress she was rapidly outgrowing would hardly have covered her knees, even if the horse's back had not hiked it up to mid-thigh. Though still boyish in face and figure, she displayed the striking features that would soon make her outstanding even among *Californio* beauties. Chance may have missed the family resemblance in her mouth and chin, but the enormous blue eyes she had gotten from her mother were unmistakable. D.C.—soon to be seven but still roundfaced with baby fat—sat behind her with his eyes downcast in the presence of strangers.

David saw where Chance was looking and walked his horse backward to clear the space between them. "I don't reckon I have to tell you who this young lady is," he smiled.

"Hello, Princess," Chance said, trying to keep the nervous uncertainty out of his voice. "You're growing up just as pretty as I knew you would."

"Hello, Papa."

Vicky Beth's tone was as flat as her stare. For a long time she had dreamed of this moment, of the vengeful pleasure she would derive from telling her father how much she hated him for the hurt he had caused her. But time and the Paiutes had taught her that it is better to accept fate unfeelingly when you can't do anything about it. She had learned how to punish an enemy with the cruelest weapon of all—indifference.

"I think a kiss might make us both feel better," Chance suggested, spurring his stallion over to her pony. Her long lashes fluttered against his cheek, but her lips remained tightly pursed even after he raised his head and smiled down at her. "Reminds me of the first time I kissed your mother."

"Did *she* ever get to like it?" Vicky Beth shot back.

Chance stared at his daughter, thinking of the stubborn broncs he had broken at the ranch. He and Teresa certainly had their work cut out for them. He turned to D.C. and rumpled his tangled blond mop.

"And this must be the Halloween boy. How are you, Pumpkin?"

"Fine, sir," D.C. answered shyly.

"Give your Uncle Chance a kiss," David ordered.

"Men don't kiss," Chance chided David. "They shake hands. Put 'er there, partner."

D.C. blushed with the pride of being treated as a man for the first time in his life. Jeremy and the *vaqueros* laughed as Chance took hold of the boy's small hand and pretended to be hurt by his grip.

"That's a fine-looking pony," Chance observed. "What's his name?"

"Coso," D.C. answered. "It means fire in Paiute."

"Yes, I can see the fire in his eye. I bet he's a fast one. Are you a good rider?"

"Pretty fair, sir. But not as good as Vicky Beth. She can go like nobody's business."

Chance cocked an eye at the girl. "That a fact? Then how about a race? Say to that lone pine tree over yonder and back."

"It wouldn't be fair," Vicky Beth answered. "Your horse looks tired."

"Old Chulo tired? Why, he's fresh as a daisy."

Vicky Beth hesitated, playing with Coso's ears, then nodded. "All right. Get down, D.C."

"Wait." Chance reached out and swung the boy over to his mount. "You're riding bareback, so I ought to have a handicap, too." He looked at David. "Is that all right with you?"

David laughed. "Go ahead. After all the deviltry them two've been through, I don't see how you can hurt 'em any."

The racers lined up and Jeremy set them off with a wave of his neckerchief. Chance gave Vicky Beth a lead of three lengths before putting the spurs to Chulo and telling D.C. to "Hang on tight, partner!"

D.C. grabbed Chance's belt with both hands as the big stallion lunged forward. His face was pressed against Chance's back and the feel of the hard muscular body filled him with a sense of excitement and security he had never known before. When they drew abreast of Vicky Beth and Coso, he felt a wild thrill and cried out to Chance to go faster. His devotion to Vicky Beth was as strong as ever, but he was riding with a *man* now and they couldn't let a mere girl beat them.

They rounded the pine and pounded back toward their cheering companions. Vicky Beth lay almost flat along Coso's back with her face in his wind-whipped mane and her bare heels kicking his flanks. Chance watched her with surging pride. What a woman she was going to be! If she and her horse had been properly trained for racing, she would have given him a run for his money.

Chance came in two lengths ahead of Vicky Beth and swept off his hat to her in the *caballero*'s salute. "Bravo, Princess! Now we'll walk the horses a ways to cool them down."

Vicky Beth's eyes sparkled in her flushed face and for an instant she came close to smiling at her father. Then she remembered herself and wiped off the expression as she slid down from Coso's back. Chance dismounted and lifted D.C. to the ground. Holding their horses' reins, they ambled along as the motley procession of cowboys, Indians and horses resumed its northward trek.

"We beat you," D.C. said smugly to Vicky Beth.

"Not by much," she retorted.

"You might've won, if you'd done the right thing to your pony," Chance said.

"What's that?"

"Talk to him. A horse needs encouragement. Tell him he's the fastest thing on four legs, and he'll try to live up to it."

Vicky Beth gave him a puzzled look, wondering how she was going to hate someone who talked to horses.

* * *

204

Chance spent only five days in Owens Valley, much to David's disappointment. David would have done anything to keep him there longer, although he sympathized with Chance's explanation that he had to get back and take care of his own affairs. But David allowed none of the time to go to waste. He used every daylight hour to show the visitors around the valley, modestly embarrassed but pleased as punch by Chance's compliments on his accomplishments.

Chance and his men were greatly impressed by David's irrigation system, judging his cultivated crops and fruit and nut trees the equal of any they had seen in California. They were impressed that he had gotten so much done with just the aid of Indians. David didn't think there was anything remarkable about that; he had always had a knack for getting along with people.

In the evenings they sat out under the stars, smoking and catching up on each other's lives and yarning about old times. Vicky Beth listened silently, trying to appear disinterested even when Chance and David discussed her mother. But D.C. was enthralled by the men's talk, asking endless questions until he fell asleep in Chance's lap or curled up at his feet with the dogs.

David apologized to Chance for his wife's absence. He couldn't understand why Rebekah had taken Bobby Buck and gone off to visit her Paiute friends when she knew company was coming. Probably it was just one of her strange heathen ways that she hadn't got shut of yet.

Chance told David not to let it bother him. He would have liked to have seen the rest of David's family, but he really didn't remember much about Rebekah except her oversized nose. His intense happiness with Teresa made it easy for him to forget the other women in his life. Also, it would have troubled Chance's conscience to recall that he had made love to a timid Indian girl who was now his best friend's wife. Therefore his mind had compassionately buried the memory so deeply that it never occurred to him that anyone but David could have fathered Bobby Buck.

But there were plenty of other Indians around. Several Paiutes, including the simple-minded Wongata, had attached themselves to David as full-time retainers. Under Winnedumah's supervision they performed field and household chores in exchange for food, clothing and whatever other items David could spare. The old woman was a stern taskmaster, particularly with Wongata, whom she treated as her personal servant.

As David's family had increased and Winnedumah had grown more irritably antisocial, she had moved out of the farmhouse to a small cabin near the river's edge. Wongata lived in a nearby wickiup, constantly at her beck and call to carry wood and water or serve tea when Lightning Tracker or some other acquaintance dropped in. Advancing rheumatism had forced Winnedumah to walk with a cane and she didn't hesitate to apply it to Wongata's back when he failed to step lively enough to suit her. Wongata accepted her bullying and beatings with his unshakable good-natured grin, which made her even more furious with him. At least Rebekah had given her the satisfaction of crying and begging for mercy when she was whipped.

Seeing Chance again only added more fuel to Winnedumah's consuming bitterness and self-pity, as she thought of the good life she could have had if Rebekah had married him instead of David. She was tempted to tell Chance the truth about Bobby Buck, just to be spiteful. But she feared Rebekah's vengeance now that the girl had outgrown her domination, thanks to David's support. That was another example of how men—especially white men—were responsible for all of her troubles, Winnedumah believed. What a curse it was to be born female in this world! That she also derived a sense of fulfillment and worth from belonging to David's family—however tenuous the relationship—was something Winnedumah would never have admitted, even to herself. Loving and caring for others were womanly weaknesses that men had always exploited. Now Winnedumah was determined to be the exploiter.

Her favorite victim, next to Wongata, was Lightning Tracker. The old chief's unrequited love for Winnedumah had grown over the years, making him vulnerable to her sharp tongue. Winnedumah took sadistic pleasure in teasing and browbeating Lightning Tracker with her superior knowledge of the world. Then she would send him home to take out his frustration on his wife. It was a paltry reward for her years of subjugation and hardship, but Winnedumah made the most of it.

Chance, sensing Winnedumah's resentment, managed to placate her with gifts of tobacco, coffee, sugar and other luxuries. Nor was she the only Indian to benefit from the heavy burdens borne by Chance's pack animals. The day after his arrival, Chance gave a feast for David's neighbors and handed out all manner of useful trade goods—knives, axes, cooking pots, blankets, trinkets. He had also brought a good supply of new farm tools and seeds for David, along with some guns and powder and lead. For Rebekah there were bolts of brightly colored cloth and sewing gear, which David said she would be tickled pink to get. D.C. and Bobby Buck received new clothes and boots they could grow into, as well as books, marbles, spinning tops and other playthings. But the gift that most fascinated D.C. was a small globe of the earth. David had explained to him that the world was round, but still D.C. couldn't understand why the people living at the bottom didn't fall off.

Naturally Vicky Beth gained the most from her father's bounty. Teresa had selected several fine dresses of different sizes that she thought would fit a girl of twelve, with plenty of underwear, shoes, and accouterments. There was even a parasol to protect a proper young lady's fair complexion from the sun—which made Chance smile when he looked into his daughter's deeply tanned face. Vicky Beth accepted her presents with polite disinterest. Chance, observing her devotion to Coso, guessed the best way to reach her.

"It's not good to ride bareback, Princess," he said. "When we get home I'll order a new saddle for your pony."

Vicky Beth's eyes flashed with pleasure, before she remembered that the "home" her father spoke of was not of the valley she had grown to love.

The feast was a great success. At sunset the Paiutes started homeward with full bellies, praising the generosity of the wealthy white chief.

"Seemed like we had every Indian in the valley here today," Chance remarked to David.

"Not quite all of 'em. You recollect Paul the Apostle?"

"Can't say I do."

"The one you got the mules off of."

"Oh, him. Is he still around?"

"Uh-huh. He lives in a canyon a few miles up north, with about twenty other renegades. Most of 'em came over from the other side of the mountains after their tribes got busted up in wars with the whites. They're a surly bunch and the Paiutes are scared of 'em, but they haven't done no harm yet."

"Well, if I were you, I'd keep the door bolted and my guns loaded anyway," Chance said, thinking of the occasional Indian troubles he had had over the years. Roving bands of desert tribesmen still swept down from the hills to steal horses and cattle from the ranchos around Los Angeles.

Chance had intended to try to persuade David to move down to Los Angeles. But a visit to the small graveyard behind the house changed his mind.

"Look who's here, Margaret," David said, hunkering down beside his first wife's grave. "Didn't I tell you he'd come back to us? Took him a little longer than we expected, but ain't that Chance all over? You used to say he was like a boy walking to school—he could always find more interesting things to do along the way."

Chance stood by awkwardly, feeling like an intruder. Gradually it dawned on him that David really believed Margaret could hear his words. Not that David was insane. Chance was sure David understood that Margaret's physical remains lay under the soil. But that did not interfere with the spiritual bonds between them. Chance thought of offering to have the body transported to Los Angeles and reburied there, but he sensed that David's attachment to Owens Valley went much deeper than Margaret's grave.

David looked up and saw that Chance had finally come to understand what he had known all along.

When Chance had passed through the valley before he had paid little attention to its natural resources. Now he and his *vaqueros*, ever alert for good cattle country, took

208

special interest in the sprawling grasslands along the river and its tributary streams.

"You could fatten a thousand head around here in no time at all," Chance pointed out to David one morning as they rested their horses on a high vantage point with good views up and down the valley. Around them, Jeremy and the *vaqueros* nodded in agreement.

"Yes, I s'pose the stockmen over the mountains'll find that out someday," David said. "Be a shame to see 'em trample so much good plow land, though."

Chance smiled. "It'll only be a shame if somebody else does it first. Why don't I send you up some of my best heifers and a bull or two, come next spring? In a few years you could build up a sizable herd."

"Why, that's mighty kind of you, Chance. But I don't know anything about raising beef cows."

"There's nothing to it, if you have enough Indians to do the heavy work. A couple of my men could teach your Paiutes the ropes."

"Major, I'd sho like to have that job, if'n y'all don' mind me leavin' the store," Jeremy said softly.

Chance looked at the mulatto in surprise. "Well, sure, Jeremy, if you think you can handle it. But why do you want to mess with something as ornery and nasty as a bunch of cows, when you're doing so well as a storekeeper?"

Jeremy ducked his head self-consciously under the other men's stares. "Well, suh, I 'preciates everythin' y'all've done for me. But I got a hankerin' to have a place of my own, an' the land hereabouts is mighty sweet. So I figgered if'n I help Mr. Wheeler with his stock, he'll help me with the writin' to take out a homestead."

"Sure thing, Jeremy," David grinned. "I'd be proud to have you for a neighbor."

"I'll hate to lose you," Chance said. "But if that's what you really want, I'll give you all the help I can to get settled here."

Jeremy beamed happily. "Thank you, suh."

They rode on without discussing the matter further. Chance could easily guess why Jeremy wanted to move away from Los Angeles. He had been secretly courting a

Californio girl named Maria Rivas and rumor had it that they planned to elope soon. In former times a mixed marriage would not have caused too great a scandal. But Los Angeles had lost much of its racial tolerance as large numbers of emigrants from the southern states had settled there. There had been angry clashes between pro- and anti-slavery factions and although no black man had ever been lynched in the pueblo, Jeremy was wise in deciding he didn't want to risk being the first one.

The more Chance thought about Jeremy moving to Owens Valley, the more it pleased him. Having two good friends living here would give him an opportunity to become firmly established in the valley, in case that should ever turn out to be an advantage.

During their yarning session that evening, Chance and David discussed the brand design for David's future cattle empire. David liked the way Chance had adapted the Rancho Agua Fria's joined initals mark—Æ—by enclosing it with a large C— Æ. After scratching and erasing several possible brands in the dirt, David took a stick and drew

"A wheel and arrow, for Wheeler and his Indian friends," Chance said, after studying the design critically. "Not bad, Davy."

"It means more than just that, Chance. I got the idea from a Paiute water sign. An Indian'll put an arrow on the ground pointed to the nearest waterhole, then make a magic circle of stones around it to keep anything from disturbing it."

"Then it's all the more appropriate. That's your brand, Davy. Don't change it a bit."

David took Chance's advice and the Circle Arrow Spread became symbolic of the Wheeler family's special relationship with the Paiutes throughout much of Owens Valley's history.

Chapter 21

"D.C. Wheeler, you come down from there this instant," Vicky Beth ordered, standing at the foot of the huge oak with her fists on her hips. "I'm not gonna wait all day for you."

She peered up into the tree's mass of twisted limbs and leafy shadows, unable to see the boy in the poor light of the rosy dawn. She had been on her feet since well before the day's first light, packing her things for the journey to Los Angeles with her father, and she had no patience for D.C.'s sulkiness. When David had discovered that the boy was not present to say goodbye to the travelers, he had searched all over the house and barn for him. But Vicky Beth knew that the oak, which had always been their playhouse and sanctuary in troubled times, was where he would be found.

"And don't pretend you ain't up there," she said. "I could hear you a mile off, making more noise than any squirrel or bird."

There was a long silence, then the sound of rustling leaves halfway up the tree as D.C.'s voice called petulantly: "Go away!"

"I'm not going anyplace until you come down here and act like a gentleman. Or else I'll climb up there and throw you down."

There was another long silence, while Vicky Beth waited confidently. She knew that D.C. knew that she didn't make idle threats. Finally the leaves trembled again and D.C. came swinging down between the branches, stopping at the low massive limb that nearly touched the ground. Standing on the limb raised his eyes several inches above hers, although normally she was a head taller. D.C. used the lofty viewpoint to look down his nose at her with a careless sneer belied by his tear-stained cheeks.

"I'm glad you're going away," he said fiercely. "I hope you never come back!"

"Why would I want to come back to a stinkhole like this?" Vicky Beth retorted. "I can't wait to shake its dust off my heels."

D.C. glared at her for another half-minute, then his eyes filled with fresh tears and he started to snivel. "But *why* can't you stay with us?" he whined.

Vicky Beth put her arms around him and swung him to the ground. "Hush, honey. You know why. It's been 'splained to you enough times."

She took his hand and they started walking around the pond of irrigation water toward the house. The pond's dead surface reflected the Sierra's gray face, while the eastern sky brightened at the sun's approach from behind the Inyo Range. D.C. wiped his eyes with the back of his free hand.

"Now dry up," Vicky Beth said. "How can you expect to grow up like a Paiute brave if you're a big crybaby?"

D.C. reluctantly dragged his feet and kicked at dirt clods as Vicky Beth hauled him along. It was only the day before, when Chance and his men had started preparing for their return to Los Angeles, that D.C. had felt the full impact of his inevitable parting from Vicky Beth. Up till then it had been an abstract idea that he could easily keep out of his mind. Now it was horrifyingly real.

How could they possibly get along without Vicky Beth? As far back as D.C. could remember, she had always been there, a big sister protecting and taking care of him and Bobby Buck. If she were taken from them, perhaps the world would come to an end, since Vicky Beth was as much a part of D.C.'s world as the river and the valley and

the vast sky above them. Uncle Chance just *had* to understand how important it was for her to remain with them.

But Uncle Chance had been too busy to listen to the
boy's pleas. So D.C. had turned to his father. David had
patiently tried to make his son understand that Vicky Beth
was a member of Chance's family, so it was only right and
proper that she live with him. Even Vicky Beth agreed
with that, despite her lack of enthusiasm for it, when D.C.
tried to talk her out of leaving. He had carried on his argument until after bedtime, and then spent the night weeping
and tossing with bad dreams. Waking early, he had slipped
out of the house and made his way to the oak. Hidden in
the dark security of the tree's embrace, he had tried to ease
his pain through hatred. But how could he hate those he
loved?

Suddenly D.C. halted and pulled Vicky Beth around to
face him. "Don't go with him," he begged. "You don't have
to."

"You know I have to," she replied. "He's my papa."

"No. We can run away." His heart raced with desperate
excitement. "We'll find Bobby Buck. Then we all can go
live in Shoshone Land. They'll never find us there!"

Vicky Beth smiled sadly, wishing she still shared D.C.'s
childish belief in Shoshone Land, the magical fairy tale
world where all dreams are fulfilled. But her rapidly ma-
turing mind had lost many of its illusions over the past few
years and she doubted that there were any safe refuges
from reality in this life. Not even Owens Valley, where she
had always felt happy and secure, had been able to protect
her from her father.

Her fearful apprehension had started building when
David had first told her that Chance was coming for her.
She had never forgiven Chance for his double betrayal of
taking her away from her mother and then leaving her
here when he went on to the gold fields. Her bitter resentment had increased over the years until she was convinced
that she hated Chance and could never accept him as her
father. If only she were grown up enough to choose her
own way in life, instead of being subject to her parent's
will! Already she was stronger and braver than many

213

Paiute youths of her age. In a few more years she would have been able to take care of herself as well as any man could.

But Vicky Beth was woman enough to respond to Chance's powerful masculine appeal, although she was too stubborn to admit it. Even David, a good father figure in his own right, paled in comparison to the rich, handsome, dashing horseman who had ridden back into her life like the shining knight of a fantasy. There was an air of romantic mystery about Chance; a tantalizing hint of faraway places and exciting adventures that aroused Vicky Beth's imagination even more than the tales of Shoshone Land.

Vicky Beth told herself that she was going with Chance only because she had no choice; it was a daughter's duty to obey her father. But would she have tried harder to resist that obligation if she hadn't been fascinated by Chance and the new life he promised her? Her feelings were so mixed up that she couldn't understand them herself, let alone explain them to D.C.

"Look here," she said. "I have to go with my papa now. But when I grow up I'll come back and we'll find Shoshone Land together."

D.C. looked as if he were going to cry again. Then he manfully decided that half a loaf was better than none. "Promise?"

"I promise."

"Cross your heart and hope to die?"

Vicky Beth solemnly took the oath and drew a cross over her heart with her right forefinger. They walked on toward the house, but D.C. wasn't quite finished with the subject.

"If you don't come back, I'll come to get you," he vowed.

"If I don't come back, I'll be dead," she reminded him. "That's what it means when you say 'hope to die.' "

"Oh." D.C. felt much better. Death was something he could understand.

Chance and his men were ready to mount up when Vicky Beth and D.C. reached the house. The moment of departure brought Chance and David close to revealing their emotions. D.C. lost several more tears and one of the

214

Indian women who had helped raise Vicky Beth wept loudly. But Vicky Beth's eyes were dry as she rode away on Coso at her father's side. She had decided long ago that she would never again cry over things that couldn't be helped.

Four days later Rebekah and Bobby Buck came home. David scolded Rebekah for her strange absence and told her how much she had missed by not being there during Chance's visit. Rebekah listened with downcast eyes, offering no explanation for her behavior. David hadn't thought she would. Finally he sighed and dropped the subject. No sense beating a dead horse. These contrary Indians would always be a puzzle to him, no matter how well he got to know them.

Their lives soon fell back into their familiar humdrum patterns, except for the constant painful reminders that Vicky Beth was no longer with them. Bobby Buck thought he would miss her the most, because she had been his guardian angel against D.C. But D.C. quickly discovered that teasing and picking on his half-brother wasn't as much fun without his big sister around to tell him to stop it. The boys became fast friends and were pleased to learn that by working together they could get into twice as much mischief as before.

Rebekah greatly admired the gifts Chance had brought. But it was a long time before she was able to touch them.

Vicky Beth found no poetry in Los Angeles, and little else that lived up to her father's glowing description of it. After having been prepared for a fabulous city of Arabian Nights splendor, she was even more disillusioned than Chance had been when he first saw the squalid pueblo. And she had a better reason to be disappointed. The school year was about to commence when they reached Rancho Agua Fria and Chance insisted on enrolling her in the new schoolhouse at Second and Spring Streets.

After the wild freedom she had enjoyed in Owens Valley, being confined to a crowded classroom several hours a day was unbearable torture. Because she had received only a sketchy home education from David, she was placed in the second grade. She learned quickly, but the humiliation of being made to sit with younger children compounded her misery. She became sullen and withdrawn, feeling more than ever that she didn't fit in with her new surroundings.

Having lived apart from her own race for so long, Vicky Beth was uncomfortable with Anglos, and her lack of Spanish prevented her from making friends among the *Californios*. Even the Indians seemed alien and unresponsive to her familiarity with their ways. Being a lone, friendless outsider made her the natural prey of schoolyard bullies— but only once. On her second day at school she was surrounded on the playground by several older pupils who tauntingly asked her how she liked being with the wetpants babies in the second grade.

Vicky Beth would probably have been reduced to tears by her tormentors, if a heavyset girl had not made the mistake of trying to push her backwards over a boy who had crouched down behind her legs. Vicky Beth was only defenseless to hurtful words; physical violence was something she understood perfectly. She tore into the heavyset girl with fists, feet, teeth and nails and drove her screaming from the playground. After that the other students respected Vicky Beth's angry demand to be left alone. She didn't want any friends, she told herself, and almost believed it. The only bright spot in the ordeal was that she got to ride Coso to and from school.

Her experiences at home were not much happier, due to her stubborn determination not to give Chance the satisfaction of thinking that she liked him even a little bit. Teresa had warmly welcomed Vicky Beth and insisted on calling her *hija*—daughter. Miguel, Ramonito, and Beatriz were lively little rascals who poignantly reminded Vicky Beth of D.C. and Bobby Buck, and the countless members of the Esperanza clan did all they could to make her feel one of them. But Vicky Beth remained coolly aloof. She was polite and respectful to her elders, performed her share of the household chores and did whatever else was expected of her. But she never let Chance and Teresa forget that she was an unwilling guest in their home.

It was only when she was with animals that Vicky Beth

was able to relax and be herself. She soon made friends with all of the horses, dogs, cats, and even some of the wild creatures on the ranch. She was fascinated by the untamed range cattle and the leathery men who handled them with skillful ease. Her every spare moment was spent with Si Darcy and the *vaqueros*, learning the infinite details of their work and helping them with it when they let her. The ranch hands affectionately tolerated the lanky girl and patiently answered her endless stream of questions.

Si grew particularly fond of Vicky Beth. He called her "Sis" and taught her how to throw *la reata* both Texas style, with a wide loop that could encircle an entire cow, and *Californio* fashion, with a loop small enough to snag a calf's hind leg. Once she was even privileged to witness the *vaquero*'s most impressively daring roping feat—the capture of a killer grizzly bear.

After slaying several cattle, the bear was tracked down and cornered in a box canyon. Three times *El Oso*'s neck was lassoed by the darting horsemen. Twice the raging beast chewed through the tough rawhide lines, before he was thrown to the ground where other *reatas* quickly snared his legs, while Vicky Beth watched excitedly at a safe distance. Then the securely bound grizzly was loaded onto a *carreta* and hauled off to the plaza bullring to provide Angelenos with their favorite Sunday afternoon entertainment, *la Batalla del Oso y el Toro*—the Fight of the Bear and the Bull.

Vicky Beth thought that an unfitting end for the noble beast. But she could not deny her pleasure when her own roping and riding skills earned her the supreme compliment from Si that she was "just like one of the boys."

Si had continued to manage Rancho Agua Fria after its ownership had passed from Don Carlos to Chance. Which was fortunate for Chance, who doubted that the place could survive without the likable Texan's ranching savvy and ability to command the *vaqueros*' loyalty. Chance had offered Si a partnership in the ranch, which Si had refused by saying that he didn't want to be tied down. That was about what Chance would have expected from such an independent cuss.

The company of Si and the *vaqueros* was all that made

Vicky Beth's new life tolerable, once she had given up hope of running away and finding her way back to the freedom of Owens Valley. Uncle David would probably just send her back anyway, she sadly concluded. So she resigned herself to daydreaming of Shoshone Land and learning the ways of the rancheros. That relieved much of her unhappiness, until one day when Chance caught her behind the stable taking a smoking break with Si and three of his men.

The *vaqueros*, with the inborn stealth of their Indian blood, silently faded away. Vicky Beth wished she could do likewise, as she frantically threw down her *cigarrillo* and stepped on it under her father's blank stare. She could not hold back a wave of cold fear that tied her stomach in knots. But at the same time she felt a thrill at having brought her defiance of Chance's authority out in the open. Let him punish her. She would show him that she could take it.

"Well," Chance said at last. "Has this been going on long?"

"Don't get the wrong idea," Si began. "We was just—"

"I'm talking to my daughter," Chance curtly cut him off.

"Don't blame Si," Vicky Beth said. "It's all my fault. I've been smoking since I was eight."

"Indeed? With your Uncle David's permission?"

"Yes, sir. I mean, no, sir. Uh, well, you see . . ."

Vicky Beth was disgusted with her frightened blushing and stammering. How her Paiute friends would laugh if they could see her now!

"I think you'd better go to your room," Chance decided. "I'll be in shortly to settle this with you."

Vicky Beth hesitated and shot a sidelong glance at Si, who urged her along with a slight nod. With a mumbled, "Yes, Papa," she turned and hurried away. Chance looked at Si with a puzzled expression, feeling more betrayed and hurt than angry.

"Si, what in God's name possessed you to—"

"Easy, Chance. It was just corn silk. You know I wouldn't let a kid touch tobacco."

"I don't care what it was. You had no right letting her sneak around behind my back and do it."

"Well, I figgered it was better to have her do it here at home, where me and the boys could make sure she didn't get into real trouble."

"I'll be the one to figure what's best for her. I'm her father."

"And you're my boss," Si said levelly. "So we both gotta do what you say. But only so long as we're in your outfit."

Chance came close to telling Si that if he didn't like working there, he knew what he could do about it. But his strong affection and respect for Si helped him hold his tongue. Besides, Si was not one to take such a challenge lightly. He couldn't be pushed any more than he could be bought, especially when he thought he was right.

"Hell, Si, I'm just trying to raise her to be a civilized lady," Chance said in softer tones. "And that's not easy, when she won't let me get close to her."

Si's features relaxed as he felt the tension between them ease. "I reckon I know a heap more about raisin' horses and cows than kids," he admitted. "But I'll tell you one thing—that filly's got more gumption than most colts. If you don't let her get it out of her system now, she'll be a handful when she grows up."

"Maybe you're right," Chance conceded. "But at least I can see to it that she doesn't grow up smoking, even if I have to take a strap to her."

"That's one way to get close to her," Si grinned as Chance turned and started toward the house.

"And after this, let me know when she misbehaves," Chance called over his shoulder.

"Right, boss."

Teresa was waiting for Chance when he entered the house. She had known something was wrong when Vicky Beth had come in and gone straight to her room without speaking to anyone. Chance told her what had happened, concluding with: "I've never laid a hand on her before, but this is different. She has to learn that she can't have everything her way."

"Please don't whip her," Teresa begged. "Let me handle it. I am sure I can get her to see reason."

"I think she already knows *how* to act reasonably," Chance said. "She just doesn't *want* to."

"Even so, I would like to talk to her first."

Chance hesitated. He wanted very much to be relieved of the ordeal of punishing Vicky Beth, but he felt it was his duty. For a long moment he peered into Teresa's pleading eyes, then decided that duty could wait a little longer.

"All right. But tell her that I'm at the end of my patience. If she pulls something like this again—"

"Thank you, darling!" Teresa rose on her toes to give him a quick kiss, then hurried off to Vicky Beth's room.

Chance stared after her, wondering if he actually could have brought himself to whip Vicky Beth.

Vicky Beth was sitting on her bed gazing out the window when Teresa knocked on her door and entered the room without waiting for an invitation.

"Your father is very concerned about you," Teresa said.

Vicky Beth did not indicate that she had heard her stepmother.

"We all think very highly of you," Teresa went on. "I wish you could be happy with us."

"You've treated me fair and square," Vicky Beth said flatly. "I got nothing against you."

"Thank you. But I would like you to feel more than that for me, now that we are both in the same family."

"Do you want me to call you Mama?"

Teresa smiled sadly, remembering what Chance had told her about Vicky Beth's mother. "No, that would not be right. But if we tried to get to know each other better—"

Vicky Beth jerked her head around to look at Teresa. "Is Papa gonna whip me?"

"Perhaps. I asked him to let me talk to you first."

"I'd rather be whipped then preached to."

"Perhaps you will get both," Teresa said shortly, and instantly regretted that she had let the girl provoke her.

Vicky Beth stood up and walked over to the cedar chest where she kept her personal belongings. On top of the chest lay her raggedy black doll, Liza Jane, the only thing from her earliest childhood that had lasted all these years. Vicky Beth picked up the doll and solemnly rocked it in her arms.

"Do you think I'm preaching to you?" Teresa asked.

"I dunno."

"Did your Uncle David preach to you?"

"Sometimes. On Sundays."

"Did he ever whip you when you were bad?"

"Uncle David?" Vicky Beth almost smiled at the thought. "No. He wouldn't hurt a fly."

"Well, I think your father will not whip you, if you promise that you will never smoke again."

Vicky Beth went to the bed and fell back on it, holding the doll at arm's length above her head. "Papa smokes."

"Of course. But he is a man."

"I wonder if he had to kill somebody to be a man," Vicky Beth mused. "That's how it is in some Indian tribes. Not the Paiutes, though. With them, a boy becomes a man when he can take a wife."

"It takes a real man to be a good husband," Teresa agreed.

"I'll never get married," Vicky Beth said confidently. "It hurts."

"Hurts?"

"Yes. Seyavi told me. It hurts when a man goes into a woman's—"

"You are too young to be talking about that." Teresa shuddered at the thought of what the poor child must have witnessed in the camps of savage Indians.

"Bulls do it to cows," Vicky Beth insisted. "It's how all of God's creatures beget, Uncle David said."

"Yes, it is nature's way, and when you are old enough—"

"Does Papa still hurt you that way?"

Teresa caught her breath and peered sternly at the girl on the bed. "I must go start supper now. You will stay here until you are ready to promise your father that you will never smoke again."

Teresa left the room feeling frustrated. Vicky Beth had deliberately antagonized her until she had taken repressive action, thereby giving the girl another excuse to wallow in self-pity and the belief that her parents were persecuting her. Why did she let herself be taken in by such common children's tricks, Teresa wondered, when she wanted so desperately to win Vicky Beth's love? If only the sullen girl could see how her heart ached to reach out to her! But she must not give up hope. There had to be some way to reach Vicky Beth, and Teresa was determined to find it.

Teresa's problems with Vicky Beth had started early. When Chance had ordered the gift he had promised Vicky Beth, Teresa had insisted it must be a sidesaddle. There was only one acceptable way for a lady to sit a horse, Teresa maintained, as Vicky Beth argued in vain the advantages of riding astride.

Teresa well understood Vicky Beth's preference. That was why she adamantly denied it to her. Teresa had grown up straddling half-broken mustangs, like her brothers. She knew the thrilling power of squeezing her thighs around hot laboring sides, and the strange excitement produced by the friction of a saddle or a horse's bare back against her body. Many times she had finished an exhilarating ride trembling with nervous tension that ached to be released in a way she did not understand. The puzzling sensation had become almost unbearable until the day, shortly before she turned fourteen, when her mother had seen her dismount after an invigorating canter with her gaze fixed hungrily on a handsome young *vaquero*. The next day Teresa was given a sidesaddle and sternly commanded to use it.

Like Vicky Beth, Teresa had felt cheated and bewildered at being deprived of a right that her brothers took for granted. It wasn't fair that boys were allowed so much more freedom than girls! Her bitterness had lingered until she grew up and understood the wisdom of preventing young unmarried women from becoming too stimulated around men. If she had continued to ride astride, Teresa did not doubt that she would have lost the precious gift she had brought to her husband on her wedding night.

Now it was Teresa's turn to safeguard the reputations of the female children in her care. She took her motherhood duties seriously and she wasn't about to let her stepdaughter's sulky resentment discourage her. Someday Vicky Beth would thank her, when she too was happily married.

When Vicky Beth had finally realized that she could not win the argument, she had grimly resigned herself to learning to ride sidesaddle. She was sure the new posture made her look like a fool. But she gamely stuck to it until she and Coso became accustomed to it, although neither of them liked it very much. Her father's proud smiles and Teresa's compliments on how ladylike she looked only added insult to injury.

Vicky Beth's angry resentment smoldered on long after she had been forced to give her word that she would never smoke again. She wasn't able to hate her stepmother with the intense hostility she reserved for her father, because Teresa was too disarmingly cheerful and warm-hearted. But in their occasional clashes, Vicky Beth almost always suffered anguished defeat. Whereas Rebekah and the other docile Indian women had been no match for the headstrong girl, Teresa firmly laid down the law. And she was fully capable of enforcing it, with or without her husband's support.

Chance's determination to educate Teresa and share control of their property with her had made her an efficient manager of the house and ranch when he was busy with other affairs. But in her heart Teresa remained a thoroughly domesticated and contented housewife, reverting to fluttery girlish femininity when Chance was around. That irritated Vicky Beth, who thought it was stupid and cowardly for women to cater to men when they didn't have to. She would never do that, Vicky Beth vowed, nursing smug contempt for what she felt was Teresa's weakness, until something happened to make her reconsider that opinion.

In January, 1857, two impetuous young men named Juan Flores and Pancho Daniel escaped from the new state prison at San Quentin. Gathering followers as they rode south, the desperados holed up in the Santa Ana Mountains southeast of Los Angeles and went to work robbing stagecoaches and rustling cattle.

At first many honest *Californios* viewed the bandits tolerantly as latter-day Robin Hoods who were giving the thieving gringos a taste of their own medicine. But that attitude changed to outrage when Sheriff James R. Barton and three of his deputies were massacred in a bandit ambush. After that the manhunt became a crusade for vengeance, with the outlaws relentlessly pursued throughout the Southland.

Chance was active in the chase, as was General Andres Pico, the fierce Yankee-fighter and treaty negotiator of the Mexican-American War. Juan Flores was captured once but managed to escape. When General Pico heard about that, he decided that none of the prisoners his men took would get away; he hanged them on the spot.

That solution was widely copied and when Flores was recaptured a noose was waiting for him. Altogether a dozen members of the gang went the way of the rope—one of them legally.

Chance disapproved of the lynchings, although he knew his rangers would probably have done the same thing if they had caught any of the bandits. Fortunately for his conscience, his troop encountered the gang only once and the outlaws got away after a running gun battle.

During the height of the bandit scare, Teresa had kept Vicky Beth home from school and turned Oakmont into an armed fort. News that the manhunt was over reached the ranch the day before Chance returned home and Teresa decided it was safe to resume their normal activities.

"I think I'll ride to school with you this morning," Teresa informed Vicky Beth at breakfast.

"Do whatever you want to do," Vicky Beth replied indifferently. She only had to live under her parents' domination; she didn't have to act as if she liked it. After the initial excitement of preparing to fight off bandits had dissipated, she had grown bored with being penned up in the house. Now she was eager to be on her own again.

It was a beautifully clear February morning aglow with spring freshness. For the first mile they let their horses amble along leisurely while Teresa poured out a cheerful stream of gossip and commentary on everything in sight. Vicky Beth had stopped listening and was absorbed in her own thoughts when Teresa suddenly glanced over her shoulder and lowered her voice.

"Don't look back. It may be nothing to get alarmed about, but there are three horsemen about two hundred yards behind us."

In spite of the warning, Vicky Beth couldn't help jerking her head around. She didn't get a very good look at the men but she could see that they were heavily armed and dressed *Californio* style.

"Pretend you don't know they are there," Teresa ordered. "When we get around the next bend in the road, we'll dash into the chaparral and shake them off."

But it was already too late for that. The men, realizing they had been seen, spurred their horses and called out to the women to wait for them.

"Vamos!" Teresa shouted, applying her riding crop to her mount's flanks.

Vicky Beth urged Coso into a full gallop, cursing the ungainly sidesaddle that made it difficult for her to control him.

"Hold him down to a canter!" Teresa called as she fell behind Vicky Beth.

"But they'll catch us!"

"No. Their horses are already tired. Hold him in until I tell you to let him out."

Vicky Beth pulled gently back on the reins and stole a quick glance over her shoulder. Teresa was two lengths back, keeping herself between Vicky Beth and the men, who were steadily gaining on them. But Vicky Beth could see that Teresa was right about the men's horses. They were lathered with sweat and their slobbering mouths bit the air. Vicky Beth did not think she was afraid. Her heart was pounding and her skin tingled, but she was sure that was only due to the excitement of the race. What an adventure this would be to tell D.C. and Bobby Buck about!

The next time she looked back, the men were close enough for her to see their faces. The man in the lead had a large droopy mustache and a black patch over his right eye. He smiled broadly and she caught the glint of gold in his mouth. Vicky Beth shifted her gaze to Teresa, who swayed gracefully in her pitching sidesaddle and looked as calm as if this sort of thing happened every day. But Vicky Beth lost some of her composure as their pursuers continued to close the gap between them.

"Here they come!" Vicky Beth cried around the lump in her throat.

Teresa glanced back and said coolly: "Wait a bit longer."

The one-eyed man was still smiling, his face screwed up tightly. He was a good ten lengths behind Teresa's horse, but it seemed to Vicky Beth that he had only to reach out and grab both of them. Her bowels felt weak and squirmy, as the bandits' laboring horses drew closer. Eight lengths . . . five . . . four . . .

"Now!" Teresa shouted, whipping her mount alongside Vicky Beth and raining blows with her riding crop down on Coso's rump.

The women's horses sprinted ahead, easily outdistancing the men's tired animals. They continued at top speed until they had put a good five hundred yards between themselves and their pursuers. Then Teresa said it was safe to ease their horses back down to a canter. Vicky Beth saw that the men were still doggedly on their trail and starting to close up again.

"We can repeat that as often as they get near us," Teresa said confidently. "Their horses will be worn out before we get to town. But if anything should happen to me, don't stop or look back. Ride on into town and get help."

"But—"

"Do as I say!" Teresa glared sternly at Vicky Beth, then dropped back to ride behind her again.

They had to perform Teresa's maneuver three more times before the men gave up the chase. When Teresa ordered Vicky Beth to slow to a trot, she looked back and saw the one-eyed man sitting on his horse on a low rise. Solemnly he swept off his sombrero and bowed to the women, before riding back to join his *companeros*.

Vicky Beth looked at Teresa with an uncertain smile. Now that the desperate game was over, she almost wished it could have gone on longer.

Teresa didn't say much during the remainder of their ride. When they reached the schoolhouse, she dismounted and held Vicky Beth in her arms for several moments. Vicky Beth was surprised to feel her stepmother's body trembling violently. Finally Teresa released the girl and wiped her damp eyes, smiling self-consciously.

"Go on into class, *hija*," Teresa said. "I will report what happened to the sheriff's office. But don't say anything to your father about it. It would just cause him unnecessary worry."

With that, Teresa climbed back onto her sidesaddle and rode off with the cool decorum of a proper lady of her class.

"*Si, Mama,*" Vicky Beth whispered.

The memory of that day stayed with Vicky Beth for the rest of her life. When she heard, a few months later, that a one-eyed bandit had been hanged near Santa Barbara, she felt a sharp personal loss. Just as she had lamented the grizzly's undignified death in the bullring, she wished the bandit's fate had been more in keeping with the violent romantic image she had of him. Also, the Paiute side of her soul wondered what had become of his gold tooth. She would have liked to have had it for a souvenir.

With the ice between them broken, Teresa had no trouble winning Vicky Beth over completely. The two of them were soon close friends and Vicky Beth became a true sister to the younger children. It took Chance longer to overcome her animosity, but he waited patiently until Teresa's love had softened her so much that she could no longer hold a grudge against anyone. By the time the spring rodeo was over and Jeremy was headed for Owens Valley with a breeder herd, Vicky Beth was so much a member of the family that no one was happier than she to learn that Teresa was going to have another baby.

At the same time, Vicky Beth made phenomenal progress in school. When she was finally promoted to the sixth grade level with the other children her age, all of their snobbish hostility disappeared and Vicky Beth suddenly found herself one of the most popular girls in school. Nancy Duvol, the heavyset girl with whom she had fought the previous fall, naturally became her best friend. Nancy's parents were vineyardists from southern France who had played a major role in establishing California's commercial wine industry. Old Jacques Duvol had a bad reputation for abusing his Indian laborers, but Chance tried to overlook that for Vicky Beth's sake. Nancy had a sixteen-year-old brother named Pierre who was a horrible tease and of course Vicky Beth saw no possible use for him in her life.

The remainder of the school year passed all too quickly. When it was over, Chance and Teresa gave a fiesta for Vicky Beth's classmates and their families. The party came off pretty successfully. At first Vicky Beth was too bashful to try out the dance steps Teresa had taught her. But she discovered to her delight that she was more graceful on her feet than most of the other children. The only unpleasant incident occurred when Pierre Duvol tried to make a laughingstock of Vicky Beth by breaking a *cascaron* on her head. But Vicky Beth got an even bigger laugh by returning the favor with an egg that had *not* been hollowed out and filled with confetti. Chance had to scold her for that, although he admitted privately that Pierre did look mighty funny with egg yolk dripping down his face.

Later Pierre got his revenge by catching Vicky Beth in a dark corner and stealing a kiss. It was the first time any male outside of her family had seriously put his lips to hers and she found the experience as disgusting as she had always thought it would be.

The summer was filled with hard work that Vicky Beth found more rewarding than play. She helped out around the house and ranch and Chance took her with him on his business activities as often as he could. He was very proud to show her off to his friends, and even more pleased by her growing admiration for his accomplishments. By winning her approval, Chance felt that he was making up for the years they had been apart, and that did a lot to relieve his guilt feelings about the separation. Maybe he wasn't such a bad father after all, he once remarked to Teresa, who replied that she could have told him that a long time ago, but she didn't want to add to his conceit.

Vicky Beth's impression of Los Angeles improved with time, although she never completely got over her original disappointment. The town's basic squalor was often made even uglier by the Angelenos' careless disregard for human rights. A glaring example of that was the weekly hiring of Indian laborers, which amounted to little more than a slave auction.

Most of the dispossessed natives who had not found positions on the ranchos were contracted out every Monday to local farmers. The vineyardists were especially eager to employ them because on Saturday they could be paid the bulk of their wages in rotgut brandy that cost nearly nothing to produce. After spending Saturday night and most of Sunday in drunken carousing, the miserable wretches were herded into the plaza on Monday morning to begin the cycle over again. Eventually Chance and other conscientious citizens were able to abolish the barbarous practice, but by then there weren't many surviving Indians to benefit from the reform.

But there were more cheerful sights, like the traveling Italian with his marvelous magic lantern and music box. For *dos rials*, young and old alike could stare enthralled at exotic scenes while the smiling showman cranked out "Yankee Doodle" and old country folk tunes.

And Vicky Beth would never forget the awesome sight of camels on Main Street. The animals had been imported from Egypt to test a theory, conceived by Secretary of War Jefferson Davis, for transporting army supplies through the American deserts. After being shipped to Texas, the camels had completed the overland journey to California in good form. Eventually they proved to be impractical for military use and were sold to private freighters, who used them extensively in the arid regions of the southwest. For Vicky Beth, few memories of Los Angeles in those days could compare with the image of the ornery beasts spitting at passers-by while the Moslem camel driver Hadji Ali (called Hijolly by his American comrades) bowed toward Mecca in prayer.

For further excitement, there were the stagecoach races from San Pedro to Los Angeles. Travelers arriving by ship at the port found two of Phineas Banning's coaches waiting to carry them to the pueblo. To each coach were hitched six bronco mules under the whips of typical California drivers. The passengers, after being fortified with welcoming drinks, were encouraged to place bets on which carriage would reach town first. As often as she could, Vicky Beth would ride down to greet the arriving ships, and then enjoy the thrilling sport of galloping Coso alongside the wildly rocking coaches while the passengers held onto their seats for dear life.

Then there was the solemn beauty of her confirmation in the Catholic faith, inspired by her stepmother's devout example. The conversion fulfilled a deep longing inside Vicky Beth and she felt serenely confident that she would always be able to live up to the highest ideals of the Church, no matter what the future might bring.

Near the end of summer, Chance took Vicky Beth along when he sailed to San Francisco on one of his trading vessels. Vicky Beth was captivated by the fabulous city on the bay, but its impossible climate made her glad that their visit was fairly brief. It was only when they were on their way back to the sunny south that it suddenly occurred to her that she had not thought about Uncle David or D.C. or anyone else in Owens Valley for over a month. Guilt stabbed her as she realized that she was not even very curious about Rebekah and Seyavi, who must have had their babies by now. She made up her mind that she would write a letter to Uncle David immediately. But then her father called her up on deck and all thoughts of Owens Valley were swept away by the enchanting vision of a school of flying fish.

Chapter 22

The second half of the 1850s decade was as eventful for California as the first half, but in different ways. The early waves of boisterous, gold-seeking, mostly male pioneers had turned to more reliable occupations and sent for their families. The foundations of greatness, laid down with youth's passionate zest for living and discovering, were ready to receive maturity's more thoughtful organization and social structure. There were still some wild and woolly times to come and the state would never entirely lose its appetite for romantic, violent, often bizarre adventures. But there was no denying that dull respectability had reached the land of El Dorado.

In San Francisco the vigilance committees and volunteer fire departments decreased the excitement of random homicide and arson. Kearny Street, once the fashionable place to sleep off a drunk, was never the same after some kind soul donated a wheelbarrow to haul the sleepers to jail.

The state capital, after wandering restlessly from Monterey to San Jose, Vallejo, and Benicia, finally settled down permanently in Sacramento, where the legislators suffered the cruel and unusual punishment of having to sober up for a tea party given in their honor by the city's leading women's club.

Even San Quentin Prison, whose first warden had conscientiously resigned when he learned that most of the inmates were old friends of his, became so securely guarded that neighboring residents missed the early mass escapes that had frequently relieved their boredom.

The southern cow counties were changing, too, although respectability and progress came about more slowly there. For some time the only Anglo communities around Los Angeles were El Monte, the western terminus of the Santa Fe Trail, and San Bernardino. El Monte was the first American town incorporated in southern California, in 1851, by Texans who vigorously spread the fame of the high-spirited "Monte boys." In the same year, Mormon pioneers established San Bernardino in Brigham Young's effort to build a second Salt Lake City. But in 1857 all Mormons were recalled to Utah and San Bernardino's reputation for morality, industry, and thrift passed to the new German farming colony of Anaheim. A year later the port of Wilmington, near San Pedro, was founded by the energetic stage and freight line owner Phineas Banning.

After that, development of the sleepy southland settled back into its unhurried pace for another decade. Chance, always seeking new markets for the products of his varied enterprises, had to reach far beyond the local area. His cannery turned out to be successful, under the efficient management of Madison Starr. The hardworking and ambitious young Virginian had not shared Si Darcy's disdain for a partnership when Chance offered it to him. And Starr eagerly agreed with Chance's dream of achieving worldwide distribution of their processed foods—a dream they optimistically launched with a large shipment of canned beef to New York via Cornelius Vanderbilt's Accessory Transit Company. Neither of them could have foreseen that their plans would be thwarted by an old acquaintance of Chance's.

In 1855 William Walker led another expedition south in his quest for power and glory. His victim on that occasion was Nicaragua, where revolutionaries fighting to overthrow the government happily welcomed his support. After helping the rebels win the war, Walker used his genius for military organization and political intrigue to make himself President of Nicaragua—the only native-born American

232

citizen ever to become head of a foreign nation. Then the daring "gray-eyed man of destiny" decided that he also wanted to control the Accessory Transit Company.

The Vanderbilt line consisted of steamships that carried passengers and cargo from New York to the east coast of Nicaragua, where they transferred to shallow-draft steamers to travel up the San Juan River and across Lake Nicaragua. From there it was but a short land journey to the west coast port where other steamships waited to take them on to California. By avoiding the long haul around Cape Horn and the equally dangerous Panama route, the transit company turned a handsome profit and Walker thought that by seizing its lake steamers he could collect some of the revenue that was making Vanderbilt the richest man in America. The plan worked, for a while, and Chance's canned beef ended up feeding filibusters who never even thanked him for it.

Eventually Walker and his men were driven out of Nicaragua and Vanderbilt regained his property. But the disruption of shipping to the east temporarily discouraged Chance and he concentrated on sending his canned goods along the more reliable routes to San Francisco and Sacramento. That was just one of the setbacks Chance suffered in the wildly fluctuating economic life of early California. Fortunately his diversified investments enabled him to absorb occasional losses better than many of his neighbors. More importantly, he had the emotional support of his family to keep his spirits up.

Teresa's third baby was a boy who took over Oakmont with the usual loud-mouthed, overbearing arrogance of infants. He was dearly loved by all, even Beatriz, whom he supplanted as the baby of the family, and Chance reluctantly allowed him to be named Kenneth, junior. Chance had never liked his given name and he felt guilty about saddling an innocent child with it. But he had discovered that he was as vain as most men about perpetuating himself in the next generation. He supposed it had something to do with getting on the wrong side of thirty-five and feeling that he should make a significant mark in the world before his life was over.

Vicky Beth's involvement with her new family and

friends grew deeper with each passing day. Teresa treated her more like a younger sister than a stepchild, guiding her along the path to womanhood so subtly that Vicky Beth scarcely noticed that she was losing interest in her tomboy activities and finding more pleasure in cooking and sewing. She quickly picked up Spanish and spent hours happily chattering with Teresa, Doña Luisa and the other rancho women. Her relations with Chance improved too, although she never got over regarding him more as a stern authority figure than the kind, loving father he tried to be.

But at least Vicky Beth came to realize that Chance had done the right thing in bringing her to Los Angeles. As the memory of her life in Owens Valley faded, she saw it realistically as a wonderful childhood that she was bound to outgrow eventually. She would always love Uncle David, D.C., Bobby Buck, Rebekah and her Paiute friends, but her years with them were only part of her growing-up experience. This was where she belonged now, where she could be exposed to a wider range of influences from the civilized world. She was sure that D.C. and Bobby Buck would benefit from living here, too, when they were older, and she resolved to write to Uncle David about that sometime. She hardly ever dreamed of Shoshone Land anymore.

Los Angeles, like Chance, had its ups and downs over the years. Severe earthquakes jolted the area in 1855 and 1857, causing much property damage but few human casualties. Other unpredictable whims of nature—floods and droughts, plagues of grasshoppers and brush fires fanned by mouth-drying Santa Ana winds—wreaked more havoc on the debilitated cattle industry. At the same time, man-made afflictions continued to hamper the pueblo's moral development. By 1858 all of the fledgling Protestant churches in town had closed their doors because of poor attendance, while the number of drinking, gambling and wenching establishments steadily increased.

In spite of that, steps were being taken to make Los Angeles more than a cesspool of sin and misery. The first hospital was started in 1858 by the Sisters of Charity from Maryland and a year later the Library Association opened a small reading room at the corner of Court and Spring streets. Teresa was active in both of those endeavors, and the town's other attempts at cultural and spiritual improvement.

After Vicky Beth graduated from grade school, Teresa insisted that she continue her education at home. Chance agreed and filled the house with books, art works, and musical instruments. Their proudest acquisition was a baby grand piano, which Teresa quickly mastered. Vicky Beth had inherited Chance's low musical aptitude, but she practiced diligently until she became a fair pianist. The other children had the Esperanzas' natural rhythm and they all sang and played almost as soon as they could talk.

In 1857 the first city water franchise was given to William Dryden, who constructed a brick reservoir in the plaza to supplant the men who peddled drinking water from horsecarts. In 1858 Don Abel Stearns erected the city's most ambitious structure—a brick and tile business complex named the Arcadia Block. Also in that year Los Angeles was put on the map by becoming a station of the Butterfield Stage Line from St. Louis to San Francisco. And in 1860 Chance had the satisfaction of seeing another of his dreams realized when a telegraph line linked Los Angeles to San Francisco.

Those and other developments encouraged the Protestant ministers to give Los Angeles one last try. Since there still were not enough worshippers of any one denomination to make up a congregation, they had to combine their resources and open a joint church. Even the most diehard hellraisers had to admit that the town's slide into respectability got a big boost when the City Council outlawed the plaza bull and bear fights. That traditional *Californio* sport was replaced by a new game that was becoming popular around the country—something called baseball.

But by far the single issue that occupied most of the Angelenos' attention in the late fifties was the growing dissension between the pro- and anti-slavery states. With so many ex-Southerners living around Los Angeles, the controversy became so heated that it was seriously proposed that California should be divided, with the southern half becoming a slave state. Chance stubbornly opposed that idea and tried to make his neighbors from the southern

235

states understand that slavery, aside from being immoral, was not a good business practice. An employer could get better service from paid workers, Chance argued, and have a clear conscience to boot.

In Owens Valley the passing years were even less remarkable than in Los Angeles. To David nothing seemed to change very much, except the sizes of his growing children. He never felt any older and Rebekah always looked the same to him. The cattle Chance had sent up to him altered the look of the valley somewhat, but he soon got used to them. David did his work, loved his family, talked to Margaret, helped his Paiute friends and feared God. As his reward, he was allowed to flow through time as smoothly as the river and the wind, and to be as indifferent as they to the shifting seasons.

Jeremy Starr had homesteaded a good piece of land a few miles to the north, with his almost-white wife. They were good neighbors. Jeremy taught the Paiutes to ride and instructed them to keep the livestock away from cultivated fields and wild growths that the Indians used for food. The Indians were pretty good about not killing the cows and horses, except in times of starvation, when no one could blame them.

Jeremy and Maria were content in the valley. For a while they were homesick for Los Angeles, as Jeremy had once longed for the lush greenery of Virginia. But they were better off here, where they could bring up their young without fear of being pestered by low-down white trash. Jeremy had been raised as a house servant and was unaccustomed to the heavy labor of farming and ranching. But he soon grew to love the challenge of wresting a living from the soil. Sometimes in the evening he would sit outside their cabin, smoking his pipe and chuckling as he stared up at the ragged Sierra crestline. Once Maria asked him what he was laughing about and he replied that he was thinking of the fools on the other side of the mountains who were still trying to scrape up golden fortunes in freezing streambeds. Any man who didn't have enough sense to be satisfied with a roof over his head, food on the table, and a woman in bed deserved to be laughed at.

David's sons were growing fast, especially D.C. He had started to shoot up the summer after Vicky Beth's departure and he carried his lean frame so proudly erect that the Paiutes called him Kahdu Waukobe, Like-A-Pine. Bobby Buck was more stockily built, like his mother's people. (And like Chance, Rebekah couldn't help noticing with a tug at her heart every time she gazed into his soft brown eyes.) Both boys were hard workers and they eagerly took to herding cattle under Jeremy's tutelage. But when their chores were over they were happy to slip away to play and hunt with their Paiute friends. Going about in nothing but loincloths for six months of the year left them so sun-bronzed that only D.C.'s blue eyes and shock of corn-colored hair set him apart from the Indians. He was comfortable in their language and customs and could handle a bow and throwing sticks as well as any budding brave of his age.

Hu-pwi was the boys' favorite companion among the Paiutes. Seyavi had given birth to a baby boy shortly after their return from Black Rocks and the badger skin had done its job of making him grow strong and healthy. Hu-pwi looked forward to teaching his son the ways of the People, when he was old enough. Until then Hu-pwi was glad to practice his fathering skills on D.C. and Bobby Buck.

Shortly after Seyavi had her baby, Rebekah had presented David with another daughter, whom they had named Rachel. The girl was healthier than her unfortunate sister had been, and there seemed little likelihood that they would lose her. But Bobby Buck was extremely protective of his little sister and he tenderly looked after her as if she were the only girl in the world. D.C. did not share that feeling. Although he cared for Rachel, he lived only for the day when he would be reunited with Vicky Beth. Every night, between prayers and sleep, he willed himself to remember every detail of their last meeting at the oak tree, so that her image would always be sharp in his mind. That was the main difference between the two boys. Bobby

Buck still loved Vicky Beth, too, but he had the Indian way of putting unattainable goals out of his mind, while D.C. was a dreamer who could never be content with anything less than the fulfillment of his dreams.

The eastern Sierras' age of isolated innocence ended in the summer of 1859 when a prospector named Cord Norst squatted in Mono Gulch, north of Owens Valley, and washed out a load of sand and gravel that left the dented bottom of his pan spangled with yellow flecks. In the same year, Ben Butler arrived at the Sacramento parlor house operated by his wife Susan O'Neal and her three grown but still unmarried sons. Ben was fresh from the Washoe Diggings over in what would soon become the state of Nevada. He brought with him some samples of heavy dark blue ore that seemed curiously familiar to him, although he could not remember seeing similar rocks on the prospecting jaunt he had taken with David Wheeler several years before.

Susan, playing a hunch, had one of the rocks secretly analyzed by a friend in the Assay Office. The friend, trembling with excitement, informed her that the ore contained only a trace of gold but was unbelivably rich in silver. Swearing the man to silence, Susan calmly started liquidating her assets in Sacramento. In a few weeks she had her family packed and headed eastward—at about the same time that another piece of Washoe ore was being assayed in the northern Mother Lode town of Grass Valley by a man who was less able to keep a secret than Susan's friend. Within days the Gold Rush was reversed by hordes of wild-eyed men swarming through the Sierra passes to the fantastically rich Comstock Lode.

Some of the fortune hunters turned south to follow up Cord Norst's discovery by founding such rip-roaring towns and camps as Monoville, Cameron, Aurora and the wonderfully wild and wicked Bodie. But none of them approached the dazzling development of the Washoe-Comstock area and its opulent mistress, Virginia City. The most popular establishment in Virginia City was the Limerick Hotel and Restaurant, owned by Susan O'Neal. Having at last achieved her desired level of social respectability, Susan devoted herself to providing her guests with the finest accommodations and meals, which required a steady supply of goods from the outside world. And the most convenient route to the new, rich, hungry mining centers lay through Owens Valley.

At first the valley Indians only stared in amazement at the trains of freight wagons and herds of livestock being driven over their lands. But the sight of cattle trampling and grazing on their precious food crops aroused Lightning Tracker and other leaders to demand tribute from the intruders. A few of the whites responded with token payments of a cow or sheep, but most of them drove the Indians away with angry threats. The Paiutes retreated sullenly, remembering what the survivors of other tribes had told them about the white man's treachery.

David also was initially stunned by the bustling activity that shattered his peaceful existence in the valley. But he quickly recovered from the shock when he realized that the newcomers were eager to pay top dollar for all the cattle he wanted to sell them. While he and Jeremy were rounding up their stock, David sent a message to Chance, who had already heard about the mining boom and dispatched Si Darcy and several *vaqueros* northward with a large herd.

Neither Chance nor David had any forebodings about the future of Owens Valley. Chance was too preoccupied with other matters and David, in his guileless, good-natured way, assumed that things would work out for the best somehow. Perhaps they would have, if all of the white travelers had been content to go on about their business. But many of the drovers following the slow-moving cattle looked over the valley's abundance of water and grass with great interest. They liked what they saw and remembered it, while the Indians withdrew to the hills to chew on the indigestible knowledge that they no longer controlled their valley.

Because the first transcontinental telegraph line was not yet completed, news of the Confederate attack on Fort Sumter on April 12, 1861, took nearly two weeks to reach San Francisco by pony express. Word that the long-feared Civil War had finally commenced was instantly wired to Los Angeles, where it provoked varied emotional responses.

The majority of the Anglo Angelenos, being southern

sympathizers, anticipated a swift victory for the secessionist states. Many of them hurried to join the Confederate Army and those who stayed behind made life so uncomfortable for their Yankee neighbors that men wanting to enlist in the Union forces had to do so evasively during the night. Only the presence of loyal army and national guard troops prevented the southern California secessionists from actually making the area a separate Confederate state.

Women and children on both sides of the controversy viewed the men's belligerent enthusiasm with mixed pride and fear, while most *Californios* coolly ignored what they regarded as a family quarrel between people who were still pretty much foreigners to them. Chance wished he could adopt the latter attitude, now that he was at last free of the urge to answer the call of military adventure. At thirty-nine he was starting to put on weight and settle into the comfortable routine of a successful, happily married middle-aged man.

This was not his war, Chance repeatedly told himself. But the thought of his fellow Americans killing each other over a stupid disagreement was so sickening that he could not get it out of his mind. Unlike his friends, Chance did not optimistically look forward to a short war with little bloodshed. He knew from experience what brave, stubborn fighters men from both sides of the Mason-Dixon Line could be. And the realization that he, being so well positioned to ship canned food and other essential supplies to the east, was sure to profit from the conflict only added a grim note of irony to his gloomy outlook.

Chance, believing that the men about to leave for the fighting should take a good memory with them, gave a fiesta in their honor. Supporters of both sides were invited, with Chance insisting that they avoid political discussions and treat each other as the friendly neighbors they had been up till then. It was a bittersweet affair charged with repressed tension and forced gaiety as the guests tried to outdo one another in respecting Chance's hospitality. The strong undercurrent of suspicious hostility depressed Chance, especially when he saw Madison Starr and Si Darcy drinking and laughing together. Starr, though proud of his Virginia heritage, made no secret of his decision to back up his antislavery sentiments by joining the Union Army. Si had even less love for the South's "peculiar institution," but Texas's entry into the Confederacy left him no choice as to which side he would serve.

Soon the two friends would be enemies, Chance reflected sadly. He was glad to have his attention diverted from that thought when Nicolas Alviso danced by with Teresa and threw him a grin. Nicolas was one of the few *Californios* who had decided to get into the gringos' war. Chance smiled at the memory of their ride down from San Francisco, nearly twelve years ago. This time the happy-go-lucky *caballero* had ridden south with the most illustrious guest at the fiesta—General Albert Sidney Johnston, a Kentucky native who had resigned his command of the U.S. Army's Department of the Pacific to join the Confederacy.

Somebody should stop these fools before they throw their lives away, Chance brooded. To cheer himself up, he gazed across the room at Vicky Beth as she stood chatting with some of her friends. Now seventeen, she had blossomed into a tall, slim, well-rounded beauty who knew how attractive she was to the opposite sex. Chance was amused by the way she pretended not to notice the frequent glances Pierre Duvol cast her way. At twenty-one, Pierre was rakishly handsome and possessed the sort of reputation one would expect in a high-spirited and somewhat spoiled young bachelor. In a year or so, when Pierre had had time to sow his wild oats, Chance would have a serious talk with his parents. It wouldn't be easy for him and Teresa to give up Vicky Beth, but he couldn't deny that the thought of becoming a grandfather pleased him.

As always, thinking about his family raised Chance's spirits. Why was he wasting time fretting about a future that he could not control anyway? Making up his mind to forget the war and have some fun tonight, he waited until Nicolas danced Teresa near him again and cut in. As he swung his wife around the floor she smiled up at him with such a radiant glow that he wondered if she was pregnant again. Well, why not? They could use another daughter, since her last two had been boys.

Much to Teresa's relief, she was not with child at that

time. She still loved children, but she thought that having five young ones and a teen-aged stepdaughter was enough responsibility for a while. Now she wanted to be free to enjoy her husband for as long as he would be with her. Chance had sworn to her that he had no intention of going off to war again, but one could never tell with a wild stallion of his unpredictable breed.

As things turned out, Teresa had no reason to worry about that. Chance paid little attention to the news of the war's slow progress in the next several months. Reports of the Union defeats at Big Bethel, Bull Run and Ball's Bluff caused him some concern. But most of his attention was on California's older and more dangerous enemy, the weather, as the long dry summer stretched into November and December.

Chapter 23

Far out over the Pacific, where some of the west coast's worst problems begin, the sun had spent the summer sucking moisture up into thick cloudbanks. Finally December winds started pushing the clouds toward land, where a massive atmospheric pressure ridge waited to halt them. Most of California enjoyed fine weather until Christmas Eve, when the rains started and seemed for a while to have forgotten how to stop.

Storm after storm drove the spongy clouds ashore and broke them up like wrecked ships. In the first two months of 1862 some fifty inches of rain fell on southern California's coastal plain, which normally received less than twenty inches in an entire year. The sun-hardened ground could not soak up the water fast enough. Torrents poured off mountains and hills, flooding the lowlands. New arroyos and gulches were carved out and rivers wildly changed their courses. Cattle drowned by hundreds or were pulled down by hungry bears, coyotes, and mountain lions that had been flushed out of their lairs. So many rattlesnakes were washed down from the hills that Chance and his *vaqueros* spent much of their time killing them.

Water stood waist-deep in Los Angeles' streets and the pueblo's ditch system was nearly wiped out. Adobe buildings became waterlogged and collapsed, making Chance glad that he had had Oakmont's walls stuccoed and white-washed. He and Teresa hosted the entire Esperanza clan when they lost their homes on the plains.

North of Los Angeles the storm's fury was even more intense. The long valley of the Sacramento and San Joaquin Rivers was transformed into a lake stretching from the foothills of the Coast Range to the Sierras, where snow accumulated to record depths.

In Owens Valley the Indians and whites suffered alike as the rain alternated with snow and the half-frozen river overran its banks like a flow of dirty lava. Winnedumah's cabin was swept away and she took refuge in David's house, where other Paiutes had already gathered. Several cattlemen and miners had chosen to winter in the valley and the Indians coveted their food supplies with eyes that had seen too many children starve.

One of the winter's casualties was Pah-ya Che-e, the Shoshone hostage and medicine man who had told Vicky Beth and D.C. glowing tales of his homeland. When three of his patients died of pneumonia in rapid succession, Pah-ya Che-e's fate was sealed. Lightning Tracker offered to help him escape, but Pah-ya Che-e said he had lived among the Paiutes for so long that he could no longer find his way back to Shoshone Land. There was only one way his soul could go home and he gladly welcomed the hatchet of the nervous brave who had been assigned to see him off.

David gave the Indians permission to kill cattle wearing his and Chance's brands when they had nothing else to eat. But it was difficult for an empty stomach to distinguish one animal from another.

The white stockmen tolerated the loss of several cows before warning the Indians that retaliatory measures would be taken if the depredations continued. The Indians, feeling that they had a right to do as they pleased on their own land, ignored the warning. They went on taking the cattle they desired until a brave was caught in the act and shot dead by Al Thompson, a herder for Henry Vansickle. That angered the Indians so much that a few days later they captured a white man named Yank Crossen, who had recently arrived from Aurora, and killed him.

That was the beginning of the First Owens Valley Water War.

We, the undersigned, citizens of Owens Valley, with Indian chiefs representing the different tribes and rancherias of said valley, having met together at San Francis Ranch, and after talking over past grievances, have agreed to let what is past be buried in oblivion; and as evidence of all things having transpired having been amicably settled between both Indians and whites, each one of the chiefs and whites present have voluntarily signed their names to this instrument of writing.

And it is further agreed that the Indians are not to be molested in their daily avocations by which they gain an honest living.

And it is further agreed upon the part of the Indians that they are not to molest the property of the whites, nor to drive off or kill cattle that are running in the valley, and for both parties to live in peace and strive to promote amicably the general interests of both whites and Indians.

Given under our hands at San Francis Ranch on this Thirty-first day of January in the year of our Lord Eighteen Hundred and Sixty-two.

David finished interpreting the peace treaty and asked the Indians if they understood it. One of the Paiutes, whom the white men called Chief George because they couldn't be bothered memorizing heathen names, murmured something to Lightning Tracker.

"He desires assurance that the white chiefs will keep their animals away from our gardens and hunting grounds," Lightning Tracker informed David.

When David translated that to the men of his race, most of them nodded.

"Tell them they can kill any cattle they find eating their crops," Samuel Bishop said. "That should make them happy, and keep our herders alert."

David then asked if there was anything else that either side wanted to discuss. No one could think of anything, so they warmed their fingers to sign their names or make their marks on the treaty. The raw blustery day and low clouds threatening more snow made them glad to have their business over with. Now they could have some of the

245

coffee and hot food that Mrs. Bishop had spent the morning preparing in the cabin.

David gazed around him, thinking how typical of the times it was for Bishop to have given the title "ranch" to a rude stone hut, a horse corral, and uncounted acres of sagebrush and grass presently blanketed with muddy snow. David felt quite pleased with the part he had played in preventing more violence in the valley. Even Chance could not have done much better, he thought as he looked over the tranquil scene of white men and Indians eating together. It had been touch and go for a while, but he and Lightning Tracker had finally persuaded representatives from both sides to meet for a peacemaking powwow near the northern end of Owens Valley.

David's inner satisfaction was reflected by the sight of Samuel Bishop hunkering beside Chief George. The two men were about the same age—the mid-thirties—and both had the dignified bearing and self-confidence that distinguishes leaders. They were also, David sensed, honorable men who could be relied on to hold their people to the terms of the treaty. As for the others—L.J. Cralley, Allen Van Fleet, Sid Graves, John Welch, Daniel Wyman, Al Thompson, Alney McGee and his four capable sons—David was not so sure. They seemed decent enough, but they had the hard, quick-tempered look that survival in a savage land tends to give men. Veterans of the Gold Rush or grueling trail drives, they had learned never to be out of reach of their guns. To them, Indians were merely parts of the hostile landscape that had to be thrust aside or ridden over. David, although happy to have white neighbors again, could have asked for more congenial ones. But he reckoned that was not important, now that the treaty had been signed. He was so eager to get home and tell Rebekah the good news that he failed to notice the worried scowl on Lightning Tracker's face.

The old chief glared across the campground, trying to catch his son's eye. But Hu-pwi was deep in conversation with Paul the Apostle, who stood with his hands resting on the hilt of the cavalry saber that he had worn proudly during the dozen years since Chance had traded it to him. Lightning Tracker wished he had had the foresight to steal the sword and cut Paul's throat with it before Paul had become a powerful influence in the valley, particularly over gullible young braves like Hu-pwi.

Lightning Tracker did not share David's hopeful outlook. He knew that he and Chief George were the only important Indian leaders present, except for Paul, who had sullenly declined to sign the treaty. The other Indian signers—Chief Dick, Little Chief Dick, and Shondow—led only small bands, and none of the other chieftains would consider the treaty binding on them and their followers. The only advantage of the agreement, in Lightning Tracker's opinion, was that it bought him more time to persuade his people that making war on the white intruders would lead to their own destruction.

Lightning Tracker was well aware of how the severe weather and famine had rendered the Paiutes eager to believe those who preached hatred and violence, claiming their medicine could make them invulnerable to white men's bullets. Crazy talk like that had pushed their eastern cousins, the Walker River Paiutes, into disastrous war two years earlier, in spite of Chief Numaga's wise warning that the whites would "come like the sand in a whirlwind and drive you from your homes."

Now bitter survivors of that war had come to Owens Valley to help other outsiders like Paul the Apostle and Joaquin Jim stir up more trouble. Jim, the bravest and smartest of the rising new war chiefs, worried Lightning Tracker the most. Paul had displayed no outstanding qualities. But Jim had the cunning determination to wage a long-running conflict with the white men whom he hated with implacable fury. A Fresno renegade who had been outlawed by his own people, Jim was said to be driven by an obsession to avenge the brutal murder of his wife and children by white gold miners.

Lightning Tracker hoped he could prevent further bloodshed for the remainder of his own lifetime, which would be difficult enough. As he was well into his sixties, he obviously could not compete physically with the younger chiefs. But he had the advantage in political experience and persuasive eloquence. He had demonstrated that by arranging this treaty conference, while making the other Indian and white leaders think it was their idea. Now he had to work out a more lasting peace between the two races before one of them decided the treaty was just a scrap of paper. That challenging prospect aroused Lightning Tracker's love of diplomatic intrigue. It was good to have some excitement in his life once more, since he had almost given up hope of ever consummating his romance with Winnedumah. Impatient to get to work, he again stared at his son and finally caught his attention.

"I must go now," Hu-pwi said to Paul the Apostle.

"Think on what I have said, brother," Paul urged. "The time of decision is rapidly approaching."

Hu-pwi nodded and made his way over to his father's side.

"What were you discussing with the foreigner?" Lightning Tracker demanded. Paul's marriage to a Paiute woman and long residency in the valley made no impact on Lightning Tracker's bigotry. In his mind, anyone unfortunate enough not to have been born a Paiute was forever of a different and decidedly inferior breed.

"Nothing of importance," Hu-pwi answered.

Lightning Tracker frowned. "Everything is important in these dangerous times. Come. We have much to do."

He turned and started walking toward the trail to the south, thinking about the teams of runners he planned to send throughout the valley. He already had a good intelligence system, based mainly on the tribal women's informative and fast-traveling gossip, but he needed a better means of communicating with the other chiefs.

Hu-pwi fell in behind Lightning Tracker, his eyes sulkily downcast. Why did his father always treat him like a child? Had he not proved his manhood many times over? He was the head of his own family, a good provider, and the major support of his aged parents. But no one would suspect that from the arrogant way his father ordered him around. Someday he would show him, Hu-pwi vowed, thinking of the exciting invitation he had received from Paul the Apostle.

Paul had explained that he was working with Joaquin Jim to organize Indian resistance against the invaders. Let these cowardly chiefs sign the white men's paper, Paul sneered. Perhaps it would give the whites a feeling of security, until the real warriors were ready to rise up and drive them out of the valley. Already Jim was on his way to meet an Aurora merchant who had agreed to sell guns and ammunition to the Indians. Soon they would have more than a thousand armed braves ready to fight, with more promised from other tribes who had reason to hate white men. Join us, Paul begged Hu-pwi, and help remove the dishonor your father has brought upon his family by encouraging his people to surrender.

Hu-pwi was strongly tempted to accept Paul's invitation, as he looked down at his moccasined feet plodding through the freezing mud. Many of the rebellious braves owned horses and Hu-pwi had a pleasing mental image of himself riding home covered with war glory and booty. That was the only way for a man to live! But two things held him back; he was intimidated by his father's domineering personality, and he did not feel right about making war on David Wheeler's family. If only there was some way to get around those obstacles, Hu-pwi thought wistfully.

As Paul the Apostle watched Lightning Tracker and Hu-pwi disappear down the trail, a white blur streaked his vision. The overloaded clouds were starting to spill more snow, reminding Paul that it was time for him to be on his way. He walked over to where his horse was tied to the corral fence, his hand nervously clasping his saber hilt, when he passed Jeremy Starr and another black man. Paul had never grown accustomed to their kind. It seemed unnatural for them to be with whites, although they obviously belonged to no known Indian tribe.

Paul rode away feeling satisfied with his day's work. All of the young braves he had contacted agreed that his cause was just and he was sure they would eventually join him. It seldom occurred to him that he might not get everything he wanted and he was curiously unable to learn from experience. Basically he was a rather stupid man who had never acquired Lightning Tracker's understanding of human nature or Joaquin Jim's organizational skill or Chief George's popularity. But he had courage, ambition, and a stubborn bullying vanity that enabled him to bring other men under his control. Of the twenty warriors in his band, most could be relied on to follow him anywhere with fanatical devotion—as long as he was victorious. Another thing Paul unfortunately lacked was a strategist's imagination to take the possibility of defeat into consideration when making plans.

Jeremy could hardly sit still in the saddle. His whole body squirmed with delight and he kept glancing over at his new friend as they rode away from the Bishop ranch. Lord have mercy! Who would've thought he would meet another black man in this forgotten corner of the world? And Charles ("Nigger Charley") Tyler was about the blackest thing Jeremy had ever seen. Jeremy's *café au lait* complexion looked positively anemic next to Charley's deep ebony hue. Seeing black like that made a man proud to have African blood in his veins.

Charley had grown up on Alney McGee's home ranch in Texas, where the McGees had been such ignorant white trash that they hadn't known how to treat their few slaves like niggers. As a result, Charley had learned to ride, shoot, and punch cattle along with the McGee boys. When the McGees had pulled up stakes and driven their herd to California three years ago, Charley had come along. Now, although he was technically a free man in a free state, Charley continued to work for the only family he had ever known.

Jeremy, attending the treaty conference with David, had instantly taken to the big black cowboy who wore a six-shooter and squirted tobacco juice as expertly as his white companions. They had spent most of the day getting to know each other so well that Jeremy had insisted that Charley come home with him for supper. Jeremy was happily looking forward to introducing Charley to his family—when Charley's deep voice suddenly rumbled up from his barrel chest like thunder in a canyon.

"Is yore hoss gunshy?"

"Not a bit," Jeremy answered. "Why?"

" 'Cause they's a big ol' rattler on the trail ahead that I'd jest as soon not leave in one piece."

Jeremy's eyes found the snake as Charley drew and cocked his single-action Colt in one fluid motion. The rattler made for the cover of a pile of rocks and was nearly out of sight when Charley casually shot its head off. Jeremy stared at him in wide-eyed admiration.

"Whoo-eee! That's some shootin'!"

Charley grinned modestly. "Jest tol'able, for Texas."

The peace treaty proved to have a life span of less than four weeks.

David learned of its demise from Barton McGee, who rode down to alert the southern valley settlers of the renewed Indian hostilities. The trouble had started several days before, Bart said, when he, his brothers, and ten other men had started driving a large herd north to the market in Aurora. When they reached Big Pine Creek, where Joaquin Jim's band was camped, there was a tense confrontation when Jim demanded payment for the right to travel through his territory. The cattlemen had refused to pay and the Indians had backed down. But for the next two nights the white men had been kept awake by the Indians' noisy war dances and suspicious movements around the herd.

On the third morning the white men discovered that 200 head of cattle were missing. When some of them went out to recover the stock, they encountered about fifty armed braves who ordered them back. The drive was completed without further trouble, with Indians hovering about the flanks of the herd.

A few days later Bart was making another cattle drive with his brother Taylor, Allen Van Fleet, Jim Harness and Nigger Charley Tyler. Near Putnam's cabin at Little Pine they saw four Indians approaching the herd and went out to meet them. The leader of the Indians turned out to be Chief Shondow, one of the treaty signers. But Shondow had heard of Joaquin Jim's successful rustling experience and he made a similar demand for tribute. The whites rejected the demand and, after a lengthy argument, Van Fleet leveled his rifle at the Indians and ordered them to be on their way.

Then Van Fleet made the mistake of turning away from the Indians and received an arrow in the side for his carelessness. Harness went to help Van Fleet and was also wounded. At that point the white men opened fire and all of the Indians were killed.

251

Bart concluded his story by saying that there were reports of Indians preparing for war throughout the valley and the whites were gathering at Putnam's to fort up against a possible all-out attack.

David was deeply disturbed by the news. "I sure wish you fellows hadn't killed Shondow," he said sadly. "He wasn't much account, but the other Indians set great store by him. There's no telling what they'll do now."

"Well, be that as it may, it was done," Bart said flatly. "Now you'll be wise to take your folks to Putnam's before the redskins get properly on the warpath."

David shook his head, looking at Rebekah, the children, and his Paiute retainers who had gathered around to hear the grim tidings. "No, we'll be better off here. If the Indians see us run, it'll make them bolder. But if we show them we're not afraid and go on like nothing's happened, they might decide to let this business blow over."

"And they might not," Bart said, mounting his horse. "Do as you please. But don't say you weren't warned."

"We're obliged to you for that. Will you swing by Jeremy's place and give him the news, before you start back?"

"Nigger Charley's already gone there," Bart called back as he rode off. "Good luck to you."

David looked uncertainly at Rebekah. She put her hand supportively on his arm. "We will be safe here. My people know you are their friend."

"I think you're right," David said. "But we'd better fortify the house, just in case."

"I can handle a gun, Pa," D.C. said eagerly.

"Me, too!" Bobby Buck chimed in.

David smiled fondly at his sons. At twelve D.C. was a gangly collection of big hands, big feet, big ears and a broadshouldered frame waiting to be fleshed out. He had inherited too many of his parents' features to be truly handsome. But with David's open-faced honesty and Margaret's winning smile, he would never lack friends. Bobby Buck was a head shorter than his brother, with the compact build of a Paiute and his father's winsome good looks. Just looking at them often made David speechless with pride and love.

"Let's have no talk of guns," David chided the boys. He

252

ordered the Indians back to work and then stared at the house, his brow creased with the effort of finding the right ways to make it secure from attack.

Rebekah watched her husband with a small tender smile. She had full confidence in his ability to see them safely through the coming ordeal. But she knew how hard it would be on him emotionally, as he agonized over every decision and wondered afterwards if he had done the right thing. And she could guess from his expression what he was going to say next.

"If only Chance was here! He'd know what to do."

Lightning Tracker listened in silence to the runner's report. A steady rain was falling and water found its way through the wickiup's brush roof to discomfort the Paiutes squatting on the earth floor. Hu-pwi watched his father's face closely, but it betrayed no flicker of emotion at the ominous news. When the young messenger finished speaking the chief remained motionless, his unblinking eyes staring at something far beyond the other men's ken. His wife, Slow Of Speech, stirred the bubbling kettle on the small fire and placed a cup of hot soup before him. She could not stop shivering and sawing the air with the ugly cough that had plagued her all winter. The years had not dealt kindly with her. She was frail and wrinkled and her hands trembled constantly. Hu-pwi did not like to look directly at her, now that death crouched nakedly in her eyes.

If only he had had a little more time, Lightning Tracker mused, absently warming his hands over the steaming cup. He had been making good progress toward convincing the other chiefs that the deaths of Shondow and his braves were their own fault and therefore not worth breaking the treaty over. But all hope of smoothing that incident over was finished now, if the runner's story was accurate. According to him, Joaquin Jim and Paul the Apostle had led their warriors against the cabin of Ezra Taylor, a prospector living alone north of the valley. Taylor had held out for two days and killed several Indians before he was flushed out and pincushioned with arrows.

That had happened yesterday, and Jim and Paul had foolishly left Taylor's body where it had fallen. When the other whites found out about the killing—if they had not already done so—they were sure to make a retaliatory attack on any Indian camp they could find. The northern Indians would have gone into hiding by then. So the white avengers would turn south, where the scattered Paiute bands would have been unaware of their danger except for Lightning Tracker's efficient messenger service.

Lightning Tracker reviewed his last meeting with Jim and Paul, a week after the signing of the peace treaty. Jim had returned from his gun-buying trip and called the other chiefs together to discuss their chances of getting rid of the white invaders. Both Jim and Paul had made rousing speeches that had fired up the younger braves. But Lightning Tracker had cooled them off by calmly pointing out how dangerous it would be for them to make war on people who could call upon nearly unlimited reinforcements and weapons. Even the few white men already in the valley were armed with new breechloading rifles that were far superior to the Indians' simple bows and lances.

That argument was especially persuasive in view of the fact that Jim had brought back only a few ancient muzzle-loaders. Jim answered that the guns were the best he had been able to obtain in exchange for the small amount of trade goods he had taken along. The merchant from Aurora had refused to extend credit to the Indians. But he promised to pay them well for cattle, since beef was at a premium in the mining camps.

"So you propose to steal the white men's cattle and trade them for guns, when we are not even able to get enough meat to feed our children and old ones," Lightning Tracker had remarked scornfully, turning to his fellow Paiute chiefs. "Those of you who find that scheme feasible may go with him. But I prefer to go back to my people and help them survive until the return of warm weather makes the land fruitful again."

With that, Lightning Tracker had turned his back on Joaquin Jim and walked away from the powwow. He knew he was taking a big gamble, but it paid off when most of the other chiefs hesitantly rose and followed him. Behind him, Jim's voice cried angrily:

"Go then, cowards, and watch your people starve! But I will never submit to the white men's outrages."

"Nor I!" Paul the Apostle echoed.

Shifting his position to a drier spot on the wickiup floor, Lightning Tracker sighed tiredly. But he had never expected his job to be easy. "Go to David Wheeler and tell him what has happened," he said to Hu-Pwi. "If he will go with me to the white men who are assembled at Putnam's, we may be able to persuade them that the Paiutes were not involved in this new violence and we wish to live in peace."

As Hu-pwi started to rise, his mother spoke.

"No. I will go. The white men may already be at Wheeler's place. If so, they will not be as likely to shoot an old woman as a young brave."

That made so much sense that Lightning Tracker wondered why he hadn't thought of it. He nodded and Slow Of Speech left the wickiup. Lightning Tracker dismissed her from his thoughts and started making plans to move his people back into the hills until it was safe for them to return.

Groaning with the effort, Slow Of Speech made her way through the stinging raindrops away from the huddled collection of wickiups. When she was out of sight of the village she turned not north toward the Wheeler farm, but south toward Chief George's camp. She would deliver her husband's message to Wheeler later, if she had time. But first she wanted to make sure that all of the Paiutes in the area knew of their danger. She didn't know why Lightning Tracker had neglected to spread the alarm, but she had learned long ago that it was better to do something herself than call it to his attention and risk his wrath at having a woman tell him his business.

The soggy ground slowed her progress and the afternoon was well spent by the time she reached the first creek between her camp and Chief George's. Ordinarily an easily waded stream, the rain-swollen torrent growled menacingly as it rushed to join the river. Slow Of Speech surveyed the scene cautiously, then picked her way downstream to a spot where, in her younger days, she had skipped across on rocks protruding from the water.

There were five rocks in all, with the middle one so low that the muddy foam boiled over its polished surface. Slow Of Speech hesitated for a long time, wondering if she could make the leap safely. The thought of losing her footing and falling into the creek's clammy grip filled her with a fear that was perversely thrilling. At last her humdrum life had been made meaningful by the service she was performing for her people. Danger only enhanced the importance of what she was doing. Drawing courage from her sense of mission, she bit her lower lip and jumped.

She almost made it.

In the first panic-filled instant of feeling her foot slip off of the rock, Slow Of Speech thought how unfair it was that she was not allowed to fulfill the one important task of her life. Death itself held no terror for her; she rather looked forward to it as a welcome release from her pain-wracked and increasingly helpless existence. There was little reason for her to continue living anyway, now that her son was grown. She had known for years that Lightning Tracker no longer cared for her. With her out of the way he would have more freedom to court Winnedumah, although she really didn't know what he saw in her.

Then the shock of the icy current caused her to fling out her arms instinctively to halt her tumbling journey downstream. Other rocks struck her, and her gasping mouth breathed water. Finally she was swept near the bank and her fingers fastened around an overhanging tree root. She clung to it, coughing her way back to consciousness. When her vision cleared she saw that, with a little effort, she could drag herself up onto the bank. Then she heard something behind her, a low murmur over the creek's roar, like an old friend calling in the distance.

She turned her head and saw the river.

Her violent shivering ceased and she was bathed in a warm peaceful glow. Of course! The River of Life, where all is cleansed and refreshed. Why had she never noticed before how near it was? How stupid she had been to struggle toward a difficult goal, when the current could easily carry her where she really wanted to go. Smiling, she released her grip on the root.

* * *

There were twenty-five riders in all.

The determined expressions of the heavily armed white men told Hu-pwi all he needed to know. Quivering with excitement, the young brave gripped his bow and tried to get even closer to the earth where he lay concealed on a low rise a quarter of a mile from David's house. He watched the troop ride up to the house and wait for David to come out, before crawling down the other side of the rise on his belly.

When Slow Of Speech had not returned home the night before, Lightning Tracker assumed she had stayed overnight with the Wheelers to avoid walking back in the rain. But when the morning passed with no sign of her, he had started to worry. He was almost positive that David would not have harmed the old woman, but he had lived long enough to learn that no one can be trusted in wartime. So he had cautiously sent his braves out to scout the countryside. When one of them had found Slow Of Speech's body washed up on the riverbank a mile downstream, Lightning Tracker had not known what to think. After much deliberation, he had dispatched Hu-pwi to spy on David.

When Hu-pwi felt it was safe to get to his feet, he ran all the way back to his father's camp. Lightning Tracker listened to him gasp out his report, then issued a few terse commands. A half-hour later the only signs of life in the camp were a few wisps of smoke from dying fires.

David listened with growing sadness as Barton McGee gave a brief account of the discovery of Ezra Taylor's mutilated body and the unanimous decision of the other white settlers to avenge his death. The horsemen had dismounted to rest their animals but they remained tensely alert. Some of them looked suspiciously at the huts of David's Paiute workers. They were keyed up from the long day's ride and David did not doubt that any of them, except Jeremy Starr, who stood beside his new friend Charley Tyler, would flare into action at the slightest provocation.

"So we elected Anderson here our captain," Bart concluded.

"We mean to teach the redskins a lesson they won't soon forget," said the lean, broken-nosed man beside Bart.

Charles Anderson was an ex-cavalryman with a reputation for being a tenacious fighter, if not a noticeably brilliant one. "Are you with us?"

David had trouble keeping his mind on the conversation. He looked westward at the Sierra crest, where the lowering sun gleamed through the broken cloud cover. The nasty weather was passing at last. Tomorrow ought to be clear and fresh with the first smell of spring. "But why come this far south?" he asked. "None of the Indians around here had anything to do with killing Taylor, as far as we know."

"That don't make much difference," Anderson replied. "Every Indian in the valley's fair game now that the treaty's been broken."

"Not my Paiutes," David protested. "None of 'em's been off the place in weeks, and I give you my word they're all law-abiding."

"All right, we'll leave them out of it," Anderson said.

"And Lightning Tracker's band, too," David urged. "I know he wouldn't do anything to break the peace, after he worked so hard to get the treaty."

There was an angry rumble of protest from several of the men.

"You can't spread your blanket wide enough to cover all of 'em," Bart McGee said with a thin smile.

"At least let me go along and talk to Lightning Tracker first."

"The time for talking is past," said Tom Hubbard, rubbing his bandaged left arm where he had taken an arrow in the fight with Chief Shondow and his braves.

"We ain't bloodthirsty," Anderson said in a more conciliatory tone. "You can have your palaver with Lightning Tracker, if he don't start anything first."

"Thanks," David said. "I'll get my gear."

He went into the house where Rebekah and the children waited. Winnedumah, having grown more stout and arthritic with the years, sat in a rocking chair near the fireplace. David explained the situation and said he would probably be away for a day or so. They had been prepared for something like this and while D.C. went out to saddle a horse for David, Bobby Buck fetched his bedroll and saddle bags.

"Go tell the workers they must stay close to home until the trouble is over," David said to Winnedumah. "If they leave, the white men may think they are going to join the war parties and kill them."

Winnedumah heaved her bulk out of the chair with a grunt of angry resignation. It was only to be expected that men would be responsible for disturbing the peace of her old age, since they had ruined the rest of her life. She waddled out silently cursing the entire male sex.

David turned to Rebekah, who stood holding little Rachel's hand. "Will there be fighting?" she asked.

"Don't you worry about that," he said, going to her. "Just keep everything under control here while I'm gone. Don't let the boys get too rambunctious."

Rebekah kept the fear out of her face until he had kissed her and Rachel and left the room.

As David went out to the men, followed by Bobby Buck carrying his rifle, D.C. came around the house leading the horse. David clapped the boy's shoulder. "Well, son, you're the man of the family while I'm away. So take good care of everybody."

D.C. thrust out his chest proudly. "You can count on me, Pa."

"Me too," said Bobby Buck.

David embraced his sons, then swung into the saddle.

They reached Lightning Tracker's camp at sunset and paused only long enough to make sure it was as deserted as it appeared.

"Let's burn the wickiups," one of the men suggested.

Anderson shook his head. "That wouldn't do any good, and the other Indians hereabouts might be warned by the smoke. Mount up. We'll go on to Chief George's camp."

Darkness had fallen when they came to the sod cabin of Ault and Sadler, not far from the hills where David had tried to end his life after Margaret's death. While most of the men ate a cold supper, Anderson sent scouts ahead to obtain more information on the Indian camp. In two hours the scouts returned to report that they had spied on the

Paiutes calmly going about their business, evidently unaware of their danger.

"We'll attack at dawn," Anderson decided.

David asked to be allowed to talk to Chief George first, but Anderson said no. The white men were spoiling for a fight and they didn't want to risk having this group of Indians slip away from them as the others had done. When David persisted, Anderson issued orders that he was not to be allowed to leave the camp under any circumstances. Then the elected captain told the men not on guard duty to turn in and get all of the sleep they could.

David unrolled his blankets near Jeremy and Charley Tyler. He felt frustrated and ashamed of himself for not doing more to prevent what was shaping up to be a bloody fight. It would be different if Chance were here! He would find a way to get around Anderson and settle this mess peacefully. But deep down David had to admit that Anderson could be right in thinking they had to hit the Indians hard before they could get organized for a major uprising.

David lay staring at the patches of clouds and stars, wishing that life was not so confusing.

Jeremy shared David's worried puzzlement. He had not wanted to join this expedition, but he couldn't refuse to come along because he was afraid Charley would think he was afraid. Jeremy could not explain the bond of deep affection that had been established between Charley and himself; he only knew that he would do just about anything to preserve it.

Jeremy tried to recapture the happiness he had felt when he first took Charley home to meet Maria and their two children. He had nearly popped his buttons with swelling pride when Charley had complimented him on the good life he had made for his family in the valley. After supper they had sat up for hours talking about what a wonderful country this California was, where even an ex-slave could become a prosperous landowner. Charley had listened interestedly as Jeremy told him how easily he, too, could homestead a farm here and get himself a good wife to help work it. When Charley had left the following day to return to his cowpunching job with the McGees, Jeremy had eagerly looked forward to having his new friend for a neighbor, as soon as the Indian trouble was settled.

All during their ride down the valley, Jeremy had hoped they would not encounter any Indians, or at least none that he knew personally. But Charley had cheerfully joined the white men's talk about the sport they would have shooting redskins. Their brutal remarks frightened Jeremy, but he knew there was no cure for war fever when it infected men. He had seen it burning in the eyes of supporters of the northern and southern states in Los Angeles. Jeremy fell asleep wondering why people could get so worked up over the notion of killing folks they didn't even know.

The sky was so clear and black when the guards passed among the men shaking them awake that the blazing stars looked within reach. David guessed from the position of Orion that it was an hour before daybreak. His blankets crinkled with frost as he crawled stiffly out of them to pull on his boots. The shivering men muttered about how good hot coffee would taste as they ate a cold breakfast from their supplies of boiled beef.

After checking their weapons, the men formed up and Anderson divided them into two squads. Leaving three men in charge of the horses, Anderson led one squad directly into the hills while the other followed a winding creekbed to outflank the Indians. David went with Anderson, who promised to use him as interpreter if they found it necessary to talk to the Indians.

In spite of the rough going through the rock-strewn hills, they made good time and were within sight of the Indians' campfires when the eastern sky started to gray out the stars. Anderson ordered them to crawl up as close to the camp as they dared, finding meager cover behind rocks and brush. David lay between Anderson and Jeremy, watching the squaws bending over cooking pots and baskets while their men squatted outside the wickiups waiting for breakfast. A few early-rising children begged morsels from their mothers. David and Jeremy exchanged helpless looks. They both recognized Chief George and several other acquaintances.

Anderson had planned to wait until the other squad joined them before launching the attack. But with each passing moment the growing light increased their danger of being spotted by the Indians. Finally he realized he could wait no longer and signaled his men to prepare to fire. David writhed in an agony of indecision, then made up his mind that he could not be a party to cold-blooded murder. Aiming his rifle over Chief George's head, he jerked the trigger and hoped the sound of his shot would give the Paiutes enough warning to run to cover.

When the other men fired an instant later, the Indians were already dashing for the shelter of the rocks behind them. A squaw and five braves fell, but the others were out of sight before the white men could get off a second volley.

"After 'em, boys!" Anderson yelled, leaping to his feet.

The squad surged forward, whooping and firing as they ran. Jeremy glimpsed Charley to his right, his black face split into a wild grin as his sixgun roared with deadly accuracy. The chase lasted for about a hundred yards before the Indians disappeared into well-shielded cavities in the rocks and sent a shower of arrows down on the white men. Tom Hubbard cursed as another arrow struck his wounded arm. Jim Harness was struck on the forehead but fortunately the obsidian arrowhead shattered without penetrating. Scott Broder caught an arrow in the shoulder and broke the shaft trying to pull it out.

Anderson saw that the Indians were too securely entrenched to be taken by a frontal assault and ordered his men back to a safe distance. Most of them found good firing positions behind rocks and sniped at the dark cave entrances, while the Indians replied with more arrows. After thirty minutes, the other squad arrived and joined the battle.

The white men kept up their harassing fire until noon, with little effect on the Indians' stubborn resistance. Several plans to flush the Indians out in the open were discussed, but Anderson judged that they had achieved enough of a victory without taking any further risks. They burned the wickiups and all other Indian property they could find, including a large supply of dried meat and pinon nuts—after filling their pockets with the latter—and started walking back to their horses. Most of them were in good spirits, including Charley Tyler, who laughingly tossed shelled pinons in the air and caught them in his mouth.

"We don't even know if George's band was on the warpath," David remarked.

"If they wasn't befo', they is now," Jeremy said grimly.

Chapter 24

March 25, 1862
James W. Nye, Governor,
Territory of Nevada
Care of Bella Union Hotel
San Francisco, California
Indian difficulties on Owens River confirmed. Hostiles advancing this way. I desire to go and if possible prevent war from reaching this territory. If a few men poorly armed go against those Indians defeat will follow and a long and bloody war will ensue. If the whites on Owens River had prompt and adequate assistance it could be checked there. I have just returned from Walker River. Paiutes alarmed. I await reply.

Warren Wasson,
Acting Indian Agent,
Territory of Nevada

Governor Nye sat facing General Horace Wright, who had succeeded Albert Sidney Johnston as Commander of the Department of the Pacific, and admired the fine view of the Golden Gate and San Francisco harbor the general's Presidio office provided. General Wright read the telegram and looked up.

"How serious do you think it is, Jim?"

"Not nearly as bad as Wasson makes it out, I'm sure,"

the governor answered. "He always was a Nervous Nellie."

"Then a couple of cavalry companies should be sufficient?"

"More than sufficient, I should think."

"Consider it done."

"Thanks, Horace. I knew I could rely on you."

"Don't mention it. Will this cause you to cut your vacation short?"

"Good heavens, no!" Nye shuddered at the thought. Presiding over the sagebrush wilderness of Nevada was such a strain on his refined sensibilities that he found it necessary to refresh them with frequent visits to the civilized fleshpots of San Francisco.

"Good. Then I'll expect you at my Friday night poker game."

General Wright summoned his secretary to transcribe the orders that he assumed would, in a part of the country that was still innocent of the Civil War madness, automatically bring about a swift end of the Indian difficulties on the Owens River.

"Wild horses couldn't keep me away," Governor Nye assured him.

David stayed close to home in the days following the raid on Chief George's camp. He tried to contact Lightning Tracker in the hope of working out another peace treaty, but the old chief was too canny to leave the Sierra canyon where his people had taken refuge.

David and Jeremy were the only remaining settlers in the valley south of Putnam's cabin—which was being called Putnam's Fort—where forty-five men and a few women and children huddled waiting for the outside world to answer their call for help. And they were going to need all the help they could get.

Chief George and several other Paiute leaders had taken their people north to join Joaquin Jim and Paul the Apostle. The Indians ravaged the countryside, killing a few lone white travelers and driving off cattle. But mainly they concentrated on obtaining more guns and ammunition and making other preparations for a full-scale war.

Twelve hundred braves were on the warpath by then, all

265

of them dedicated to the proposition that the only good white man was a dead white man. As a fighting force they lacked only good organization, as Joaquin Jim vainly tried to convince the Paiutes who refused to accept him as their commander-in-chief. It took a stupid blunder by the enemy to unite the Indians and make them, for a little while, the most serious threat to white dominance in California that the state had yet seen.

The men at Putnam's, having grown dissatisfied with Charles Anderson's leadership, elected William Mayfield as their new captain. In Mayfield's opinion, Anderson had been too timid in his battle with Chief George. He believed that a swift hard blow against the Indians would break the back of their rebellion. Putting theory into practice, Mayfield led out a mounted force of thirty-two men to find and engage the hostiles.

Shortly before that, John J. Kellogg had started from Aurora with seventeen volunteers to relieve Putnam's, which he had heard was being besieged by Indians. The two parties met and joined forces near Samuel Bishop's San Francis Ranch, as Indian scouts in the hills looked on. The next day, April 6, the whites encountered nearly every hostile Indian in the valley on the creek that has since worn Bishop's name.

The Indians still possessed only a few ancient muzzle-loaders and were ignorant of their proper use and care. So the well-armed white men could have achieved a decisive victory, if they had had a good leader. But Mayfield mismanaged his command so badly that three of his men were killed and several more were wounded in a battle that lasted most of a day and a night. Indian casualties were much higher, but under Joaquin Jim's skillful direction the warriors drove the whites back and almost succeeded in capturing their pack train. Under cover of a brave rear guard action fought by Nigger Charley Tyler, Bart and Alney McGee, and a few others, the whites were able to retreat safely to Big Pine Creek.

While the Battle of Bishop Creek was in progress, two military forces were entering Owens Valley from opposite directions. Lieutenant-Colonel George S. Evans, leading eighty troopers of the Second California Cavalry from

Camp Drum near Los Angeles, passed through the southern end of the valley and stopped at David's house to ask about the situation further north. David was unable to provide much information, but he offered to go along with the soldiers and give whatever help he could in the way of talking the Indians into making peace. Colonel Evans gladly accepted the offer and David once more left D.C. and Bobby Buck to defend the homestead.

Acting Indian Agent Warren Wasson, after receiving an affirmative reply to his telegram to Governor Nye, had gone to Fort Churchill, Nevada, where Company A of the Second California Cavalry was stationed. Captain Edward Rowe, the ranking officer, had instructed Lieutenant Herman Noble to accompany Wasson with fifty men and do everything possible to pacify the Indians.

The two cavalry detachments met at Big Pine Creek while the civilian Indian fighters under Mayfield were still there licking their wounds. The white leaders had a powwow of their own, with Wasson and David arguing in favor of meeting the hostile chiefs under a flag of truce. Wasson was especially eager to talk peace with the Paiutes when he learned that David spoke their tongue and knew many of them as old friends. But Mayfield, enraged by his shameful defeat, urged a campaign of extermination against the Indians.

Colonel Evans tended to agree with Mayfield. An experienced soldier who knew something about Indian psychology, Evans shrewdly guessed that the Paiutes and their allies would be too puffed-up with their victory to come to a peace conference. They would have to be soundly beaten before they could be persuaded to get off of the warpath, Evans surmised. However, he compromised with Wasson by promising to scout out the Indians to see if they were peacefully disposed before taking action against them.

Being the senior officer present, Colonel Evans assumed command of the combined military force and asked for volunteers from the Mayfield and Kellogg commands. Most of the uninjured civilians agreed to serve under Evans, who then sent the wounded men back to Putnam's with a cavalry escort. Two days after the Battle of Bishop Creek, Evans dispatched scouting parties in different directions and ordered the bulk of his 153 men to rest and clean their weapons. Indian Agent Wasson sat under a pine tree with David and three cavalry officers. One of them—Captain Garfield Winne, a strange, brooding man in his late thirties—was often seen jotting things down in a notebook that he never allowed anyone to read.

"What do you think of the situation, Mr. Wheeler?" Wasson asked.

David peered up at masses of dark, fat-bottomed clouds settling over the Sierra peaks. "Bad weather coming. Wouldn't surprise me if we had snow before dark."

"I mean about the Indian situation," Wasson said.

"You can't discuss Indians without taking the weather into account," Captain Winne remarked in a dry monotone. "The weather, the land, water, animals—all the elements of nature are inseparable parts of the primitive man's makeup."

The other men looked at Winne in surprise. His fellow officers had never heard him voluntarily comment on anything before. David was pleased to hear some of his own feelings about Indians expressed so well. Wasson was impressed, and a little jealous, at hearing a military man speak intelligently about what was supposed to be his specialty.

"Well, what do *you* think the weather has to do with the present Indian situation?" the Indian agent challenged Winne.

"It means we'll have to fight them, if there's snow," Winne answered. "Storms favor savages. They're inured to harsh weather and can function better in it than civilized men."

"Oh, come off it, Winne," Lieutenant Oliver scoffed.

"He's right," David said. "The last time I talked to Chief Lightning Tracker, he said Joaquin Jim needed two things to make him big medicine with the Indians—a victory over the whites and more bad weather and starvation to keep the Paiutes desperate enough to fight."

"We'll have to wait and see about that," Wasson said. "At any rate, I believe Colonel Evans is clever enough not to let the Indians provoke him into a fight when the advantage is with them."

268

"Children believe in Father Christmas, too," Winne replied.

They were reminded of that a few hours later when an excited shout called their attention to the return of a scouting party with one of its blood-smeared members slung over his saddle.

Joaquin Jim leaned on his long rifle, savoring the sharp burnt-powder aroma of the recently fired piece. He also savored the anticipation of what he believed was going to be his finest hour.

"My warriors will act as bait," he said, concluding the description of his plan to the other chiefs. It was a simple yet effective stratagem designed to lure the attacking cavalrymen across Round Valley and into the narrow canyon where a deadly ambush would be waiting for them. Jim was certain the soldiers would be too emotionally eager to fight when they arrived to pause and cautiously examine the battlefield. He had made sure of that when he personally shot the sergeant leading the scouting patrol up from Owens Valley.

Paul the Apostle smiled and lovingly polished the blade of his saber. But most of the other chiefs—George, Dick, and Little Dick in particular—did not look so enthusiastic for the coming fight. George peered up at the steep mountain range, where the first light snow flurries were dusting the highest foothills.

"It is not a good time to fight," Chief George said. "The storm will break shortly, then darkness will fall. Our braves could become confused and shoot at each other."

Chiefs Dick and Little Dick expressed agreement with George.

"But those are the best conditions for us," Joaquin Jim argued. "It is the white men who will be confused. We will easily cut them to pieces. And if the battle should go against us, the snow and darkness will cover our withdrawal."

"Do not be frightened women," Paul sneered when the chiefs continued to look unconvinced. "This is our chance to crush the whites and drive them out of our land forever."

269

"That was what we were told two days ago," Chief Dick said. "But we were unable to destroy a force much smaller than that which advances against us now."

"This is an even better opportunity," Jim insisted. "These are not just ordinary white men, but their finest warriors. When we defeat them, the entire white race will regard us with fear and respect."

"They will be too terrified ever to come back," Paul added.

"And how many of our people will have to die for that purpose?" George asked.

"If the glory of victory was cheap, it would not be worth having," Paul answered carelessly.

Jim could have killed Paul for that. The other chiefs' expressions did not change, but it was obvious that they resented having their braves' lives treated so lightly. Bitter anguish welled up in him as he felt his chance of greatness slipping away just as he had finally come within reach of it. When the whites had retreated from Bishop Creek, the Indians had hailed Jim as their heroic leader. But even as he had enjoyed the thrill of victory, he had known he must act fast to consolidate his power. Only by engineering a defeat of the cavalry could he hope to achieve supreme command of all Indian forces in the valley.

Chief George looked once more at the approaching storm. "No, this is not a good time to fight, I think."

He turned and walked away to where his braves were waiting. The other Paiute chiefs followed his example, as Jim's hands twisted the barrel of his rifle in frustration.

"What kind of dogs are you?" Paul called scornfully after the departing chiefs. "If you enjoy being cowards, why don't you wait for the white men to come and watch them lie with your wives?" He turned to Jim with a look of cool indifference. "Well, there will be other days to kill white men."

Jim glared at Paul. His inferior mind could not grasp the tragic consequences of the Paiutes' withdrawal. The Owens Valley Indians were not a close-knit, cooperative people either by government organization or social custom. Only an exceptionally fortunate chain of events had assembled their full fighting strength here today. Without the bond of a great military victory to hold them together, the individual Paiute bands and family groups would drift back to their home territories. In time the braves would lose their war fever and the chiefs would accept peace terms dictated by the white leaders. Only those who, like Jim, had seen their families and tribespeople slaughtered could continue fighting with relentless hatred until stopped by total victory or death.

"Where to now, brother?" Paul asked.

"You may go wherever you please," Jim answered, turning away to join his handful of loyal followers. "But I have a war to fight."

A light shower of wet snowflakes was falling by mid-afternoon, when Colonel Evans's cavalrymen and civilian volunteers rode into Round Valley. The wind carried the smell of smoke and they followed it up to the northwestern end of the valley, where they found the smoldering remains of a campfire in the mouth of a winding canyon.

"Why would the Indians have left a fire burning here?" Evans wondered aloud to David and Indian Agent Wasson.

"No sensible reason for it," David answered.

"Unless they *wanted* us to find it," Wasson offered.

"Yes, it's obviously intended to draw us into the canyon, where an ambush has most likely been prepared for us. I must congratulate the leader of the savages on his strategy, if we take him alive."

"You're not going into the canyon, are you?" Wasson asked.

"Not the way the Indians hope we will," Evans said, ordering Bugler John Hubinger to ask his officers to join him.

Sending Lieutenants Noble and Oliver along the top of the north wall of the canyon with forty men, Evans took an equal number up the opposite ridge with Lieutenant French's assistance. The remainder of the men were left at the canyon mouth under Captain Winne's command, to welcome the Indians that Evans hoped to drive back down with his pincer maneuver.

David and Wasson hunkered in the melting snow with Captain Winne, after he had finished deploying his men.

Wasson pulled off his gloves and blew on his fingers, then put them under his armpits.

"After our conversation this morning, I'd be interested in hearing any other observations you care to make about Indians," Wasson said to Winne. "Have you known many of them intimately?"

"Only my wife," Winne answered.

Wasson peered curiously at him. "What was her tribe?"

"I'm really not very cognizant of the Paiutes," Winne said. "Wheeler here is your best authority on them."

"I've already told him all I know about 'em," David said. "I just wish I could tell him a way to end this awful fighting."

"The most efficacious solution would be to invite all of the Indians to a feast," Winne suggested. "Then massacre them."

David stared speechlessly at Winne. "That's a rather drastic proposal, don't you think?" Wasson inquired.

"The Paiutes are finished anyway," Winne's expressionless voice continued. "There simply is not enough water in the valley to satisfy the needs of Indians and whites, who are the stronger of the two groups. So we can do one of three things with the Paiutes: kill them outright, drive them into the desert to starve, or make them slaves to work the land that was once theirs. The first course of action is the most humane."

"The government doesn't see it that way," Wasson said. "That's why we have the reservation system."

"You only confirm my assertion. As you no doubt can testify from your own observation of the inadequate water supplies of most southwestern Indian reservations."

"You make much of the most common liquid resource," Wasson countered, uncomfortably aware of the truth in Winne's last statement.

"Common, but vital. This is a water war we are fighting, as are all of the conflicts out here. Men may think they contend for other gifts of nature—grass, fertile soil, minerals or timber. But without water, all other products of the land are meaningless. In the end, it is always those who control the water who determine the fate of the land."

David struggled to understand a concept that had never

before been put to him in quite those terms. "You might as well say we're fighting the Indians for their air, since everybody needs that as much as they need water."

"Men have not yet found the means to take possession of air and dole it out," Winne said. "But it's only a matter of time."

"Yours is a bleak judgment of mankind, Captain," Wasson commented.

"It merely reflects the course of human progress. Property tenancy inevitably passes to the stronger. The former Indian and Latin masters of California who resent our Anglo-Saxon usurpation can take comfort in the certainty that we in turn will be supplanted by other races. As the Japanese haiku puts it:

> Love your conquerors.
> In a thousand years they too
> will be conquered."

"A thousand years can be a long time for a Paiute with an empty belly," David murmured.

Sergeant McKenzie approached and spoke in the captain's ear.

"Excuse me," Winne said, rising and following McKenzie through the thickening snowfall toward the line of troopers guarding the canyon.

Wasson watched him go. "A man of unsuspected depths."

"Seems to be a lot of hurt in him," David agreed.

Colonel Evans kept his men scrambling over the slippery rocks flanking the canyon until the storm reached full gale force. Snow driven by the abrasive wind howling down the Sierra wall turned to icicles in the soldiers' beards. As they moved, the icicles broke and left jagged edges to chafe their faces. When they could see no more than a few feet ahead of them in the swirling whiteness, Evans drew his revolver and fired two quick shots in the air. From across the canyon echoed the sound of a single shot, as Lieutenant Noble acknowledged the colonel's prearranged signal to turn back.

"This storm is a lucky break for the Indians," Lieutenant French shouted in Evans's ear over the wind's roar.

"Yes, it's damned frustrating to think they may be within range of our guns, and we can't see them," Evans replied, unaware that Joaquin Jim's rifle was leveled at his back. But the weapon misfired on damp powder and before Jim could fit an arrow to his bowstring the colonel was out of sight.

The soldiers withdrew to the valley and made camp. An hour after nightfall the storm abated somewhat, enabling the exhausted men to get a little sleep. As David crawled into his blankets near Captain Winne, he heard a gurgling sound and caught the scent of alcohol. Colonel Evans had strictly forbade drinking on duty, but David didn't think it was his place to report the captain. He figured that anyone who had managed to carry a bottle this far without breaking it deserved to enjoy it.

Garfield Winne only occasionally needed the aid of strong spirits to blank out the past. Most of the time he could move fast enough to stay ahead of it. The Mexican-American War had first aroused his wanderlust, when he was studying for the ministry at Harvard. When he returned from the war, his parents were dead and he had no desire to continue his education. He obtained a position as a law clerk and married a quiet, pleasant girl, but she soon died in childbirth.

Winne eventually reached California and panned for gold, went to sea for a few years, worked at various jobs around San Francisco and then tried his hand at desert prospecting. On the Gila River he lived with a Papago squaw and treated her as a wife. But she took his kindness for weakness and ran away with a man of her tribe who beat her and kept her pregnant much of the time. Winne made his way back to California and rejoined the Army.

During the night Joaquin Jim gazed down on the white men's campfires and entertained himself with fantasies of what he would do if he had more than twenty-four warriors with him. He was angry enough to attack the enemy camp alone, but he kept himself under control. This was not the right time for him to die. Even without the Paiutes' help, he must go on fighting as long as possible. Leaving one brave to keep the enemy under observation, he returned to his men in the canyon.

By morning the weather had cleared and the wet snow had frozen to an icy crust over the soldiers' tents and blankets. They awoke complaining about the futility of spending another day searching for unseen Indians. But Colonel Evans briskly led them back to the canyon mouth.

"Them Indians're long gone by now," William Mayfield muttered sourly within the colonel's hearing.

"Perhaps, but we can't go on without making sure," Evans said. He ordered Lieutenant Noble to take nine men and scout the canyon, then sent similar details up the next two canyons along the upper rim of the valley. The remaining cavalrymen and civilians waited without speaking, occasionally flinging their arms across their chests to stir sluggish circulation. The rising sun warmed the rocks and started a liquid chorus dripping from the melting snow and ice.

Lieutenant Noble's men advanced along both sides of the creek that flowed down the floor of the canyon, their eyes carefully scanning the scattered boulders and the nooks and crannies in the rocky walls. Trooper Christopher Gillespie looked up and smiled at a golden eagle sliding across the blue roof of the gulley. Sergeant McKenzie told him to keep alert, as their horses carried them around a bend to within sight of a side ravine. Gillespie was wondering if sighting the eagle so early in the day was a good omen, when a bullet rudely interrupted his thoughts.

Sergeant McKenzie felt a sharp blow strike his chest as Gillespie was knocked from the saddle. McKenzie thought he would be all right once he caught his breath. More gunshots reverberated from the canyon walls and puffs of smoke rose from behind rocks. An Indian sprang out in the open holding a drawn bow, released his arrow and darted back under cover. Lieutenant Noble, remembering that his orders were only to locate the enemy, not engage them, ordered a retreat. He emptied his revolver in the direction of the Indians to cover his men as they wheeled their mounts around and dashed back down the canyon. Gillespie's horse trotted after them, leaving its rider lying motionless beside the stream.

Halfway back to the canyon mouth they met Evans leading the rest of his command up to find out what the shooting was about. Noble explained what had happened, reloading his pistol with trembling fingers.

"Was anyone else hit?" Evans asked the scouts.

"Got a bullet in my left arm, sir," Corporal John Harries answered.

Evans looked at the hole in the front of McKenzie's coat. "What about you, Sergeant?"

"I'm all right, Colonel."

McKenzie pressed his hand to his chest, stared in astonishment at the blood on his fingers, and slumped over his saddlebow. When his comrades lifted him down, he was dead.

"Come with me, Lieutenant Noble," Evans said. "Captain Winne, keep your troop to the right. Lieutenant French, yours to the left. Lieutenant Oliver, cover the rear until we know how many we're up against."

Mayfield spurred his horse forward. "I'm going with you! I owe those red bastards something for Bishop Creek."

Several of the other civilian volunteers insisted on going along, too, and Evans made no effort to stop them. At Noble's direction, Evans ordered his men to halt and dismount just short of coming into view of the Indians' positions. As they crept around the final bend, they received fire and returned it. Wasson, with David's help, climbed to the top of a tall rock where he had a good view of the battle. He could see the Indian riflemen clumsily recharging their weapons while their bowmen distracted the soldiers.

"We can take 'em, boys!" Mayfield yelled, waving his revolver. "Let's go!"

He ran forward and the other civilians followed him, ignoring Evans' command to halt. Firing wildly, Mayfield almost made it to the entrance of the ravine when an Indian stood up and shot him through the body. John Welch, just behind Mayfield, killed the Indian, then helped another man pick up the wounded citizen captain. As they were carrying him back under the cavalrymen's covering fire, another bullet struck him with fatal results.

Seeing Mayfield's attack beaten back confused Evans's judgment. Thinking that he was facing a large number of Indians in a confined area where he could not effectively deploy his troops, Evans ordered a retreat. As the soldiers fell back, they picked up the body of Trooper Gillespie.

"Why is that fool pulling back?" Wasson demanded of David. "He could easily overrun those few Indians."

Wasson shouted that information to Evans. But by the time he had made the colonel understand that there were less than thirty Indians in the ravine, Joaquin Jim had successfully withdrawn his band. Another cavalry scouting party failed to locate them and, it being nearly noon by then, Evans ordered his command back to the valley for lunch. While they were eating, Evans announced that he had decided to withdraw from Round Valley and start evacuating all of the white settlers from Owens Valley. Wasson was dumbfounded by the news.

"But there are only a handful of Indians up there," he insisted. "Probably a rear guard left to cover the others' escape. If you leave now, you'll increase the Indians' confidence and add to the likelihood of further outbreaks."

"It will only be a temporary withdrawal," Evans answered, "until we can return better prepared for a long campaign. I only brought along enough supplies to last forty days, and I distributed much of that to settlers in need on the way up here. I had hoped for a quick victory over the Indians that would make them willing to talk peace. Now I can't afford to waste time chasing them up and down the valley."

Wasson argued for more time in which he could try to contact the Indian leaders. But Evans's decision was final. They left Round Valley that afternoon, trying not to feel ashamed when Joaquin Jim and his warriors came out of the canyon to shout defiant taunts after them.

The evacuation of Owens Valley began at once. In the following days the cavalry escorted nearly all of the white settlers and their livestock over Walker Pass to the safety of the San Joaquin Valley. David, after much hard thinking, decided that he could not leave Margaret's side even for a little while. Nor could he persuade Rebekah to take the children away until the Army could make the valley secure again. However, he was able to talk Jeremy, who also refused to leave the valley, into moving his family in with them.

As Wasson had predicted, the Indians became bolder and more aggressive when the soldiers were gone. For a while the Paiutes held Joaquin Jim in high esteem for his successful resistance to the cavalry. But without a common enemy present, Jim was unable to unite all of the Valley Indians. When he tried to lead them in an attack on David's farm, most of the Paiutes refused to fight an old friend and the others were disheartened by the strong fortifications David and Jeremy had constructed. Jim had to content himself with killing and plundering the few whites who were imprudent enough to travel through Owens Valley without adequate protection.

The next two months passed tensely for everyone at David's. One day when David was out doing some spring planting, dark clouds of smoke billowing over the ridgeline told him that spiteful Indians had fired Jeremy's house and barn. Jeremy was heartbroken by the news, after the hard, loving care he had put into developing his property. Then he cheered up at the thought of Maria and their children safe in David's house. Buildings could always be replaced.

Chapter 25

Chance left Alexander Bell's house tingling with the anticipation of seeing action again at last. It had been an exhilarating evening for the nearly fifty leading Los Angeles citizens gathered in Bell's *sala*. The high point of the meeting
had come with General Andres Pico's announcement that
he had asked Governor Stanford's permission to organize
an expedition against the warring Indians of Owens Valley.
Chance had been promised a high-ranking position in the
expedition, perhaps even as Pico's second-in-command.

It was about time something definite was done about the
Paiute uprising, Chance reflected as he mounted his horse.
Only his absence from town on business when Colonel Evans had departed from Camp Drum had prevented Chance
from joining that campaign. When he had learned, upon
Evans's return, how serious the Owens Valley situation had
become, Chance had been beside himself with eagerness to
rush to David's aid. It had been easy to stick to his vow
never to get involved with military adventures again when
only the Civil War had tempted him, but knowing that
David and his family were in danger drastically altered his
outlook. In fact, if Pico had not put forth his plan, Chance
was prepared to lead a volunteer force of his own to rescue
David.

Chance was halfway to the plaza before he realized that he had turned his horse north instead of west, toward home. He well understood why he had made the subconscious decision and, after a brief hesitation, figured he might as well take care of something he had been putting off for several months. There would never be a better time for it, now that he was about to leave on a dangerous mission.

Chance's horse turned into Nigger Alley and he saw the familiar front of La Marseillaise. He smiled at the memory of the good times he and Si Darcy had known there. Unfortunately the establishment was no longer graced by the colorful presence of Madame Moustache. She had saved enough money to return to France in style and two years later the news of her death had reached Los Angeles.

Chance reined up before the dilapidated adobe building that he had often approached, then turned away telling himself not to stir up the dead past. The sign over the door said it all: The Glory Hole.

Chance dismounted and gave a coin to one of the Alley's ever-present urchins to hold his horse. Then he stood hesitantly as emotional memories crowded his mind. Gloria Holt had arrived in Los Angeles ten months ago with three fairly attractive girls and soon hired two more. She was said to be doing well enough as a madame to support her male companion—Willis Trent, the faro-dealing gambler who had killed one of the Gookin brothers in the gunfight at Goldcock.

There were many rumors about Gloria and Willis, some of them so fantastic that they were probably true. Somehow they had gotten back together after Chance had left Gloria in San Francisco and their combined skills enabled them to live well in California's golden boom. Eventually they joined the Australian gold rush and prospered even more in New South Wales. By providing high-spending pleasure-seekers with sophisticated vice, they became famous throughout the western Pacific, operating sumptuous sporting establishments in Hong Kong, Manila, and Singapore. Flushed with success, they moved on to London and Paris, where they entertained the cream of European society. But finally a decline in their fortunes and Willis's health had forced them to seek the beneficial climate of southern California.

Chance did not fully understand the strong force that drew him to the Glory Hole. He was certain he had done the right thing in breaking off with Gloria when he realized he could not overlook her past. But the pleasure of their single night together had remained with him all these years. He had to see Gloria again, to make sure he had really gotten her out of his system.

It was nearly eleven and the Alley's social activities were in full swing. Two men, snickering and making lewd jokes about the good times they were about to have, shouldered open the door of the Glory Hole and disappeared inside. Chance hesitated a little longer, then cursed his nervously racing heart and walked up to the door.

It was a sordid imitation of a high-class parlor house, where the girls sat around trying to look demurely seductive while the customer decided which one he'd take upstairs. But there was no upstairs here; just a dark hallway to stuffy little cubicles at the rear of the house. The room was filled with expensive red velvet furniture and tasteful nude paintings left over from the proprietors' more affluent years. A faded blonde on the sofa looked up hopefully at Chance. His gaze swept over her to a disheveled, beard-stubbled man playing solitaire at a low table with a half-empty whiskey bottle and two glasses handy. The man ignored Chance, who glanced at the room's only other occupant, an Indian maid sitting silently in a corner. Then he looked at the back of a woman who was ushering the two recently arrived men and their girls down the hall. He knew the woman was Gloria even before she turned around.

A broad smile of recognition spread over Gloria's face. "Chance! How wonderful to see you again. You haven't changed a bit."

"Nor have you, Gloria. Still as beautiful as ever."

"And you remember how much I love flattery, too," she laughed.

But Chance did not have to tell flattering lies. Gloria, now in her early thirties, retained much of the fresh beauty of her youth. Her auburn hair was immaculately groomed and artfully applied makeup under her eyes concealed dark circles that, Chance was sure, were caused by fatigue rather than age. Holding her hands out before her, she walked swiftly to him with a soft rustle of skirts and petticoats. Her low-cut burgundy gown showed off her lovely white shoulders and full breasts. She gave Chance's hands a welcoming squeeze and peered into his eyes.

"Did you see who's here, darling?"

The man playing solitaire looked up and Chance was shocked to recognize him as Willis Trent. Somehow the dapper, swarthily handsome young gentleman-of-fortune had gotten lost in this slovenly, wasted wreck with a flabby gray complexion and sunken eyes that swam in a pink haze. Only his disarmingly guileless smile remained unchanged as he rose unsteadily to his feet.

"Hello, Chance. Long time no see."

"Hello, Willis. Sorry to hear you've been sick."

"Nothing that the right medicine won't cure." Willis picked up the bottle with one hand and both glasses with the other. "Let's have a drink to old times. I need some company, now that Gloria's gone temperance."

Gloria frowned as Willis sloshed whiskey into the glasses and thrust one at Chance. He downed his drink in two swallows, then burst into a violent fit of coughing. Chance caught his arm as he staggered weakly.

"You'd better rest a while, dear," Gloria said, taking Willis's other arm.

"I don't wanna be put to bed and miss the fun," Willis protested in the petulant whine of a spoiled child.

But Willis had no strength to resist when Gloria steered him toward a side door that opened into another hallway. Halfway down the hall, which led to the kitchen, a door opened into a large bedroom. With Chance's help, Gloria stretched Willis out on the bed and pulled off his boots. Willis muttered unhappily, but his eyes were closed and he was breathing in raspy gasps when they left him.

"Will he be all right?" Chance asked.

"Yes, until the coughing wakes him in a few hours. I wish he could get a full night's sleep without drinking himself blind."

They returned to the parlor and Gloria spoke to the

maid, who soundlessly floated out of the room. The blonde girl, introduced as Sylvie, obligingly vacated the sofa for them. Chance sank down stiffly with his hands gripping his knees. Gloria sat half-turned to him and demanded:

"Now tell me about that beautiful family of yours. I've heard so many good things about you since I've been in town that I've been dying to see you. But of course I understand why you haven't called before this."

Chance was spared the awkwardness of explaining that it was not the difference in their social standings that had kept him away by the maid's return with a wine bottle and glasses.

"I'm not entirely temperance," Gloria smiled, pouring the wine.

Chance was glad to sip something less abrasive than Willis's whiskey. His tension relaxed as he gave her a lengthy account of his personal and business affairs. Gloria's sincere delight at his good fortune was touching. Their conversation was frequently interrupted by the arrival and departure of customers and the girls returning to take their places in the parlor. The maid was kept busy making the beds between sessions.

During a lull in the business traffic, when Chance had run out of things to say about himself, Gloria asked: "Would you mind telling me something? Why did you walk out on me in San Francisco? Not that I blame you. I realized eventually that you and I weren't right for each other. But I can't help being curious."

"Well, I, uh . . . " Chance stammered as he groped for the right words to explain his revulsion at seeing the ugly T-shaped scar burned into her flesh. "When I thought of how I'd feel every time I saw the way Tassie Llewellyn had marked you—"

"You thought Tassie had done that to me?" Gloria broke in, staring at him in surprise.

"What else could I think?"

Gloria smiled thinly. "Was he the only man you and I knew who had a 'T' as one of his initials?"

Chance's confusion slowly turned to shock as her words sank in. "You don't mean Willis Trent . . ?"

"He could never get over knowing that, of the only two

men I've ever really loved, you were the first," Gloria said sadly. "After you left Goldcock, I told him that nothing had happened between us. But he couldn't control his insane jealousy. One night he got drunk and tied me down and said he was going to make sure I never forgot that I belong to him."

Chance had never dreamed that Willis's soft-spoken, cold-blooded professional gambler's manner could conceal so much passion. "I'm sorry," he muttered.

"That's all right. It stopped hurting a long time ago." Gloria smiled and rubbed her right flank. "And strangely enough, it does make me feel closer to Willis. I guess I'm the kind of woman who needs a strong man to own her. Now if he would try harder to regain his health, I'm sure we'd be back on top of the world in no time."

"I'm sure you will, too," Chance said. "If there's any way I can help . . ."

"Thanks. Just knowing I have your friendship is enough."

"Don't ever doubt that."

They continued talking for another half-hour, to Chance's increasing pleasure. With all physical desire between them dead, he could finally appreciate Gloria's other attributes. He considered inviting her and Willis out to the house for dinner sometime when he was finished with the Owens Valley trouble. But he decided he had better hold off on that for a while. Although he and Teresa often felt so closely linked that they could almost read one another's minds, no man ever completely knows his wife and Chance did not want to make the dangerous mistake of thinking he did.

When he at last rose to leave, Gloria regarded him with a wistful twinkle in her eye. "Can you spare a kiss for an old friend?"

"I'd be honored."

Chance took her in his arms and pressed his lips to hers as innocently as he would kiss Vicky Beth or any of his other female relatives. Gloria put her hands on his cheeks and held his face to hers for a long moment.

"Did you give him a discount for old times' sake, my dear?"

284

Willis's voice was a hoarse explosion behind Chance. Gloria broke away with a startled gasp and he turned to stare at Willis standing in the hall doorway. "Now Willis, don't think—"

"I think we'll all meet in hell eventually." Willis smiled as his derringer came smoothly out of his sleeve. "But you'll be there first."

Chance's hand went automatically to his gunbutt, as he continued trying to reason with Willis. Gloria cried out something that was lost in the derringer's bark. Chance's right leg went out from under him and he drew his pistol as he pitched forward, trying to ignore the paralyzing but not yet painful shock that came with the wound. He heard a woman screaming and guessed it must be the maid or one of the parlor girls, because he could see Gloria standing with her hands pressed to her bosom in horrified silence. Willis's derringer was leveled at Chance's face, but a sudden coughing fit caused his second shot to go wild. Chance brought up his Colt and fired an instant before realizing that the gambler's two-shot weapon was empty. The bullet hit Willis over the heart and knocked him back against the wall. He slowly slid down to a sitting position and placed his right hand over the wound, without losing his smile.

"Thanks, Chance. That's the one I've been looking for." Blood bubbled from his mouth and his head flopped limply forward.

Gloria rushed across the room and flung herself down beside Willis. She took his head in her arms and hugged it to her breasts, sobbing hysterically. Chance stared at her, unable to speak as the pain crawled up from his thigh to overpower his mind. He heard more women screaming and men cursing as they poured out of the business cubicles in the back. Then he no longer saw or heard anything.

For several days Chance lingered in painful semiconsciousness while Doc Holyrod fought to keep him alive. Teresa and Vicky Beth hovered at his bedside. At first the doctor thought he would have to amputate Chance's right leg to halt the spread of blood poisoning. He finally managed to save the leg, but he warned Chance that he would have to spend several months in bed if he ever hoped to walk again. Even so, he would always limp because some of the shattered femur bone had been removed, making the right leg shorter than the left.

At Governor Stanford's direction, General Wright in San Francisco ordered Colonel Evans to prepare for the Mono and Owens River Military Expedition. Accordingly, Colonel Evans started from Fort Latham, between Los Angeles and Santa Monica, in mid-June with 157 men and enough supplies for a prolonged campaign. Captain T. H. Goodman served as his second-in-command, replacing Captain Garfield Winne.

A few days before, Winne had made the mistake of letting the past catch up with him. They found him in a small hotel-boardinghouse operated by Mrs. Lydia Graves, a devout middle-aged widow. His pistol was in his right hand and the top of his head was blown off. His only luggage was a small carpetbag, which Mrs. Graves kept for several months while she tried to locate Winne's next of kin. When she could find no one to claim the bag, she gave away the clothes in it and burned Winne's notebooks, which contained one of the most comprehensive first-hand observations of Indian life in the southwestern United States ever recorded.

Chapter 26

Colonel Evans's expedition found the southern portion of Owens Valley fairly peaceful. Some hostile Indian bands were spotted but they fled northward before the superior white force, losing a few warriors to the soldiers' marksmanship. When the troopers reached David's farm, everyone who had gathered there to wait out the bad times cheered their arrival. David told Evans he was sure the Indians would sue for peace when they realized that further resistance was hopeless.

Evans said he hoped David was right, and moved on to establish a permanent camp on Oak Creek. Because the date was July 4, 1862, the new military base was named Camp Independence. It was located a few miles northeast of the site of the future town of Independence, the seat of Inyo County. Evans was soon joined by Acting Indian Agent Wasson, who had come down from Fort Churchill with Captain Rowe's cavalry company.

David's prediction was confirmed when Chief George's warriors captured a white man named Cox and sent him to Evans with a message saying that the southern Paiutes wanted peace. They had never wanted to fight anyway, George insisted. All of the trouble had been caused by the northern bands and outsiders like Joaquin Jim and Paul the

Apostle. Evans and Wasson agreed to meet with the Indian leaders for a peace conference and the terms for a temporary armistice were worked out.

By then Governor Stanford had been reminded that Owens Valley was in his state, so the Indian affairs there should be handled by J.H.P. Wentworth, Indian Agent for the Southern District of California. Wentworth sent word to Wasson that he would arrive as soon as possible to negotiate a lasting peace treaty with the Indians. Wasson said he would be glad to be relieved of the problem so that he could get back to his duties in Nevada.

Wentworth arrived late in September with a large quantity of supplies and presents. Runners had been sent out to summon the scattered Indian bands to Camp Independence and even Lightning Tracker led his people down from the hills to attend the big powwow. David was surprised to see the chief looking so old and frail. Actually Lightning Tracker's tough physical constitution had seen him through the ordeal pretty well, but his spiritual strength was greatly depleted. The death of Slow Of Speech had hit him much harder than he would admit and he had become cranky and overly domineering with his followers, especially his son.

Lightning Tracker was aware of Hu-pwi's desire to join his tribesmen on the warpath and he used all of his political and parental tricks to keep the young man under his control. Hu-pwi, too intimidated to resist his father, sullenly retreated into dreams of battlefield glory. Lightning Tracker also had his dreams. That was why he needed the emotional support of his son's family, now that he was at last free to pursue Winnedumah openly. Far more clearly than Hu-pwi, Lightning Tracker understood the pleasure of thinking about how bravely he would overcome challenges to his heart's desire—while being safely prevented from facing the challenges. The thought of being rejected and ridiculed by Winnedumah's merciless tongue was so humiliating that Lightning Tracker used every excuse he could imagine to put off proposing to her.

The peace conference was conducted to the satisfaction of all who attended it. Wentworth, after feasting the Indians and generously distributing presents among them, assured them that the cavalry was not in the valley to punish them. He promised that they would be protected and given farming tools, seeds, and other means of supporting themselves. But they must learn to live amicably with their white brothers. Any further acts of violence on their part would be severely dealt with. The Paiutes solemnly promised to keep their end of the bargain and a formal treaty was made on October 6, with Chief George agreeing to remain in Evans's camp as a hostage.

White settlers began returning to the valley immediately. Gold found by a prospecting soldier east of Camp Independence led to the birth of the mining camp of San Carlos and the discovery of a nearby galena vein rich in lead and silver drew more fortune hunters.

David was too busy throughout the rest of the year helping Jeremy rebuild his house and replace the stock and other property the Indians had stolen to take much notice of other events in the valley. Because of the damage and neglect of the crops, they reaped a poor harvest. But David was confident they would make it through the winter in good shape. He was so happy to have peace restored that no hardship or sacrifice was too high a price to pay for it. He wrote long letters to Chance describing their joyful Thanksgiving and Christmas celebrations and predicting a bright future for the entire West. He only wished the darned fools back east could be as smart as the Indians and whites out here, instead of getting so many boys in blue and gray killed.

David's enjoyment of the peace would have been diminished somewhat if he had known how miserably disappointed D.C. and Bobby Buck felt over not having been allowed to take part in the fighting. After Lightning Tracker's band had moved back to its old campground, the boys resumed visiting their Paiute friends and matched boasts with Hu-pwi about how bravely they would have performed in combat. It never occurred to D.C. and Hu-pwi that, had they participated in the war, they would have fought on opposing sides, while Bobby Buck would have had difficulty deciding which of his mixed bloodlines to follow. Young imaginations seldom allow inconvenient facts to interfere with their fantasies.

Indian Agent Wentworth, while waiting for Commissioner of Indian Affairs William P. Dole and Secretary of the Interior J.P. Usher to approve his plans for the Paiutes, had a proposed reservation surveyed. He felt that the area would be ample for the Indians' needs, while leaving the rest of the valley for white exploitation. But Senator Milton Latham countered with a bill to turn Owens Valley into a reservation for all of the Indians in southern California. Wentworth strongly objected to that, pointing out that the 16,000 Indians in his district were far more than the valley could possibly support.

Nothing came of Wentworth's or Latham's recommendations and while the bureaucratic quarreling over them dragged on, the Paiutes waited impassively, subsisting on insufficient government handouts. The year ended peacefully in Owens Valley, although isolated parts of it remained dangerous for white men. Joaquin Jim, Paul the Apostle, and other renegades refused even to discuss the new treaty. Malcontents from other tribes along the Kern River, in the Tehachapis and the lower desert areas remained equally unreconciled and reports of fresh depredations reached Camp Independence as 1863 got under way. There were rumors of growing restlessness among the Paiutes and efforts to organize another uprising.

Colonel Evans and Captain Goodman had been transferred by then, with several of their troops, leaving recently promoted Captain James Ropes in command of Camp Independence. Accompanied by David, Ropes rode around the Paiute camps to investigate the alleged war preparations. But they learned very little, as the Indians claimed they were scrupulously sticking to the terms of the treaty.

About that time, Hu-pwi finally managed to slip away from his father and Seyavi long enough to attend a secret powwow conducted by Paul the Apostle as he traveled through the southern valley recruiting action-hungry braves to his cause. Paul's work was expedited by a jug of whiskey, the first that Hu-pwi had ever tasted. As his war excitement burned brighter on the alcoholic fuel, Hu-pwi was held back by the nagging fear that he might be required to fight David, D.C., and his other white friends. But Paul eased his conscience on that score by saying:

"Do not worry, brother. We will kill the Wheelers for you. You can kill other white people."

Greatly relieved, Hu-pwi took another drink and pledged his loyalty to Paul.

"And I believe that is checkmate, my son."

Chance studied the chess pieces intensely for several moments, then laughed and held up his hands in surrender. "Did you invent this game, Padre? I thought I knew something about strategy and tactics, before I met you."

Father Diego smiled modestly. "It's just one of my many worthless talents. Now I must be going." He rose gracefully from the small table in a corner of Oakmont's *sala* and came around to help Chance out of his chair.

"Teresa will be disappointed that you aren't staying for lunch," Chance said, leaning heavily on his cane.

"Thank you, but there are so many I must visit today. I'm delighted to see you back on your feet."

"I had no choice. My backside was starting to grow to the bed."

As Chance limped alongside the priest toward the front door, Teresa came out of the kitchen. Her two younger sons, Roger Juan and Luis Paul, were almost hidden behind the spreading bulk of her sixth pregnancy. She had not been overjoyed to learn of the unexpected addition to her family, which she secretly hoped would be the last, but she accepted it with her normal good nature. When she was unable to persuade Father Diego to share their noon meal, she asked:

"You will call on *Tia* Ignacia before you leave, won't you?"

"Of course. How is she feeling?"

"Better, I think."

There was more hope than conviction in Teresa's voice. *Tia* Ignacia had been bedridden for the past few days and everyone carefully avoided mentioning what they suspected was the cause of her illness. Along with the drought that had plagued southern California since the end of last year's devastating floods had come smallpox. Already the epidemic had claimed several victims and Doc Holyrod and the other few physicians in the area were working tirelessly to vaccinate everyone they could reach. But many of the older *Californios*, like *Tia* Ignacia, did not believe in the preventative medicine technique developed by the English physician Edward Jenner in 1796. The old woman stubbornly maintained that if the disease came to her, she preferred to receive it through the will of God instead of a nasty little needle poked into her arm.

Chance and Teresa, followed by the two boys who had become uncharacteristically speechless with shyness, walked the priest out to the front of the house where his mule was tied. Chance's painful limp was an annoyance, but at least he no longer had to lean on someone's arm to get about.

Teresa pushed Roger Juan and Luis Paul forward to receive the priest's blessing. Chance smiled at Father Diego's solemn expression as he admonished the boys to be good because God was always watching them. The priest was only in his mid-thirties but he took his duties as spiritual father of his flock seriously. Chance had enjoyed the clergyman's cheerful visits during his long convalescence. The new shepherd of the Church of Our Lady of the Angels came from lowly Spanish and Indian origins and he had spent all of his ministry in rural Mexico and the American southwest. But he had read extensively and could converse intelligently on many topics, when he wasn't beating Chance at chess.

"Tell Vicky Beth I'm sorry I haven't seen much of her lately," Father Diego said, hitching up his cassock to straddle his mule.

"Neither have we," Chance replied.

During the months when he had lain helpless, with Si and his other best men away at war, responsibility for conducting the family's business affairs had fallen to Chance's wife and eldest daughter. While Teresa had helped Chance look after the cannery and other concerns, Vicky Beth had taken over the management of the ranch. With such a good excuse for spending most of her time in the saddle, the girl was seldom seen around the house.

"I'll see that she attends Mass on Sunday," Teresa promised.

"If they'll let her take her horse into the church,"

Chance muttered. *"Vaya con Dios, Padre,"* he called after the departing priest.

When Teresa had returned to the kitchen, Chance took a short walk around the house with Roger and Luis. He wished he could take a ride before lunch, but his mended thighbone was still too weak for vigorous exercise. And he decided it wasn't worth the bother of having a horse hitched to the carriage. Even with his growing eagerness to resume his normal activities, Chance had sense enough to follow Doc Holyrod's instructions to rest his bad leg when pain and fatigue told him he had overused it. So, sending the boys to the stables to check on the progress of a new colt, he went into his study to read until Teresa called him to the table.

He was well into a new translation of Homer's *Illiad* that Heinrich Schliemann had sent him. Chance had started corresponding with the German merchant a few years after their meeting in San Francisco, when a visiting sea captain had mentioned that he had run across Schliemann in Europe. Now Schliemann wrote happily, he was at last on the verge of becoming financially independent enough to organize an expedition to search for the ruins of Troy. That news excited ten-year-old Miguel Zachary, who was developing into a bright scholar. Chance still doubted that Troy was more than a myth, but Schliemann was probobly as skeptical of his belief that Los Angeles would someday become a great city. Everyone had to follow his own dream, until life revealed which was closest to reality.

Although Chance had never been fond of pondering abstract ideas, his long period of forced inactivity had enabled him to do a lot of thinking and he had become more content with the world and his place in it.

He even thought he could understand and sympathize with the death wish that had driven Willis Trent to draw on him. He had been helped along that course by Gloria's forgiveness and comforting visits. At first Gloria had been stiffly formal with Teresa and Chance was apprehensive about how his wife would receive a woman of her reputation. But Teresa, as Chance later told himself he should have known, had graciously welcomed the grieving widow and quickly put her at ease. The two women got along so well together that Chance looked forward to having Gloria as a frequent guest at Oakmont. He was disappointed when Gloria announced that she was moving to San Francisco because Los Angeles was a reminder of her tragic loss.

Teresa also expressed regret that they would not be seeing Gloria again. But Gloria did not miss the flicker of relief in Teresa's eyes when they said goodbye. However much Teresa had matured from the naive girl who had been swept off her feet by the dashing gringo, she was still, as Gloria shrewdly observed, a respectable married woman with territorial rights to defend. Even the most generous wife does not care to have her husband exposed to an old flame who has no man of her own. Gloria liked Chance and Teresa too much to want to cause trouble between them—something that a faint stirring of her old feeling for Chance told her was definitely possible. So it would be best for all of them if she left Los Angeles. Besides, a woman who lived as she did never knew when she might need help from old friends, and experience had taught her to give just enough of herself to keep the receivers always desiring more.

But it was not always easy for Chance to use his bedridden time constructively. The helpless confinement, after a lifetime of good health and vigorous activities, had been unbearable at first. He felt especially frustrated by not being able to help David when he most needed him.

After hearing that the cavalry had pacified Owens Valley, Chance found other things to worry about, the Civil War in particular. With things going so badly for the Union side, the conflict seemed capable of dragging on for years, tearing the country apart and killing many of Chance's friends. Already General Albert Sidney Johnston had fallen at Shiloh.

Only the knowledge that Si Darcy and Madison Starr were unlikely to meet in battle gave Chance any peace of mind. Si and Nicolas Alviso had joined the Texas Cavalry, while Mad was with the Army of the Potomac.

Then Chance started feeling guilty about the money he was making from his shipments of canned food to the Union Army, when the Confederate raiders didn't get it. How could he stand to be a profiteer from a war that was causing so much death and destruction?

Whenever he tired of stewing about that, Chance could always berate himself for his failure to look after family and business affairs. What would become of the ranch and his other enterprises without his constant supervision? They would lose everything and end up in the poorhouse—all because of his stupid carelessness.

He even wallowed in remorse for not being able to perform his most important duty as a loving husband. Luckily Teresa was too pregnant and distracted by the other children to be overly bothered by sex urges. But even so Chance was sure it must be a strain on her. In his lowest moments he even thought he wouldn't blame her if she was unfaithful to him. He wasn't good enough for her anyway.

Even after his business affairs had been effectively taken over by Teresa and Vicky Beth, Chance continued to torture himself with reminders of his shameful failure. It was unmanly for him to be so dependent on women. What must they think of him, lying there like a useless lump while they had to work so hard? That question was answered for him one day by a scrap of conversation between Teresa and Vicky Beth that he happened to overhear.

Vicky Beth mentioned how disappointed she was that Papa didn't seem pleased with the way she was running the ranch.

"Oh, he is just jealous at seeing a girl doing his work," Teresa assured her stepdaughter. Then she said that reminded her of a joke about a rooster who fell ill and the farmer wondered how he was going to wake up in time to do his chores. But one of the hens told him not to worry; she would crow before sunrise to wake him.

"You mean hens can crow just like roosters?" the farmer exclaimed in surprise.

"Of course we can," said the hen. "But don't tell the rooster, or he will think he doesn't have to do *anything* around here."

Vicky Beth laughed and Teresa said that *Tia* Ignacia had told her the joke to illustrate how a woman can get a man to do almost anything for her, as long as she lets him think that she is unable to do it herself.

Chance had to laugh too when he realized how aptly the joke suited him. Like an arrogant rooster, he had thought he was so all-fired important that the world must come to a halt when he wasn't able to help it go around. The truth of the matter, when he could get his silly pride to admit it, was that Teresa, Vicky Beth, David and everyone else— even the Civil War generals—were quite capable of managing things without him. Once he accepted that ego-deflating fact, he was able to relax and think in more practical terms about the problems that troubled his conscience. That was brought home to him when David wrote describing the pitiful plight of the Paiutes and his efforts to help them.

How typical, Chance thought ruefully, that he had been ready to rush off half-cocked and kill every Indian he saw, while David had reacted with his instinctive decency and love for people. Now that Chance understood that the poor savages were only trying to defend their land and get enough to eat, he could help out by sending a beef herd up for David to distribute among them. And his war profits could be used to help the veterans get a fresh start when they came home. Hell, there were all kinds of ways he could use his money and energy to make life better for his fellow men, if he just set his mind to it. He had been thinking about organizing a fund to restore the neglected mission buildings and preserve other aspects of the *Californio* culture before the rush of progress swept it away.

Chance spent many happy hours discussing his philanthropic plans with Teresa, blissfully unaware that they would be thwarted by forces beyond his control. There was no way he could have guessed that the present dry spell was merely the beginning of a prolonged drought that would be the death blow of the already weakened cattle industry in southern California. Economic hard times were coming that would have even Chance struggling desperately to keep from going under. Most of Chance's hopes for Los Angeles' social and cultural improvement would have to be left for future generations to fulfill. The town's pioneering era still had many years to run, and pioneers are almost always too busy taming their wild frontiers to spare much time for more genteel pursuits.

But for the time being, Chance and Teresa could enjoy their dreams of finer things for their pueblo. Only one troubling thought remained in his mind as he steadily regained his strength and started to get back into the swing of things. He had never stopped envying David and others who seemed to derive so much satisfaction from religion and he had spent a lot of time over the years on theological studies. But still the ultimate reward of piety eluded him. Once, when trying to explain how he felt to Teresa, he concluded:

"I guess what it boils down to is that I'm sorry I've never been able to find God."

Teresa gave him the soft, patient smile she often used with her children. "Fear not, *esposo mio*. When the time is right, God will find you."

Chapter 27

The fight was going well for the Indians.

Hu-pwi smiled at the white soldiers' confusion from his vantage point high up in the Black Rocks. He squinted along his rifle barrel and fired at an overly bold cavalryman who was trying to work his way up the slope by dashing from one boulder to another. Dust spurted at the soldier's feet and he ran back downhill under covering fire provided by his comrades.

Hu-pwi laughed exultantly. This was the way for a real warrior to live! He had no regrets for the way he had sneaked out of Lightning Tracker's camp to join Paul the Apostle's band. He only wished Seyavi were here to share his triumph and praise his bravery. But it was better that she and the boy had remained safely at home. When the war was over he would return to her covered with glory and the tales of his victories would be repeated around the hearth fires.

He had been with Paul for over two weeks and was growing bored with their apparent inability to find the enemy when, three days before, a small scouting party of cavalrymen had ridden into their ambush. Paul had shot one of the soldiers from the saddle and Hu-pwi finished him off with an arrow through his left eye. The Indians had wounded four more soldiers as they retreated and a tasty horse was killed. As they feasted on the animal's flesh, Paul grinned at Hu-pwi.

"Did I not tell you how easy it is to kill white men, brother? Now that they know where we are, they will return in greater numbers. And we will be ready for them."

Paul had prepared a fine trap, but this time the whites were too wary to be taken by surprise. After a brief skirmish, Paul had given the order to fall back into the broken lava spill, where every niche and cavern was familiar to them. If the soldiers tried to rush them, they would disappear like raindrops in dry sand. And as long as the cavalrymen remained cautiously outside of the natural stronghold, a few well-placed braves with rifles could keep them pinned down. Paul had thought of everything, even of having his men eat and rest in relays to keep them fresh while their enemies were gradually worn down.

Hu-pwi called out to his fellow warriors not to fire so often, unless they had clear targets. They were running low on ammunition and, although he estimated there were only about thirty white men facing them, they were well-armed and led by Captain Ropes. What a coup it would be to kill him, Hu-pwi thought, as another Indian crawled up to relieve him for a rest period. Hu-pwi hated to leave the battle. But he was very hungry and besides it did not seem that the soldiers were going to do any more fighting for a while.

Hu-pwi gave the other Indian his rifle and picked his way through the narrow twisting corridors between the rocks to the spring where he and Seyavi had brought Rebekah and Bobby Buck several years ago. A cook fire was smoking near the spring and Hu-pwi squatted to gnaw on a chunk of roasted horsemeat, ignoring Chief George seated a few yards away. George appeared equally oblivious to Hu-pwi's presence, except for a slight deepening of the contemptuous scowl he directed at all of Paul's men.

George had escaped from Camp Independence when he heard about the new clash between the whites and Indians. He had not been happy about breaking his word as a hostage, but he thought he might be able to talk the warring Indians into restoring the peace before the white men became angry enough to launch a general massacre against the Paiutes. Two days of futile argument with Paul had cured George of that dream. Now he only wanted to wait until darkness and slip away to join his people in the south. He hoped the soldiers would chop Paul and his men into small enough pieces for the rats to dine on. They weren't good enough to be fed to the coyotes.

It was nearly sunset when David and Lightning Tracker reached Captain Ropes and his troopers. Ropes had sent for David shortly after hearing about the skirmish between his scouting party and the Indians, thinking that a good interpreter would improve his chances of persuading the hostiles to surrender. Lightning Tracker had accompanied David in hope of finding his son and convincing him to come home before he got into serious trouble.

With darkness coming on, Captain Ropes decided to postpone attempting to parley with the Indians until morning. The soldiers pulled back a mile from Black Rocks and made camp. It was early March, still cold enough to make sleeping on the ground unpleasant. But even so, Chief George had no trouble stealing around the cavalry camp on his way home. Even the men on guard duty were dozing a few hours later, when Hu-pwi and four other braves slipped down and stole five of the soldiers' horses. Hu-pwi passed within six yards of where his father lay, without waking him.

When Paul received the fresh horses, he decided to go looking for more lucrative game than the soldiers. The following morning, when David and Lightning Tracker made their way up into the Black Rocks carrying a white flag, their calls were answered only by echoes. After Ropes's scouts had assured him that the Indians had indeed gotten away without leaving a traceable trail, he concluded that there wasn't much he could do except return to Camp Independence.

David was not sure what he should do. Several days before, Jeremy Starr had gone with his friend Charley Tyler, Alney McGee, and Jesse Summers to Aurora. Mrs. McGee and Summers's family had spent the winter there and now the men planned to bring them back along with two wagon loads of badly needed supplies. David thought he should ride north to intercept the travelers and warn them that a hostile band was roving the area. But Captain Ropes told David there was no need for him to expose himself to such danger; messengers had already been sent to Aurora to spread the word about Paul's marauders. David struggled with his conscience for a while, then decided Ropes was probably right. He and Lightning Tracker went with the soldiers to Camp Independence, spent the night there, and got an early start for home the next morning.

"No, that ain't right," Jeremy objected, and broke into song with the lyrics to "The Bluetail Fly" that he had learned as a tad in Virginia.

> "Jimmie crack corn an' I don't care,
> Jimmie crack corn an' I don't care,
> Jimmie crack corn an' I don't ca-re,
> Ol' Massa's gone away."

"Ree-dik-a-luss," Charley sneered, leaning to one side to squirt tobacco juice at the ground their horses were ambling over. "Wuffo would a massa care if'n his slave jest cracked corn? That ain't nothin'. Lissen now, yo dumb nigger, an' see kin yo learn somepin." His rich bass boomed out:

> "Jimmie drink corn an' I don't care,
> 'Cause ol' Massa's gone a-way."

Charley gazed triumphantly at Jeremy. "It's *drinkin'* a massa's corn liquor that gets a darky's ass whupped."

"I reckon yo knows all about drinkin' liquor," Jeremy conceded, remembering the bottles they had happily emptied in Aurora. "Too bad yo don't know nothin' about singin'."

Charley started to protest again and Alney McGee, riding up from the wagons behind them, called out:

"Can't you two ever stop arguin'? I swear if you ain't the feistiest niggers I ever seen."

301

"It's this fool an' his aggervatin' foolish ways," Charley insisted. "I can't teach him nothin' about how we does things in Texas."

"Yo ain't in Texas now," Jeremy reminded him.

"I don't care about that," Alney cut in. "Just try to keep your mouths shut and your eyes open. I don't want no Injuns surprisin' us."

"Yes, suh," Charley agreed.

Alney tossed the two black men a grin to show that he wasn't really put out with them, then dropped back to exchange a few words with Jesse Summers and his wife in the first wagon. Then he smiled at his mother, who was driving the second wagon with her nine-year-old granddaughter Martha on the seat beside her. Assured that everything was all right, Alney fell back further to bring up the rear of their small train. He still felt uneasy about his mother's decision to leave Aurora before they could convince other travelers to join them. But it was beginning to look as if she had been right. Already they had come more than halfway to where the rest of the McGees were tending their herd, without seeing a single hostile Indian. Even so, Alney loosened his revolver in its holster and carefully swept his gaze over both sides of the trail along the Owens River's west bank.

Jeremy and Charley spurred their horses away from the wagons to scout the trail ahead. Jeremy thought about explaining to Alney that he and Charley were not really feisty. In fact, Jeremy was in especially good spirits today because Charley had promised him that he would start staking out a homestead in the valley as soon as the McGees could drive enough cattle to market to pay him his back wages. It was going to be wonderful having another black man living near him, Jeremy thought, as they topped a rise in the trail and startled a dozen deer making their way across the valley from their winter browsing grounds in the Inyo Mountains. It was past time for the bucks to drop their antlers and the does could only be distinguished by the signs of the fawns they would bear in June.

Charley reined up and raised his rifle to sight in on a deer that had paused to stare fearlessly at him. Then he lowered the gun and stared at several vultures and ravens circling low in the southern sky. Jeremy followed his gaze and said hopefully:

"Maybe jest a dead animal."

"We'll see." Keeping his rifle ready for action, Charley cautiously led the way forward.

They found the body on Big Pine Creek. It was a white man, stripped of all clothing and bearing several gaping wounds where arrowheads had been cut out for reuse. Death had occurred several days before, but the cool weather had preserved the flesh for the scavengers. Charley and Jeremy found several signs of a running battle and a dead campfire about a quarter of a mile away. Evidently the victim had had a few companions, but there was no telling what had become of them. After looking around to make sure no Indians were still in the vicinity, they rode back to the wagons.

Charley's report made Alney McGee even more anxious to hurry on to the safety of Camp Independence. But he knew without asking that his mother would insist on giving the corpse a decent burial. They paused just long enough to scrape out a shallow grave and cover the body with stones, then whipped up their horses. As they neared the low lumpy hills—later named the Poverty Hills—below Fish Springs, smoke signals rose in the windless sky.

"That mean anything to you?" Alney asked Jeremy, thinking he might have learned to read Indian smoke talk during his years in the valley.

"Uh-huh. Means trouble," Jeremy answered.

"Do tell?" Charley said drily.

They pushed on, squeezing between the hills and the river and splashing across Tinemaha Creek. Suddenly the hills erupted with howling Indians both mounted and afoot. Alney estimated that there were about 100 warriors in the band. But to Jeremy it seemed that many times that number spread out in a line to block the trail ahead. Alney hesitated only a moment before signaling Jesse Summers to turn his wagon left, toward the river. With Red Mountain behind them, they raced past a low mound and plunged into the water where a shallow ford was known to lie. But in their excitement they miscalculated and the wagons bogged down in deep mud before they were halfway across the river. A few of the Indian riflemen opened fire and their archers were hurrying up to get within bow range.

"Cut the horses loose!" Alney shouted.

"But the wagons," Mrs. Summers protested. "All of our things . . ."

"No time! We gotta run for our lives!"

Jeremy's hands were shaking so badly that he could hardly control his horse. He drew closer to Charley for moral support as he dismounted to cut the traces of Jesse Summers's horses. They put the two women and the little girl on the unhitched horses and Alney and Jesse started leading them toward the opposite bank. By then the Indians had nearly reached the western bank and bullets and arrows fell in the water around them. Charley's horse, which had always before remained calm under fire, bolted when a bullet grazed its flank. Charley and Jeremy got in each other's way trying to grab the frightened animal's reins and it galloped away downstream.

"Climb up behind me!" Jeremy shouted.

Charley, standing waist-deep in water, shook his head and instead grabbed Jeremy's horse's mane with his free hand. "Ride like hell! I'll hang on."

Jeremy dug in his spurs and his horse leaped ahead with Charley running alongside. They waded on to the eastern side of the river and started up the sloping bank after their white companions. As they reached level ground, the horse stumbled and fell. Charley sprang aside and Jeremy was thrown clear. Charley caught the horse's reins, but as it started to rise a bullet struck it in the neck and it fell back screaming and kicking. Jeremy, gasping for breath, crawled over to Charley.

"You two all right?"

Charley and Jeremy looked up. Alney sat on his halted horse fifty yards away, looking back at them. Charley stole a glance back at the river. The first five mounted Indians were nearly across.

"Yo get the ladies an' chile outa heah, boss. We'll hold 'em off a bit, then ketch up wif y'all."

Alney hesitated, then raised his rifle arm in a salute to the black men and rode on after the others.

"Oh, Lawd, I wish we was wif 'em," Jeremy groaned.

Charley grinned confidently and picked up Jeremy's rifle and put it in his hands. "Don't yo fret, brother. We's gonna have us a right smart of fun." He crouched down to take aim at the charging Indians. "Yo take the leadin' one on the right. I'll get t'other."

Jeremy pointed his rifle toward the Indians, but he was still gasping and trembling and he couldn't get his eyes to focus. Then, just as the two leading Indians rode up out of the water, everything became amazingly clear. He did not know the leading braves, but one of the three behind them was waving a saber, so that had to be Paul the Apostle. The man beside him was easily recognized as Joaquin Jim. And Jeremy thought the fifth horseman looked like Hupwi. But he was sure Lightning Tracker would never allow any of his people to go on the warpath.

Charley's rifle cracked and the rider who was his target pitched backward off of his horse. Jeremy fired and saw his Indian also go down. The other three riders halted at the water's edge and the Indians who were fording the river on foot behind them paused to wait for orders. Charley had started to draw his revolver, but when he saw the Indians hesitate, he scrambled to his feet.

"Let's vamoose!"

He pulled Jeremy to his feet and they sprinted away to the southeast, reloading their rifles on the run. They gained a lead of several hundred yards before they heard the whooping Indians coming after them again. When their pursuers started to gain on them, they wheeled about on Charley's command and fired another volley to slow them down. They repeated that maneuver several times with such effectiveness that the three mounted Indian leaders soon learned to stay behind the cover of their infantry.

But the long grueling race gradually took its toll on the black men. As they tired the Indians gradually closed the gap between them and arrows started to fall at their feet. Suddenly Charley cried out and Jeremy turned to see an arrow shaft sticking out of his back.

"It ain't nothin'," Charley panted. "Keep goin'."

It was soon obvious that Charley was hurt more than he would admit. His pace slowed to a walk, but he shook off Jeremy's helping arm.

305

"Go on to the fort for help." Charley's words came in rasping spurts. "I'll hold out till yo gets back."

"I ain't leavin' yo to them devils," Jeremy insisted.

"Ain't nothin' else yo can do."

Jeremy soon realized that Charley was right. When they came to a pile of boulders washed down by spring floods from the Inyo foothills, Jeremy helped Charley take cover in the rocks. He gave Charley his rifle, then decided to leave his revolver as well, so that he could run faster.

Trying not to think of what might happen to his friend, Jeremy trotted on toward Camp Independence. He heard several shots exchanged, and wild yells from the Indians. He ran another mile, then cut back to the river and waded along the bank until he found a rock overhang where he could squat down with just his nose and eyes above water. After half an hour, he heard Indian voices on the bank, but they soon moved on.

By the time Jeremy felt it was safe for him to crawl out of the water under cover of the gathering dusk, he was almost too chilled to move. He slowly got his blood circulating again as he made his way back to where he had left Charley. Receiving no reply to his whispered calls, he groped in the darkness on his hands and knees until he found some empty cartridge casing and smelled dried blood.

Jeremy hunkered there indecisively for a long time, before resigning himself to doing what he had to do.

Creeping along in the darkness, cringing with terror at every sound, Jeremy made his way upstream until he saw the glow of campfires across the river near the mound he recalled passing in their flight from the Indians. Crouching low in the water, he forded the river and crawled toward the fires, unobserved by the singing and dancing Indians.

He got within fifty yards of the main campfire and lay behind a clump of sage to watch the goings-on. Somehow the Indians had found a long stout pole in that treeless area and planted it upright in the ground. Charley was tied naked to the stake, his ebony body gleaming with sweat and blood. Paul the Apostle stood before him, lovingly holding his saber with both hands. Smiling slightly, Paul reached out with the saber and pricked Charley's left biceps. Charley glared at Paul, but refused to give him the satisfaction of flinching or uttering a sound. Paul didn't seem to mind that; he had all night.

After making a few more small cuts in Charley's torso, Paul lowered his blade and casually sliced off the black man's right little toe. Charley's throat muscles worked jerkily and he hawked up a gob of spittle that fell just short of Paul's face. Paul raised the swordpoint to Charley's face and teasingly flicked it at his eyes.

Jeremy bit his lips and clutched his only weapon—his Bowie knife. The distance was too great for an accurate throw at Paul's back. Not that Jeremy dared to risk his own life in such a futile gesture anyway. Maria and the children needed him too much for that. He could only watch the sickening atrocity continue, and remember the faces of those involved in it. At one point he saw Hu-pwi approach Paul and try to persuade him to stop torturing the captive, to no avail. That was one good mark in Hu-pwi's favor, but not enough to save him when the time of retribution arrived.

Paul went on with his amusing game for another two hours. His saber worked slowly down from Charley's head and up from his feet, until it finally reached the tender target midway between the two.

Jeremy turned his face away, but Charley's scream drew a far more vivid picture than anything his eyes could have seen.

When it was over, Jeremy crawled away to spend the rest of the night in sleepless hiding. In the morning, after the Indians had left the camp, he gathered up all he could find of Charley and buried him at the foot of the mound, which ever since then has been known as Charley's Butte.

Chapter 28

Twice a year, in the time of white butterflies and again when young quail ran neck and neck in the chaparral, the women of Lightning Tracker's band cut willows to make baskets. Winnedumah had adopted their practice when she first came to the valley and was now grateful she had, for many of the white newcomers were willing to pay well for her gracefully woven and beautifully ornamented baskets. She had done little basketweaving during her long period of slavery in New Mexico. But among Indian women the art of fashioning household utensils, once learned, is never lost.

On this day she had sent her servant, the simple Wongata, to invite Seyavi to go with her to the little willow-lined creek that struggled toward the river against the thirsty sun and winds. It never quite reached the river except in flood times, but it tried bravely and the willows encouraged it as much as they could.

But Seyavi was in no condition to leave her wickiup. In the night she had dreamed of Hu-pwi's death and all day she sat with her blanket over her head, speaking to no one.

So Winnedumah had gone with only Wongata to fetch and carry for her. She knew there was danger, with warrior bands and white soldiers ranging the valley. But men were always doing something to discomfit women. That was such an inescapable fact of life that Winnedumah accepted it without thinking too much about it any more. Except when she wanted to add a little more seasoning to her favorite emotional diet of hating the male sex.

They reached their destination, a few miles north of David's farm, and spent several hours gathering willow withes. Winnedumah was very particular about the materials that went into her baskets and she kept Wongata busy clambering up and down the creek in search of twigs of the right size and pliancy for her use. She could still split the long slender sticks into strips of any desired size with her teeth, as she had often done in her younger days. But now she preferred to save her few remaining teeth for eating. Wongata enjoyed his work and Winnedumah was having such a good time screeching instructions and curses at him that neither of them noticed the three white horsemen who topped a ridge behind them.

Fletcher Whitlow, Ethan Herbert and Harlan Pitt had just come over from Visalia to help the cavalry put down the Paiute uprising they had heard so much about. Amusements were scarce in the San Joaquin Valley and they had thought that the excitement of an Indian hunt would be just the thing to cure their boredom. But they had been disappointed and increasingly frustrated at not having encountered any hostile savages yet. Now they sat on their resting horses and watched the oddly matched Paiute couple.

"Well, Fletch, you said you could use a plump squaw," Herbert said. "There she be."

Whitlow snorted at the suggestion and Pitt chuckled. "If you don't want to bed her, you could render her down for lard. Looks like enough fat on that carcass to last a family through the winter."

"That's about all a man could use her for," Whitlow agreed. "The buck looks like he might be good for some sport, though."

"Why not?" Herbert asked with a slight shrug. "We ain't gave the horses a work-out all day."

Whitlow put the spurs to his mount and dashed forward with a loud yell, his companions following closely.

Winnedumah, sitting cross-legged beside the creek,

looked up in surprise at the horsemen bearing down on her. Wongata, a few yards above her, watched the riders approach with his standard lopsided grin. It was only when Whitlow leaped his horse over Winnedumah and she fell flat screaming with terror that Wongata felt alarmed enough to turn and run. The white men came after him in a rough V-formation, laughing and calling instructions to one another as their game twisted and feinted like a frightened rabbit.

Wongata was a strong runner and he could have eluded his pursuers on the uneven ground that he knew so well. But in his fear he could only think of finding safety with the person who had taken care of him ever since his mother's death. Waiting until the white men were nearly upon him, he swiftly reversed his course and dashed between their horses, heading straight toward Winnedumah. The old woman had gotten to her feet when he reached her. She looked for a place to hide as he cowered behind her skirts and the white men turned their horses around for another charge.

Winnedumah shuffled down the incline and the white men hooted with laughter at the sight of her ponderous body trying to run. Catching her hand, Wongata tugged her along ahead of the plunging horses until they came to a narrow dry wash about eight feet deep. Without thinking, Wongata leaped across the gap and landed safely on the other side. Winnedumah tore her hand free of his and tried to halt on the brink of the wash, but momentum carried her forward and she tumbled down to the rocky bottom.

Whitlow, watching Wongata racing away for all he was worth, reined up at the dry wash. No sense in taking a chance of crippling his horse by leaping over it. "That's enough," he said as his friends pulled up beside him. "Let him go."

"Yeah. There's one Injun that'll be too scared to scalp any white folks for a while," Pitt opined.

They turned their horses and rode away feeling proud of having done a good day's work in the war to bring civilization to Owens Valley. It did not occur to any of them to look down at the twisted body that lay groaning on the bottom of the dry wash.

310

Wongata, whimpering and brushing tears from his sting-ing eyes, continued running at top speed toward David's farm. He had gone about a mile when he met David and Lightning Tracker returning from their unsuccessful mis-sion to the Black Rocks. At first they could make no sense out of his terrified babbling, but finally Lightning Tracker understood that Winnedumah was in danger and urged David to hurry to her aid.

Winnedumah was still conscious when they reached her, but she screamed with pain when David tried to move her. He examined her body the best he could, asking her where she hurt the most. As near as he could tell, her back ap-peared to be broken. While he was trying to find a tactful way to break that news to her, she stopped sobbing long enough to ask him if she was dying.

"That's about the size of it," David confessed.

Lightning Tracker touched David's arm. "Is there noth-ing you can do?"

"I'm afraid not. We'll kill her if we move her."

"But if she is dying anyway—"

"I'd rather leave that to God."

Lightning Tracker nodded fatalistically and sat down be-side the last person on earth for whom he really cared. Wongata squatted on the other side of Winnedumah, not understanding what was happening, but grinning again now that friendly adults were in charge of the situation.

So this was how her cord of life was to be unwound, Winnedumah thought bitterly. How fitting. Always she had been used and abused by men and now they were to be the death of her. And there was no way she could pay them back for their cruel treachery. Then her eyes turned thoughtfully to David. Perhaps she could enjoy a little re-venge on the hateful creatures before she died.

"Your son, Bobby Buck," she gasped, "is not really yours. When Don Chance was here—"

"I know," David said calmly, patting her hand.

Winnedumah was mildly astonished. "You knew? For how long?"

"Ever since he was born. Don't take me for an even big-ger fool than the good Lord made me."

"But how could you—"

"Hush. You're wasting valuable strength."

David held his canteen to her lips and made her take a few swallows of water. It would be pointless for him to try to explain to her that knowing that Chance was Bobby Buck's father had only made him love the boy more. Watching D.C. and Bobby Buck grow up together had enabled him to recapture some of the wonder of his own happy childhood with Chance. That experience was far more rewarding than any price he might have had to pay in jealousy or hurt pride, if it were possible for him to feel anything like that toward Chance. He only regretted that Chance had not been able to share the joy of the boys' upbringing with him. But Chance would have insisted on taking Bobby Buck away with him if he had known the truth, and David could not have brought himself to cause Rebekah that much pain.

Winnedumah glared at David, dredging up the last drop of poison she could find to inject into his mind. "And did you know that when your first wife died, I did it, so that you would marry my granddaughter?"

David blinked as the thrust hit home. But it was only a momentary reopening of an old wound. "That was long ago," he murmured. "I'm sure Margaret forgives you." Being incapable of spitefulness himself, he was sure that the old woman was making a dying confession to clear her conscience.

Winnedumah wept with anguish. She had used up the last of her ammunition against men in a fruitless attack. David's unshakable goodness had defeated her. She could fight no more. She could only surrender unconditionally to the final humiliation that she had scornfully resisted for years. Humbly she asked David to give her the Christian God that had made him invincible to life's evils.

David baptized her with canteen water and talked comfortingly to her as she slipped into mental confusion and then unconsciousness. She went out with the sun and it took the three men's combined strength to get her out of the dry wash and onto David's horse. They took her home and buried her not far from Margaret's grave, where spring wildflowers always bloomed and the wind would never forget her. David read a Christian service over her and Lightning Tracker sang the Paiute death chant.

Lightning Tracker spent the night beside Winnedumah's grave, reviewing the major turning points in his unsatisfied life. So the almost forgotten dream of long ago had been a true vision. The deadly longhorned gods he had seen in his fevered mind had indeed come to destroy everything in the valley. Thus the old gods had punished him for his refusal to accept his gift of prophesy. If he had obeyed their will and become a medicine man, he might have been able to save his people. Perhaps he would have been given Winnedumah as a reward. But instead he had fed his vanity by playing the great leader and statesman—much to the gods' amusement, no doubt.

Now it was too late. He had lost everything and he was too old to start over. But he wasn't quite finished yet. His rebellious spirit still had the strength to challenge the immortals in a way that even they could not resist.

Lightning Tracker never returned to his people, who judged by his strange behavior that he had gone mad. Freed at last from his fear of Winnedumah's rejection, he was able to court her more passionately in death than he had dared in life. He became a wandering poet forever composing paeans to his lost love and singing them to the wind. For many years afterwards people mentioned running across him in all parts of the valley, his eyes burning as he labored to add Winnedumah to the land's legends. For evidence of his success, look east from Independence to the Inyo crest where a tall granite spire points like a finger to heaven. It is called Paiute Monument, or Winnedumah.

What finally became of Lightning Tracker is not known. He was last seen heading into the White Mountains above Bishop. No one ever reported finding his remains, so he could still be up there with those other gnarled ancients, the bristlecone pines.

Two days after David buried Winnedumah, Chance and Teresa were in Los Angeles to say goodbye to *Tia* Ignacia, who was being laid to rest in the plaza church's *campo santo*. The old woman had indeed been stricken with small-pox. But she expressed no regret for having refused to be vaccinated, as she died blessing her loved ones and promising to see them again someday *"con el favor de Dios"*—if it pleases God.

Teresa had wept during most of the long carriage ride from the ranch, but she was somberly dry-eyed as she stood between Chance and her mother at the graveside. Nearly 300 mourners crowded into the cemetery. Many of them had been related to the deceased. All of them were deeply moved by their overpowering sense of loss. *Tia* Ignacia, one of the few remaining children of the first pioneering *Californios*, had lived almost as long as the *pueblo* itself, and there was an oppressive feeling that she was taking an important part of it with her as she left.

Father Diego moved to the head of the grave. The murmur of the crowd died away and everyone waited for the priest to read the funeral service. Instead, he looked at Chance.

"Before I begin, Don Chance has asked permission to say a few words in honor of Doña Ignacia. So, if you will give him your attention . . ."

Chance gave Teresa and Vicky Beth a reassuring smile as they peered curiously at him. Limping over to join Father Diego, Chance was self-consciously aware of the dozens of eyes fixed on him. He cleared his throat and took a small, slender book from his pocket.

"I'll try to make this brief, *amigos*," he promised. "As you know, I've had a great deal of idle time on my hands recently, and I've used much of it thinking about things that are most important to me. Naturally I thought about *Tia* Ignacia. Moreover, I thought of those whom she had inspired with her love and unselfish consideration. In particular, I thought of one who was with us for all too short a time—my friend and brother, Ramon Esperanza. Remembering his fondness for poetry, I took down his copy of Shakespeare's sonnets and found one that seems to express how we all felt about *Tia* Ignacia."

Chance opened the book and read:

314

"Shall I compare thee to a summer's day?
Thou art more lovely and more temperate:
Rough winds do shake the darling buds of May,
And summer's lease hath all too short a date:
Sometime too hot the eye of heaven shines,
And often is his gold complexion dimm'd;
And every fair from fair sometime declines,
By chance, or nature's changing course, untrimm'd;
But thy eternal summer shall not fade,
Nor lose possession of that fair thou owest;
Nor shall Death brag thou wander'st in his shade,
When in eternal lines to time thou growest;
So long as men can breathe, or eyes can see,
So long lives this, and this gives life to thee."

Chance closed the book and clasped his hands around it. *Tia* Ignacia was a summer's day, brightening the lives of all who knew her. Now that she is gone, our world is a darker and colder place. But, as she would have pointed out with her practical good sense, there will always be another summer. As time heals the pain of our loss, we will walk in the light and warmth of her memory. And that memory will give life to her, as it gives hope to us."

The crowd remained silent as Chance made his way back to Teresa and Vicky Beth. When he passed Teresa's mother and father, Doña Luisa smiled up at him with brimming eyes. Beside her, Don Carlos, remembering the time Chance had broken the *cascaron* over *Tia* Ignacia's head, whispered: *"Bravo, hijo. Muy galante!"*

When the service was over and the last spadeful of earth had been patted down over the coffin, Father Diego walked Chance, Teresa and Vicky Beth to their carriage. "I was very touched by your words," the priest said to Chance. "They made me think of my mother, for the first time in years."

"Is she still living?" Teresa asked.

"I have no way of knowing. We were separated when I was twelve, in New Mexico, and I have never been able to trace her."

"Well, maybe you'll meet her again someday," Vicky Beth said hopefully.

"Perhaps. Only God knows." The priest bade them good-day and went to talk to some of the other mourners.

That was the nearest Chance ever came to knowing that he had met Winnedumah's son Diego, who had been sent to Mexico City to study for the priesthood.

In the days following Charley's death, Jeremy was a changed man. He brooded in his cabin, burning with lust for revenge against the devils who had killed his friend. Sometimes he stalked up and down in a violent rage, cursing and shouting that all of the Indians in the valley should be slaughtered. His wife and children were afraid to approach him on those occasions. It was almost as bad for them when he sat hunched over in deep silence with his mind conjuring pictures of Paul the Apostle suffering agonizing torture that kept him in constant pain without ever giving him the merciful release of death. Jeremy had heard that Paul had a young son and he took sadistic pleasure in planning how he would tie the boy to a stake and force Paul to watch him being slowly cut to pieces before his own torment commenced.

David was unable to get Jeremy out of his savage mood when he called to say how sorry he was to hear about what had happened to Charley. Nor did Jeremy take much notice of the other white men who dropped in with praise for the brave roles he and Charley had played in saving the McGee-Summers party. Alney McGee gave Jeremy a new rifle and revolver and said that Charley had been the greatest hero of the war. "He was whiter than any of us," Alney concluded, paying Charley the highest compliment a Southerner of that period could offer a black man.

Alney said he was working with the cavalry to run down Paul's band. When they were finally located, he would send word to Jeremy so that he could be in on the kill.

That was the only news that interested Jeremy. He kept his guns loaded and his saddlebags packed, prepared to hit the trail at a moment's notice. But the days dragged by with no encouraging reports on the war's progress. Bands of hostile Indians were spotted throughout the northern half of the valley and a few indecisive skirmishes were fought. But the Indians always managed to slip away from the soldiers, often reappearing shortly afterwards several miles away to make lightning raids on isolated white camps. It was almost always Joaquin Jim who was reported to be leading the raiders. Paul the Apostle and Hu-pwi seemed to have dropped out of sight, much to Jeremy's disgust. It was starting to look as if he never would have a chance to even the score for Charley, until one day he suddenly received the joyful news that his hour of vengeance was at hand.

Toward noon of March 19, 1863, Alney McGee rode up to Jeremy's cabin with a dozen cavalrymen and civilian volunteers. Grinning broadly, Alney told Jeremy that Captain Ropes had been informed by a friendly Paiute that Paul's band had stolen down the valley during the night. They were believed to be heading for a rendezvous with some Kern River Indians who were coming up to join the fight against the whites. Ropes had dispatched Lieutenant Doughty with a forty-man troop, of which Alney and his companions were the vanguard, to find the Indians and subdue them.

Jeremy was instantly galvanized into action. He wanted to set out at once after his hated enemy, but Alney persuaded him to wait for the other troopers to join them. Word of the cavalry mission was sent to David, who arrived shortly before Lieutenant Doughty's column trotted up. All of the men were well armed and eager to fight. But Doughty, with a good officer's foresight, insisted that they take time out to eat lunch and rest their horses before pushing on.

During the break several of the men boasted about the Indians they would kill, if only the red cowards would stand and fight. One of them, a Polish sergeant named Janusz Katowice who had only recently arrived in the valley, asked if it were true that Chief Paul fancied himself a swordsman.

"Yeah, when the other feller's tied to a stake," Alney answered.

"Then perhaps I will have an opportunity to match skills with him." Katowice drew his saber and gave the troop a dazzling display of swift thrusts and parries, then slid the blade back into its scabbard without looking down at it. He claimed to have been a colonel in the Russian army until the British captured him in the Crimean War and induced him to change sides.

"Jeremy's got dibs on that Injun," Alney said, and related Charley's fate to Katowice.

The Pole looked at Jeremy and nodded sympathetically. "Yes, it is fitting that you punish your friend's murderer. But if you should need any help . . ." He touched his saber hilt.

"Much obliged, suh," Jeremy said. "But I wants to do it my own self."

David drew Lieutenant Doughty aside and requested that he be allowed to try to talk Paul's band into surrendering, when the soldiers made contact with them. Doughty shook his head sternly.

"If the hostiles throw down their weapons and hold up their hands when they see us coming, I may feel inclined to be merciful," the officer said. "Otherwise, I don't care much about taking prisoners, and neither do they." He indicated his men. "White people will never be safe in the valley as long as Paul and his braves are alive. But you don't have to come with us, if some of them are your friends."

"I ain't sure I've got any Indian friends left," David said gloomily, thinking of Winnedumah and Lightning Tracker. He wished he could accept Doughty's offer to let him stay behind. But he had promised Rebekah that he would do all he could to save Hu-pwi's life, for Seyavi's sake. So he would have to go along and perhaps see more good men injured or killed. If only Chance were here!

They picked up the Indians' trail and followed it south past the site of the raid on Chief George's camp. At a point about two miles north of Cottonwood Creek, an unseen sniper removed a trooper's hat and gave his hair a new part. Jeremy, Alney McGee and five other men charged the Indian's position and Doughty, suspecting an ambush, ordered his command to prepare to attack. But the sniper had already taken to his heels. David waited tensely at Doughty's side as the sound of shooting grew more distant. The sudden absence of action around them made Doughty even more uneasy. He cautiously ordered a slow advance. Before they had gone very far, Alney and his bold followers came galloping back to report that the Indians were strongly posted in a ravine about five miles south of the head of Owens Lake.

The attackers continued on horseback until they drew fire. Then they dismounted and crawled from rock to rock, exchanging shots with the Indians. David stayed with Doughty as he directed his men from the rear of their ragged line. It was almost impossible to get clear shots at the Indians, who stubbornly held their positions in the ravine for over an hour. Finally Jeremy ran out of patience. Calling to the others to cover him, he leaped up and ran straight at the ravine, hollering and firing his revolver. Several bullets and arrows came his way without finding their mark, before he reached the ravine and came face to face with an Indian who was frantically trying to reload his rifle. Jeremy killed him with a shot between the eyes and looked around for more targets, as the soldiers came charging after him.

That broke the Indians' resistance and they ran for their horses. The troopers pursued them with fire, killing a few of them and several of their horses. Jeremy's pulse was racing with bloodlust. He kicked the body at his feet and howled triumphantly. At last they were paying for Charley! But where was Paul? He hoped Paul would hold out till the end, so that he would see all of his braves die before he received his own just desserts.

Doughty ordered the troop's horses brought up so they could pursue the surviving Indians. But he neglected to uncock his revolver as he mounted and the weapon discharged, killing his horse. That gave his men some amusing diversion from their bloody business. Corporal McKenna laughed so hard that he shot himself in the foot. It was later reported that the whites suffered more casualties from mishandling their own weapons than were inflicted by the enemy.

But somehow the cavalrymen and their civilian auxiliaries got mounted and chased the Indians to another ravine a mile away. Once more the Indians dug in and the white men had to go through the laborious process of rooting them out, as the sun dipped low toward the Sierra crest. Always Jeremy was in the thick of the action, fighting furiously and trying to catch a glimpse of Paul. He exposed himself to enemy fire so recklessly that twice Alney saved his life by shooting Indians who were about to put an end to his bold career as a warrior.

Finally the Indians were driven out in the open again and retreated to the next defensive cover they could find. By then both sides had lost so many horses that most of the running battle that ensued was fought on foot. The Indian riflemen were having trouble returning the white men's fire. Their gun barrels were so foul from the black powder they were using that they could only get bullets in them by pounding the ramrods with stones. But their bows continued to be accurate at close range. Corporal McKenna, limping painfully on his gunshot foot, caught an arrow in the chest. An Indian, coming up to finish him off with an ax, ran straight into Sergeant Katowice's saber. Katowice then put his foot on McKenna's chest and yanked the arrow out.

"You've killed me, you dirty Polack sonofabitch!" McKenna screamed.

"A Cossack would have smiled," Katowice said. "Battle wounds give them more pleasure than making love." He called a trooper over to take care of the wounded man, then went on after the retreating Indians with McKenna's curses following him.

Slowly but steadily, the Indians were driven back toward Owens Lake's bitter waters. Doughty, temporarily penned behind a rock with David, scowled at the setting sun. "Damn! If we don't finish 'em off soon, they'll stand a good chance of getting away in the dark."

"No," David said. "There's a full moon tonight, and it'll be up before the daylight's gone."

Doughty smiled exultantly. "Then we've got 'em! There won't be a savage left alive by morning."

Won't there? David wondered, looking around at the bloodstained, wild-eyed white men who pressed on viciously with hoarse yells and grunts.

They fought on in the thickening dusk until the landscape started to lighten again from an orange glow in the east. Jeremy was exhausted, but the thrill of victory carried him on. He was using his clubbed rifle and Bowie knife now, saving his few remaining pistol rounds for his meeting with Paul. He had not yet seen the Indian leader, but he could sense his nearness so strongly that he almost thought he smelled him. Soon, very soon, he would savor the ecstasy of draining the last drop of pain from Paul's evil body. Only after that would he be able to rest and once more think sweet thoughts without hate constipating his soul.

What was that?

Jeremy blinked and wiped sweat from his eyes, trying to fathom the deep shadow of a tall rock several yards ahead. He was certain he had seen movement there. Yes, something—no, *someone*—was trying to hide in the shadow. He looked around to see if any of his comrades were near, but the battle had moved far beyond him. Good. This would be all his. He drew his revolver and crept up to the rock.

"Come out, Paul." Jeremy *knew* it had to be Paul. "They ain't nobody here but yo an' me an' Gawd, an' He can't help yo."

A faint scratching sound came from the shadows and Jeremy barely made out a huddled form on the ground. There was no response when he repeated his order. He cocked his gun and started to take aim, as the moon's golden rim peeped over Inyo and illuminated the frightened face of an Indian boy of seven or eight.

Jeremy quickly recovered from his surprise, recalling that Paul's son was about that age. This would make his revenge complete, just as he had dreamed of it. His gunhand wavered when the boy started to whimper, but he steadied it by thinking of Charley's agonized screams. Nothing could stop him now. His finger tightened on the trigger. The boy's wet cheeks captured moonlight and his chest jerked with silent sobs.

"Stop that!" Jeremy snarled. "That won't help yo none."

The boy continued to cry without a sound. Jeremy gripped his gun with both hands, fighting to keep the image of Charley's bloody naked body in his mind. Then suddenly it was the boy tied to the stake and something snapped inside of Jeremy, purging his heart with even

321

more relief than tears could bring. He sank to his knees and gathered the small trembling body into his arms, gently rocking back and forth.

"Don' cry, Charley," he whispered. "It's all right now."

He started to croon a lullaby his mother had sung to him.

> "Don' yo cry, chile,
> Jest sleep a li'l while.
> An' don' fear the night,
> Ever'thin' will be all right."

He continued soothing the boy until he stopped sobbing and relaxed in his arms. There were still occasional gunshots and screams in the air, but Jeremy no longer heard them as he turned his back on the war and took his adopted son home.

David's legs felt rubbery and his rifle seemed impossibly heavy as he tried to keep up with the running soldiers. The moon was above the mountains now, setting the lake's surface on fire and silhouetting the surviving Indians, who realized too late that they were trapped. From somewhere David heard Lieutenant Doughty shouting:

"We got 'em! We got 'em! Keep after 'em, boys!"

Then abruptly an Indian directly before David turned and struck a defiant pose. Everything about him was black against the moonglare, even the saber he held challengingly above his head.

David stopped and stared at Paul the Apostle's last stand, too dumbstruck to raise his rifle. Paul waited motionlessly for his fate, which suddenly appeared as Sergeant Katowice dashed past David with his saber drawn.

The clash of blades reminded David of the sounds of trees being split by frozen sap during the severest winters back in Oneonta. Paul's wildly slashing strokes were no match for Katowice's delicate fencing moves.

But the Indian put up a spirited fight and the Pole enjoyed playing with him. Katowice was truly sorry when Paul stepped in too close and caught a parry on the inside of his elbow and the blade sliced cleanly through the joint.

David looked at the severed arm on the ground, still clutching the sword hilt. Paul stood calmly watching Katowice as if he were merely taking a rest from their game. Katowice turned to David.

"Do you think the black man still wants him? I can put a tourniquet on his arm."

David raised his rifle and shot Paul through the heart.

"I suppose that is just as well," Katowice said, and bent down to pry Paul's fingers from the saber hilt.

David walked past the sergeant and stood peering down at the first man he had ever killed. He had once asked Chance what it felt like to take a human life. He did not remember what the answer had been, but he was sure that Chance must have felt more than the numb, empty sensation that clenched like a fist inside his stomach. Katowice put the saber in David's free hand.

"This is rightly yours, since you killed him. A prize of war."

David nodded. He supposed Chance would be happy to get his saber back.

Down at the lakeshore, the surviving Indians had plunged into the water and were trying to escape by swimming to the opposite side. Their dark heads bobbing against the moonsilvered wavelets made good targets for the troopers, who lined up on the beach and placed bets on which ones they could pick off. A strong east wind was blowing and when the shooting was finished small waves licked the shore, making sounds like nursing babies. The white men waited patiently until the bodies were washed back to them. Thirty-six dead Indians were counted, and the troopers guessed there were probably a few more at the bottom of the lake.

In the morning a search was made around the lake. But the only sign they found that anyone had gotten out of the water alive was a damp moccasin a quarter of a mile from the northern shore. David recognized it from its beautiful beadwork as part of Rebekah's wedding gift to Hu-pwi and Seyavi.

Chapter 29

After David had left his farm to join Lieutenant Doughty's troop, D.C. and Bobby Buck exchanged bitter complaints about their father's refusal to take them along. D.C., feeling supremely confident of his untested military competence, relieved his frustration by belittling Bobby Buck's similar claims.

"You wouldn't be any good fightin' Indians," the older boy said scornfully. "You'd be too scared."

"I would not!" Bobby Buck protested. "I bet I could kill more Indians than you."

"Don't talk crazy. War is man's work. It's not for runty little kids like you."

Rebekah turned from the stove where she was preparing supper, while six-year-old Rachel set the table. "And are you already a man, my son?" she smiled at D.C., who blushed and drew his lanky body up to its full height of nearly six feet.

"Well, I'm bigger than most men hereabouts," he boasted.

"And he can work harder'n any of 'em," Rachel proudly added.

In one of the mysterious ways of childhood, the little girl had developed a severe case of hero-worship for her eldest brother. All of her life Bobby Buck had taken care of her with tender loving protectiveness. D.C. had barely tolerated her, yet it was he who now received her love and loyalty. Rebekah, while sympathizing with Bobby Buck's hurt puzzlement, remembered with ironic amusement the times Vicky Beth had mercilessly teased and cuffed D.C., only to have him follow her around like a devoted puppy.

"Then perhaps you are strong enough to fill the woodbox for morning," Rebekah suggested.

"It's Bobby Buck's turn. I did it last night."

"You did not!" Bobby Buck cried. "I did."

"D.C. did it. I saw him." Rachel lied without a twinge of shame to back up D.C.

Bobby Buck glared at D.C.'s triumphant smirk. As he started to argue, D.C. said condescendingly:

"I'll do it, even if it's not my turn, since some folks are too lazy to pull their own weight around here."

He swaggered out into the semidarkness to the woodpile and was swinging the ax vigorously when he heard approaching hoofbeats. Looking up, he made out three or four horsemen coming from the north. D.C. did not think they looked like Indians, but David had warned him not to take any chances. He dropped the ax and ran to the house, calling to Rebekah to fetch his father's shotgun.

When the four white men reached the house, D.C. was standing protectively out front with the shotgun ready. He told himself he had not really been afraid, in spite of his sweaty palms and twitching belly. But still it was good to know that Bobby Buck was behind him at the window with another gun and Rebekah stood ready to yank open the door if he should have to beat a hasty retreat. He stared up at the men lounging in their saddles and tried to look brave.

" 'Evenin', son. You here alone?" one of the men asked.

"No, sir. My four big brothers are in the house, and my Dad'll be home directly."

Two of the men smiled at D.C.'s transparent attempt to make it appear that the farm was well defended. "Put down the cannon, boy," a second speaker said in a friendly tone. "We're loaded for Injuns, not white folks."

"What's that over yonder?" Another member of the

group squinted at the cooking fires of David's farmhands.

"Friendly Paiutes," D.C. answered. "They work for us. If you want to fight bad Indians, you ought to be with the cavalry."

"That's what we aim to do," the first speaker said. "They told us at Camp Independence that a troop had headed out this way after a gang of renegade savages an' we're tryin' to catch up with 'em."

"Oh, I can tell you how to do that." D.C. gave them directions to where they could find Doughty's trail and said they would easily be able to follow it when the moon had risen.

"Thanks. We'll get right after 'em," the man said, then added off-handedly: "That cabin we seen down by the river—anybody live there?"

"Just an Indian simpleton," D.C. answered without wondering why the stranger was curious about the cabin. "Used to belong to an old Paiute woman, but she died."

"Too bad," the man said. "Well, thanks again."

As they started to turn away, the man who had not yet spoken walked his horse a few paces toward D.C. "If that's supper I smell cooking, I'll be happy to pay for a bite of it."

D.C., not sure of how to respond to the offer, looked at the other men.

"Oh, I ain't an Indian fighter," the fourth man explained. "I just rode with these gentlemen for safety. I'm a reporter for the Virginia City *Territorial Enterprise*, sent down to write up the war. Name's Sam Clemens."

"Honest?" D.C. was immensely impressed. He had never met a journalist before.

"Honest, and I'm more accustomed to the composing room than the saddle. So I'd be much obliged for a chance to get this one out from under me for a while."

"Oh. All right, sir, we'd be proud to have you stay to supper." D.C. looked at the other men in embarrassment. "Uh, we ain't got much to eat, but . . ."

"Never mind about us," the leader of the three other men said. "We can't waste time eatin' when there's Injuns to be killed."

The three men rode away and Clemens dismounted stiffly. D.C. led him into the house and introduced him to his family. Rebekah welcomed the journalist to her table and tried in her shy, quiet way to make him feel at home. Clemens proved to have a conversational talent to match his appetite and they all were enthralled by his amusing stories. He spoke with a thick drawl that so intrigued D.C. that he asked if he were a Southerner.

"Born in Missouri of old Virginia and Kentucky stock," the guest answered. "And worked a spell on the Mississippi, which cuts deeper into the South than good sense will take you."

"Are you for the Union or the Confederacy?" Bobby Buck asked.

Clemens gave the boy a level stare that made him regret his tactless question even before the newspaperman replied: "To avoid that inquiry was my motive for leaving Missouri."

"What if it ain't the same one?" Ethan Herbert wondered as he and his two companions circled back to come up on Wongata's cabin from the river side.

"Then we'll keep lookin' till we find him," Fletcher Whitlow answered.

"Damn lot of bother over a village idiot," Harlan Pitt grumbled.

"He's the only one that saw us," Whitlow reminded him. "And you heard what they was sayin' at Camp Independence about a drumhead court-martial."

"Puttin' white men on trial for killin' Injuns!" Pitt snarled. "I never heard such nonsense in my life."

"Makes a body wonder what the country's comin' to," Herbert agreed.

Pitt's tone softened a bit. "I'm glad we got rid of the newspaper feller. I'd hate to have to kill a white man just 'cause a fat old squaw didn't look where she was runnin'."

"I'd kill anybody to keep from facin' a firin' squad myself," Whitlow said, and cautioned the others to be quiet.

Wongata, hearing the approaching horses, thought that David and Jeremy were returning and hurried out of the cabin smiling. He recognized the men an instant before Pitt's lasso tightened around his neck, preventing him from crying out.

When supper was over, Clemens relaxed with a cigar and bottle of whiskey from his saddlebags. As the drink mellowed him, he told the Wheelers how he had come west with his brother Orion, who had been appointed Secretary of the Territory of Nevada. He had prospected in Nevada and California for a while, before beginning his journalistic career as the *Territorial Enterprise*'s political correspondent to the Nevada Legislature in Carson City.

"Orion was soon very popular with the legislators because they found that whereas they couldn't usually trust each other, nor anybody else, they could trust him. He easily won the belt for honesty in that country but it didn't do him any good in a pecuniary way because he had no talent for either persuading or scaring legislators.

"But I was differently situated. I was there every day in the legislature to distribute compliment and censure with evenly balanced justice and spread the same over half a page of the *Enterprise* every morning; consequently I was an influence. I got the legislature to pass a law requiring every corporation doing business in the territory to record its charter in full, without skipping a word, in a record to be kept by the Secretary of the Territory—my brother. All the charters are framed in exactly the same words. For this record service he is authorized to charge forty cents a folio of one hundred words for making the record; five dollars for furnishing a certificate of each record, and so on. Everybody has a toll road franchise but no toll road. But the franchise has to be recorded and paid for. Everybody is a mining corporation and has to have himself recorded and pay for it.

"And so we prosper. The record service pays Orion an average of one thousand dollars a month—in gold. Not Mr. Lincoln's nearly worthless greenbacks."

Clemens paused and looked at D.C. to see if the boy had grasped the significance of what he had said. D.C. had tried to keep his mind on the newspaperman's rambling discourse, as he fought off increasing drowsiness. Rebekah had slipped away to put Rachel to bed and Bobby Buck was nodding with his eyes nearly closed. D.C. wondered if Clemens knew how early farming families had to get up in the morning.

"Words!" Clemens rolled the sound lovingly around in his mouth before releasing it with a cloud of cigar smoke. "The power of the word is the greatest force in the universe. Nothing can stand against it. The invention of the printing press made the word invincible and its rapid distribution by telegraph and railroad renders no spot on earth secure from it. The politicians who carelessly added the First Amendment to our Constitution would have cut off their hands if they had known what they were signing away. With that, they transferred all of their authority and prestige to organs of public opinion whose owners and operators are a law unto themselves."

Clemens thrust a long finger at D.C.'s face. "Mark my words, boy. The day will come—I may not live to see it, but you will—when presidents, kings, generals, captains of industry, princes of the church and all others who think they have power will quake in terror before thin, myopic scribes who can make or break them with a single stroke of the pen."

D.C. struggled to hold back a yawn. "Well, I guess you're right, sir. But . . ."

"Oh, sorry I kept you up so late." Clemens's air of self-exultation vanished as he remembered that he was talking to two very young country boys. "Go on to bed. Don't worry about me. I'll just unroll my blankets here on the floor."

"But ain't you goin' on to see the fight?" D.C. asked.

"If all the reports of battles were written by men who actually *saw* the battles, there would be precious few battles written about," Clemens said. "Battlefields are sadly short on hospitality. It's much better to wait until the fighting is over, then get your information from the survivors. Or better yet, wait until all the survivors are dead, too. Then you can write whatever you please."

When D.C. slipped into bed beside the already snoring Bobby Buck, he tried to think over what Clemens had said. But his mind was still filled with pictures of cavalry-and-

Indian fights. It was unfair that there were two perfectly good wars going on now and he was missing out on both of them just because his father said he was too young to be a soldier. He fell asleep brooding about that, forgetting to perform his nightly ritual of envisioning the day when he would rescue Vicky Beth from Los Angeles and take her away to live happily ever after in Shoshone Land.

He was enjoying a heroic war dream when a noise aroused him. After having been prepared for an Indian attack for more than a year, D.C. was instantly alert. He sat up reaching for the shotgun as he heard the sound again— a faint scratching on the wall outside the window. Creeping out of bed, he made his way silently over to the brilliant splash of moonlight at the narrow window and peeked out.

An Indian was crouching against the wall.

As D.C.'s hands tightened on the gun, the Indian raised his face to the moon and he recognized Old Firestealer, one of the farmhands. The Indian motioned for him to come outside.

D.C. quickly got into his clothes and slipped out the window to join the Indian.

Firestealer signaled D.C. to be quiet and follow him. D.C., knowing better than to question a Paiute when he didn't want to talk, fell in behind Firestealer and followed him up over the rise to the irrigation pond and the towering oak that held many fond memories of Vicky Beth for him. But when he saw what was hanging from one of the tree's limbs, he knew he would never be able to think of it as a happy place again.

Clemens was awakened by the sound of running footsteps when D.C. came back to the house for the ax. Thinking that something was amiss, the journalist pulled on his boots and went outside in time to see the boy disappear over the ridgeline. When he reached the pond, D.C. was hacking furiously at the oak trunk and sobbing because the ax could do so little damage to the hard wood. Clemens went over and gently put his hand on the boy's shoulder.

"Don't punish the tree. It's only an innocent bystander."

When they had cut Wongata down, D.C. knelt beside the body and swore:

"I'll never be a soldier. Never!"

"You're learning," Clemens drawled, remembering his own brief hour of cowardice and compassion in a too-tight gray uniform. "Try not to forget this lesson."

In the morning Clemens stayed long enough to help bury Wongata. Then he went to find the veterans of the Battle of Owens Lake. He reckoned it wouldn't do any harm to interview them before writing their story under the pen name he had appropriated from the well-liked riverboat Captain Isaiah Sellers—Mark Twain.

Chapter 30

After swimming the lake to safety, Hu-pwi made his way back to his clan's camp, where he was told of his father's strange disappearance. For several days he hardly stirred from the wickiup, while Seyavi tenderly cared for him. He had suffered no serious wounds and his healthy young body quickly recovered from his exhaustive ordeal. But his spirit was broken by the knowledge that he had fled in abject fear while his comrades fought and died gloriously. His shame was so painful that he spent most of his time huddled under his blanket, mourning for his dead manhood.

"You must keep up your strength," Seyavi said, urging him to eat.

"Why?"

"There may be more fighting. The white soldiers have returned to their camp, but the northern bands are still at war."

"Let others do the fighting. That is a job for warriors, not cowards."

"You are not a coward."

"Be silent. What does a woman know of such things?"

"I know of my needs, and our child's."

Hu-pwi looked at the boy. He was stronger than the daughter they had lost, but even so there was some doubt that he would survive to adulthood. They had named him Badgerskin, hoping the reference to his first covering would give him that animal's tenacious power to endure.

"Find another father for him," Hu-pwi grunted. "You are the same as widow now."

Seyavi went outside to spare him the further shame of seeing her cry.

But in a Paiute habit is stronger than humiliation and as the days passed Hu-pwi automatically began to make fresh arrows for the extra bow he had left in the wickiup. Seyavi, hiding her relief, told herself that he just needed time to let the bad memories fade. Eventually he would be able to hold up his head among his tribesmen once more. Perhaps the war would be over by then and he would never be tempted to leave her again. Just as she started to believe that, word arrived that soldiers were coming to arrest Hu-pwi as an accessory to Paul's murder of Charley Tyler.

"I will go north to join Joaquin Jim's band," Hu-pwi said, gathering his weapons.

Seyavi picked up her seed-gathering basket and took Badgerskin by the hand. "We will go with you."

"That is unwise. I must travel fast."

"We will not hamper you."

Hu-pwi scowled. "Do you require a beating to remind you of your place? There is no room for women and children in a warrior band."

Seyavi modestly lowered her eyes and Hu-pwi assumed that the matter was settled. But when he was a mile from camp, he looked back and saw Seyavi and the boy following a few hundred yards behind. He shouted angrily and shook his fist at her. He even threw a few stones. But she clung stubbornly to his trail until he finally relented and waited for them to catch up with him. He had to punish her disobedience, to save his pride, but the blows were so light that Seyavi knew he was glad to have her along.

They moved along the valley's western rim, where they could take cover in the gorges of the Sierra foothills. But that did not prevent the eight horsemen traveling the valley floor from spotting them early in the afternoon. Hu-pwi, his hand on his son's neck, watched the soldiers start to work their way up the rocky incline toward them.

"If you surrender, you will be taken to their camp alive," Seyavi said. "And David Wheeler will testify that you only killed in battle, as an honorable warrior."

Hu-pwi did not bother to comment on the suggestion. Seyavi offered another plan.

"Take the boy and escape over the mountains. Leave me here to delay them."

Hu-pwi's expression was so reproachful that Seyavi wondered how she could have dared to insult his honor even before he had fully recovered it from the defeat at Owens Lake. Too speechless with shame to look into his face again, she took Badgerskin's hand and started up the mountainside.

Hu-pwi scrambled over the uneven slope, trying to appear to be seeking refuge in the gullies while staying in view of the men below. He smiled when he saw them alter their course to continue angling over toward him. The story of how Hu-pwi the coward had regained his honor by leading the enemy away from his wife and son would make good entertainment for the People.

The men steadily drew closer, calling to him to surrender. They fired warning shots, but the range was so great that Hu-pwi only laughed derisively and bent over to show them his buttocks. The white men dismounted and came after him on foot. Hu-pwi ducked in and out of the cover of rocks to draw their fire, responding with arrows and invitations for them to come up and fight if they were men, or open their legs for him if they were women. The joy of combat was singing in his blood again and he looked around for some way to cause the white men more consternation. A boulder appearing to rest loosely in the soil caught his eye. He crouched behind the rock and strained so hard to send it rolling down on the soldiers that he hardly felt the ricocheting bullet enter his left side.

Noticing blood pouring down his leg, Hu-pwi scooped up handfuls of earth and pressed them to the wound until the red mud sealed off the flow. But he could not keep the seal from cracking every time he used his bow to slow the white men's advance.

Soon he started seeing things with a lightheaded clarity that told him he was losing too much blood. It angered him to think that the game was about to end just when he was enjoying it so much. But he managed to hold his position for another hour, exhausting his arrows and all of the throwable stones within reach. As the world became more unreal, he heard the wind whisper comfortingly: "Poets and warriors should always die young." Turning his fading vision inward, Hu-pwi found no great faults with his life. He would not be reborn a coyote.

When the soldiers finally crept up to Hu-pwi, he was seated with his back to a rock and looking east toward the sacred range of Inyo. Some of the white men wanted to scalp the body. But their leader insisted on leaving it to the valley's continuing chain of life with no further loss of grace. As they turned away, one of them muttered the funeral oration:

"Maybe heaven'll give the poor devil a better shake than he got here."

So died Hu-pwi, the Desert Thorn, son of Lightning Tracker and Slow Of Speech, that his mate and heir might live.

And live they did, somehow. Too terrified even to approach David and Rebekah, Seyavi took the boy to the caverns at the Black Rocks, where they survived the remainder of the war furtively digesting mussels, tule roots, seeds, grubs and what little else was afforded them by the small mercy of the gods of frost and rain. It was an existence that stayed so close to nonexistence for so long that Seyavi was able to squeeze it all into a single sentence.

"A man must have a woman, but a woman who has a child will do very well."

Many years later, when her son had gone his own way and she was a sun-dried object of charity, Seyavi told her story around the hearth fires. One of those who heard it was a remarkably unattractive white woman named Mary Austin, who immortalized Seyavi and Owens Valley in her neglected masterpiece, *The Land of Little Rain*. And sometimes, to amuse her friends, the old woman would sing:

"I am the white flower of twining,
Little flower by the river.
Oh, flower that twines close by the river.
Oh, trembling flower!
So trembles the maiden heart."

Then she would lay her arms upon her knees and laugh into them at the recollection. It is not recorded if she still thought of Hu-pwi at those times.

Epilog

In July of that year the cavalry rounded up nearly a thousand Owens Valley Indians and marched them over the mountains to a reservation near Fort Tejon. Most of them eventually ran away and returned to the valley to work for or beg handouts from the new white masters of lands that had once been theirs. Sporadic clashes between the two races continued for several more years, with atrocities committed by both sides.

But for all practical purposes, the First Owens Valley Water War ended with the Battle of Owens Lake. Chief George and most of the other Paiute leaders made peace with the conquerors and tried to live in harmony with them. Joaquin Jim was never defeated and remained a fierce hater of all white men for the rest of his life.

By the late 1860s, the Indian and Spanish cultures of California were becoming history. The day of the Anglo, first seen in the gray stain of the Mexican-American War and the rosy glow of the Gold Rush, had at last fully dawned.

The total number of people killed in the Owens Valley fighting was estimated at sixty whites and about 200 Indians, hardly enough to qualify the conflict as a real war, if it had not been fought by human beings. Perhaps all of

337

their souls went to the Christian heaven with Winnedumah. There was enough water and blood in the valley to baptize them. We know only that their bones have long since joined the indifferent grains of sand that serve as their monument and their voices sing in the mournful wind that tells the story of how they helped Los Angeles fulfill her poetic destiny. Whatever else was left of them flows on in the river—the ever-trickling River of Life that began in God's tears and knows no barrier, be it mountain or desert or the weak hearts of men.

More Bestselling Fiction from Pinnacle

MORE
BEST-SELLING FICTION
FROM PINNACLE